The Stone Diaries

Chosen as 'Book of the Year 1993' by:

> Joanna Trollope, *Daily Telegraph*
> Anita Brookner, *Spectator*
> Paul Bailey, *Kaleidoscope*, BBC Radio 4
> Shena Mackay, *Sunday Express*
> Stephen Spender, *Independent on Sunday*
> Penny Perrick, *Sunday Times*
> Penelope Lively, *Daily Telegraph*
> Margaret Forster, *Kaleidoscope*, BBC Radio 4
> Carl MacDougall, *Glasgow Herald*

'I can think of few novels containing so much that is resonant and unforgettable, or that invite the reader to participate so fully and rewardingly. *The Stone Diaries* is a triumphant and important book, and deserves a wide audience.' – *Sunday Telegraph*

'Shields is an exceptionally sympathetic and involving novelist but her books are also finely plotted: after the pleasure of the first reading, subtle patterns emerge; beauties of construction are perceived.' – *Independent on Sunday*

'Anyone who hasn't yet discovered Carol Shields is in for a treat. She is one of a number of Canadian writers – Alice Munro and Michael Ondaatje are among the others – who have been gaining a reputation here. Her new novel . . . can only help secure that reputation.' – *Tatler*

The Stone Diaries

Carol Shields was born and raised in Oak Park, Illinois, a suburb of Chicago. She studied at Hanover College and the University of Ottawa. Except for three years in Manchester in the 1960s, Carol Shields has lived in Canada since 1957. She is married with five grown-up children, spends her summers in France, and has recently completed the screenplay for *The Republic of Love*.

Though none of her novels was published in the UK until 1990, *Mary Swann* immediately established Carol Shields as a major writer. *Happenstance* (1991) and *The Republic of Love* (short-listed for the Guardian fiction prize 1992) also received huge critical acclaim.

The
Stone Diaries

Carol Shields

TED SMART

This edition produced for The Book People Ltd,
Hall Wood Avenue, Haydock, St Helens WA11 9UL

This paperback edition first published in 1994

15 16

First published in Great Britain in 1993 by
Fourth Estate Limited
6 Salem Road
London W2 4BU

A catalogue record for this book is available from the
British Library.

ISBN 0 00766 623 3

Printed and bound in Great Britain by
Clays Ltd, St Ives plc

For my sister
Babs

A number of people have read the manuscript for this book and offered encouragement and suggestions. I thank Blanche Howard, Joan Clark, Jim Keller, Anne Giardini, Catherine, Meg and Sara Shields, and, especially, Miss Louise Wyatt of London, Ontario.

nothing she did
or said

was quite
what she meant

but still her life
could be called a monument

shaped in a slant
of available light

and set to the movement
of possible music

(From "The Grandmother Cycle" by Judith Downing, *Converse Quarterly*, Autumn)

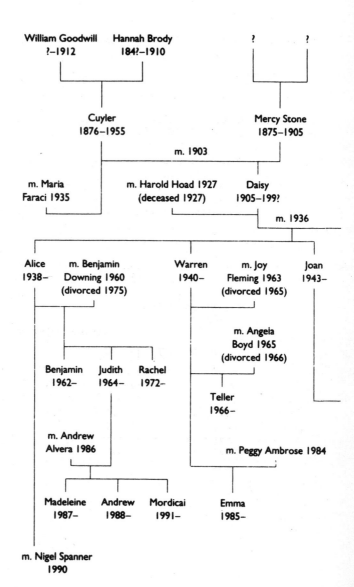

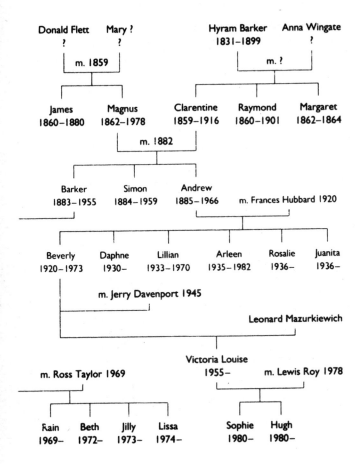

Donald Flett | Mary ?
? | ?
m. 1859

Hyram Barker | Anna Wingate
1831–1899 | ?
m. ?

James
1860–1880

Magnus
1862–1978

Clarentine
1859–1916

Raymond
1860–1901

Margaret
1862–1864

m. 1882

Barker
1883–1955

Simon
1884–1959

Andrew
1885–1966   m. Frances Hubbard 1920

Beverly
1920–1973

Daphne
1930–

Lillian
1933–1970

Arleen
1935–1982

Rosalie
1936–

Juanita
1936–

m. Jerry Davenport 1945

Leonard Mazurkiewich

Victoria Louise
1955–

m. Ross Taylor 1969

m. Lewis Roy 1978

Rain
1969–

Beth
1972–

Jilly
1973–

Lissa
1974–

Sophie
1980–

Hugh
1980–

CONTENTS

Family tree

CHAPTER ONE: *Birth, 1905*   1

CHAPTER TWO: *Childhood, 1916*   41

CHAPTER THREE: *Marriage, 1927*   79

CHAPTER FOUR: *Love, 1936*   121

CHAPTER FIVE: *Motherhood, 1947*   157

CHAPTER SIX: *Work, 1955–1964*   197

CHAPTER SEVEN: *Sorrow, 1965*   229

CHAPTER EIGHT: *Ease, 1977*   265

CHAPTER NINE: *Illness and Decline, 1985*   309

CHAPTER TEN: *Death*   343

Birth, 1905

MY MOTHER'S NAME was Mercy Stone Goodwill. She was only thirty years old when she took sick, a boiling hot day, standing there in her back kitchen, making a Malvern pudding for her husband's supper. A cookery book lay open on the table: "Take some slices of stale bread," the recipe said, "and one pint of currants; half a pint of raspberries; four ounces of sugar; some sweet cream if available." Of course she's divided the recipe in half, there being just the two of them, and what with the scarcity of currants, and Cuyler (my father) being a dainty eater. A pick-and-nibble fellow, she calls him, able to take his food or leave it.

It shames her how little the man eats, diddling his spoon around in his dish, perhaps raising his eyes once or twice to send her one of his shy, appreciative glances across the table, but never taking a second helping, just leaving it all for her to finish up – pulling his hand through the air with that dreamy gesture of his that urges her on. And smiling all the while, his daft tender-faced look. What did food mean to a working man like himself? A bother, a distraction, perhaps even a kind of price that had to be paid in order to remain upright and breathing.

Well, it was a different story for her, for my mother. Eating was as close to heaven as my mother ever came.

(In our day we have a name for a passion as disordered as hers.)

And almost as heavenly as eating was the making – how she gloried in it! Every last body on this earth has a particular notion of paradise, and this was hers, standing in the murderously hot back kitchen of her own house, concocting and contriving, leaning forward and squinting at the fine print of the cookery book, a clean wooden spoon in hand.

It's something to see, the way she concentrates, her hot, busy face, the way she thrills to see the dish take form as she pours the stewed fruit into the fancy mold, pressing the thickly cut bread down over the oozing juices, feeling it soften and absorb bit by bit a raspberry redness. Malvern pudding; she loves the words too, and feels them dissolve on her tongue like a sugary wafer, her tongue itself grown waferlike and sweet. Like an artist – years later this form of artistry is perfectly clear to me – she stirs and arranges and draws in her brooding lower lip. Such a dish this will be. A warm sponge soaking up color. (Mrs. Flett next door let her have some currants off her bush; the raspberries she's found herself along the roadside south of the village, even though it half kills her, a woman of her size walking out in the heat of the day.)

She sprinkles on extra sugar, one spoonful, then another, then takes the spoon to her mouth, the rough crystals that keep her alert. It is three o'clock – a hot July afternoon in the middle of Manitoba, in the middle of the Dominion of Canada. The parlor clock (adamantine finish, gilded feet, a wedding present from her husband's family, the Goodwills of Stonewall Township) has just struck the hour. Cuyler will be home from the quarry at five sharp; he will have himself a good cheerful wash at the kitchen basin, and by half-past five the two of them will sit down at the table – this very table, only spread with a clean cloth, every second day a clean cloth – and eat their supper. Which for the most part will be a silent meal, both my parents being shy by nature, and each brought up in the belief that conversing and eating are different functions, occupying separate trenches of time. Tonight they will partake of cold corned beef with a spoonful of homemade relish, some dressed potatoes at the side, cups of sweet tea, and then this fine pudding. His eyes will widen; my father, Cuyler Goodwill, aged twenty-eight, two years married, will never in his life have tasted Malvern pudding. (That's what she's preparing for – his stunned and mild look of confusion, that tender, grateful male mouth dropping open in surprise. It's the least she can do, surprise him like this.) She sets a flower-patterned plate carefully on top of the pudding and weights it with a stone.

A cool place, the recipe says: "Set the mould in a cool place." (The book is an old one, printed in England more than thirty years ago, its pages limp, but the author's tone vigorous and pungent.) Yet where on a day like today is Mercy Goodwill to find a cool place? Even the dark stone floor under the cellar steps where she stores her milk and butter and lard has warmed up, giving off this last fortnight a queer sour smell. The Flett family, next door, has recently purchased a Labrador Ice Chest, zinc-lined, and Mrs. Flett has spoken shyly of this acquisition to Mercy, mentioning its features, its ventilating flues, the shining tin provision shelves, how a block of ice is able to last through two warm days or more.

Some sharp thought, the worry over how to keep the pudding cool, or perhaps envy for the Fletts' new ice chest, brings on my mother's first spasm of pain. She gives a little cry. Her eyes pull tight at the corners, as though someone has taken hold of her hair and yanked it upward so that her scalp sings. A witness, had there been a witness present in the little back kitchen, might have feared a fainting spell coming on, even though my mother is not much given to faintness. What she feels is more like a shift in the floor of her chest, rising at first, and then an abrupt drop, a squeezing like an accordion held sideways.

She looks down and observes with wonder how the blue and white stripes of her apron are breaking into colored flakes. Her hands fly straight out in the air, a reflex meant to hold back the crushing pressure, and she steadies herself by settling her shoulders and placing her palms flat on the table, leaning forward and letting go a long, soft whimper. The sound that comes from her lips is formless, loose, a wavy line of bewilderment. (Later, these words, more than any others, will attach themselves to my image of my mother: looseness, bewilderment.) For a heavy woman she perspires little, even during the height of summer, and she takes, if the truth were known, a shy pride in her bodily dryness – only now a broad band of dampness is spreading beneath her apron and down the channel of her back. She breathes rapidly, blinking as the pain wraps a series of heavy bands around her abdomen. Down there, buried in the lapped folds of flesh, she feels herself invaded. A tidal wave, a flood.

All spring she's been troubled with indigestion. Often in the morning, and then again at night after her young husband has gone to sleep, she's risen from her bed and dosed herself with Bishop's Citrate of Magnesia. When she drinks ordinary milk or sweetened tea or sugary lemonade she swallows it down greedily, but Bishop's cool chalky potion she pours into a china cup and sips with deep, slow concentration, with dignity. She doesn't know what to think. One day she's persuaded her liver's acting up, and the next day her kidneys – she's only thirty years old, but kidney trouble can start early in life, especially for a woman of my mother's unorthodox size. Or perhaps the problem stems from constipation. Mrs. Flett next door has suggested this possibility, recommending rhubarb tablets, or else, speaking confidentially, some woman's trouble. Excessive loss of blood, she tells Mercy, is the cause of discomfort for many young ladies – has Mercy spoken to Dr. Spears? Dr. Spears is known for his sensitivity to women's complaints; he has a way of squeezing his eyes shut when he phrases his delicate inquiries, of speaking almost poetically of nature's cycles and balances, of the tide of fertility or the consolation of fruit salts.

No, Mercy has not approached Dr. Spears, she would never speak to Dr. Spears of such a thing, she would speak to no one, not even her husband – especially not her husband. Her monthly blood has appeared only twice in her life, springing out of the soft cushions of her genital flesh, staining her underclothes with its appalling brightness, and mocking the small decencies and duties that steady her life: her needlework, her housekeeping, her skill with a flat iron, her preserves and pickles and fresh linens and the lamp chimneys she polishes every single morning.

The doses of Citrate of Magnesia help hardly at all. Fruit salts only make her suffering worse. Her abdominal walls have continued to cramp and heave all spring, and she's wondered at times if her inner membranes might burst with the pressure. Bile rises often in her throat. Her skin itches all over. She experiences scalding attacks of flatulence, especially at night as she lies next to my father, who, out of love, out of delicacy, pretends deep sleep – she can tell from the way he keeps himself curled respectfully to his own side of the bed.

Only bread seems to ease her malaise, buttered bread, enormous slabs of it, what she's heard people in this village refer to as doorsteps. She eats it fresh from the oven, slice after slice, sometimes not bothering with the knife, just tearing it off in handfuls. One day, alone in this kitchen, she consumed an entire loaf between noon and supper. (One of the loaves burned, she explained to her husband, anxious to account for the missing bread – as though a man of my father's dreamy disposition would notice so small an item, as though any man would notice such a thing.) Frequently she sprinkles sugar on top of the buttered bread. The surface winks with brilliance, its crystals working between her teeth, giving her strength. She imagines the soft dough entering the bin of her stomach, lining that bitter bloated vessel with a cottony warmth that absorbs and neutralizes the poisons of her own body.

Her inability to feel love has poisoned her, swallowed down along with the abasement of sugar, yeast, lard, and flour; she knows this for a fact. She tries, she pretends pleasure, as women are encouraged to do, but her efforts are punished by a hunger that attacks her when she's alone, as she is on this hot July day, hidden away in a dusty, landlocked Manitoba village (half a dozen unpaved streets, a store, a hotel, a Methodist Church, the Canadian Pacific Railway Station, and a boarding house on the corner of Bishop Road for the unmarried men). She seems always to be waiting for something fresh to happen, but her view of this "something" is obscured by ignorance and the puffiness of her bodily tissue. At night, embarrassed, she gathers her nightdress close around her. She never knows when she blows out the lamp what to expect or what to make of her husband's cries, which are, thankfully, muffled by the walls of the wood-framed company house where she and my father live. Two rooms up, two down, a privy out back. She knows only that she stands apart from any coherent history, separated from the ordinary consolation of blood ties, and covered over and over again these last two years by Cuyler Goodwill's immense, unfathomable ardor. Niagara in all its force is what she's reminded of as he climbs on top of her each evening, a thundering let loose against the folded interior walls of her body.

It's then she feels most profoundly buried, as though she, Mercy Goodwill, is no more than a beating of blood inside the vault of her flesh, her wide face, her thick doughy neck, her great loose breasts and solid boulder of a stomach.

Standing in her back kitchen, my mother's thighs, like soft white meat (veal or chicken or fatty pork come to mind) rub together under her cotton drawers – which are wet, she suddenly realizes, soaked through and through. There are double and triple ruffles of fat around her ankles and wrists, and these ridged extremities are slick with perspiration. Her large swollen fingers press into the boards of the kitchen table, and her left hand, her wedding ring buried there in soft flesh, is throbbing with poison. She seems to see a weak greenish light unfolding like a fan in front of her eyes. This is worse, far worse, than ever it's been before. She wonders if her body will break apart, the bones drawn out from under the flesh, blood spilling on the floor and walls. She imagines her blood to be yellow rather than red, a thick honey-colored sludge slowing her down, keeping her from crying out to Mrs. Flett next door.

Mrs. Flett, as it happens, is within easy earshot, no more than forty feet away, pinning her rough sheets and pillowcases on to a clothesline. She would come running if she only knew of Mercy Goodwill's distress; she would be there in a trice, exhorting the poor dear soul to be calm, begging her to lie down on the kitchen couch, bathing her broad, damp, blank face with a cool cloth, easing her clothing, pulling off the tightly laced shoes and heavy stockings. She loves Mercy, loves her ways, her solid concentration, though on the whole (it must be admitted) her love is churned from fascination, and also from pity – pity for that large, soft, slow-flowing body, the blurred flesh at the sides of Mercy's young face, and a blinking prettiness that shows itself in certain lights, in the curve of her upper lip or the tender spilt panic of her hazel eyes. When she looks into Mercy's calf eyes she does not think "childish," but "child." Poor thing, poor lost thing. Never a mother to call her own, and now, from the looks of it – though who could tell such things, who can read the future? – no little ones of her own to rock and sing to.

Mrs. Flett – her Christian name is Clarentine – has three grown sons, Simon, Andrew, and Barker, but no daughter. The eldest of these sons, Barker, has gone to Winnipeg to study at the College, and the other two work at the quarry alongside her husband Magnus, a master stonecutter, a cold, lean Orkneyman who immigrated to Canada at the age of nineteen. His Orkney ways have stayed with him. He prefers simple things. A plainly furnished house. A carefully tended garden. Ordinary food on the table, a supper of porridge or smoked fish or even a plate of bread and butter washed down by tea. The sight of a Malvern pudding unmolded on a glass plate and covered with cream would distress him deeply, particularly a pudding set out on what is, after all, an ordinary Monday evening in high summer in the year 1905 (the year of my birth, the day of my birth).

Mrs. Flett, Clarentine, a neat-bodied woman whose skin is the color of mushrooms and whose memory of her sons' infancy has been washed clear by disappointment, dreams of taking Mercy's large dry hand in hers and saying, "A woman's life isn't worth a plateful of cabbage if she hasn't felt life stir under her heart. Taking a little one to nurse, watching him grow to manhood, that's what love is. We say we love our husbands, we stand up in church saying as how we'll love them forever and ever, till death do we part, but it's our own blood and sinew we really love."

She likes giving Mercy things. Only last spring, while cleaning house, she came across an old tinware jelly mold, and this is the vessel Mercy uses today to provide shape for her Malvern pudding. She gives Mercy flowers from her garden, sweet peas, nicotiana, dianthus, candytuft, snapdragons. Also lettuce when it's in season, new radishes, carrots, broad beans. Also pots of berry jam or rhubarb pickle. Once a set of tea towels with embroidered corners, another time an appliqued sham with an open-work centre. Why, she's even given Mercy the cookery book the girl's so everlasting fond of and has nearly worn out with use. At Christmas she gave her a bar of heliotrope soap fresh in its paper wrapper, and once, out of the blue, a hairpin glass trimmed with ribbon. These objects, passing out of her hands into Mercy's, seem momentarily ringed with light, though the phrases she employs along with her gift-giving are calculated to diminish her generosity. "I've no earthly use for this myself." Or "I've more here than would feed an army" or "Too fancy for us, but it'll suit you" or "Mr. Flett don't hold with sweet-smelling stuff, and I do hate to throw a thing away what's perfectly good and useful."

Mercy's softly focused gratitude, her slow-forming smile with its hint of bewilderment and her look of being unspotted by the world make Mrs. Flett long to take her in her arms. She can imagine Mercy's compacted fullness pressing up against her own tidy dress front, heaving with emotion and surrender. "My dear," she would like to murmur into the pale bulk of Mercy's neck, into Mercy's soft shoulders and curling brown hair.

The moment lies in the future, it will come. This is what she thinks as she stands under the blazing sun, pegging her clean wash to the line – the linens first, then her aprons and shirt waists, then the men's summer overalls. There is so little breeze that the clothes will dry stiff and hard – in two hours they'll be dry, it's that hot. She's late with the wash today, and there's still the garden to weed, and peas to pick for supper. She's always running late, and always there's a shrewish tune skirling away inside her head: now the stove to polish, now the mending, next the curtains to starch. The scolding voice is her own, so abrasive and quick, yet so powerless to move her. The men, her husband and sons, leave for the quarry at seven o'clock sharp and return at five. What do they imagine she does all day? It makes her shiver to think of it, how not one pair of eyes can see through the roof and walls of her house and regard her as she moves through her dreamlike days, bargaining from minute to minute with indolence, that tempter.

God sees her, of course. He must. God observes her at the window where she stares and stares at the shadows of the caragana blowing across the path, or sitting on one of the kitchen chairs, locked into paralysis over her mending basket, watching a fly creep across the table. The minutes tick by, become an hour, sometimes two. These segments of time are untied to any other time she recognizes. It happens more and more frequently, these collapsed hours, almost every day since the summer weather came on. She wakes up fresh enough, but as the hands of the clock move forward she feels a force beckoning, the teasing seduction of ease and secrecy, and then, with the next breath, she's lost the battle.

Whatever it is that encloses her is made up of tenderness. It rises around her like a cloud of scent. There's no face or voice to it, only a soft, steady, pervasive fragrance, a kind of rapturous wave that enters her throat, then moves downward through her body, bringing tightness to her female parts and the muscles of her softened thighs. The silence is perfect, and yet a torment, and always a dry little thought plucks away at her – that God is not interested in her lapses. He has not spoken out to her in any way, has not given a sign, not even troubled Himself to betray her, even though she has baited Him with a scrap of embroidered linen on her kitchen wall:

> *Christ is the Head of the House*
> *The Unseen Guest*
> *at every Meal*
> *The Silent Listener*
> *to every Conversation*

It is frightening, and also exhilarating, her ability to deceive those around her; this is something new, her lost hours, her vivid dreams and shreds of language, as though she'd been given two lives instead of one, the alternate life cloaked in secret.

Or does she deceive herself? Dr. Spears, when she met him by accident walking on the Quarry Road, did catch hold of her wrist and speak to her in a most curious and candid manner. "Women need the companionship of other women," he burst out after some polite talk about the weather. "A little laughter is a great comfort, a little harmless gossip. The Needlework Auxiliary or the Mothers' Union – and I believe, Mrs. Flett, you were once a member of the Ladies Rhythm and Movement Club, that you used to find enjoyment in an afternoon of cheerful company. My own wife tells me the recent talk on the Chinese missions was diverting, as well as edifying."

"I'm very busy at home," Clarentine Flett told Dr. Spears.

"Of course, of course," he nodded quickly. "Or perhaps you're thinking of a few days' visiting in Winnipeg. I believe you spend a few days there every year with your son Barker. He is still there, is he not, engaged in his studies? Botany, if I remember, his field of endeavor."

"Yes," she answered. "Flowers. Plants."

"I'm sure he does you credit. A fine young fellow. If you remember, I was one of those who put his name forward for the Epworth Scholarship."

"I do remember, indeed I do, and –"

"Why not surprise him, then, with the pleasure of a visit? We all need a change of scene now and then, especially after a long hard winter. I could mention it to your husband, if you like – indirectly, of course. I could suggest the healthful benefits of a little holiday."

"Please," she'd said. She was thinking of the oval of silence she would enter as soon as she left Dr. Spear's presence, the smooth pearl gloss of it. "There's no need of that. I can speak to him myself."

The Mothers' Union. A few days in Winnipeg. Only months ago these diversions would have held some attraction. She might actually have spoken to her husband, Magnus, about a week away in the city. The words would have come forward – while she was engaged in

some ordinary task, drying the supper dishes or taking
the dead leaves off the fuchsia that hung by the window.
Her husband was not a man who wasted words, but the
two of them had managed over the years the simple,
necessary marital commerce required for the rearing of
three sons, for the ordering of supplies, the discussions
concerning weather, illness, what manner of vegetables
should be planted in the garden. And she guessed –
though how was she to know such a thing? Who in this
world would tell her? – she guessed her husband was no
rougher in his ways than other men. "If you're willing,
Mother," he says in the darkness of their back bedroom,
one hand working up her nightdress. A thousand times,
five thousand times – "If you're willing, Mother." The
words have worn a groove in her consciousness, she
hardly hears them. And afterwards there's silence, like
falling down a hole, or a kind of grunt that she takes to be
satisfaction.

"Shall we marry then?" These were the words of his
marriage proposal delivered some twenty-five years ago,
the phrase riding upward in a way she found disarming.
At that time he had been less than one year in Canada,
eight months working in the old granite quarry at Lac du
Bonnet near to where her father farmed; his Orkney
accent was pronounced and exceedingly harsh, though
she fancied she heard something softer beneath it. He
walked her home from a prayer meeting at Milner's
Crossing. It was a warm April night with stars spread
thick across the sky. She felt she could gulp the clean air
in like a kind of nourishment. This was the third time he
had walked her home, and she knew – and he knew – that
he was entitled to ask for a kiss. Out of curiosity she

assented. His upper lip, moving quickly, too quickly, grated against her mouth and cheek. And then he spoke: "Shall we marry then?"

His presumptuousness moved her, it was so childlike. She had an urge to laugh, to tease him – she knew how to be merry in those days – but his face was too close.

"What do you say, then?" he pressed her. His features were covered over by darkness, but she felt his warm breath on her neck, and it weakened her terribly. She readied herself for words of tenderness.

"I make a good enough wage," he said, "and I work regular."

This was true. She could not contradict what he said. She never did learn to contradict what he said. He had a particular way of putting a thing that disallowed contravention. The new ice box, for instance. He had written away for it, secretly sent an order in to Eaton's Mail Order, and now it occupied a corner of the kitchen. Suddenly it was there. Months earlier, for reasons of economy, he had refused to consult Dr. Spears about the lump behind his ear, and then he had to go and waste eleven dollars on an ice box, eleven dollars plus shipping. The neat metal plate attached to the ice box door said "New Improved Labrador Ice Chest." She had never asked for such a thing. She watched him on that first day run his fingers over the smooth wood and polished hinges, and against her will thought: those same fingers have touched me, my naked body.

Such thoughts are more and more with her. Her brain has been running wild these last months. She is a woman whose desires stand at the bottom of a cracked pitcher, waiting.

Even now, hanging out the wash, she is faint with longing, but for what? Embrace me, she says to the dripping sheets and pillowslips, hold me. But she says it dully, without hope. Her wash tub is empty now, an old wooden vessel sitting there on a piece of outcropping rock. The sky overhead is wide and blue; it makes her dizzy looking up. She feels a tweaking in her nostrils, and reaches in her apron pocket for her handkerchief. The smell of washing soda affects her, makes her want to sneeze. "I am not willing," she says inside her head. "I am no longer willing."

It is three o'clock already, she judges. She will dispense with weeding the garden for today. If anyone asks, her husband or one of her sons, she'll blame the heat. Why put her health at risk under a strong sun like this? She'll seek out the coolness of the front room instead, the tapestry chair in the darkened corner. She's done this before, unable to stand up to this sorrow of hers. Her prized star of Bethlehem sits rooted in its china pot; she likes to study its gray-green leaves for secrets. The wallpaper, too, holds her attention with its rows of flowers, its browns and pinks alternating and repeating. The little beveled mirror in its oak frame sends back her image, her flattened-down hair and her eyes, hot as stones in her head.

"I love you," she heard young Cuyler Goodwill say to his immense, bloated wife, Mercy. "Oh, how I love you and with all my heart."

It was an early evening when she heard this declaration, a Monday like today. She had been standing beside the Goodwills' kitchen door, a basket of early lilacs in her arms, a neighborly offering. (In truth, she finds it hard to stay away; the houses of the newly married, she senses, are under a kind of enchantment, the air more tender than in other households, the voices softer, the makeshift curtains and cheap rugs brave and bright in their accommodation.) The Goodwills' kitchen window was wide open to the fresh spring breezes. They were at table (she could see them clearly enough) – Mercy on one side and Cuyler on the other, the white tablecloth and the supper dishes as yet uncleared.

Light from the doorway fell on my mother's broad face, giving it a look of luster. My father was leaning toward her, his hand covering hers. The two of them, Clarentine Flett thought, might have been the subject of a parlor picture, a watercolor done in tints of soft blues and grays.

My mother, as I have already said, was an extraordinarily obese woman, and, with her jellylike features, she was rather plain, I'm afraid. It's true her neighbor, Mrs. Flett, glimpses a certain prettiness behind her squeezed eyes and pouched chin, but the one photograph I possess, her wedding portrait, tells me otherwise. My mother was large-bodied, heavy fleshed. My father, in contrast, was short of stature, small-boned and neat, with a look of mild incomprehension flitting across his face. It can perhaps be imagined that among the men of the community coarse jokes were made at his expense.

With all my heart, Mrs. Flett heard him say to my mother. He seemed exhausted by the utterance, leaning back now in his chair. With all my heart. This was the sort of phrase that lovers in books invent. Love talk, sweetheart talk. The poetry of rapture. Occasionally Clarentine Flett has read cheap novels – hiding them from her husband who would think them time-wasting –

in which people speak to each other in soft ways, but she had never suspected that such pronouncements might be uttered in the houses of ordinary quarry workers in a village such as Tyndall, Manitoba. Nor had she imagined the enrichment of voice or tone that could be brought to these offerings. "Oh, how I love you," Cuyler Goodwill said to his wife Mercy, crying out to her with a pitch of entreaty which Clarentine Flett has been unable to wipe from her remembrance. It's been with her all spring, raining down on the dry weave of her daily comings and goings. It's with her now as she stands beside the clothesline, sneezing and blinking in the brilliant sunshine and fighting a temptation to withdraw for the afternoon.

And then an idea comes to her. She would boil up a kettle for tea and invite Mercy to come across and share it.

Yes, a nice pot of tea, Clarentine Flett decides. And she'll take down the best rose tea cups, Royal Albert, that belonged to her mother, and while she's at it, she'll set out a plate of jam biscuits. Women need companionship – that was the very thing Dr. Spears was fussing her about. Maybe that was all that was the matter with her, nothing but loneliness, not the unhappiness of life itself, but only a seasonal attack of loneliness. And Mercy Goodwill, the poor dear young soul, was lonely too – Mrs. Flett knows, suddenly, that this is true. She divines it. Never mind Mercy's secret hoard of tenderness and the soft words her young husband pours into her ear, never mind any of that. She and Mercy are alone in the world, two solitary souls, side by side in their separate houses, locked up with the same circle of anxious hunger. Why had she not seen it before? This is what's been keeping Clarentine Flett close to home these last weeks, away from the Mothers' Union and the Needle-work Auxiliary, away from the possibility of a few days' visiting in Winnipeg; she cannot bear to travel outside the ring of disability that encircles the two of them, herself and Mercy Goodwill – a pair of Christian sisters uniquely joined.

Something must at last be done, and she will do it; she'll knock on Mercy's door this very minute and call her over. She'll make the tea light and sweet the way Mercy prefers it. And she might – she feels suddenly bold at the thought of an afternoon tea party, the sort of tea party Dr. Spears's wife might have with Mrs. Hopspein, the Quarry Master's wife – she might, after a cup or two, ask Mercy to call her by her Christian name. "Why don't you call me Clarentine," she'd say. "I wouldn't mind one bit, I'd welcome it, in fact. We've been neighbors these two years now. Why, you're like a daughter to me, that's my feeling, and if you could only bring yourself –"

But this is the moment when her reverie is inter-rupted. She hears a voice, a man's high-pitched yipping, and looks up to see the old Jew stumbling toward her across the garden.

It's hard nowadays to talk about the old Jew. It's a tricky business. The brain's got to be folded all the way back to the time when the words "old Jew" could be said straight out: old Jew; here comes the old Jew.

And there he was with his dirty black clothes flapping in the heat, his hair all wild and strange about his head.

He wears a hat of some kind, shredded and filthy and pushed to the back of his skull. His cheeks, high up under his eyes, are brown and wrinkled as walnuts. The long eroded lines of his face are seamed with dirt, either that or it's the queer foreign tint of his skin.

His horse, poor creature, stands by the roadway, tied to the little bent aspen by the side of Mercy Goodwill's door. Trust him to tie up carelessly like that when he might have chosen the fence-post just as well. And that wagon, all broken down and shabby, so that it hardly deserved to be called a wagon, the way it rattles, and creaks as it jerks along its way, scattering the very crows in the fields.

His arrival is everywhere dreaded, for almost invariably he asks for the refreshment of coffee or a swallow of cold water, and then there are the cups and glassware to be scalded after him. Traveling in winter, in the remote countryside around Arborg where the Icelanders have settled, he often dares to beg a roof for the night. Bedding, then, will have to be produced, and boiled the next day, and the windows opened wide for airing. He carries into those clean, frugal households the stink of garlic, onions, mildew, and unwashed skin. The buttons and bootlaces and needles he sells, though hard to come by, are scant compensation for the risk of bedbugs and vicious unnamed diseases. His tongue is thick and sour, his eyes bewildered. He wheedles. He addresses every woman in the region as "meesus," their husbands as "meester." To the young men in the boarding houses he sells filth. He might be forty years of age or sixty. He carries a selection of pills and lotions, pocket knives and small toys, tobacco and hard candy, all poison. He looks no person in the eye. It's said he helps himself to fresh eggs from the hen houses, pinches tomatoes from gardens, slips teaspoons under his coat and carries them off. He reaches forth a black hand and pats young children on the head, catching them before they can run away, discomfiting their mothers and fathers.

He can be seen on back roads putting a whip to that poor nag of his. He shuffles up to doorways and knocks in a way that is obsequious and yet demanding. You hear that knock and you know who it is. His gait is damaged, a slow uneven shuffle that calls up memories of old-world contagion. Yet here he is on a July afternoon, running raggedly toward Mrs. Clarentine Flett, who stands beside her clothesline – her banner of bedsheets and towels – like a figure burned into a wood panel.

He grabs first at the sleeve of her dress. Instinctively she pulls away, gasping, protesting, but of course he grabs again, this time catching her roughly by the wrist. His face is screwed up with sorrow, and he's sobbing, wailing, "Meesus, meesus," his face so close to hers she can smell the rankness of his breath and body.

"Come, meesus; meesus, come."

The voice is demented; it has the creak of terror in it, too high-pitched for a man's voice, and the words nothing but gibberish. He has no more than three teeth in his head – she registers this with something like awe. A sore blackens his upper lip. Clarentine Flett, pulling herself away from him, feeling faint with disgust, is unable to take her eyes from that dried scab, which she unaccountably longs to reach out and touch.

He refuses to let go.

"Come, meesus."

She is made queasy by the roughness of his hand on her wrist, but the sight of his thready coat sleeve, and the way his pale arm shoots out beyond its length, gives her pause.

It is an ordinary man's arm, Mrs. Flett observes, and it is only mildly grotesque, not that different really from her husband Magnus's arm as it slips free of its underwear casing on a Saturday night and plunges into the scum of soapy water – exposed, scarred, knotted with veins, tightened with exertion, yet surprisingly, touchingly, womanlike.

She wonders – and all these images of hers crowd together in the space of a few seconds – wonders if the old Jew might possibly have relations somewhere in the neighborhood, a roof, a warm stove, a bed of his own to return to. If so, he might also have a woman's body next to his under the bedclothes, and a sack of loose blue flesh between his legs like every other man. These thoughts are repellent, she must shift her gaze to what is wholesome and good. And a name, of course he must have a name, you can't enter this country and become a citizen without a name. Two or three names perhaps. Unpronounceable. Unspellable. Someone would have given him those names, but who?

These questions rush at her, depriving her of air. At the same time, overlapping like an eddy of fresh water, comes the thought of her darkened front room, the armchair with its cool felt seat cushion, the way the green tapestry cloth is worn away at one corner, and how careful she is always to keep that corner turned from view.

The old Jew hangs on to her, and with his other hand gestures wildly in the direction of Mercy Goodwill's kitchen door. "Meesus sick," he manages, "sick, sick," and finally she understands.

The ground between the two houses is uneven, full of rocks and roots and tufted grass. They run together toward the open doorway, awkwardly, bumping up against each other, the old Jew's fingers never once letting go of the woman's wrist.

It is a temptation to rush to the bloodied bundle pushing out between my mother's legs, and to place my hand on my own beating heart, my flattened head and infant arms amid the mess of glistening pulp. There lies my mother, Mercy Stone Goodwill, panting on the kitchen couch with its cheap, neat floral cover; she's on her side, as though someone has toppled her over, her large soft trunky knees drawn up, and her woman's parts exposed. Like seashells or a kind of squashed fruit.

Her blood-smeared drawers lie where she's thrown them, on the floor probably, just out of sight.

There's nothing ugly about this scene, whatever you may think, nothing unnatural that is, so why am I unable to look at it calmly? Because I long to bring symmetry to the various discordant elements, though I know before I begin that my efforts will seem a form of pleading. Blood and ignorance, what can be shaped from blood and ignorance? – and the pulsing, mindless, leaking jelly of my own just-hatched flesh, which I feel compelled to transform into something clean and whole with a line of scripture running beneath it or possibly a Latin motto.

And there is my father to consider, for here he comes now, walking home down the Quarry Road. He's whistling, slapping at the sandflies, kicking up dust with his work boots. He is exhausted. Who wouldn't be exhausted after nine hours of hacking at the rock shelf, fourteen cents an hour, which is less than the cost of the pound of Vestizza currants his wife, Mercy, put in her Christmas pudding last winter? But he's whistling some merry tune, "Little Cotton Dolly" or perhaps "Zizzy Zum, Zum." At Pike's Road, which leads to the grave-yard, he stops and empties his bladder.

The distance between Garson and Tyndall is two miles. The other quarry workers, after a day in the lime kilns or working with their picks at the stone face, ride home to Tyndall in the company wagons, their boots hanging over the side. Sturdy teams of horses – those beautiful, thick-muscled, ark-worthy beasts scarcely seen nowadays – pull them homeward. But not my father. He prefers to walk. He's an odd sort, that's what's said of him in these parts. A loner. Daft-looking. Goes his own way. A runt. A quick worker though, no flies on *him*. Smart with machinery. Has a touch. Quiet, sober, comes from Stonewall Township, himself and his wife too. As for his wife, well (this said with a wink, a poke of the elbow), there's enough woman there to keep two or three fellows busy all the night long.

He likes to stretch his legs after a day spent bending over the limestone face or peering into the innards of the cantankerous old steam channeler. The quarry is only a few years old, discovered in 1896 by a farmer digging a well behind his house, and sold four years later (a steal, an outright swindle, some say) to one William Garson, owner and proprietor. Already 100,000 tons of stone have been cut and carried away, and already the landscape has been transformed so that the earth steps down in tiers like an open air arena, the shelves measuring some 12 to 36 inches in height. There is controversy about how much stone actually lies beneath the ground. Some say, the way things are going, the place will be quarried out in five or ten years; others, more optimistic, and more knowledgeable, estimate the seam to be half a mile wide and to run all the way to Winnipeg and beyond.

The stone itself, a dolomitic limestone, is more beautiful and easier to handle than that which my father knew growing up in Stonewall, Manitoba. Natural chemical alterations give it its unique lacy look. It comes in two colors, a light buff mixed with brown, and (my favorite) a pale gray with darker gray mottles. Some folks call it tapestry stone, and they prize, especially, its random fossils: gastropods, brachiopods, trilobites, corals and snails. As the flesh of these once-living creatures decayed, a limey mud filled the casings and hardened to rock. My father has had only limited schooling, but he's blessed with a naturalist's curiosity and not long ago he hacked out a few of the more interesting fossil pieces and carried them home to show to his wife, Mercy. (The stone with which she weighted her Malvern pudding on the day of my birth contained three fused fossils of an extremely rare type, so rare that they have never to this day been properly classified.)

What is it that makes Cuyler Goodwill walk home at the end of the day with the sun still hot and yellow overhead, what makes him whistle the way he does? I've already said he likes to stretch his cramped muscles after his hours of toil, and I imagine – this is a particular fancy of mine – that he likes to extend his very limbs, to feel himself grow taller, bigger, stronger as he moves closer to home, closer to the man he is about to become. A husband. A lover. He is awaited. This is an unlooked-for gift of happiness – to be awaited. He possesses a roof (rented to be sure but a roof none the less), and a supper table already set, and a wife he worships. Body and soul, he worships her.

Nothing in his life has prepared him for the notion of love. Some early damage – a needle-faced father, a dishevelled stick of a mother, the absence of brothers and sisters – had persuaded him he would remain all his life a child, with a child's stunted appetite.

His family, the Goodwills, seemed left in the wake of the stern, old, untidy century that conceived them, and they give off, all three of them, father, mother, child, an aroma of impotence, spindly in spirit and puny of body. The house they lived in faced directly on to the lime kilns of Stonewall. It sat at the end of a dirty road, its porch askew. The windows, flecked with yellow ash from the kilns, went unwashed from one year to the next, and the kitchen roof leaked; it had always leaked. In rainy weather the chimney smoked. Bread baked in this house was heavy, uneven, scarce. Wages that might have been spent on repairs or small luxuries were kept in an old jam pot, the dollar bills heaped up there like crushed leaves, soiled, aromatic. In the summer time the men of the town might gather at the corner of Jackson and Maria for a game of horseshoes, but the Goodwill men, father and son, were seldom asked to take part. The reasons for their exclusion are not clear. Perhaps it was assumed that they were indifferent to forms of recreation or that they lacked essential skills, or that they might contaminate the others with their peculiar joyless depletion. Sharp-eyed Mrs. Goodwill, on the other hand, out of some worn Christian persuasion, pinned a felt hat to her head each Sunday morning and attended services at the Presbyterian Church, but no one suggested that Cuyler come along.

No inquiries, in fact, were ever made as to his spiritual or physical health. His opinion was not sought on any issue. His growing skill as a stone worker was seldom remarked on. Until the day of his marriage, not one person had given thought to taking his photograph. No mention was made of his birthdays (November 26) – there were no gifts forthcoming, no cakes, no bustle of ceremony, though when he turned fourteen his father looked up from a plate of fried pork and potatoes and mumbled that the time had come to leave school and begin work in the Stonewall Quarries where he himself was employed. After that Cuyler's wages, too, went into the jam pot. This went on for twelve years.

It has never been easy for me to understand the obliteration of time, to accept, as others seem to do, the swelling and corresponding shrinkage of seasons or the conscious acceptance that one year has ended and another begun. There is something here that speaks of our essential helplessness and how the greater substance of our lives is bound up with waste and opacity. Even the sentence parts seize on the tongue, so that to say "Twelve years passed" is to deny the fact of biographical logic. How can so much time hold so little, how can it be taken from us? Months, weeks, days, hours misplaced – and the most precious time of life, too, when our bodies are at their greatest strength, and open, as they never will be again, to the onslaught of sensation. For twelve years, from age fourteen to twenty-six, my father, young Cuyler Goodwill, rose early, ate a bowl of oatmeal porridge, walked across the road to the quarry where he worked a nine-and-a-half-hour day, then returned to the chill and meagerness of his parents' house and prepared for an early bed.

The recounting of a life is a cheat, of course; I admit the truth of this; even our own stories are obscenely distorted; it is a wonder really that we keep faith with the simple container of our existence. During that twelve-year period it is probable that my father's morning porridge was sometimes thin and sometimes thick. It is likely, too, that he rubbed up against the particulars of passion, snatched from overheard conversations with his fellow workers or the imperatives of puberty, or caught between the words of popular songs or rare draughts of strong drink. He did attend the annual Bachelors' Ball, he did shake the hand of Lord Stanley when the old fellow steam-whistled through in 1899. My father was not blind, despite the passivity of his youthful disposition, nor was he stupid. He must have looked about from time to time and observed that even in the dead heart of his parents' house there existed minor alterations of mood and varying tints of feeling. Nevertheless, twelve working years passed between the time he left school and the day he met and fell in love with Mercy Stone and found his life utterly changed. Miraculously changed.

Stonewall in those days was a town of a mere two thousand souls, but some accident of history or perception had kept the two of them apart, and he had never, as a child and then a man in that town, laid eyes on her, had never heard mention of her name. She grew up, cloistered as any nun, in the Stonewall Orphans Home, an austere, though by no means heartless, establishment at the eastern edge of town. Here at the Stonewall Home, out of an impulse for order or perhaps democratization, all constituents lacking family names of their own, that is to say infants given over to the institution's care by their unmarried mothers, were called Stone – thus the register ran through the likes of Bertha Stone, Caroline Stone, Gareth Stone, Hyram Stone, Lamartine Stone, and so forth, coming down to my mother, Mercy, whose lineage, like the others, was entirely unknown, though her coloring, her fine hair and hazel eyes, suggested Ukrainian parentage, or perhaps Icelandic. She was left when only a few days old, wrapped in a flannel blanket – for the June nights could be cool – and placed in the old flour barrel that sat close by the back door of the institution. These flour-barrel babies, as they came to be called, were looked after by the township, given an elementary schooling, taught a trade, and sent at fourteen or fifteen into employment – except for my mother, whose housekeeping skills made her too valuable to part with. At the age of sixteen she was assisting the housekeeper on a regular basis; four years later, when the old housekeeper died, she assumed full command.

Her body reflected her diet of bread and porridge, but despite her girth – by age ten she was "heavy," at twenty she was elephantine – despite this she liked to get down on her hands and knees and polish a floor till it shone. Sometimes, bending over to take a rack of pies from the warm oven, she felt herself grow dizzy with pride – the gold of crisp pastry, the bubbling of sweet fruit, the perfection of color and texture. She took only a passing interest in the dozen or so boys and girls who lived in the Home – "Mercy Stone weighs forty stone" was chanted as a skipping rhyme among the foundling girls – but she loved to lay a table, thicken a sauce, set a sleeve, to starch and iron and fold a stack of neat linens. She was gifted. And her gifts were put to use. Worse lives can be imagined. When she stepped into a room, the girls' dormitory, for instance, her eyes went round to take in whatever was disorderly or broken or in need of a good buffing, and then she rolled up her sleeves and went straight to work.

On a spring day in her twenty-eighth year, a day of brilliant sunshine and cold breezes, it came to her notice that the door sill at the main entrance of the Home had heaved upward, displaced no doubt by severe frost, so that the door now opened with difficulty, making a wretched screeching sound. A mason was called to reset the stone. He turned out to be my father, Cuyler Goodwill.

He was at once taken with my mother's gentleness, a certain graciousness in her face, and the way her hands moved distractedly, one circling inside the other as she stood beside him, prompted perhaps by some obscure notion of social obligation – but he was moved beyond anything he had imagined by her sheer somatic presence. Her rippling generosity of flesh and the clean floury look of her bare arms as she pointed out the irregularity in the door framing stirred him deeply, as did her puffed little topknot of hair, her puff of face, her puffed collar and shoulders – framing an innocence that seemed to cry out for protection. He yearned to put his mouth against the inside shadow of her elbow, or touch with his fingertips the hemispheres of silken skin beneath her eyes, their exquisite convexity.

As he worked, she stood close by, keeping him company, speaking in her halting way of the harshness of the winter, the worst in years, bitter winds, deep frosts, and now it seemed there was flooding in the fields south of Tyndall.

Yes, my father replied, looking up at her, studying her solemn mouth, he had heard news of the flooding, the situation was very grave, but then – he lifted his small shoulders – flooding occurred every year at this time.

He noticed that my mother's corpulence had swallowed up much of her face but had spared her pure, softly fringed eyes.

He refused payment for the work, saying it had taken him less than an hour to set the stone right, that it was work he took pleasure in, a change from the monotony of the quarry, and besides – nodding vaguely in the direction of the door, the roof, the facade of the Home, the cluster of noisy children playing near the road – besides, he said, he felt moved to offer what he was able. She insisted, then, that he come into the big warm kitchen, where she served him coffee and one of her brown sugar slices, just out of the oven. These slices were a miracle of sweetness, of crispness, their pastry layers neat and pretty, and the filling richly satisfying.

He held his cup and saucer on his knee. Later he remembered looking down at his thumbnails and at the dark outline of dirt that defined them. His hands shook, but he managed to say, "May I come again?"

She stared hard, imagining the bony plate of his chest beneath his shirt, then busied herself clearing away the crockery, moving away from him. This pleading man made no sense to her. Words flew out of his mouth and melted into the warm kitchen air. She liked him better, though, for his trembling hands and the faint oniony smell of his sweat. Despite herself, she turned and offered him a strained smile.

"We could go walking?" he suggested.

"I'm not," she said helplessly, turning toward him and gesturing weakly, "much of a one for walking."

"Please," he said, astonishing himself with his courage. "We could sit and talk, if you like."

She gave him a dry, shy look which he interpreted as a form of assent.

Ahead of him, turning over like the pages of a heavy book, he saw the difficulty of all he would have to learn, of courtship, of marriage itself and its initiations, of a new way of speaking. The thought of so much effort brought him close to discouragement, yet he felt driven to carry on, to learn what he needed to know and to test his strength. Within a month he had exacted a promise from her. She would become his wife. They would move to the village of Tyndall thirty miles away where he had been offered a job in the new quarry. He announced his intentions to his mother and father – who were stunned into silence – and a wedding day was set.

People smiled to see them together, this timid, boy-bodied, besotted young man leaning attentively toward the immense woman, taking her wide, heavy hand on his lap and stroking it delicately. It was observed that he was an inch or two shorter than she. Standing at the doorway of the Home, saying goodnight, he placed his fingers on her broad cheek, tracing the outline of her curved pink untroubled skin.

From the beginning he knew that Mercy Stone's ardor was of a quality inferior to his own, of a different order altogether, and this seemed to him to be natural, rightful. The potency and fragrance of erotic love that overwhelmed him so suddenly in his twenty-sixth year was answered by Mercy with mild bewilderment. She was not cold toward him, not in the least, but returned his first shy eager embraces with a sighing acquiescence. About their future life together she seemed incurious, almost indifferent, though the fact that they would be let a modest company house did stir a response – her own home to order and arrange and run as she pleased. She would like that, she told Cuyler shyly. It was something she had not expected ever to have. She was, you might say, a woman who recognized the value of half a loaf.

When, in 1903, he married Mercy Stone, my father knew nothing of women, the hills and valleys of their bodies or the bent of their minds, and he had no idea at all how to organize a household, where to begin, what might be expected. Certainly he could not look to his laconic parents for an example, though they did rouse themselves to the extent of attending the simple marriage ceremony and presenting a wedding gift, the adamantine clock which chimed the hour, never failing to remind him of his luck in throwing off his old comfortless arrangements for a new set of pleasures, all the bleak rooms of his life freshly ordered and radiant.

He was changed. The tidal motion of sexual longing filled him to the brim, so that the very substance of his body seemed altered. He felt that he carried in his head some ancient subtle strand of memory, a luminous image of proof and possibility, the coast and continent of achieved happiness. He had no learning, knew little of history or of literature, had never been told that men in medieval times were put to bed with a disease called lovesickness, which was nothing more than a metaphysical assault too strange and powerful to be absorbed by simple flesh.

All day, at work in the quarry, breathing in clouds of mineral dust, my father thinks of his Mercy, the creases and secrets of her body, her fleshy globes and clefts, her hair, her scent, her way of turning toward him, offering herself – first bashfully, then finding a freer ease of movement. She sighs as their bodies join – this is true, he cannot deny it – but he loves even her sigh, its exhaustion and surrender. Lying together in their shallow bed, she is embarrassed about the attentions of his hands, though by accident her own fingers have once or twice brushed across his privates, touching the damp hair encircling his member and informing him of the nature of heaven. He is not repelled by the trembling generosity of her arms and thighs and breasts, not at all; he wants to bury himself in her exalting abundance, as though, deprived all his life of flesh, he will now never get enough. He knows that without the comfort of Mercy Stone's lavish body he would never have learned to feel the reality of the world or understand the particularities of sense and reflection that others have taken as their right.

He dares not concern himself with the future for fear of disturbing the present – but the thought sometimes comes of a satisfaction even fuller than what he knows – of a more commodious house, lit in the evenings with brighter lamps and perhaps – why not? – children asleep in the rooms overhead. In his early married days Cuyler Goodwill came close to weeping as he observed the arrangement of his wife's kitchen shelves, the stacked plates and separated cutlery, the neatly stored foodstuffs – rice, flour, sugar – that represent her touching, valiant provisioning for the future, but, in fact, it is only the present that he requires.

It is miracle enough to find that love lies in his grasp, that it can be spoken aloud, that he, so diffident, so slow, so thwarted by the poverty of his own beginnings, is able to put into words the fevers of his heart and at the same time offer up the endearments a woman needs to hear. The knowledge shocked him at first, how language flowed straight out of him like a river in flood, but once the words burst from his throat it was as though he had found his true tongue. He cannot imagine, thinking back, why he had believed himself incapable of passionate expression.

This is what he thinks about as he walks home from the quarry, how in a mere two years he has been transported to a newly created world. (With the toe of his boot he kicks along a loose stone, exactly as a schoolboy might do, and he draws into his lungs the dry smell of dust suspended over the fields. Nothing will ever seem so fine to him as the air on the Quarry Road in July of the year 1905.) His body at the end of the afternoon is pleasantly tired, but he cherishes each minor ache of bone and muscle, knowing that his day, even an ordinary Monday like today, will be rounded by rapture. He will wash himself clean when he arrives home, eat a good supper washed down by tea, and enter forthwith, before the sun has sunk from view, that other reality, wider and richer than any mere bed might be thought to afford: the gathering of tenderness, rising blood, a dark downward swirl of ecstasy, and then – this seems to him particularly precious – the miraculous reward of shared sleep, his beloved beside him, her breath dissolving into his. A coil of her hair will be loosened on the shared pillow and without waking her he will kiss the tips of this hair.

What a distance he has come! Now when he looks into the faces of other men, even his own dull-witted father, he thinks: so this is what the world offers us in exchange for our labor – this precious spark of joy!

A breeze is coming up. He's walking faster now. The Quarry Road takes him across flat, low-lying fields, marshy in spots, infertile, scrubby, the horizon suffocatingly low, pressing down on the roofs of rough barns and houses. A number of Galician families have settled lately in this area, building their squat windowless cottages which the women plaster over with a mixture of mud and straw. At one time he would have looked at such houses and imagined nothing but misery within. Now he knows better. Now he has had a glimpse of paradise and sees it everywhere.

Life is an endless recruiting of witnesses. It seems we need to be observed in our postures of extravagance or shame, we need attention paid to us. Our own memory is altogether too cherishing, which is the kindest thing I can say for it. Other accounts are required, other perspectives, but even so our most important ceremonies – birth, love, and death – are secured by whomever and whatever is available. What chance, what caprice!

My own birth is attended by Clarentine Flett, a woman half-crazed by menopause and loneliness, and in mourning for her unlived life, who two months later will climb aboard a train for Winnipeg and leave her husband forever, not because he beat her or betrayed her, but because he withheld the money (two dollars and fifty cents) she required in order to consult Dr. Spears about an abscessed tooth.

Another witness, wringing his hands most terribly and wailing loudly, is Abram Gozhdë Skutari, aged thirty-four, known locally as the old Jew, a peddler of trinkets, born in the Albanian village of Prizren, the son of a Sephardic maker and trader of nails, who was the son of a professional scribe who was the son of a rabbi who was – the history (compiled by Skutari's Canadian grandson, and later published, McGill University Press, 1969) goes back to the fifteenth century – born of a woman famous in her region for having given birth to twenty-eight children, all of whom lived to an old age and who paid her tribute at the time of her death, then quarreled viciously over her bedcoverings and pots.

Also present at my birth is Dr. Horton Spears, aged fifty-five, who had been hurriedly fetched by the old Jew, interrupted while taking a cup of coffee, a mid-afternoon indulgence, with his wife, Rosamund, who had returned, buoyant, from the woods north of the village with a new butterfly specimen for her collection, and who was attempting, with her spectacles sliding down her long, narrow, unlovely nose and her books spread wide on the dining-room table, to find its name and correct classification. Dr. Spears is a man of ardent sanity and tact who possesses a rich, secret, almost feminine sensibility.

And there too is my father, Cuyler Goodwill, young, brave-chinned, brimming with health and with gratitude for what life has so unexpectedly given him, hungry for the supper already prepared, eager for whatever tenderness the evening will bring. His small dark face and sinewy body burst through his back door, the tune he has been whistling dying on his lips as he falls upon this scene of chaos, his house with its unanticipated and unbearable human crowding, a strange sharp scent rising to his nostrils, and a high rhythmic cry of lamentation – where is this coming from, where? – these terrifying vowel sounds, iii-yyeeee, spiraling upward and joining the derangement of linen and of air, at the center of which lies his wife – on the blood-drenched kitchen couch, its gathered cretonne cover – my mother, her mountainous body stilled, her eyes closed. "Eclampsia," Dr. Spears says solemnly, pulling a sheet – no, not a sheet but a tablecloth – up over her face, and staring at my father with severity. "Almost certainly eclampsia."

Shadows from the open door are printed upon the floor. And there lay I on the kitchen table, dragged wet from my fetal world, tiny, bundled, blind, my heartbeat contingent upon a series of vascular valves which are as fragile as the petals of flowers and not yet, quite, unfolded. Where, you ask, is the Malvern pudding, weighted with its ancient stone? It has been set aside, as has my mother's cookery book. They will not be seen again in this story. I am swaddled in – what? – a kitchen towel. Or something, perhaps, yanked from Clarentine Flett's clothesline, a pillowslip dried stiff and sour in the Manitoba sun. My mouth is open, a wrinkled ring of thread, already seeking, demanding, and perhaps knowing at some unconscious level that that filament of matter we struggle to catch hold of at birth is going to be out of reach for me.

Everyone in the tiny, crowded, hot, and evil-smelling kitchen – Mrs. Flett, the old Jew, Dr. Spears, Cuyler Goodwill – has been invited to participate in a moment of history.

History indeed! As though this paltry slice of time deserves such a name. Accident, not history, has called us together, and what an assembly we make. What confusion, what a clamor of inadequacy and portent. Mourners have the power to charge the air with blame, but these are not yet mourners. A delirium of helplessness binds them together, or rather holds them apart.

The adamantine clock chimes six, and on the final stroke these witnesses turn and look at each other, and at me, the uninvited guest. The mysteries, secrets, and lies of their separate selves dance like atoms across a magnetic field so that the room, this simple low-ceilinged country kitchen, is charged with the same kind of vibrancy that precedes a cyclone. I am almost certain that the room offers no suggestion to its inhabitants of what should happen next, what words might be spoken, what comforts are available, tea, whisky, or the jointed, stuttering rhetoric of piety. These good souls, for that's what they are, are borne up by an ancient shelf of limestone, gleaming whitely just inches beneath the floorboards, yet each of them at this moment feels unanchored, rattling loose in the world between the clout of death and the squirming foolishness of birth.

Embarrassed, or perhaps ashamed, they cast their gaze one last time on the great white covered form of Mercy Stone Goodwill who lies before them, silent and still as a boat, a stranger in the world for all of her life, who has given her child the last of her breath.

It's this wing-beat of breath I reach out for. Even now I claim it absolutely. I insist upon its literal volume and vapors, for however hard I try I can be sure of nothing else in the world but this – the fact of her final breath, the merest trace of it lingering in the room like snow or sunlight, burning, freezing against my sealed eyelids and saying: open, open.

CHAPTER TWO

Childhood, 1916

BARKER FLETT AT thirty-three is stooped of shoulder and sad of expression, but women who set their eyes on him think: now here is a man who might easily be made happy.

They yearn to take a pressing cloth to that cheap worsted jacket he wears while lecturing to his students on the life cycle of the cyclamen or the prairie crocus. His shirts could be fresher too, and his collars properly attached, and those scuffed oxfords of his are crying out for a coat of polish, and so forth and so on. All Professor Flett needs is a little womanly attention. Affectionate attention, that is. Don't laugh at him; pity him, love him.

Distracted, he arrives at the College, five or sometimes ten minutes late for his classes, a look of dazed surprise in his eyes as he peers out at the waiting faces and rummages in his satchel for his lecture notes. There, he's found them. He arranges them on the lectern, fussing, frowning. His spectacles, he's forgotten his spectacles. No, there they are, folded in his breast pocket. He removes them, hooking the wire temples around his nicely shaped ears, first the left, then the right – then, with his middle finger placed firm on the nose bridge, brings them straight. He blinks twice. Clears his throat. And begins.

His voice is beautiful. Its texture is fine-woven wool. If it had a color it would be a warm chestnut. In tone, in fluidity, in resonance, it is all that a man's voice should be, with just that hint of Scottish burr, thinner than the skin of varnish on his oak lectern, giving necessary hardness. He rides straight up the walls of his sentences. His little pauses are sensuous gateways, without which his listeners would fall into a trance.

As it is, they keep their eyes fixed on him, focusing especially on his handsome, sorrowing, scholarly mouth, bending their heads only when it becomes necessary to write down the lists of words he unspools for them: the parts of a particular flower: pistil, stigma, style, ovary, stamen, anther, filament, petal, sepal, receptacle. Often he uses the blackboard, but today, having forgotten to bring his chalks along, he sketches these shapes in the air. His long fingers open and close around the airy forms. What a pity his shirt cuffs are in such a state, and it looks as though – yes, definitely – there is a button missing from his left sleeve; but he is oblivious to its absence – which is precisely what his female students find so compelling in Professor Barker T. Flett, his fine manly gift for self-forgetfulness.

The time is autumn, 1916, and twelve out of the fourteen students enrolled in Introductory Botany are young women. The men of Wesley College, all except for Edward Wood, an epileptic, and tiny misshapen Clarence Redfield – forty-eight inches high with one foot bent out sideways – have put on the uniform of the Dominion and gone to war. Why is it that Professor Flett is not himself away fighting at the Front?

Rumors abound. It is hinted that he is perhaps a pacifist, but one who has yet to declare himself. Or that he has a weakened heart, as suggested by the near-translucence of his skin. Or else his eyesight has disqualified him; a man who wears spectacles can scarcely be expected to confront the Kaiser, and then there is the diamond-willow walking stick he carries – which might be either an affectation or a necessity. Or possibly his ongoing work on new strains of wheat has been deemed crucial to the war effort. (Back in 1905, when studying for his Master of Science degree, Barker Flett helped perfect the new improved "Marquis" hybrid, a hearty red spring wheat which he is now attempting to cross with the remarkable "Garnet" strain that can be harvested a full ten days earlier, thus avoiding damage wrought by an early frost.) Or perhaps he has been ruled ineligible for active military duty because he is the sole support of his elderly mother and a young niece, a girl of eleven years. (This last is the favored explanation and, moreover, it is true, or almost true.)

How is it his students know of the elderly mother and young niece, for certainly he never mentions their existence? Because one of the students, the lively fair-haired Bessie Perfect, boards in a house on Downing Street, which is just two streets away from Simcoe Street where the three members of the Flett family reside. Another student, Jessie Saltmeyer, attends the First Methodist Church where the Flett family worships each Sunday morning. And then there's the student Miss Lena Ballentyne; Lena Ballentyne's father, a dentist, is acquainted with old Mrs. Flett, and has in fact fitted her, twice, for false teeth. And who else? Well, tiny Clarence

Redfield, out for a weekend stroll, once encountered the three members of the Flett family walking on the banks of the Red River. They were carrying a picnic basket and a folded bit of carpet to spread on the ground. The feebleness of small families! But also the compensating weight of their self-sufficiency.

In the halls of Wesley College these scraps of information are pooled and savored. It is pointed out by Miss Saltmeyer, almost as an afterthought, that Professor Flett's mother is not all that elderly after all, and that during the spring and summer season she raises a good-sized crop of flowers on the vacant land next to the Simcoe Street house and purveys them to the various flower merchants who have opened shop around the city. Someone else contributes the information that the "niece" is not a true blood relation, but only the daughter of a family acquaintance whose wife died in childbirth. All this lore is fascinating to the students of Introductory Botany, but chief among the fascinations is the fact that Barker Flett is an unmarried man. This curious and wonderful anomaly offers them hope for their own lives: a handsome thirty-three-year-old man who has yet to find his life's companion.

They can't help wondering if there might not be a tragic broken engagement in his past – and this possibility has been so often discussed by succeeding waves of students that it has acquired by now the hard sheen of authenticity. It exists in several versions: a sweetheart snatched from life by summer fever, a fiancé judged unsuitable because of high church leanings, because of tainted character, because of madness in the family, because the salary of a professor at Wesley College would never stretch to meet her material needs.

In fact, there is no broken engagement in Barker Flett's past, no severed union of spirit and body. Professor Flett, who is perfectly aware of the legends that romance around him, smiles at the thought. His smile, like his voice, is beautiful, but it is a smile hatched from a frustrated asceticism, and the suspicion that love is no more than a diminutive for self-injury. His own society is what he favors. A quiet winter room, a chair, a book opened under a circle of lamp light, a comfortable austerity. Or else a solitary hike in a summer meadow, botanizing all the day long with just his pocket knife and specimen bag and a sandwich or two for company. True, he has three times in his adult life visited the rooms of prostitutes on Higgens Avenue, but these he thinks of as educational episodes which touched nothing in him that might be termed authentic. It may be that he is one of those men who feel toward women both a delicate sensibility and a deep hostility. He is not, in any case, in mourning for a lost love, as his students want to believe; he mourns only a simplicity of life that was briefly his, and now is lost.

Never was happiness more firmly in his grasp as in the summer of 1905, his twenty-second year, living alone in two back rooms at the top of a Simcoe Street boarding establishment, bent over his small student desk and completing his dissertation on the western lady's-slipper, genus *Cypripedium*.

He loved this flower. (The "lady," of course, was Venus.) He could have drawn its sensuous shape even in his dreams. Dorsal sepal, column, lateral sepal, sheath, sheathing bract, eye, and root. A common plant, yes, but belonging to the exotic orchid family. This delicate, frilled blossom was his. He had worked on it (her) for months, and now he possessed the whole of its folded silken parts and the pure, classic regenerative mechanics that lift it out of the humble mid-continental clay and open its full beauty to the eye of mankind – and to his eye in particular. (He believed this without vanity.)

The intensity of his gaze on this single living thing awakened in him other complex longings. He ached anew for release from his body – those ladies of Higgens Avenue – and the obliteration of all he had found brutal in his life thus far, beginning with the dumb, blunted angers of his parents and brothers, a family from whom the supports of education, culture, and even language had been withdrawn. He longed to separate himself from the mean unpaved streets of Tyndall, Manitoba, where he spent his boyhood, and from the crude groping for salvation and sex he apprehended everywhere around him. Bliss lay in the structure of this simple flower he was attempting to reproduce on a sheet of white rag paper: a petalled organism, complete in itself, obedient to its own rhythms and laws and to none other. Years later, looking back, he remembers how tenderly he held the watercolor brush in his hand, how the sun falling through the windowpane struck the top of his wrist and the edge of the water glass, and how the whole of his existence lightened correspondingly.

His euphoria was to be short-lived. Principal Mac-Intosh at the College asked him to redirect his research toward the development of hardier grains, reminding him that Methodism was a social, as well as spiritual, religion and thus concerned with the quality of human life – and here the old man underlined his words with fervor – human life on this earth. For the enlightenment of young, impressionable Barker Flett, he quoted the words of Jonathan Swift: "Whoever could make two ears of corn grow upon a spot of ground where only one grew before, would deserve better of mankind, and do more essential service to his country, than the whole race of politicians put together."

Young Flett was obliged to give up his dabbling in lady's-slippers and to concentrate on hybrid grains. Moreover, as if that were not sacrifice enough, he was to be burdened with the teaching of introductory chemistry and physics as well as botany, and one year later, after poor Blaser was discharged (having been found to be a "user of alcohol"), he was assigned to teach the elementary zoology course as well. Overnight, it seemed, the singleness of his concentration had been shattered.

Worse, he returned to his rooms on Simcoe Street one evening in late September to find his mother installed. On her lap lay a tiny infant, arms thrashing, legs kicking, stomach arching, its lungs inflated, howling out against the injustice of the world.

Have I said that Clarentine Flett deserted her husband Magnus in the year 1905? Have I mentioned that she took with her the small infant who was in her charge, the young child of Mercy Goodwill, her neighbor who had died while giving birth?

The month of Mrs. Flett's departure was September; a series of night frosts had turned the air chilly, and the infant – a little girl of placid disposition – was clothed in a tucked nainsook day-slip topped by a plain flannel bar-rowcoat, which in turn was topped by a buttoned vest in fine white wool, and all these many layers were wrapped and securely pinned inside a commodious knitted shawl.

It was a sparkling morning, 9:07 by the clock when Mrs. Flett stepped aboard the Imperial Limited at the Tyndall station, certain that her life was ruined, but managing, through an effort of will, to hold herself erect and to affect an air of preoccupation and liveliness. Those who saw her purchase her ticket for Winnipeg – with a dollar bill taken the night before from her husband's collar-box – failed utterly to mark the fact that she paid for one-way accommodation only. These witnesses may, if they were standing close by, have sniffed about her person a sharp but not unpleasant scent, which emanated from the wad of cotton wool she had soaked in oil-of-cloves and packed tight against her throbbing molar. Her hat was not worth a second glance, trimmed as it was with ordinary mercerized satin and Japanese braid, but it was pinned nevertheless at a becoming angle on her small, stern head, giving her the jaunty look of a much younger woman; in fact, she was forty-five. The great armful of fall flowers she carried would have seemed to onlookers a mere womanly fancy, and anyone peeking inside her small valise would have found only a folded woolen coat for herself, a dozen napkinettes in fine canton flannel for the infant, and a baby's feeding bottle with three black rubber teats. An awkward arm-load, to be sure – bag, bouquet, and baby – but she took her seat by the window with an air of assurance.

The journey was short, a mere fifty-three minutes over flat stubbled fields and through a series of sunlit villages – Garson, East Selkirk, Gonor, Birds Hill, Whittier Junction – and during that time, with the infant asleep on her breast, Clarentine Flett began making plans for her survival. Her breakfast of oatmeal porridge lay heavy in her stomach, but her imagination soared. She saw that her old life was behind her, as cleanly cut off as though she had taken a knife to it (that note for her husband tucked under her handkerchief press, a single scratched word, goodbye). Ahead waited chance and opportunity of her own making. She would step from the train into the busy street in front of the Canadian Pacific Station in Winnipeg and offer her flowers to passers-by; city folks were fools for fresh flowers, even flowers as common as these that grew wild in every wasteland of the region, though you had to know where to look; she would make four separate sprays of them – these deep blue asters, or Michaelmas daisies as they were frequently called – then add a few thin leathery leaves and tie them prettily with some ribbon she'd brought along and sell each one for ten cents, earning enough to hire a cab to take her and the child to the rooming house on Simcoe Street where her son, Barker, lived. Once there, she would ascend the half-dozen wooden steps, knock on his door, and gain admittance. After that she would wait, watchful and alert, to see what came her way.

"My dear Mr. Goodwill," Clarentine Flett wrote in her large, loopy, uneducated hand, "I thank you for your message, and I am writing at once to assure you that Daisy, as I have taken to calling her, is well looked after and in excellent health. I am happy that you are in agreement with me that such a small infant will thrive more readily under female care, at least for the time being, and I am only sorry that my distracted state of mind last Tuesday morning prevented me from leaving you a note of explanation. You need have no worry about your dear child, since our situation in my son's household is very comfortable and hygienic. Your present state of bereavement touches me deeply, for, as you know, I loved your dear wife Mercy with all my heart. I have enclosed with this letter a lock of the child's hair which I trust will bring you some measure of comfort. It is, I fear, a very small lock, only a half-dozen hairs in plain truth, for she has as yet little to spare."

Barker Flett, that tall, gaunt, badly clothed student of botany, sat hunched over his cluttered desk, the angle of his bent head signaling misery. Sighing with vexation, he picked up a steel-nibbed pen, dipped it in the inkwell, and scratched: "My dear Father, I thank you for your letter, though it grieves me to learn of your unwillingness to write to my Mother directly, since I can't help believing that an appeal on your part, if sincerely expressed and softly worded, might encourage her to reflect on her situation and eventually return home." (Here he paused for a moment, staring out at the rain which was rattling against the window.) "In the meantime, I beg you to find it in your heart to make her some small allowance, perhaps one or two dollars a week. As you know, I have had to engage an additional room to accommodate her and the child, and my scholarship income from the College scarcely covers these new and totally unforeseen expenses. There have been a number of doctor's bills also, as Mother has suffered from severe infection following the extraction of her teeth, and the infant has been troubled day and night with what Dr. Sterling calls a tight chest. Perhaps you are aware that your neighbor, Mr. Goodwill, has agreed to provide the sum of eight dollars a month for the child's maintenance. Generous as this is, it barely suffices. I send you, and to my dear brothers as well, my affectionate regards. Barker Flett"

My dear Mr. Goodwill,

Your monthly letter is always welcome, and I thank you most warmly for your Express Money Order, which is much appreciated. I am pleased to write that Daisy continues plump and happy, and her legs are grown strong indeed. My son and I are of the opinion that she will be walking before the month is out. I enclose the photograph you requested. (And again I thank you for sending the necessary money.) You will be able to see for yourself that the photographer has captured the exceptional curliness of her hair, which is of a very pretty color that I have heard described as "strawberry." I am anxious to assure you that, contrary to what you may have heard, the air in Winnipeg is fresh and healthful. In addition, we are fortunate in having a fine big garden next to our house where little Daisy will be able to run about when the summer weather arrives.

With kind regards,
Clarentine Flett

My dear Father,

I have spoken to my Mother as you requested, but I am afraid she is firm in her refusal to return to Tyndall, despite your generous offer to accept her back into the household, even forbearing mention of her sudden leave-taking and long absence from home.

As to your other question, I must regretfully answer in the negative, for I think it would only excite her nerves to receive you here. Her state of mind is relatively tranquil at the moment, and she is much occupied with the garden and with running after young Daisy. We must not, however, give up hope of a future reconciliation.

I regret, also, your decision in the matter of money, which has become, for me, a never-ending source of distress.

Your son,

Barker

My dear Mr. Goodwill,

You will scarcely believe that Daisy is to start her first level at school in a mere ten days. Already she has her alphabet by heart, also Our Lord's Prayer, the Twenty-third Psalm, and a number of simple hymns. She is, moreover, able to recite the common names of all the flower varieties in our garden, of which there are some twenty-five. I am happy to say that these two months of fine weather have improved her chest, as has the regular application of a mullein-leaf poultice at bedtime. As for myself, I keep very well.

Yours faithfully,

Clarentine Flett

Dear Mr. Goodwill,

I thank you for yours of the 28th, and assure you that Daisy is in excellent health. Her school recitation, "A Sailor's Lament," was given with the greatest feeling and enthusiasm.

We were most interested to read of you and your famous tower in last week's *Tribune*. My son, Professor Flett, regarding the tower's rather blurred likeness on the page, grew most curious to see it as it really is, but as you know he never travels anymore to Tyndall since his brothers have gone West.

Yours most sincerely,
Clarentine Flett

My dear Father,

It gives me pain that I must once again apply to you for money. I do beseech you to search your conscience and give a thought to the many years in which you and my Mother lived in harmony, during which time she served most dutifully and lovingly with never any thought of compensation. Our day-to-day situation here is exceptionally insecure at the moment, and I now fear that my decision to purchase the Simcoe Street house, as well as the land that adjoins it, was premature, particularly with the city moving southward, and now talk of war. My actions, I assure you, proceeded from the wish to provide Daisy, who is growing into a fine young girl, with a reliable and respectable home of which she need never feel ashamed. It is true that my Mother does earn some income from the sale of plants and herbs, but the cost of constructing a greenhouse has been considerable. It is also true, as you say, that my own earnings have been augmented by the licensing of the "Marquis" wheat hybrid, but fully three-quarters of these earnings remain the property of the College. I look forward, with hope, to your favorable reply.

You may be interested to know that "Goodwill Tower," as it is known in the city, is much talked of these days, and I am told it draws visitors from all over the region, and even from the United States.

Your son,
Barker

Dear Mr. Goodwill,

This little note will, I hope, bring you the assurance that Daisy is now fully recovered from the attack of measles. It has been a most distressing time, and very tiresome indeed for her to remain so many weeks in a darkened room, particularly as she is by nature an active and healthy child. She was much cheered, however, to discover a photograph of you in the pages of last week's *Family Herald*, standing in front of your tower. "Is that truly my father?" she demanded of me, and I assured her that indeed it was. She became most anxious to pay you a visit, and would talk of nothing else for days, but we believe, Professor Flett as much as myself, that such a visit would cause too much excitation in one so recently recovered from a serious illness.

We remain grateful for your monthly contribution to our household. We manage the best we can on a limited purse, and happily my little garden enterprise is beginning to thrive. It is as if all the world has discovered the happiness that simple flowers can bring to an otherwise dreary wartime existence.

Yours,
Clarentine Flett

Dear Mr. Goodwill,

I thank you most sincerely for your prayers and for your words of condolence. I can tell you truthfully that my dear Mother did not suffer in her final days, having entered into a state of unconsciousness the moment the dreadful accident occurred. Those friends and acquaintances who kept vigil at her bedside found in her repose a source of strength and inspiration. She was laid to rest, finally, amid friends and family, both my brothers arriving from the West in time to pay their respects. Our Father, as you know, remained hardened in his heart to the end, and it is for him we must now direct our prayers. Regarding the young cyclist who struck my Mother down, he has been fined the sum of twenty-five dollars, and I am told the poor fellow is fairly ill with remorse.

I have been thinking much these last days about the question of Daisy, whom my Mother has loved as dearly all these years as if she were her own child – doted on her, in fact. You will agree, I am sure, that it is not in any way desirable for a young girl of eleven years to share a household with a man of my circumstances who has neither a wife nor the means to engage a person who would look after her needs. In any case, it seems I must leave Winnipeg very soon in order to pursue my work with the Dominion Cerealist and his committee in Ottawa. Will you be kind enough to write me the full expression of your thoughts on the subject of Daisy and what we can arrange between us to ensure her future accommodation and happiness.

Yours faithfully,
Barker Flett

Having known rapture, my father, Cuyler Goodwill, could not live without it.

Once awakened, he was susceptible. It might have been poetry he embraced after the untimely death of his wife – or whisky or the bodies of other women – but instead, like many young working men of his time, he found God. In his case, God was waiting in the form of a rainbow east of the Quarry Road, not far from the plot where my mother lay buried.

This event occurred in the month of October, an early morning following a night of heavy rain.

In a cloth sack slung over his shoulder he carries an octagonal-shaped piece of limestone (about the size, say, of a cantaloupe) which he intends to place on his dead wife's grave. He climbs the fence at Taylor's Corners, taking a shortcut through a field of stubble, over the soaked uneven ground, when suddenly the sun bursts through, weakly yellow at first, but quickly strengthening so that the heat reaches through the fibers of his gray cotton shirt. He looks up, and there it is: the rainbow.

Of course he has seen rainbows before in his life, always stopping, in the way of country people, to admire the show of watery iridescence. Rainbows, after all, do not occur so frequently in southern Manitoba that they go unremarked. "Look at that," someone or other is always sure to exclaim, pointing skyward, and then a wishful thought might rise up, a vague notion of impending good fortune or at least an alteration of mood.

At this time in his life Cuyler Goodwill had not yet begun his long immersion in Bible study, and could not have quoted, had you asked him, God's post-flood declaration to Noah: "I do set my bow in the cloud, and it shall be for a token of a Covenant between me and the earth."

At the same time, he is not by any means an ignorant or superstitious man (though limited in formal schooling), and he understands the general principles of rainbows, that the prismatic effect is caused by the refraction, reflection, and dispersion of light through droplets of water. He understands, too, the evanescence of the phenomenon, its insubstantiality – he is, after all, a man who works with stone, with hard edges and verifiable volume. The arc of a rainbow cannot be touched; its dimensions are not measurable, and its colors fade even as they are apprehended. There is a belief, for that matter, widely subscribed to by simple people, that a rainbow cannot be photographed, that its fugitive and transitory composition resists the piercing lens and the final proof of chemically treated paper.

But the rainbow that appears before my father on that October morning in 1905, a mere three months after his wife's demise, is different, its colors more vibrantly distinct, its shape as insistent as a child's crayon drawing. This rainbow seems made of glass or a kind of translucent marble, material that is hard, purposeful, pressing, and directed. Directed at him, for him. He has not observed the bands of color taking shape; he knows only that it is suddenly there, solid and perfect, and through its clean gateway shines a radiant slice of paradise.

At the moment the rainbow makes its appearance he is standing, and the next moment kneeling, by the grave of his wife, Mercy.

He, a stonecutter by trade, has set her gravestone himself, a mottled wedge split thin and polished, with her name and dates deeply incised on its center.

Mercy Stone Goodwill
1875–1905
Greatly Beloved
&
Deeply Mourned

The work of engraving had distracted him in the first terrible days, but almost immediately he perceived that the monument was pitifully inadequate, too meagre and insubstantial for the creature who had been his sweetheart, his wife, his treasure. Now, each day, he carries one or two small stones from the quarry, caching them carefully behind a clump of willow at Taylor's Corners, not far from the turning at Pike's Road. He chooses the stones carefully, for he has formed an odd resolution, which is that he will set them without mortar. Gravity alone must hold them in place, gravity and balance, each stone receptive to the shape of those it rests against and in keeping with the abstraction that has lately filled his head like a waking reverie, a dream structure made up of sorrow mingled with bewilderment. Again and again he hears a voice, the same voice, asking the same question: why had his wife not told him a child was expected?

Already the walls of the tower have risen to shoulder-height. Some of the stones he sets are no bigger than his thumb or his fist, some measure eight or ten inches across or more. This morning, in the rainbow's garish light, their surfaces seem to dance in rhythm with the clusters of goldenrod that had opened up everywhere in recent days. Sun and rain, cloud and light, flower and stone – they are each so closely bound together, so almost prophetically joined, that he experiences a spasm of joy to find himself at the heart of such a holy convergence. His chest fills up with his own noisy relief, a cry of ecstasy, a wild howl of joy.

He had thought himself alone in the world, but in fact he is a child of this solid staring rainbow, and of the persevering forms of light and shadow, of substance and ephemera. A child of the earth.

Only later, walking home across the rutted fields, does he recall and give honor to the author of his happiness, uttering God's blameless name aloud.

For days at a time he is able to forget that he is the father of a child, a little girl named Daisy, and then something will jangle a bell to remind him. He might glance at the calendar on the kitchen wall and observe that the fourth Tuesday of the month is fast approaching, the day he sends off a money order to Mrs. Clarentine Flett in Winnipeg. Or he will observe, when the weather turns warm, how young children from the village bring lunches to their fathers at the quarry, lingering there to play for an hour or two with pollywogs or with chips of waste stone, and always this sight will set him wondering what manner of child his daughter might be.

Or Mrs. Flett might send a photograph of the girl along with a letter describing her steady growth, her genial disposition, or her cleverness at school. Daisy in her pictures appears an obedient child, careful of her dress, and possessed of a spare, neat body – and for this he supposes he should feel grateful. Her smile is neither forward nor timid, but something in between. (For some reason he is unable to determine whether or not she is pretty. Probably she is not.) The most recent photograph includes Mrs. Flett and Professor Barker Flett as well, one sitting on either side of Daisy on what looks like a grassy stretch of river bank, the three of them colored into character by soft gray tones, the family at ease, the family in love with itself, no trace of disharmony.

Occasionally he will wake from sleep with his body trembling and his head soaked with the sweat of memory. There, dancing in the darkness, as plain as life, are the walls of the resurrected kitchen with its tumult and confusion, its circle of shocked faces, and the silent, sheeted body of his dear Mercy. The clock is striking the hour, and the striking seems to go on and on without ceasing, clanging behind his eyes, and muffling with its clamor the distance between that which is dreamed and what is remembered. While the others stand and stare like statues, he runs out the kitchen door and throws himself on the ground, rolling over and over, shouting and weeping and pounding his fists on the baked earth. "She didn't tell me," he roars to the vacant sky, "she never told me."

This is what he is unable to comprehend: why his Mercy had seen fit to guard her momentous secret.

He supposes he must look upon her silence as a kind of betrayal, or even an act of hostility, but he is reminded, always, of her old helplessness with words and with the difficult forms the real world imposes. He tries to imagine what she felt while this ball of human matter was growing inside her, how she accommodated its collapsed arms and legs and beating heart, whether she feared its intrusion or if she perhaps loved it so deeply she was unable to speak its name, to share its existence or plan for its arrival.

He admits to himself that his love for his dead wife has been altered by the fact of her silence. More and more her lapse seems not just a withholding, but a punishment, a means of humbling him before others who see him now, he imagines, as an ignorant or else careless man. What manner of husband does not know his wife is to bear a child?

Yes, it must be confessed – years later this is clear to me – that my father's love for my mother had been damaged, and sometimes, especially when waking from one of his vivid dreams, he wonders if he is capable of loving the child. Daisy Goodwill, eleven years old, frozen in a camera's eye. A little girl in a straw hat. A child perched on a river bank, solid, stiff, an unreadable smile playing on her lips. It would be unnatural if a father did not love his child, but what Cuyler Goodwill feels is only a pygmy love produced by the ether of custom. He has responsibilities. He sends money for her keep. He writes Mrs. Flett letters in which he expresses his concern for the child's health and happiness, but, in fact, he seldom thinks in such terms. Who is this being, flesh of his flesh? (Daisy is not a name he would have chosen, but the child had to be called something, and he was in no fit state after my birth to turn his mind to names.) He studies her photograph. He thinks of her at odd times of the day. He is mildly, intermittently curious about her, and a little afraid, and lately, learning that she has suffered from the scourge of measles, he has wondered if it might not be expected of him to take the train into Winnipeg one Sunday morning and reassure himself as to her condition.

But he shrinks from this awkward meeting. And from the confusion of travel – he has never been to the city, has never seen any reason for going – and is reluctant, anyway, to sacrifice the whole of a Sunday. On Sundays he reads his Testament, prays for forgiveness and works on his tower.

It's Sunday morning now, a fine June morning, and the iron bell in the steeple of the Tyndall Methodist Church is calling the faithful to worship, but my father is not drawn by this clanging and banging.

Religion has not made a church-goer of Cuyler Goodwill. In the early days of his conversion he attempted, three or four times, the morning service in Tyndall, and once, once only, he walked seven miles west to the settlement at Oakmidden where he sat, bewildered, through the arcane rites of a Greek Orthodox mass. The noisiness of public worship – singing, praying, chanting, preaching – make him uneasy. The vestments of holy men, even the simple white Methodist collar, abrade his sensibilities, crowd him to the edge of his belief, and the dusted, raftered, churchy spaces assault him with their perfume and polish, belittling him, taunting him. Moreover, his natural instincts feel constrained by the order of holy service, the breathy invocations and amens and numbered hymns, and afterwards the obligation to shake hands with others of the congregation, to greet them soberly, to engage his tongue in social exchange – all this rubs the man the wrong way.

Instead, almost by accident, he has fallen upon a mode of sustained personal meditation which is not so far removed from that practiced for centuries on the Asian subcontinent, a trance of concentration which was to become fashionable in our own culture later in the century, the foolish sixties, the seventies.

In his case it is an ecstatic communion. On Sundays he approaches his Maker by a series of ritualized steps, rising at dawn, taking a breakfast of tea and bread, then walking out, and in all weathers, to the burial grounds off the Quarry Road. As he walks he recites to himself a scrap of scripture, a single verse usually, which he repeats over and over.

> *There is none holy like the Lord,*
> *there is none beside thee.*

Again and again. The words beat at his temples like a secondary pulse. His boots strike the surface of the road-way in an answering rhythm that draws him behind the scrim of ordinary consciousness. He meets no one coming and going – the hour is too early for man or beast. In a small handcart, which he has cobbled together himself from odds and ends, he transports the stones he intends to set. He has come to believe that the earth's rough minerals are the signature of the spiritual, and as such can be assembled and shaped into praise and affirmation. He also conveys, hooked into the loops of his belt, a mallet and a number of small chisels. His tools, his music, his offering – he carries all that he needs on his body.

Where my mother's solitary gravestone once sat, now

rises a hollow tower some thirty feet in height and still growing. The stones that constitute its fabric have been chosen for their strength and beauty and for their effect on the overall design. A spiral of cantilevered stones protrudes, and these allow him to ascend the steep sides as easily as an insect or a lizard might scale a wall.

More and more my father chooses to decorate the stone surfaces with elaborate cipher, even though Tyndall stone, with its mottled coloring, is thought to be resistant to fine carving. Patterns incised on this mineral form seem to evade the eye; you have to stand at a certain distance, and in a particular light, to make them out. This impediment is part of the charm for him. What he carves will remain half-hidden, half-exposed, and as such will reflect the capriciousness of the revealed world. Here he inscribes a few holy words, there the image of a bird, a flower, a fish, a face, a sun or moon. An angel half the size of his hand freezes on a worked limestone sky. A tiny stone horse grazes in a stony meadow. Cupids, mermaids, snakes, leaves, feathers, vines, bees, cattle, the curve of a rainbow, a texturing like skin – the tower is a museum of writhing forms, some of which he has discovered in the *Canadian Farmer's Almanac* or the Eaton's catalogue or in his illustrated Bible.

The carving is done on winter nights in the warmed untidy cave of his widower's kitchen, where he has set up a workbench and vise and a good gas light. He has already, after a day at the quarry, eaten his supper of fried eggs and tinned peas, and is ready to make the stonedust fly. His tools are simple, and his technique somewhat unorthodox – he is after all, a self-taught carver, grown skillful through long periods of trial with the wooing of relief and shadow and with the spare particularity the stone is able to release. Working slowly, he feels the world shrink around him, small as a pudding basin. His attention becomes concentrated as he moves from scratch to groove, as he joins line and curve, elaborating an image that is no more at first than an atom flickering in his brain, bringing to it all its possibilities while guarding its pure modality, its essence – this, always, is the hardest part – and preparing himself for the moment when the worked stone is complete. (I wish somehow you might see these carved surfaces, how they send back to the eye a shiver of yielded revelation, so full of my father's sad awkwardness and exertion, yet so cunning in their capture of precious light.)

Despite his gifts, the act of carving never ceases to be a labor for him – the whole of his body bends into the effort, and his face takes on that twisted monkey look of concentration you see on the faces of real artists or musicians. (Of course he never thinks of himself as an artist – his innocence is wide open like air and water.) Only when he finishes a piece and carries it to the site of the tower does he experience the fever of transcendence (though transcendence, like art, is not a word he would utter or even recognize). What he feels when the finished stone slips finally into its waiting space is the hand of God upon his head, the Holy Ghost entering his body with a glad shout.

The religious impulse, as everyone knows – certainly I know – is hard to pin down. There are ecstatics, like my father, who become addicted to the rarefied air of spiritual communion, and then there are cooler minds who claim that religion exists in order to keep us from feeling our own absurdity.

For Cuyler Goodwill, a man untrained in conventional theology, the human and the divine are balanced across a dazzling equation: man's creation of God being exactly equal to God's creation of man, one unified mind bending like a snake around the curve of earth and heaven. (It has taken him years to work all this out.)

For those seven pacifists forced out of the Methodist ministry in the city of Winnipeg in the year 1916, religion finds its net worth between the hard rock of private conscience and the equally hard place of the political platform.

For those farmers and their families who are – right now, in the month of June – rebuilding the Chain Lakes Meeting House after it was burned to the ground by so-called patriots – for this congregation of Friends, religion is the cement that seals shut their door on the world.

For Clarentine Flett, lying in a coma after being knocked down by a bicycle at the corner of Portage and Main, religion is a soft flurry of petals drifting and settling peacefully on the evening of her life. And for the seventeen-year-old butcher's boy, Valdi Goodmansen, whose bicycle (exceeding the legal speed of eight miles per hour) was responsible for the accident, religion is the bottled broth he sucks like a starved infant in the middle of the night. *Seek ye forgiveness and it shall be given.* For Abram Skutari, who sold the boy the bicycle (twenty-five dollars), religion is an open window, as well as the curtain with which he darkens the window.

For Magnus Flett of Tyndall, master stonecutter and abandoned husband of Clarentine Flett, religion is both the container and water of remembrance, holding sacred (that is leaving untouched) the shriveled leaves of a particular parlor plant of hers called the star of Bethlehem; also the vivid tactile memory of loose beds of stone from his native Orkney; also an image he recollects of his own father and mother, the two of them at dusk, dragging hay into a barn, and his father stopping to extract a foreign object that had flown into his wife's eye, leaning down and removing it with the tip of his tongue.

For Principal MacIntosh of Wesley College religion is the physic for right thinking, correct living, and earnest praying. "One thing this war has done," he writes in a letter to the *Free Press*, "is shaken us out of our self-sufficiency and brought us nearer to our Maker."

For Bessie Perfect, a Wesley College student ardently in love with her botany professor, Barker Flett, religion is a painful obstruction that forms in her throat when she whispers his name against her pillow, and also when she sings, "Keep the home fires burrrrning / While our hearts are yearrrrning."

Left to himself, Barker Flett, professor, scholar, collector of some seventeen different species of lady's-slippers, believes religion to be a glorious metaphor for the soul's desire. There is no God, no Son of God, no Holy Family, no resurrection, there is only desire. Desire for more. For perfection. For self-knowledge. Desire to possess all fifty known varieties of lady's-slippers. Desire for sleep and forgetfulness. Desire for good and for evil. Desire for rapturous union, the object of which, he knows, can be, and often is, fraudulent. Lately he has been reading about a pollinating mechanism in which a male insect is attracted to certain small orchids, the lip of which simulates the sexual parts of the female insect. As a man of science, Flett finds the phenomenon obscurely disturbing, particularly the copulative gestures the excited male performs at the edge of the mute petal. He is also disturbed, though he has yet to acknowledge it, by the presence of eleven-year-old Daisy Goodwill in his household, the bold unselfconscious movement of her body, her bare arms in her summer dresses, the unnatural yearning he experienced recently when he entered her darkened sick room and observed the sweetness of her form beneath the sheet.

Winnipeg in the year 1916 is an agreeable place. One can live a decent life in this city – despite its geographic isolation, despite the war across the ocean. Even the long hard winters are cheerfully borne by the complacent, generally law-abiding population, and indeed winter brings a benign, clean countenance to the raw look of wooden buildings and laissez-faire planning.

Increasingly, though, the city is growing mannerly. A series of wide, new boulevards has been proposed, and an immense new legislative building in the neo-classical style is underway. Ground was broken back in the year 1913. The vast amounts of stone required for this ambitious undertaking have kept the Tyndall Quarry working full-tilt and the stonecutters steadily employed and well out of the Kaiser's reach. Churches now stand on many of the downtown corners, sometimes two or three different sects represented at one crossing. ("Let us hope God has a sense of humor," quipped a well-respected Baptist pastor at a recent civic meeting.)

These churches are made of stone, as are the many fine banks and insurance companies, also the well-known Wesley College and the new Law Courts. Scanning the municipal horizon, you can't help thinking: isn't this astonishing! A stone city rising up out of our soft prairie loam! (An eminent Chicago architect, on seeing the blocks of polished Tyndall stone, declared that American builders would be clamoring for the material, were they but to lay eyes on its beauty.)

During the winter season Winnipeg offers a variety of theatrical productions, skating parties, balls, and dinners. In the summer the well-to-do flee the heat for the Lake of the Woods, and the less privileged make do with day trips to Victoria Beach or to various other interesting attractions of the region. Among the young people, those, say, between eighteen and twenty-five years of age, a railway excursion to the village of Tyndall has become exceedingly popular of late. The cost of a train ticket is moderate, and the young people, picnicking on sandwiches and bottles of cold tea, grow very merry. The ladies greatly outnumber the gentlemen during these war years, but the gender imbalance, far from dampening spirits, produces an oddly exhilarating effect. Many bring along bathing costumes, since the old abandoned part of the quarry provides a sunken cube of clear, cold water which is ideal for swimming. But it is really Goodwill Tower they come to see.

To be sure, getting to the tower requires an energetic half-hour's tramp along a country road, and then a further stretch to the east, down a dirt trail. But this exertion is part of the day's pleasure for these lively young people. They are full of ginger and fizz, invigorated by fresh air and the relief of having escaped for a few hours their more sober responsibilities in the city, not to mention the horror of a war being fought across the sea.

Across the low-lying fields the tower can be easily spotted. "There it is," someone will shout. (For some of them this is the second or third visit.)

When the sun is high overhead the tower appears white; later in the afternoon it takes on a blue-gray softness.

Always, one or two of these young people will break into a run. *First man there is a starving bear.* They reach the low stone cemetery wall, scramble over it – never mind the gate with its rusted hook – dodging the gravestones and stands of thistle. There! At last! They pat the tower's bumpy sides, which are surprisingly warm from the sun's rays, and clamber up and down its stepping stones – the young women often have to be coaxed, or assisted, before they'll go all the way to the top, being fearful of heights, or of exposing their undergarments. They persevere, however, since the view of the surrounding countryside is said to be superb, and they are curious, every last one of them, to peer down into the tower's hollow core at the circle of weeds, beneath which lies a small gravestone – or so it is said.

There is a good deal of shrieking and laughing on these excursions. Someone locates the mermaid stone. Someone else finds the carved cat, and the little stone down near the bottom which is inscribed with the single word "woe." The most knowledgeable person in the party will recount the history of the tower: a beautiful young wife dead of childbirth. A handsome young husband, stunned by grief – a man who can still be glimpsed occasionally, working away on the tower in the early morning hours, although he is no longer young, no longer handsome by the day's standards, and no longer building with his original fervor; he is happy enough, in fact, to stop work and pass the time of day with visitors. And the baby, what happened to the baby? No one seems to know. It touches the heart. It does.

And now, just look at the time; the day-trippers must head back to the village and catch their train. The sun is dipping low. They walk more slowly; some of the couples hold hands or go arm in arm. One or two of them may turn, on an impulse, and look back at the tower. They are heard to comment aloud on the almost medieval look of the structure, and how strange it is to see a sight like this poking up in the middle of the prairie horizon. A remark will be made about the beauty of the limestone, how nearly it resembles Italian marble. One of the young men has pocketed a small carved nugget, which he fingers as he walks along. Someone else, one of the more bookish of the young women, murmurs something about the Taj Mahal in faraway India, how it too is a monument to lost love.

How does a poet know when a poem is ended? Because it lies flat, taut; nothing can be added or subtracted.

How does a woman know when a marriage is over? Because of the way her life suddenly shears off in just two directions: past and future. Ask Clarentine Flett.

We say a war is ended by a surrender, an armistice, a treaty. But, really, it just wears itself out, is no longer its own recompense, seems suddenly ignoble, part of the vast discourtesy of the world.

Things begin, things end. Just when we seem to arrive at a quiet place we are swept up, suddenly, between the body's smooth, functioning predictability and the need for disruption. We do irrational things, outrageous things. Or else something will come along and intervene, an unimaginable foe. Abe Skutari, after years and years of peddling door-to-door in rural Manitoba, is drummed out of business by Eaton's Mail Order. Who would have expected such a thing? So what does he do but borrow money from the Royal Bank – the first such loan ever made to a son of Israel – and open his own retail establishment on Selkirk Avenue in Winnipeg, specializing in men's workclothes and footwear, garden supplies and bicycles. A door closes, a door opens; Mr. Skutari's own words.

Professor Barker Flett in 1916 is at the end of his Winnipeg chapter. His mother is dead. His faith is exhausted. His thirty-three-year-old body frightens him with its perversities. The world frightens him, too, even as it beckons to him brightly, offering him whatever he desires, or almost. He must turn a page now, and move forward, eastward, Ottawa to be precise, the capital of the Dominion.

And my father, Cuyler Goodwill of Tyndall, Manitoba, has finished his tower. How does he know it is finished? The proportions tell him so, the wholly pleasing correspondence of height, width, circumference; one more course around the top and the thing would grow unbalanced; he looks at it and his thoughts become easy, almost lazy. And there have been so many visitors lately, and so many newspaper reporters. (He suspects that visitors are carrying away pieces of his worked stone, and all he can do when he hears such gossip is shrug.) These visitors have distracted him to the extent that lately he has forgotten the impulse that launched the tower. He talks willingly, even eagerly, with those who come, but shies away from the root of his obsession. Why exactly have you persevered with your tower, Mr. Goodwill? Well, now, a person starts a piece of work and the work takes over. God has receded, a mere shadow, and as for Mercy – her grave so sunken and grown over – he cannot recollect the look of her face or the outline of her body. His brief marriage, his conversion – these seem no more than curious intersections in a life that is stretching itself forward.

A letter has come from Professor Barker Flett in Winnipeg concerning the breakdown of guardianship arrangements and the problem of what is to be done for Daisy's future care.

Another letter has come, only yesterday, from the president of the Indiana Limestone Company of Bloomington, Indiana, in the United States. Expert stone carvers are urgently needed. An extravagant wage has been named. A comfortable apartment on Cross Street in Vinegar Hill (whatever that may be) is available for his occupancy. Transportation will be arranged for himself, his family, and his household effects. Does Mr. Goodwill have a family? Immediate reply requested. Please wire.

Bessie Perfect got blamed for giving Daisy Goodwill the measles. With her fever and sore throat, Bessie should have been home in bed instead of standing at the Fletts' very doorstep, handing Daisy her overdue botany notes, apologizing in great girlish splutters, and sneezing into the child's susceptible eleven-year-old face.

The disease went wafting through Daisy's respiratory passages, and soon she had all the symptoms. Aunt Clarentine (for this is how Daisy has always addressed her) peered into the child's mouth and leapt back with horror – spots everywhere. The poor little thing was put to bed in a darkened room. The door was kept shut, with Aunt Clarentine her only visitor, and no one could say the woman was not a devoted nurse. She brought the sick child cool, wet rags to soothe her fever, a solution of boracic lotion to douche her eyes morning and night, herbal creams of her own making to assuage the itching, and trays of soft food to pick at – poached eggs, stewed fruit – after which Daisy was adjured to cleanse her mouth with a forefinger wrapped in cotton wool. She began to get better, and, simultaneously, to grow bored. And then, suddenly, she became much, much worse.

The doctor – whom I am unable, or unwilling, to supply with a name – announced bronchial pneumonia, and sketched, for Aunt Clarentine's edification, a drawing of the bronchial tree. Nowadays a course of sulfono-mide or antibiotic drugs would make short work of the girl's condition, but at that time bed rest, fluids, and heat constituted the only treatment. This went on for some weeks, and since no one remembered to open the curtains or provide a light, the period of Daisy Goodwill's secondary illness was also spent in darkness. In addition, the blocked smell of dust and feather pillows imposed a kind of choking suffocation, the beginning of what was to be a lifelong allergy.

She must have slept a good deal – for how else could an active child have endured such a width of vacant time? – and whenever she woke it was with a stiff body and a head weakened by nameless anxiety. This had to do with the vacuum she sensed, suddenly, in the middle of her life. Something was missing, and it took weeks in that dim room, weeks of heavy blankets, and the image of that upside-down tree inside her chest to inform her of what it was. What she lacked was the kernel of authenticity, that precious interior ore that everyone around her seemed to possess. Aunt Clarentine with her tapping footsteps in the upstairs hall, bustling and cheerful and breaking out in laughter over nothing at all and talking away in a larky voice about how grateful she was that "God who so loved the world" had chosen to let her go her own way. And Uncle Barker, as Daisy called him in those days, setting off for the College with his diamond-willow cane in hand and his old scuffed shoes striking the pavement, purposeful in his young manly intent even while he sighed out his reluctance. Other people were held erect by their ability to register and reflect the world – but not, for some reason, Daisy Goodwill.

She could only stare at this absence inside herself for a few minutes at a time. It was like looking at the sun.

Well, you might say, it was doubtless the fever that disoriented me, and it is true that I suffered strange delusions in that dark place, and that my swollen eyes in the twilight room invited frightening visions.

The long days of isolation, of silence, the torment of boredom – all these pressed down on me, on young Daisy Goodwill and emptied her out. Her autobiography, if such a thing were imaginable, would be, if such a thing were ever to be written, an assemblage of dark voids and unbridgable gaps.

Lying in her bed, she apprehended life going on around her – which only worsened her sense of mourning. She could hear dogs barking in the neighborhood, and bird song welling up, and the sound of the milkman going his rounds on Simcoe Street, his horse making a whinnying sound at the corner and stamping his heavy feet and dropping down his water and turds. Doors opened and closed, letters arrived, people came and went in the house, voices murmuring, the kettle coming to a boil, the hall clock ticking on and on.

In the solipsistic way of children, the girl was amazed that all this should continue without her. Aberdeen School would not recess – no, it would not – because of her illness; the schoolyard would remain as full of life as ever, and the bell ringing on and on with the same punctual ferocity. She knew, too, that Aunt Clarentine's garden by midsummer would fill up with snapdragons, even if, by chance, she wasn't there to pick off their heads and make the little blossoms "bite" at her fingers. That was what she kept coming back to as she lay in her hot, darkened room: the knowledge that here, this place, was where she would continue to live all her life, where she had, in fact, always lived – blinded, throttled, erased from the record of her own existence.

She understood that if she was going to hold on to her life at all, she would have to rescue it by a primary act of imagination, supplementing, modifying, summoning up the necessary connections, conjuring the pastoral or heroic or whatever, even dreaming a limestone tower into existence, getting the details wrong occasionally, exaggerating or lying outright, inventing letters or conversations of impossible gentility, or casting conjecture in a pretty light. (When her beloved Aunt Clarentine died late in the month of June, after lying one solid week in a coma, Daisy floated her to heaven on a bed of pansies, and, at the same time, translated her uncle's long brooding sexual stare, for that was what it was, into an attack of indigestion.)

She willed herself to be strong, and when at last she met her real father, Cuyler Goodwill – he arrived at the Simcoe Street door with sweat on his brow, wearing an ill-fitting suit, looking disappointingly short and dark-complexioned – she braced herself for his kiss. It didn't come, not on that first meeting. He never so much as took her hand. His face had a poor, pinchy look to it, but the mouth was kind. They sat downstairs in the parlor, he in the leather armchair, and she on the sofa, two strangers in a glare of silence. Daisy was wearing a yellow striped dress made of Egyptian cotton. Her father cleared his throat politely. This was enough to loosen his tongue. He went on and on after that, explaining to her about the train journey they were about to take, and the place where they would be living when they arrived in Bloomington, Indiana. An apartment, it was called. He said the word cherishingly, as though to persuade her of its worth.

The two of them were drinking lemonade from tall tumblers.

Who made this lemonade? Someone must have squeezed the lemons and stirred in cups of sugar and added chipped ice, but Daisy can't think who this person might have been. Nevertheless her fingers will always remember the feel of those tumblers, the pale raised bands on thin pink glass, but it is the sun she will chiefly remember – how yellow like corn meal it was, sifting through the fine summer curtains and filling up the whole of the room. These, at least, were things she might believe in: the print of sunlight on her bare arm. The cool sweet drink sliding down her throat. The buttons on her father's shirt, glittering there like a trail of tears.

Her knees formed little hills, poking up through the yellow cloth. Her father's words came toward her like a blizzard of dots.

On that day she liked the world.

CHAPTER THREE

Marriage, 1927

MRS. JOSEPH FRANZMAN entertained at luncheon yesterday in honor of Miss Daisy Goodwill of Bloomington. Covers were laid for ten.

Mrs. Otis Cline received at tea this afternoon in honor of Daisy Goodwill, a June bride-elect. Miss Goodwill is a graduate of Tudor Hall and of Long College for Women.

Mrs. Alfred Wylie entertained at a kitchen shower Thursday afternoon in honor of Daisy Goodwill, a June bride-to-be. The rooms were prettily decorated with wisteria, bells, and streamers. Guests included Mrs. Arthur Hoad, Mrs. Stanton Merrill, Mrs. A. Caputo, Mrs. B. Grindle, Mrs. Fred Anthony, Miss Labina Anthony, Miss Elfreda Hoyt, and the Misses Merry Anne and Susan Colchester.

During the afternoon, Miss Grace Healy contributed several delightful vocal and piano selections.

A "white" dinner in honor of Bloomington bride-elect Daisy Goodwill and groom-to-be Harold A. Hoad was held at the Quarry Club last night. The menu included bay scallops, fillet of Dover sole, supreme of chicken served with an accompaniment of creamed onions, and a dessert of vanilla chantilly ice molded in the form of twin doves. Guests were Mrs. Arthur Hoad and sons Lons Hoad and Harold A. Hoad, Mr. and Mrs. Horton Graff, Mr. and Mrs. Hector MacIlwraith, the Misses Labina Anthony and Elfreda Hoyt, Mr. Dick Greene, Mr. and Mrs. Stanton Merrill, and Mr. and Mrs. Otis Cline. The artistic table, centered with a profusion of summer blooms and lighted by ivory tapers, was presided over by Mr. Cuyler Goodwill, the host for the evening and the father of the bride-elect. The silver-tongued Mr. Goodwill, a partner in the firm Lapiscan Incorporated, concluded the evening's festivities with a few eloquent and thought-provoking words on the benefice of time and coincidence.

"Time," Cuyler Goodwill tells his audience of fifteen, that genial after-dinner assembly who sit now with their chairs pulled back from the table a comfortable inch or two, a burr of candlelight softening their features, "time teams up with that funny old fellow, chance, to give birth to a whole lot of miracles. It was, after all" – and here Mr. Goodwill lifts an expository finger – "it was the lucky presence of a warm, clear and shallow sea, some three hundred million years ago, only think of it, my friends – that combination produced the remarkable Indiana limestone which has served all of us here so well." (At this there is appreciative applause all around.) "Now, if that water," Mr. Goodwill continues, "had been just a little cooler, the billions and trillions of little sea creatures might never have got themselves born, and their shells wouldn't have got piled up down there on the seabed like they did. And if the water in that peaceful old ocean had been less clear, there would sure as anything have been clay and other deposits to affect the sedimentation. Finally, my good friends, if those ancient marine-waters had been an inch or two deeper, there wouldn't have been any wave action to break down the shell material to uniform size and spread it across the many square miles of the sea floor. In short, ladies and gentlemen, our beautiful white Salem stone, our great gift from the earth, would never have existed. It was a miracle, and I think you'll agree, all these various afore-mentioned items coming together at the very same time and bestowing on us the triumphant trinity of challenge" – he pauses dramatically – "of prosperity" – another pause – "and happiness."

The port is low in the glasses now; the lovely candles flicker – for a window has been opened to the breezes of the night. Mr. Goodwill pulls back his small compact shoulders and warms to his thesis.

"By a similar stroke of luck, my good friends, it is exactly eleven years this month since my daughter, Daisy, and I arrived in Bloomington. I think often how providential was our timing, since this last decade, as we all know, has been one of unprecedented expansion for the limestone industry. But it seems to me even more remarkable that my daughter and I should have been welcomed" – here he lifts his arms in a magnanimous gesture to suggest an embrace – "welcomed by friend-ship and by opportunity. And, of course, I was honored, some years ago, when Mr. Graff and Mr. MacIlwraith, both of them present at this table tonight along with their charming wives, invited me to join with them in their new enterprise, and I believe all of you here will attest to the good fortune that smiled on our venture. Not that we can claim credit for our success. We have time itself to thank." Here he stops, looks slowly around the table, meeting each set of eyes in turn. "Time. And chance. Those twin offspring of destiny. That wondrous branching of our fates."

The waiters hover in the shadows, anxious for the evening to conclude so they can go home to their beds, but Mr. Goodwill has not yet finished.

"And, looking at our young couple here this evening – Daisy, Harold – how can any of us believe that they are not also favored by time and chance. We are living in the extraordinary year of 1927 AD. The modern era has truly begun, and if any of us had harbored doubts about the future, we have been convinced otherwise one month ago by a certain Mr. Charles A. Lindbergh Jr." (This timely allusion touches the very pulse of the gathering, and Goodwill himself leads a round of enthusiastic applause, the ladies clapping spiritedly, their lovely white hands uplifted, and the gentlemen thumping the table top.) "Furthermore, my friends" – he is winding down now, his coming-home cadence beautifully calculated – "at this very point in history the remarkable profile of a great building is about to rise in the Empire State of our nation – as noble a testimony to the powers of Salem limestone and to human ingenuity as any of us would have dreamed. From this moment we can only go forward."

Hear, hear!

"And now, may I ask you to rise, one and all, and drink to the happiness of our young couple. Chance has brought the two of them together, and time has smiled warmly on them both."

How did my father, Cuyler Goodwill, come by his silver tongue?

At fifty, he is quick of movement, all pep and go, all point and polish. He wears marvelous shirts of English broadcloth, dazzling white, professionally laundered, a fresh one every single day of the week. His suits are made for him in Indianapolis or Chicago, and they fit his form – no ready-to-wear for him: he has shed such embarrassments as a snake sheds its skin, not that there is anything snakelike or sly about Goodwill's open, energetic businessman's countenance. His physiognomy, naturally, has changed very little. He will always be a man who is short of shank and narrow of shoulder, but this rather abbreviated body is not what people register. People look into Cuyler Goodwill's small dark compacted face, wound tight like a clock, full of urgency and force, and think: here stands a man who is vividly alive.

Energy shoots from his very eyes – which have kept their youthful whiteness, their intensity of fixation. He is an impressive figure in the community, respected, admired. But it is when he opens his mouth to speak that he becomes charismatic.

That silver tongue – how was it acquired? The question – would anyone disagree? – holds a certain impertinence, since all of us begin our lives bereft of language; it is only to be expected that some favored few will become more fluent than others, and that from this pool of fluency will arise the assembly of the splendidly gifted. Call it a dispensation of nature – a genetic burst that places a lyre in the throat, a bezel on the tongue. A dull childhood need not disqualify the innately articulate; it would be arrogance to think so; a dull childhood might indeed drive the parched intelligence to the well of language and bid it drink deep.

Cuyler Goodwill himself believes (though he does not bruit this about, or even confess it to himself) that speech came to him during his brief two-year marriage to Mercy Goodwill. There in the sheeted width of their feather bed, his roughened male skin discovering the abundant soft flesh of his wife's body, enclosing it, entering it – that was the moment when the stone in his throat became dislodged. An explosion of self-forgetfulness set his tongue free, or rather a series of explosions ignited along the seasonal curve: autumn Sundays in the tiny village of Tyndall, Manitoba, a crispness in the air. Or a string of cold January nights. And spring evenings, the breezes moist, the sun still present in the western sky, slanting in through the window across the pale embroidered pillow covers and on to the curves of wifely flesh – his dear, dear, willing Mercy. Words gathered in his mouth then, words he hadn't known were part of his being. They leapt from his lips: his gratitude, his ardor, his most private longings – he whispered them into his sweetheart's ear, and she, so impassive and unmoved, had offered up a kind of mute encouragement. At least she had not been offended, not even surprised, nor did she appear to find him foolish or unnatural in his mode of expression.

My own belief is that my father found his voice, found it truly and forever, in the rhetorical music of the King

James scriptures. During the years following his conversion by my mother's grave – that sudden rainbow, that October anointing – he applied himself to his Bible morning and night. Its narratives frankly puzzled him – the parade of bearded kings and prophets, their curious ravings. Biblical warnings and imprecations flew straight over his commonsensical head. But scriptural rhythms entered his body directly, their syntax and coloring and suggestive tonality. How else to explain his archaic formal locutions, his balance and play of phrase, his exotic inversions, his metaphoric extravagance. Language spoke through him, and not – as is the usual case – the other way around.

Another theory holds that the man grew articulate as the result of the great crowds who traveled northward to see the tower he built to his wife's memory, a tower constructed with his own hands. A fair proportion of these visitors, after all, were journalists, journalists who stood by Cuyler Goodwill's side with a notebook and pencil in hand. Just a few questions, Mr. Goodwill, if you don't mind. Young, clear-eyed, ready to be astonished, they came from all across the continent, and from as far away as London, England, bringing their journalists' sheaf of queries, their hows, whens, their whys. Cuyler Goodwill had become a public person. Eccentric perhaps, an artisan *naif*, but not unapproachable, not in the least. He was a man, on the contrary, who could easily be sounded out, given space. This was his moment, and he must have recognized it. His tongue learned to dance then, learned to deal with the intricacies of evasion and drama, fiction and distraction. His voice, you might say, became the place where he lived, the way other people live in their furniture or gestures. At the same time he developed the orator's knack for endurance, talking and talking without exhaustion, not always (it can be confessed) with substance.

More and more of late, his stamina on the platform has been exclaimed over, his lungs, his bellows, those organs of projection, that chest full of eager air. His hands dance a vigorous accompaniment. At the Lawrence County Businessmen's Luncheon last winter he spoke for sixty minutes without notes, his remarkable tenor instrument never seeming to tire. And, standing before the Chamber of Commerce's annual smoker in Bedford, he carried on – delightfully so, according to the *Star-Phoenix* – for a full hour and a quarter. And just one year ago, a fine June morning, he presented an inspiring address to the graduating students of Long College for Women on the banks of the Ohio River, his daughter, Daisy, being one of those receiving the degree *artium bacheloreus*. His talk, entitled "A Heritage in Stone," a mythopoetic yoking of commerce and geology, stretched to an unprecedented two hours, and it was said afterward that scarcely half a dozen of the young ladies dozed off in all that time. "What a set of pipes the man's got," the college president remarked at the strawberry shortcake reception that followed. "What exuberance, what gusto."

But Cuyler Goodwill's longest oration, his longest by far, took place in the year 1916 aboard a train traveling between Winnipeg, Manitoba, and Bloomington, Indiana, a distance of some thirteen hundred miles. His audience consisted of one person only, his young daughter, Daisy, who was then a mere eleven years of age. They traveled, by day, in a first class lounge car, courtesy of the Indiana Limestone Company, Cuyler Goodwill's new employer. The green plush seats were roomy, luxurious, and could be tipped back and forth for comfort. An ingenious mahogany panel pulled down to form a table, and one could order tea brought to this table, tea with a wedge of lemon perched on the saucer's edge. Side by side the father and daughter sat, with only a little wood arm rest between them. They were virtual strangers, these two, and hence each avoided placing an arm on the barrier of polished wood. The journey lasted three full days – with confused, hectic changes at Fargo and Chicago, and again at Indianapolis – and for all that time the father talked and talked and talked.

A switch had been shifted in his brain, activated, perhaps, by sheer nervousness, at least at first. He had not "traveled" before. The world's landscape, as glimpsed from the train window, was larger than he had imagined and more densely compacted. The sight filled him with alarm, and also with excitement. The forests and fields of North Dakota, Minnesota, and Wisconsin seemed to him to be swollen with growth, standing verdant and full-formed against a bright haze. The land dipped and rose disconcertingly, and he was amazed to see that haying was taking place so early in the season. Towns sprang up, one after the other, the spaces between them startlingly short, and the names unfamiliar. He was discomfited to see how easily men (and women as well) stepped from the train to station platform, from platform to train – with ease, with levity, laughing and talking and greeting each other as though oblivious to the abrupt geographical shifts they were making, and disrespectful of the distance and differences they entered. Many were hatless, their clothes brightly colored. The cases they carried appeared, from the way they handled them, to be feather-light, and made of materials – straw, canvas – that mocked his own dark brown Gladstone, purchased only days before and as yet unscuffed.

South, and further south the train went, an arrow of silver cutting through the uncaring landscape. The sun shone brilliantly. As the miles clicked away, it seemed to Goodwill that the seriousness of the world was in retreat. Singing could be heard from the club car: "Ain't She Sweet," round after round, as they crossed the Illinois border into Indiana. Rivers, rounded hills, paved roads, fenced fields. Advertisements for chewing tobacco appeared on the sides of barns. The towns grew larger and dirtier. Electric wires slashed the bright air like razors.

The first day was the worst. He talked wildly, knowing that shortly he and his daughter would be called to the dining car for the second sitting, and he deeply feared this new excitement. Soon after that the sun would sink from view, and he would be confronted with the aberration of a Pullman bed, of the need to arrange his body in a curtained cubicle, yielding it up to the particles of displaced time and space.

It was against all this terror that he talked.

He told the child about his boyhood in Stonewall, laying out for her the streets of that town, the site of his parents' house by the lime kilns, the smell of burning lime on a winter morning, how sometimes he was wretched and sometimes joyous. He confessed to her his simple amusements, his liking for tasks, his ready adaptation to the trade of quarrying, his curious bond with rock and earth.

On and on. Dinner came and went. The little girl felt faintly sick, the train lurching this way and that, and the heaviness of chicken and gravy in her stomach. In the dining car she had spilled a trail of this yellow gravy on the white table cloth, and her father had pulled the linen napkin from his shirt front where it was tucked, and covered the spot over, never breaking for a moment his flow of words. He was talking now about his dead wife, the child's mother; her name was Mercy – Mercy Goodwill, a young woman uniquely skilled with pies and preserves and household management.

Some of this the young Daisy took in and some she didn't. The hour was late. She drifted in and out of sleep, but even awake her mind kept coasting back to the surfaces of the Simcoe Street house in Winnipeg where she had lived most of her life, its snug-fitting windows and doors and its flights of wooden steps, down into the cellar or out to the side garden where Aunt Clarentine's flowers grew in their rows. The face of Aunt Clarentine floated by, smiling. (This face must now be returned to dust, a comforting thought, dust being familiar, ubiquitous, and friendly and not at all threatening.) Uncle Barker would be packing up his instruments and specimens and preparing for the journey to Ottawa, another train journey, but eastward instead of southward. He had pointed out on a map where Ottawa was placed, a small black dot sitting in a nest of intersecting waterways.

Dreaming her way backward in time, resurrecting images, the young girl realized, with wonder, that the absent are always present, that you don't make them go away simply because you get on a train and head off in a particular direction. This observation kept her hopeful about the future with a parent she had never known, a parent who had surrendered her to the care of others when she was barely two months old.

Her eyes nodded shut, but still her father talked. It seemed to her that his voice continued all night long, but that was impossible, for she woke once or twice to find herself alone on a smooth cool cotton sheet and a mattress of wonderful thickness, with darkness all around.

In the morning it began again, the two of them breakfasting in the dining car (soft poached eggs, triangles of buttered toast), and her father talking, talking. His restlessness was stirred up now, stirred up so it couldn't be put down. The child had to shut her ears; she needed calming, not this assault of unsorted recollections. Sealed in, she reconstructed in her head the patches of grass and gravel that lay behind Aberdeen School back in Winnipeg, and the bushes that rubbed up against the rough fence of the schoolyard. Her father was going on about the intricacy of stone carving, how the right chisel had to be selected, and how carefully it must be held, how too much pressure in the wrong place can split and ruin good material, how every piece of stone in the world has its own center with something imprisoned in it.

Green corn filled the passing fields, every row made perfect as it swung around out of sight, each stalk a long-leafed gentleman or lady bending toward its neighbor, chattering there in the breeze, so tall and polite. Her father was explaining the difference between sandstone and limestone, between granite and marble. She felt his voice filter into her veins and arteries, and spread out in her memory.

Deeper and deeper into the well of his life he went: a rainbow, a gravestone, a slant of morning light.

He talked to fill the frightening silence and to hold back the uncertainty of the future, but chiefly he talked in order to claim back his child. He felt, rightly, that he owed her a complete accounting for his years of absence. Owed her the whole of his story, his life prised out of the fossil field and brought up to the light. Every minute was owed, every flutter of sensation. There was so much. He would never be able to pay it all back.

When we think of the past we tend to assume that people were simpler in their functions, and shaped by forces that were primary and irreducible. We take for granted that our forebears were imbued with a deeper purity of purpose than we possess nowadays, and a more singular set of mind, believing, for example, that early scientists pursued their ends with unbroken "dedication" and that artists worked in the flame of some perpetual "inspiration." But none of this is true. Those who went before us were every bit as wayward and unaccountable and unsteady in their longings as people are today. The least breeze, whether it be sexual or psychological – or even a real breeze, carrying with it the refreshment of oxygen and energy – has the power to turn us from our path. Cuyler Goodwill, to supply an example, traveled in his long life from one incarnation to the next. In his twenties he was a captive of Eros, in his thirties he belonged to

God, and, still later, to Art. Now, in his fifties, he champions Commerce. These periods of preoccupation are approximate, of course, for naturally there is a good deal of overlapping, some spiritual residue in his business activities, some memory of erotic love to sweeten his art. But on the whole, his obsessions, growing as they do from the same tortuous biographical root, then branching and proliferating, are attended by abstinence: "One thing at a time" is the rule for Cuyler Goodwill. He is like a child in that way.

And he is oddly unapologetic about his several metamorphoses, rarely looking back, and never for a minute giving in to the waste and foolishness of nostalgia. "People change," he's been heard to say, or "Such-and-such was only a chapter in my life." He shrugs with the whole of his small, hardened body and smiles out from that little leather purse of a face. He has, after all, in his life as a quarryman, seen star drills give way to steam channelers, and hand-powered cross-cut saws to mechanized gang saws. Back in the year 1916 he had been hired as a carver for the Indiana Limestone Company and he is now a principal partner in his own subcontracting firm. He has seen limestone overtake softer sandstones as the nation's favored building material. (Last year, 1926, 13 million cubic feet of Indiana limestone were quarried and sold, much of it for the dazzling new monuments of New York City and Washington D.C.) One thing leads to the next, that's life.

You should know that when Cuyler Goodwill speaks, as he often does these days, about "living in a progressive country" or "being a citizen of a proud, free nation," he is referring to the United States of America and not to the Dominion of Canada, where he was born and where he grew to manhood. Canada with its forests and lakes and large airy spaces lies now on the other side of the moon, as does the meagreness of its short, chilly history. There are educated Bloomingtonians – he meets them every day – who have never heard of the province of Manitoba, or if they have, they're unable to spell it correctly or locate it on a map. They think Ottawa is a town in south-central Illinois, and that Toronto lies somewhere in the northern counties of Ohio. It's as though a huge eraser has come down from the heavens and wiped out the top of the continent. But my father, busy with his carving contracts and investments and public speaking schedule, has not spent one minute grieving for his lost country.

That country, of course, is not lost at all, though news of the realm only occasionally reaches the Chicago and Indianapolis dailies. The newspaper-reading public of America, so preoccupied with its own vital and combustible ethos, can scarcely be expected to take an interest in the snail-like growth of its polite northerly neighbor, however immense, with its crotchety old king (sixty-two years old this week) and the relatively low-temperature setting of its melting pot. Canada is a country where nothing seems ever to happen. A country always dressed in its Sunday go-to-meeting clothes. A country you wouldn't ask to dance a second waltz. Clean. Christian. Dull. Quiescent. But growing. Yes, it must be admitted, the Dominion is growing.

Seven hundred settlers, representing nearly every European nationality, reached Montreal last week, arriving aboard four rather motley steamers: the *Letitia*, the

Athiaunia, the *Pennland*, the *Bergenfjord*. But what difference, you say, can a mere seven hundred citizens make in
all that vastness? A grain of sand added to a desert. A
teaspoon of water dribbled into the ocean. Moreover,
reverse immigration must be taken into consideration,
those settlers who fail to adapt and who, in a year or two,
or sometimes twenty or thirty, return to their countries of
origin.

Such a one is Magnus Flett of Tyndall, Manitoba,
retired quarry worker, who is on his way "home" to the
Orkney Islands. What a misery that man's existence has
been – these exact words have been said of him by at least
a dozen acquaintances, for he has no one who might be
called a friend: the poor man, the unfortunate soul, his
tragic, lonely life. A life that carries in its blood a
romantic chill, or so some might think.

Born in 1862, the man is now sixty-five – sore of spirit,
toothless, arthritic, deaf in his left ear, troubled by
duodenal ulcers, his great frame bent, his hair grizzled,
his skin broken, his muscles atrophied, his testicles
shrunken, his feet yellowed. He has lived in the Dominion since he was a mere lad. Here is where he brought his
strong, young body, which was all he possessed, and his
skill with stone. Here is where he sought his fortune.
Where he met and married one Clarentine Barker of Lac
de Bonnet Township, a farmer's daughter. Where he
sired three sons, Barker (now a fancy-talking civil servant in Ottawa), Simon (a machinist in Edmonton, a
drinker), and Andrew (a Baptist preacher presently
living in Climax, Saskatchewan, himself the father of a
daughter). You would think old Magnus Flett would be
rooted in this new country, that the ties of family and

vocation would bind him tight, and that he would wish, when the time came, to be buried in Manitoba's thin saline soil under a chunk of mottled Tyndall stone. Instead he has forked out a hefty portion of his savings for passage back to his homeland in the Orkneys, a place where he has no remaining blood connections that he knows of, and very few memories.

He doesn't know what he'll do with himself when he arrives. He's cranked up the courage to leave Canada, but he's waiting for the bare Orkney landscape to rise up and inform him, to advise him, of what he must do next. Something will emerge from his past, he's sure of it, some wisdom to rescue his last days. This faith comes out of a vacuum, an absence of recollection, though he does dimly remember the stripped hills and vales of home, their sudden, minor angles of incline, and the freshness of the wind diving about, and a remnant of other sensations too, none stronger than the smoky, blocked airlessness of his parents' kitchen, the blackened ceiling and the way the breath caught in the throat, offering a promise of safety, yet a threat too. There was a good deal of loud quarreling under that low roof, he's certain of that, it went on for years, but over what? His parents and an older brother are buried in the church-yard at Sandwick, and he imagines that he will join them there sooner or later. Dust to dust. A gathering of spirits. Something anyway.

He traveled first to Montreal by train, four days, and then boarded ship for the eight-day crossing to Liver-pool. He has his savings, which are respectable. He has a trunk packed with warm clothing, enough to last him the rest of his days, and with a few mementos of his forty-six years in Canada: some stone specimens, Tyndall dolomites, beauties, carefully wrapped round in woolen underwear. His tools. His pipe. Five pounds of his favorite tobacco. Four books – these protected in triple layers of newspaper – from which he is never parted. Some family papers too, immigration certificates, birth documents (the three sons, his progeny, his only trace in the wide world), and his wife's goodbye note, left for him under her handkerchief press in the year 1905. Goodbye, it said; that was all, after twenty-five years of marriage; goodbye. A penciled scrawl.

And there are a few photographs too. His wedding photo: a formal pose, 1880, his young bride seated on a carved studio chair, her hands stiff in her lap, her hair whisked back flat, her expression blank. And he, a fine figure of a man – impossible to deny it – six feet three inches, standing behind her, his left hand raised to his ear lobe, tweaking it somehow, or scratching it. Was it the photographer who instructed him to fool with his ear in this manner? And, if so, why had he obeyed?

Another photo: the three boys. Barker, at six years, staring sullenly into the lens: Simon, four (in short velvet pants, unimaginable those pants, where had they come from?), sitting cross-legged on a cushioned bench; and Andrew, two, squirming – unmistakably squirming – at Simon's feet. His sons. His dear sons. Lost.

And one more photo.

It is a group portrait, undated, but he believes it was taken in 1901 or 1902. Before his wife went "strange." Before everything altered. On the back of the photo someone – the handwriting is unknown to him – has written the words: "The Ladies Rhythm and Movement

Club." There are six women in the photo. He recognizes the doctor's wife, Mrs. Spears. He recognizes Maude Little and Mamie Heftner standing at the back. He recognizes each of those staring ladies. Oh, aren't they just chuffed with themselves. It makes you laugh to look at the lot of them. They're all got up in identical skirts and waists, some kind of colored border around the collar, and a wide sash wrapped around the waist. They are daft in their expression, but oddly stern too, saying with their teeth and lips and with the lift of their shoulders: aren't we swell though, aren't we just something else. Clarentine Barker Flett, his wife, is in the front row, a wee bit shorter than the others, slim, pretty, mischievous, cheeky; it's hard to believe she is in her early forties and has borne three sons, she looks so like a fresh girl. She's biting down on her lower lip as if life was one wonderful lark. Happy, yes, she seems irreverently happy.

Magnus Flett has looked at this photograph of the Ladies Rhythm and Movement Club a thousand times, searching from face to face, moving from left to right, from top to bottom, and always he comes down to this: the proven fact of his wife's happiness.

A painting will lie, but the camera insists on the truth, he's heard this said. His beleaguered mate, her little bones and covering of soft flesh, occupied a place in the world in those days; no sane person, examining this photograph, would deny that fact. She had, the evidence says, floated upward toward moments of exaltation or else foolishness, it came to the same thing. His wife. Her sassy smile, her knees bent, her sash catching the light. She does not look anything at all like the wife of a brutal husband. She cannot have been oppressed and ill-used twenty-four hours a day for twenty-five long years, the idea is unthinkable.

He consoles himself with this thought.

He remembers, too, that she had had a kind of pride, a respect for her own labor, refusing, for instance, to pit the prunes that went into her prune pudding, letting those who ate her steamed offerings wrestle with the stones in their own mouths. He admired her for that, that curious disinclination to exhaust herself.

And he denies and denies – but who is there to listen? – that he forbade her to visit Dr. Spears about an abscessed tooth in the early autumn of 1905. It was not true. No. He would have paid out the two dollars and fifty cents gladly. He had only reminded her, when her toothache came on so sudden, as to how his own ear infection the previous spring had cleared up on its own without the need for costly medical consultation. (This is true, though it is also true that he eventually lost half his hearing in that ear.)

For all the years of their wedded union he provided her with a respectable home, and was careful always that the woodpile be stocked and dry kindling carried in each morning before he set off for the quarry. Unlike a good many men, he had handed over to her each week a sum of money to buy provisions. And he had given thought to her comfort, to her womanly yearnings. Once he brought her a ribbon-trimmed hairpin glass from Winnipeg, and what did she do but give it away to fat Mercy Goodwill next door. What kind of wife was that? He surprised the woman with an ice box, the most up-to-date model, a beautiful thing, and it only made her fly into a rage and accuse him of throwing away good money.

Twice he offered to receive her back under his roof, never mind what the neighbors would have to say, never mind the looks he'd get. Several times in the years after she left home he took the train into Winnipeg and skulked like a common criminal near the corner of Simcoe Street and Aberdeen Road, catching glimpses of her figure coming and going, and working in that garden of hers with her back bent over double like the Galician women did. Once he saw her appear in the doorway of that house – still slender under a full white apron – and heard her give a shout, calling the girl, Daisy, into the house, saying supper was on the table and she'd better hustle herself inside, lickety-split. Her voice was sharp, merry, affectionate, utterly changed – and the child not even her own blood, a neighbor girl whose mother had died.

A woman who abandons her husband must have reason, must be able to show reason, but all his wife would ever say was that he'd been mean with money. And wanting in soft words and ways. Well, she knew good and well when she married him that he wasn't a man for womanish blathering and carrying on.

She'd been gone a year when he turned out the parlor, the carpet, the chairs all dusted and aired, and there at the bottom of her sewing basket he'd found four little books. Romantic books, he supposed they were called, ladies' books with soft paper covers. Nine cents each, the price was stamped on the back. The Nine-Penny Library. He wasn't sure how she'd come by these books, but guessed she'd bought them from the old Jew peddler, bought them and read them in secret, as if he would ever have denied her so trifling a pleasure.

He began to read these books himself on winter nights. It was better than watching the clock. Hearing it tick. Or listening to the ice falling from the branches on to the roof. By now he had installed a sturdy little wood-burning heater in the parlor to take off the chill, something his wife had always gone on about. He read slowly, since, truth be told, he'd never before in his life read the whole of a book, not cover to cover. It pleased him to think he could puzzle out most of the words, turning the pages over one by one, paying attention: *Struggle for a Heart* by Laura Jean Libby, *What Gold Cannot Buy* by one Mrs. Alexander, *At the World's Mercy* by Florence Warden, and *Jane Eyre* by Charlotte Brontë. This last was his favorite; there were turnings in the story that filled the back of his throat with smarting, sweet pains, and in those moments he felt his wife only a dozen heartbeats away, so close he could almost reach out and stroke the silkiness of her inner thighs. It astonished him, how these books were stuffed full of people. Each one was like a little world, populated and furnished. And the way those book people talked! Talk, talk, they lived in their tongues. Much of what they uttered was foolish, but also reasonable. Talk had a way of keeping them from anger. It was traded back and forth like cash for merchandise. Some of the phrases were like poetry, nothing like the way folks really spoke, but nevertheless he pronounced them aloud to himself and committed them to memory, so that if by chance his wife should decide to come home and take up her place once more, he would be ready. If this talky foolishness was her greatest need, he would be prepared to meet her, a pump primed with words full of softness and acknowledgment: O beautiful eyes, O treasured countenance, O fairest of skin. Or phrases that spoke of the overflowing heart, the rising of desire in the breast, the sudden clarities of one body saluting another or even the simple declaration of love. I love you, he whispered, into her waiting ear. I worship your very being.

Or if these utterances proved too difficult for him, as he suspected they would, he would simply gaze into her eyes and pronounce her name: Clarentine. He tried it out on the cozy wood-scented air of the parlor, feeling himself blush from head to toe: Clarentine. Saying it softly at first, the way you calm a tetchy creature, forcing his voice to remain gentle, speaking straight out toward that face that belonged forever to the Ladies Rhythm and Movement Club, but not to him, that dear staring face. Clarentine. Clarentine.

And later – this was after she'd been run down by a reckless cyclist in the city of Winnipeg and thrown against the foundation wall of the Royal Bank building – the word became a broken cry: Clarentine, come home, come home, my darling one, my only, only love.

A week before Daisy Goodwill's wedding in Bloomington, Indiana, the groom's mother, Mrs. Arthur Hoad, had a kind thought. She would entertain the bride-to-be for luncheon, just the two of them at a card table on the side veranda: the ordinary china, the oyster linen cloth and napkins, and perhaps a single pink peony floating in a little glass bowl. Lobelia-May, who came to clean and bake on Wednesdays, would serve up one of her famous tunafish salad plates and a pitcher of iced tea, and after that the good soul would tactfully withdraw, leaving the future daughter-in-law and mother-in-law alone to talk over those things which women must settle between them.

Not wanting to overwhelm the girl, Mrs. Hoad dressed informally for the occasion in a floral printed porch dress and white reindeer-skin pumps.

"I hope you won't think I'm speaking out of turn, Daisy. My feelings toward you are filled with nothing but affection, but those feelings do acknowledge the fact that you have grown up in a household without a mother, which can, as we know, be a handicap along the road of life. Your father is a fine gentleman, an adoring parent, you could not have asked for a better, but there are certain spheres of the world where women hold sway. First, let me say that you have had the benefit of a college education, and have acquired a certain range of familiarity in the liberal arts, but I do hope you won't let this advantage impinge on normal marital harmony. That is, I hope you won't be tempted to parade your knowledge before those who have not elected the same path. It was a great disappointment to me personally when Harold decided to leave his engineering studies after one year, but then he has always been one for practical concerns, and clearly he saw his place in the family business, particularly in view of his father's early death. By the way, Daisy, it is always preferable to say 'death,' rather than 'passing on' or 'passing away.' By the same token – I feel I must mention this – we invite people to dinner, not for dinner. When you set the table, be it breakfast, lunch, or dinner, be sure the knife blade is turned in. In. Not out. Salad forks, of course, go outside the dinner fork. Harold always takes Grape-Nuts for breakfast. A question of digestion and general health. I feel I should make myself clear on this point. I'm speaking of b.m.'s. Bowel movements. He has been troubled in that particular department since he was a very young boy, and so Grape-Nuts are a necessity, also a very economical food. We must never be ashamed of economy, Daisy. By the way, tomato juice ought never be served at breakfast, but only before luncheon or dinner. For breakfast, orange juice is preferred. Canned is quite acceptable, if fresh oranges are not available or if time is a consideration. Harold is very particular about his brushes and combs, that they are cleaned regularly. He likes a hard rubber dressing comb. I always keep an extra one or two on hand in case he misplaces his. I wonder if you have discovered Venitian Velva Liquid for your own skin. I don't suppose you give much thought to your complexion, not at your age, but facial skin coarsens quickly in the twenties and thirties. Apply it before bed, rubbing it in carefully, using a circular motion. And never soap, never. Why not, you might ask? Because soap is excessively drying. For bath powder, I suggest Poudre de Lilas. Some powders can be overwhelming. Men are offended by strong odors. I see you are not eating your olives, Daisy. If you should at any time find something on your plate which is not to your liking, try to avoid giving offense by sliding it under something else. In this case, your lettuce leaf will do nicely. Are you aware that sheeting can be ordered by the yard, and that hemming is generally done free of charge? White shoes are worn only between Memorial Day and Labor Day. Be careful of the term 'entrée.' It is not the main course, as many people think, but the course that precedes the main course. Harold is particularly sensitive about his father's history. His father's untimely demise, I mean, and I believe you have been told the necessary facts. Harold finds it upsetting to be reminded of this sad event. I think it best that you don't refer to his father at all. We never do. We always stay home on Sunday evenings. It is a very, very strong family tradition. We absolutely do not go out. Be sure to acknowledge your wedding gifts within two months. Some people allow three months, but I am old-fashioned enough to hold with two. Plain note cards are best, with perhaps a raised band around the edge. Once Harold was eating a handful of popcorn and began to choke. I always keep a close eye on him when we have a popcorn evening. Finally, a word about your honeymoon. You have not been to Europe before, and so you may be surprised to find a rather curious device in your hotel rooms. I am speaking of France and Italy, not England, of course. This little porcelain bowl is not what it appears to be, but is used by continentals for reasons of personal hygiene. You must be careful not to touch these things, since they are covered with germs, completely and absolutely covered. Germs of the worst sort. The kind of germs that can bring you a lifetime of suffering, suffering that is passed from one person to another, and even to the next generation. When a woman marries, she must be constantly alert to the possibility of harm. She no longer thinks only of herself. From the moment the marriage vows are exchanged at the altar, a woman's husband becomes her sacred trust."

*

"She means a bee-day," Elfreda Hoyt told Daisy. "A bottom washer. You fill it up with water and sort of squat over it and scrub your Aunt Nelly clean."

She and Daisy and Labina Anthony have assembled in a curtained-off back room of Marshall's Ladieswear a few days before the wedding for their final fittings. The fitter has gone to the storeroom to fetch a fresh paper of pins. It is a hot afternoon, but a little electric fan blows up the young women's billowing skirts, helping to keep them cool. Elfreda (Fraidy) and Labina (Beans), the two bridesmaids, are to wear identical dresses of powder blue crêpe de chine trimmed at the sleeves and neckline with ivory lace. Daisy's dress is in crêpe-backed satin, *en traine*, embroidered in pearls and brilliants. The veil is chiffon and lace. Her bouquet will consist of lilies of the valley, orchids, and fern.

Fraidy had traveled to Europe the summer before. She had had two shipboard romances, one on the way over and one coming home, and in between she studied art history in Florence for five weeks, on one occasion visiting a life drawing class in which a young man posed, naked and sprawling, on a platform. In addition, she traveled to Paris and climbed to the top of the Eiffel Tower and stood beside the eternal flame at the Arc de Triomphe and ate an artichoke in a French bistro by tearing off its leaves one by one, dipping them into a little dish of vinegar and scraping them hard against her bottom teeth. "The thing you need to know about the French," she tells Daisy and Beans, "is that they're absolutely filthy about certain matters. And religiously *propre* about others. For them a bidet is a necessity. For before. And after."

"Before what?" Beans asked. "And after what?"

"Before and after intercourse."

"Oh."

"They have intercourse much, much more often than American women do. Or English women for that matter."

"Why?" Daisy asked. "Why do they?"

"They're much more highly sexed. They think sex is a very important part of being a woman. They're very keen on it, very creative."

"What do you mean, creative?"

"They do it other ways."

"What?"

"Other ways than the normal ways, I mean. Last summer, at one of the hotels where we were staying – in this little bureau drawer – I found a book, a kind of pamphlet. With pictures. Of couples, you know, making love. In different ways."

"You never told us this before."

"You never asked."

"What exactly were they doing?"

"Who?"

"The couple, in the pictures?"

"Yes, what?"

"Well." Fraidy looks down at her fresh nail polish. "From the pictures in this little book, it looked as though" – she pauses – "as though they were kissing each other. Down there."

"Where?"

"Here." Pointing at her lap.

"Oh, my God."

"You mean men kissing women down there or women kissing men?"

"Both."

"Oh, my God."

"I couldn't."

"I'd be sick to my stomach, I'd throw up."

"I feel sick right this minute, just thinking about it."

"For them it's perfectly natural. They're not half as puritanical as we are in America. They're used to it. And, of course, it's one way to, you know. To make sure you don't get pregnant."

"I hope Dick doesn't know anything about that kind of thing," Beans says. She will be marrying Dick Greene on the first Saturday in July.

"My goodness, you don't think Harold would ever try –" Daisy looks at Fraidy and then at Beans. There is a moment of solid conspiratorial silence, and then the three of them burst out laughing.

Not one of them understands the reason for this sudden hilarity; it's just something that descends on them sometimes, like gusts of weather. "Stop making me laugh," Beans gasps, "or I'll split my gee-dee seams open." "And I'm going to wet my gee-dee underpants," screams Fraidy.

They're always laughing, these three, laughing to beat the band – as Fraidy's mother puts it. Sometimes Daisy thinks that she and Fraidy and Beans are like one person sitting around in the same body, breathing in the same wafts of air and coming out with the same larky thoughts. This has been going on forever, all the years they were at Tudor Hall in Indianapolis, and then going off to Long College together, and pledging the same sorority and getting their diplomas on the same June morning. And whenever Daisy stops and thinks about her honeymoon, about actually standing in front of the Eiffel Tower or the Roman Coliseum, she always somehow imagines that Fraidy and Beans will be there too, standing right next to her and whooping and laughing and racketing around like crazy.

But this afternoon, with the electric fan blowing up her silk underskirt, she realizes that of course this isn't true. She'll be standing in those strange foreign places all alone. Just herself and her husband, Harold A. Hoad.

Harold A. Hoad's middle initial, A, stands for Arthur, which was his father's name, the same father who shot himself when Harold was seven years old in the cellar of his stone castle on East First Street.

This is the street where the important quarry owners live, a cool, straight, sane-looking street with over-arching trees and the houses set well back. The Hoad house, which is situated across the street from the Kinsey house, was built in the English Domestic Revival style with a steeply pitched roof and tapering chimney. The structure is solid stone, not merely dressed with ashlar facing. The windows are leaded glass. The massive front door is oak, and the delicate carving around the door was done by Horton Graff, the most renowned of the Bloomington carvers, who was later to become a partner in the firm Lapiscan with Hector MacIlwraith and Cuyler Goodwill. (Graff had done this work while still a young man, and the intertwined leaves, vines, and grape clusters are considered a beautiful example of adapted art nouveau.)

After the suicide in the basement, early on a Sunday evening, Mrs. Hoad gathered her two sons, Lons and the young Harold, around her and told them what had transpired. "Your poor father had recently consulted a specialist about his eyes, and was told he would soon be totally blind. He could not bear to become a burden to me, and so he chose this path of deliverance."

How had she known of the impending blindness? Had the specialist confirmed the diagnosis? Had the dead man left a letter of explanation for the family? (It was some years after the event when these questions occurred to Harold.) But no. For "insurance purposes," it seemed, Arthur Hoad had allowed his departure to remain somewhat clouded. But Mrs. Hoad always swore that she knew what she knew. And she understood and forgave, and so must they, the dead man's two young sons.

Later, growing up in Bloomington, in this selfsame house (for the family quarry continued to prosper right up until the depression), Harold was to hear rumblings about his father's financial irregularities and about a woman "friend" in Bedford, and not one pellet of this bitter information greatly surprised him. A congenital cynicism was rooted in his heart. It would never go away. He feels sure that his own life will be a long waiting for the revelation of a terrible truth which he will both welcome and dread.

Meanwhile he hungers for details, all of which are denied him, or which, rather, he feels he has no right to demand. He would like to know, for example, the excuse his father gave for descending into the basement on that particular Sunday evening. Exactly what type of gun had he used, and had it been bought specifically for this act of self-destruction? How large was the hole the bullet made and where precisely was it located? The head? The chest? What about blood. How much had there been and who had been assigned the task of cleaning it all up. Had the fatal trigger been pulled in that little shadowy place behind the furnace or in the fruit cellar or perhaps over by the washing boiler under the little curtained window? Had his father died at once, or perhaps lingered for an hour or two, regretting his decision and calling out weakly for help?

Precisely what were the events of that evening? He needed to know, but at the same time his neediness shamed him. What kind of morbid creature was he? Wasn't this unseemly, unhealthy, grotesque, this unnatural slavering after documentation? Wasn't this, well, unmanly? Unmanliness – in the end the questions always came down to that.

His father's suicide had been speedily transformed by his mother into a sacrificial act – a loving father and husband sparing his family. In much the same way she steadfastly maintained that her son Lons was "artistic" rather than mildly retarded and she firmly put the blame for Harold's expulsion from the Engineering School (for cheating) down to the maliciousness of one particular neurotic professor. Her creative explanations had the effect of making Harold feel perpetually drunk. He stumbled under the unreality of her fantasies. His head felt thick nearly all the time. It became harder and harder, as he grew to manhood, for him to think clearly, and he was driven in his early twenties to real drink, whisky sodas in the afternoon, a bottle of wine in the evenings, often two, with brandy to follow. For his own wedding to Daisy Goodwill in June of 1927 he came drunk to the church – St. Luke's Episcopal Church on Second Street – and to his surprise he was admitted. His best man, Dick Greene, propped him up during the ceremony. The wedding guests, that sprawling pinkish blur, seemed to yawn at him from the pews, some of them blinking sentimental tears from their stupid eyes.

Such a handsome youth, the handsomest young man in Indiana, it was said. A first-class example of America's young manhood. Full of prosperity and promise. Love and family. God and duty. Blessings, blessings.

There are chapters in every life which are seldom read, and certainly not aloud.

Barker Flett in Ottawa, receiving a letter from Daisy Goodwill about her impending marriage to a young man named Harold A. Hoad, experiences a persistent light ache in his chest which he recognized as being similar to the pains of restlessness or of guilt. He remembers vividly the last time he saw her, an eleven-year-old child in a straw hat boarding a train, but he refuses to rehearse – and why should he? – his perverse, momentary desire to crush her young body close to his, her delicately formed shoulders and budding breasts. He's shut that particular shame away, a little door clicked shut in his skull. Closed.

It is said of Barker Flett, who is the newly appointed Director of Agricultural Research, that his spirit, his very spine, is Latinate. He is now forty-three years old, a bachelor who is thought to have frosty reservations in the matter of sex, intimacy, and *la vie personelle*. Occasionally, at staff picnics or dinner parties, he demonstrates a shiver of vivacity, which is undercut always by a tug of repression. "I have eaten bitterness," he rather pompously wrote in his private journal, "and find I have a taste for it." His social manners are clumsy, but appear curiously sweet, a serious man always anxious to seem less serious than he is, and that pale famished face of his is still considered by women to be handsome. He can talk on and on about his collection of lady's-slippers, twenty-seven varieties, each beautifully preserved, but he knows nothing about the importance of the foxtrot in America, and he is too self-occupied to have registered anything but the dimmest impressions of Charles Lindbergh's recent heroics. His long, solitary weekend rambles in the countryside have, at least, kept his body fit, and even in his forties his head of hair remains thick and dark. (Beneath his woolen trousers and underwear there is a wild pubic sprouting like a private garden.) For years there have been whispers in the city that he is homosexual, a rumor that, thankfully, has never reached his ears, for he would have been bewildered by such an allegation. He feels nothing for the bodies of men. Toward women he feels both a profound reverence and a floating impatience, and from his random reading on the subject, he understands that this impatience stems from a resentment toward a punishing, withholding, enfeebling mother, the mother who gives and then withdraws the breast.

But when he remembers his own bustling, narrow-chested little mother, her attention to the cost of articles, to the contrivance of her own life, he feels only warmth.

Clarentine Flett had been deficient in a sense of probity. Yes, she had distorted and remade her own history, abandoning a husband and her wifely duties. Her spiritual growth had ended with childhood, with a mild dislike for the God of Genesis, God the petulant father blundering about in the garden, trampling on all her favorite flowers. But still . . .

Oh, yes, he thinks of his mother often, and always tenderly. Just as he thinks of young Daisy and the happy, blurred years when he and his mother had looked after her.

Today, when he sits down and writes Daisy a letter of good wishes for the future, he encloses a bank draft for $10,000, explaining that this was the amount realized from the sale of his mother's florist business in 1916, quadrupled now by judicious investment. "This is your money, my dear Daisy," he writes. "It is what she would have wanted, believing as she did that every woman, married or otherwise, must have a little money of her own. Pin money, she would have called it, in her simple way."

For his own wedding gift he sends Daisy a complete, hand-colored edition of Catherine Parr Traill's *Wild Flowers of Canada*. He cannot imagine any finer or more fitting gift for a young woman about to begin her life.

The wedding gifts are arranged for viewing in the dining room of the Cuyler Goodwill home on Hawthorne Drive. Four chafing dishes. Crystal for twelve. Two sets of china. Silver, both plate and sterling. A waffle iron. Linens. Thick woven blankets. A Chinese jardinière.

Candy dishes, nut dishes, relish dishes, candelabra, a coffee service, a tea service. From the groom to the bride, a platinum wristwatch. From Cuyler Goodwill to his daughter, a three-foot-high limestone lawn ornament in the shape of an elf.

He has made this little creature himself, the first piece of carving he has attempted in some years, and it seems he has no idea of its embarrassing triviality or crudeness – this from the same hand that carved the spry little mermaid embedded in his tower in Manitoba, now sadly eroded, and the Salem stone angel who supports the central pillar of the Iowa State Capitol. His gift for carving has left him. His sensibility has coarsened. He has become a successful businessman, true enough, but has grown out of touch with his craft, hopeless with the languid tendrils of art nouveau which is all the rage, and deficient with the new mechanized tools of the trade. "The miracle of stone," he said a year ago in his commencement address at Long College, "is that a rigid, inert mass can be lifted out of the ground and given wings."

Yes, but the miracle of the sculptor's imagination is required. And freshness of vision.

Neither imagination nor freshness touch this ludic-rous little garden sprite. It grins puckishly – its round O of a mouth, its merry eyes twinkling above pouched stone cheeks – and the over-sized androgynous head balanced atop a body that suggests a cousinage of deformity. Furthermore, this object might have been cast in cement, so smooth and bland is its surface texture. This "work of art" is about to become one of those comical,

tasteless wedding presents, like the ceramic lobster platter and the atrocious bisque wall plaque, that are con-
signed, and quickly, to the basement or garage, and
which eventually become the subject of private family
jokes or anecdotes.

No matter. It has been executed with love, and with
endearing innocence. Cuyler Goodwill's eyes swim with
tears as he presents this ugly little gnome to his adored
daughter.

Daisy's own eyes fill up in response, but she sighs,
knowing her father is about to deliver one of his sonorous
and empty speeches.

What he doesn't realize is that his gift of speech is
exhausted too. He has entered his baroque period.
Whatever fluency he has evolved has turned against him,
just as his arteries would do later in his life. His tongue's
inventions have become a kind of trick. Even his address
at Long College a year ago had filled Daisy with embarrassment, so that she squirmed and scratched beneath
her pale gray cap and gown – his preacherly rhythms, his
tiresomely rucked up sentences and stale observances.
He approaches stone not as an aesthete – that would be
tolerable – but as a moralist. Words in their thousands,
their tens of thousands, pouring out like cream, too rich,
too smooth. Doesn't he see the yawning faces before
him, doesn't he hear the sighs of boredom, or observe
her own scalding shame? Only look at him, waving his
arms in the air. A bantam upstart, pompous, hollow.
How does such spoilage occur? She knows the answer.
Misconnection. Mishearing.

On and on he went that June morning, standing on
tip-toe so as to see over the lectern, introducing and

expanding his favorite metaphor. Salem limestone, he tells his captive audience, is that remarkable rarity, a freestone – meaning it can be split equally in either direction, that it has no natural bias. "And I say to you young women as you go out into the world, think of this miraculous freestone material as the substance of your lives. You are the stone carver. The tools of intelligence are in your hand. You can make of your lives one thing or the other. You can be sweetness or bitterness, lightness or darkness, a force of energy or indolence, a fighter or a laggard. You can fail tragically or soar brilliantly. The choice, young citizens of the world, is yours."

"Don't," she remembers saying to him.

"Don't what?"

"Don't do that."

Daisy Goodwill and Harold A. Hoad were out walking in Bloomington's public gardens a few days before their marriage. "Don't do that with your stick," she said to him.

Idly, he had been swinging a willow wand about in the air and lopping off the heads of delphiniums, sweet william, bachelor buttons, irises.

"Who cares," he said, looking sideways at her, his big elastic face working.

"I care," she said.

He swung widely and took three blooms at once. Oriental poppies. The petals scattered on the asphalt path.

"Stop that," she said, and he stopped.

He knows how much he needs her. He longs for correction, for love like a scalpel, a whip, something to curb his wild impulses and morbidity.

She honestly believes she can change him, take hold of him and make something noble of his wild nature. He is hungry, she knows, for repression. His soft male mouth tells her so, and his moist looks of abjection. This, in fact, is her whole reason for marrying him, this and the fact that it is "time" to marry – she is, after all, twenty-two years old. She feels her life taking on a shape, gathering itself around an urge to be summoned. She wants to want something but doesn't know what she is allowed. She would like to be prepared, to be strong.

But she is unable to stop her young husband from drinking on their wedding night. He chugs gin straight from a bottle all night long as the train carries them to Montreal, drinks and sleeps and snores, and vomits into the little basin in their first-class sleeper. He stops drinking during the eight days of the Atlantic crossing, but only because he is seasick every minute of the time, as is she. It is late June, but the weather on the North Atlantic is abominable this year. The sea waves heave and sway, and the rain pours down. They arrive in Paris shaken. Her college French proves useless, but they manage somehow to find their hotel on rue Victor Hugo, and there on a wide stiff bed they sleep for thirty-six hours. When they wake up, sore of body and dry of mouth, he tells her that he hates goddamned Paris and loathes foreign wogs who jibber-jabber in French and pee on the street.

He manages in the space of an hour to rent an immense car, a Delage Torpedo, black as a hearse with square rear windows like wide startled eyes. Grasping the steering wheel, he seems momentarily revived, singing loudly and tunelessly, as if a great danger had passed, though his tongue whispers of gin: Daisy, Daisy, give me your answer true. I'm half crazy all for the love of you. He shoots out through the Paris suburbs and into the countryside, honking at people crossing the road, at cows and chickens, at the pale empty air of France. They hurtle down endless rural avenues of trees, past fields of ravishing poppies and golden gorse, and eventually, after hours and hours, they reach the mountains.

She keeps pleading with him to stop, whimpering, then shouting that he oughtn't to be driving this wildly and drinking wine at the same time, that he is putting their lives in danger. He almost groans with the pleasure of what he is hearing, his darling scolding bride who is bent so sweetly on reform.

They stop, finally, at the sleepy Alpine town of Corps, their tires grinding to a halt on the packed gravel, and register at the Hotel de la Poste. A hunched-looking porter carries their valises up two flights of narrow stairs to an austere room with a sloping ceiling and a single window which is heavily curtained.

Daisy lies down, exhausted, on the rather lumpy bed. Her georgette dress, creased and stained, spreads out beneath her. She can't imagine what she's doing in this dim, musty room, and yet she feels she's been here before, that all the surfaces and crevasses are familiar, part of the scenery sketched into an apocryphal journal. Sleep beckons powerfully, but she resists, looking around at the walls for some hopeful sign. There is a kind of flower-patterned paper, she sees, that lends the room a shabby, rosy charm. This, too, seems familiar. It is seven o' clock in the evening. She is lying on her back in a hotel room in the middle of France. The world is rolling over her, over and over. Her young husband, this stranger, has flung open the window, then pushed back the shutters, and now the sun shines brightly into the room.

And there he is, perched on the window sill, balanced there, a big fleshy shadow blocking the sunlight. In one hand he grasps a wine bottle from which he takes occasional gulps; in his other is a handful of centimes which he is tossing out the window to a group of children who have gathered on the cobbled square. He is laughing, a crazy cackling one-note sound.

She can hear the musical ringing of the coins as they strike the stone, and the children's sharp singing cries. A part of her consciousness drifts toward sleep where she will be safe, but something else is pulling at her, a force she will later think of, rather grandly, as the obligation of tragedy and its insistence on moving in a forward direction. She stares sternly at the ceiling, the soiled plaster, waiting.

At that moment she feels a helpless sneeze coming on – her old allergy to feather pillows. The sneeze is loud, powerful, sudden, an explosion that closes her throat and forces her eyes shut for a fraction of a second. When she opens them again, Harold is no longer on the window sill. All she sees is an empty rectangle of glaring light. A splinter of time passes, too small and quiet to register in the brain; she blinks back her disbelief, and then hears a bang, a crashing sound like a melon splitting, a wet injurious noise followed by the screaming of children and the sound of people running in the street.

She remembers that she lay flat on the bed for at least a minute before she got up to investigate.

CHAPTER FOUR

Love, 1936

THE REAL TROUBLES in this world tend to settle on the misalignment between men and women – that's my opinion, my humble opinion, as I long ago learned to say.

But how we do love to brush these injustices aside. Our wont is to put up with things, with the notion that men behave in one manner, and women in another. You might say it's a little sideshow we put on for ourselves, a way of squinting at human behavior, a form of complicity. Only think of how we go around grinning and winking and nodding resignedly or shrugging with frank wonderment! Oh well, we say with a knowing lilt in our voice, that's a man for you. Or, that's just the way women are. We accept, as a cosmic joke, the separate ways of men and women, their different levels of foolishness. At least we did back in the year 1936, the summer I turned thirty-one.

Men, it seemed to me in those days, were uniquely honored by the stories that erupted in their lives, whereas women were more likely to be smothered by theirs. Why? Why should this be? Why should men be allowed to strut under the privilege of their life adventures, wearing them like a breastful of medals, while women went all gray and silent beneath the weight of theirs? The stories that happen to women blow themselves up as big as balloons and cover over the day-to-day measure of their lives, swelling and pressing with such fierceness that even the plain and simple separations of time – hours, weeks, months – get lost from view. Well, this particular irony haunts the existence of Daisy Goodwill Hoad, a young Bloomington widow, whose thirty-first birthday looms – she who's still living in the hurt of her first story, a mother dead of childbirth, and then a ghastly second chapter, a husband killed on his honeymoon. Their honeymoon, I suppose I should say.

Her poor heart must be broken, people say, but it isn't true. Her heart was merely squeezed and wrung dry for a time, like an old rag.

Yet wherever she goes, her story marches ahead of her. Announces her. Declares and cancels her true self. Oh, she did so want to be happy, but what choice did she have, stepping to the beat of that ragbag history of hers?

Of course, the same might be said of the famous Dionne quintuplets, born to an ordinary Canadian farm couple just two years ago. First there's the children's humble origins to consider. Add to that their miraculous survival, and you've got a story so potent and compelling that the little girls themselves are lost, and will always be lost, that's iny opinion, inside its convolutions.

Another example, less dramatic, but more pointed. A woman named Bessie Perfect Trumble (1896–1936) was killed at midnight last night. It was in the morning papers, even for some reason in the *Bloomington Phoenix* – well, it was summer and real news was scarce. It seems this person jumped, or fell, from a Canadian Pacific stock car just one mile from Transcona, Manitoba. What was she doing there in the deserted switching yards? Her left arm and leg were completely severed. She died within minutes of the accident, her last words being, "I am so bloody." Her beauty, her intelligence, her years of inspired teaching in the Transcona school system, her marriage to Transcona fireman Barney Trumble – all are lost to history. She will always be "that woman who jumped or fell" (such tantalizing inconclusion) and at midnight, that unlikely hour, a witch's hour, and her arm and leg – imagine! – followed by her fearful, final, enigmatic statement: "I am so bloody." The rest is a heap of silence. We nod in its direction, but keep our eyes on the flashpoint.

The unfairness of this – that a single dramatic episode can shave the fine thistles from a woman's life. But then the world is bewitched by the possibility of sudden reversal, of blood, of the urgent need to reframe simple arrangements. Daisy Goodwill Hoad's honeymoon tragedy, so strange in its turnings, so unanticipated, blurs the ordinary outlines of her ongoing life which, if the truth were told, is quiet, agreeable and not all that different from the next person's. Since the tragedy in France she's continued to live with her father, also widowed, in the large gloomy Vinegar Hill house with its circular driveway, stone pillars, and that awful misbegotten garden dwarf grinning away on the front lawn, next to the snowball bush.

You might like to believe that Daisy has no gaiety left in her, but this is not true, since she lives outside her story as well as inside. The seasons turn: golf, tennis, her friends, the garden – that and the helpless, secret love she gives her body. There's something touching, in fact, about the way she's learned to announce pain and dismiss it – all in the same breath, so that she's able to disappear, you might say, from her own life. She has a talent for self-obliteration. It's been nine years now, nine years since "it" happened, and she's becoming more and more detached from her story's ripples and echoes and variations. Still, they persist.

"Isn't she the one who –?"

"In this little French hotel, or was it Swiss? The second floor, anyway –"

"The summer of 1927. I remember that wedding like it was yesterday."

"Gorgeous."

"A gorgeous man, the pink of health, handsome as a movie star."

"Rich as Croesus. Both of them. Of course, this was before the crash. But what's the use of money if –?"

"She heard it happen. His head. Splitting open. Like a ripe melon, she said. Or was it a squash? Of course there was an inquest, or whatever they call them over there."

"My God, she must have been in her early twenties then –?"

"– and in a foreign country."

"Didn't know a soul. Couldn't speak a word of the parley-doo."

"He was distributing money, you see, to these poor little street children, tossing coins out the window –"

"When it happened –"

"They hadn't even unpacked. The suitcases were still –"

"She was resting there. On the bed. When all of a sudden she heard . . . "

"There she goes now."

"Is that her?"

"The nightmares that woman must have."
"After all this time."
"You never really recover from –"
"Poor thing."

Besides Daisy, there are two people in the world, Fraidy Hoyt and Beans Anthony Greene, who know that her marriage to Harold Hoad was never consummated: "He was always drunk," she told them plainly not long after she got home from Europe, "or sick. Or just not very interested."

She recounted the intimate details of her honeymoon while sitting on the edge of Fraidy's bed, pleating the pineapple crocheted bedspread between her fingers. (Poor Fraidy was down with a summer cold.) Daisy told her dear old trusted school friends everything – everything except the fact that she had sneezed just before Harold fell out the window, also that she had remained frozen on the bed for a minute or more afterward, her eyes staring at the ceiling, feeling herself already drifting toward the far end of this calamity.

These shared confidences at Fraidy Hoyt's bedside rekindled their old laughter – which came slowly, at first, in a nervous pah-pah, then a burst; concerned glances flew between Fraidy and Beans, but it was heavenly when it finally ran free, their wild girlish hooting. It lifted the heaviness right off Daisy's heart – or rather her stomach, for it is here in her middle abdomen that she's stored her shock and grief.

Grief? Grief for what? For Harold? Well, no. For her own bungling. For what she allowed. For the great story she let rise up and swamp her.

"My, God, that means you're a gee-dee virgin," said the no-longer virginal Beans Greene, her eyes popped open, laughing.

"The only virgin in our midst," said Fraidy, who had recently "tried out" sexual intercourse with a well known Bloomington professor of Fine Arts, a married man old enough to be her father.

What a blessing Daisy doesn't know that there are others in Bloomington who are acquainted with the state of her intact hymen, quite a few others: old Dr. Maldive, for one, who examined her after she returned to Bloomington. Shortly thereafter this same Dr. Maldive, in good conscience, communicated the curious fact of non-consummation to Daisy's father, Cuyler Goodwill (it seemed the responsible thing to do, a man-to-man thing), and the good doctor had also, with a less good conscience, spoken of it to his wife Gladys who let the fact slip, framing it in the form of an eyebrow-lifting speculation, to her bridge club acquaintance, Mrs. Arthur Hoad, who concluded, and announced her conclusion at every social opportunity Bloomington presented, that young Daisy Goodwill was an unnatural woman of profound frigidity, who had trapped and then frustrated the ardor of a healthy young man, her son, and perhaps had driven him to an act which must remain forever unarticulated.

All Daisy knows is that her mother-in-law treats her coldly. They scarcely see each other. Never, in fact. Daisy has been encouraged to renounce claims on the Hoad estate, and this she has willingly done. She has no need for money. She is comfortable in her present circumstances; she is still reasonably young; and she is not particularly unhappy.

Back in the bad old days of the Great War, my Aunt Clarentine Flett saw her wholesale flower enterprise unexpectedly prosper. And now, in 1936, with the limestone industry in the doldrums and most of the old quarries shut down, the art of stone carving is thriving. It seems as though people in hard times need something decorative and pretty to ease the heaviness of life's offerings. What a paradox it is, that in the midst of a worldwide economic depression, my father, Cuyler Goodwill, and his partners in Lapiscan Limited should be busier than ever. Prestigious contracts roll in day by day. The new Ohio State University Library. The giant war memorial in Little Rock, Arkansas. The frieze of the Grain Exchange in Chicago. You could go on and on.

Mr. Goodwill is forever complaining that there aren't enough good carvers to be had. The old fellows are dying out, he says, and the youngsters are too impatient. Recently, Goodwill traveled all the way to Italy in search of new talent, and came home to Bloomington with three new craftsmen for Lapiscan and a new bride for himself.

Her name is Maria. What else would a young Neapolitan bride be called? But how young is she, exactly? No one knows for sure, and no one knows how this question can be posed. Twenty-eight is the age given on her immigration papers, but who trusts such official information, particularly when the papers themselves look phony – overly crisp and too heavily fixed with seals and signatures. She might be anywhere between thirty-five and forty, certainly not more than forty-five, but in any case she is many years younger than her husband, who is close to sixty.

He adores her, that's plain as the nose on your face.

Since his first wife died in childbirth back in 1905, he has done without the solace of sex. He cannot himself explain how or why he had chosen to live all these years apart from the comfort of women. He has been busy, he might say, if asked. Other concerns took over his mind: his business, his rise to prominence, the fact that he had a young daughter to bring up. He would – should you question him – shrug, smile, glance upward in that sweet befuddled way of his; most people who cut themselves off from love commit themselves to lies, hypocrisy, and discouragement, but it seems Cuyler Goodwill is one of those rare beings who is happy enough to travel along where the wind blows him. And now the wind of good fortune has brought him Maria.

A woman whose body is full of complications and puzzles. Broad-breasted, slim-ankled, narrow-waisted, heavy-hipped. She is indeed an aberration, walking the polite, leafy streets of Bloomington, Indiana, walking always rapidly, with an air of purpose – for she is not just taking the air, no, she is on her way to do the marketing, ever hopeful of what curiosities and bargains she may uncover. She walks home with a canvas sack slung on her arm, and this sack is weighed down with treasure – red onions, fresh parsley, cauliflower, tomatoes. She carries all this as though it were an armload of feathers. Her muscular calves suggest an acquaintance with rough country roads. Her face, on the other hand, is sweetly formed, a pair of liquid eyes, a large but narrow nose and shapely mouth. A nasty scar nested into the left side of her face disappears, almost, when she smiles. She scorns lipstick. Whores wear lipstick. But her heavy dark hair with its henna highlights is clearly dyed. Cuyler Goodwill describes, for anyone kind enough to ask, how he and Maria met – at a seafood restaurant in Naples where she was employed as a hostess. "One look," he tells his Bloomington friends, innocently, "and that was that."

She jabbers and jabbers, and no one understands one word she says – except for her husband who claims he can usually get the "gist." The "gist" apparently is enough for him. His own tongue is suddenly stilled. He looks at his bride, shakes his head with wonder, and grins the grin of a happy man, especially when she bends down – for she is taller than he by a good three inches – and kisses with a loud smack the bald spot on the top of his head. This bending and smacking she does even in public places, at the Quarry Club where they go to dinner, at the Bloomington Foundation for a civic reception, and what does he do on these embarrassing occasions but go on smiling and smiling, as if this were normal behavior between husbands and wives.

Cora-Mae Milltown who has kept house for the Goodwills, father and daughter, all these years gives notice. It's not that she doesn't like Maria, she says, it's only that she feels useless. Maria, with the wearingly buoyant effervescence of a child, is up and about by six-thirty; she likes to get the kitchen floor mopped clean before the others come down to breakfast. Then she'll shuffle about vacuuming for an hour or so, wearing a robe of red silk that shows the division between her long brown-streaked breasts. Later in the day, much later, she may change to a loose cotton house dress and apron, and often she answers the front door wearing this apron, sometimes still clutching a paring knife or dustpan or toilet brush or whatever she happens to have in her hand, her mouthful of teeth ready to welcome anyone who comes, not that she's able to offer a word of common English. "Allo," she shouts, sweeping her arms forward and upward in a hectic gesture. All day long she drinks thick black coffee that she boils up on the back of the stove, and in the evening she serves her husband and her new step-daughter Daisy hot, wet, stewy platefuls of food. These meals are taken in the kitchen, not the dining room, because the dining room table is covered now with the yard goods and paper patterns for the dresses she is always in the middle of making. Talk, talk, talk, her hands waving, gesturing: a second helping? a third? She sulks when they refuse food, and beams like an angel when they accept. A regular dago-squaw, says one of Goodwill's associates, down at the Quarry Club. Crudely. Unkindly.

Between Daisy and Maria grows an intricate rivalrous dance which can never, never be brought to light.

You'd think she'd be lonely, Daisy tells Fraidy and Beans, you'd think she'd be lost in a foreign country where she doesn't speak the language and hasn't got a single friend. "She's got your father," says Fraidy. "Maybe that's all she needs."

"Oh, Lordy," says Daisy, rolling her eyes and thinking of the night noises, the wild love cries. His as well as hers.

"People have different requirements." This from Beans. From Mrs. Dick Greene. "She never stops," Daisy tells them. "Cooking, cleaning, sewing. She keeps wanting to make me a dress. She yanks at my skirt, just yanks, and makes these barking noises and wrinkles her nose and then she gets out her dress patterns, Butterick, and holds them up to me."

"Maybe you should let her if it would make her happy," says Beans, who, now that she is settled into married life with two babies, is always going on about making other people happy.

"Maybe you should think about finding a place of your own," Fraidy says. "Personally, I couldn't stand living in the midst of an ongoing operetta."

"She's always kissing me. Morning, noon, and night, kissing."

"On the mouth?"

"Yes."

"Ugh." A social shiver from Beans.

Fraidy stares. "Well, tell her you don't want to be kissed morning, noon, and night."

"Of course, physical affection is natural for certain nationalities," Beans contributes in her new sweet expository tone that makes Fraidy want to throw up.

"I say, move out. It's time. You're over thirty, for crying out loud."

"They'd both be so hurt."

"They'll get over it. My mother cried for a month when I moved to my own apartment, and now she'd hate it like *h-e*-double toothpicks if I came back."

"Well, actually –"

"Yes?"

"Actually" – Daisy looks from one to the other, seeking approval, encouragement, and wanting to surprise them too – "I was thinking of going on a trip."

"Alone?"
"Yes."
"You lucky thing."
"Where to?"
"Canada," she answers

She surprised herself. She sat down with a pile of train schedules and travel booklets and planned a two-week vacation. Her itinerary was eccentric, with a certain amount of doubling back and forth: Niagara Falls first, then Callander, Ontario, to see the quints, then Toronto to visit, on her father's behalf, the site of a great new bank building, and finally Ottawa to call on her Uncle Barker whom she hasn't seen since her childhood. Her arrangements were modest, touristy even, and yet she regarded her schedule with wonder, as if this little venture of hers were a kind of mythic journey – and perhaps it was, for she has never traveled alone before, and, except for a few hours in Montreal boarding ship on her honeymoon, she has never visited Canada, the country of her birth and early childhood. "I feel as though I'm on my way home," she wrote in her travel diary, then stroked the sentiment out, substituting: "I feel something might happen to me in Canada."

It was summertime. Her train moved northward through the bright little towns of eastern Michigan. In between these towns were cultivated hills and groves of trees. Beyond those hills, she thought, just behind those trees and clouds lies the Dominion of Canada. The Dominion; she repeats the word solemnly to herself, rolling it on her tongue. Do-min-i-on.

Please, please let something happen.

A cool clean place, is how she thinks of it, with a king and queen and Mounties wearing red jackets and people drinking tea and speaking to one another in polite tones, never mind that these images do not accord in any way with her real memories of the hurly-burly of the Winnipeg schoolyard and the dust and horse turds of Simcoe Street. It seemed to her that June day, as the train slid at last over the Michigan State line and entered Canada, that she had arrived at a healing kingdom.

No one here could guess at her situation. No one here knew her story. Here she was simply one more young woman wearing a linen dress and matching jacket and standing by the railing at Niagara Falls, catching a fine spray on her cheek.

She felt agonizingly alert as she attempted to swallow the thunder and majesty of this natural marvel. But why should all this ravishing beauty make her sad? A good question. Because it was not beautiful enough, nor was it quite as large as she had imagined. Moreover, the strewn rocks at the bottom of the falls gave a look of untidiness. Something seemed lacking in the overall design. At any rate, she was not "seized with rapture" as the travel booklet had promised. The next minute, though, she was made cheerful, for she perceived a man standing beside her, standing so close she could feel the cloth of his jacket scratching her bare arm. "Jeez," he said brightly, in a New York-accented voice, "it makes ya thoisty, don't it, lookin' at all dat water."

She stared with great pleasure into the side of his upper sleeve and shoulder, beyond which floated clouds and a clean wipe of blue sky. She resisted an impulse to lean into the man's chest, to shelter there, crying out her joy at having fallen upon this unexpected intimacy. Instead she inclined herself toward his lightness of spirit, thinking how suddenly merry the world could turn if you only let it. The gaiety of this encounter, its private looks and smiles and shared observation, is more indelibly fixed in her mind than the chronology of her tragic honeymoon; there are words to accompany this Niagara scene, there is a fresh breeze, there is mingled disappointment and mirth, there is the eloquence of a man's gaberdine sleeve randomly brushing against her skin.

Two days later, in Callander, Ontario, she lined up in the hot sun with hundreds of other tourists. As they at last approached the viewing area, they were ordered to remain silent so as not to disturb the young quints who were playing in an enclosed garden. She caught only a glimpse of little white dresses and sun bonnets against the vivid green grass. At least one of the infants was wailing. People behind her pushed up against her, and she was obliged to move on. She felt herself part of a herd of absurd creatures observing other creatures, and dwelt with a part of her mind on the need to set herself at a distance from all these sunny, chatting people, women in summer cottons with cardigans thrown over their shoulders, men nattily dressed in linen jackets, determined to be entertained. There was something comical about this, and something deeply degrading, but why should she be surprised? She had come to see this spectacle knowing she would go away filled with a satisfying sense of indignation – and so she did.

In Toronto, in a solemn-as-a-church corporation boardroom, she delivered a sheaf of blueprints from her father's company, and was patronized by the bank president – "What a fine wee girlie you are coming all this way" – and propositioned by the bank vice-president – "Here we are, two lonely people on a beautiful summer's afternoon."

"But I'm leaving," she told him, "on the four o'clock train."

"You just arrived."

"I'm on my way to Ottawa," she said, "to see an old friend."

"A he-friend or a she-friend?"

She stared hard. She wanted to reach out and slap the smile off his silly shining middle-aged face. At the same time she wanted this conversation to go on and on, to see where it might take her. "A he," she said boldly.

"I knew it, I knew it."

"And how did you know?" This was obscene, continuing like this. And frightening.

"Your face. Your perfume. The way you said 'friend.' I have a nose for these kinds of things."

"What? What kinds of things?"

"I think you know what I mean."

"Well, I don't," she said turning.

"I think you do."

Of course Barker Flett met Daisy's train. As a matter of fact, he had had his new Hudson specially washed and waxed for the occasion, and drove it to the station slowly, as if it might explode under him, as if it were carrying him toward a punishment of biblical proportions.

The night was hot, though a vivifying breeze drifted up from the canal and entered the car windows. As a rule he disliked driving, but had learned, as he later told Daisy, to appreciate the feel of the polished steering wheel in his hands, and he liked, too, the sensation of this large quiet vehicle pushing its way through the summer dusk whose violet-tinted air was bordered at the top with a darker purple, so utterly different from the skies of his boyhood, from Manitoba's abrupt evening light.

Thinking of Daisy, how he would greet her, his courage rose and fell, an echo, he supposed, of the clenching and release of memory. He clearly remembered her as an infant, how she had slept for several months in an old dresser drawer lined with cotton batting, and how, for some reason, this arrangement was always spoken of as a sentimental joke, the young infant and her improvised accommodation. After that, there is a great gap in his recollections, unflavored, flat, for Daisy is suddenly eleven years old and lying in a darkened room, recovering from a serious illness (measles? what?), looking up at him with eyes that seem no longer the eyes of a child. On the other hand, he might easily have imagined the entire scene, acquainted as he is with the existential insult of failed memory – though he can't quite believe this is the case: Daisy's young, possibly naked, body beneath the sheet – he is unable to clear his mind of it. He rehearses the moment again and again, not lasciviously, but in the hope that he may be wrong. He is fifty-three years old. And it is nineteen years since he saw the child. No, not a child. A woman of thirty-one years. A widow.

"Dear Daisy," he wrote to her less than one month ago, "It's been so long. I am immensely pleased that you should be planning a visit to Ottawa."

What else had he written?

He can't remember, and he's not a man to make carbon copies of personal correspondence – he draws the line on self-consciousness there – but probably he had penned the same hashed civilities he always imposed on her. Courteous sentiments. Inquiries about her health, her activities. Dull summaries of his own circumstances, the weather in Ottawa (extremely hot or unbearably cold), the vexations of bureaucracy, occasional higher thoughts on nature, life, progress, the twentieth century, and more and more in recent years, paragraphs of hypocritical avuncular counsel. Counsel from him, her elder, her advocate, he who travels once each month to Montreal in order to relieve his body of its sexual tensions, he, a fifty-three-year-old man who occasionally still weeps at night into his pillow, who is obliged to pinch himself alive with a glass of spirits after a day of papers and meetings and putting out small administrative fires, he who keeps a cushion of awe between himself and women, pretending reverence but requiring protection. He who struggles over his letters to her, to Daisy Goodwill, his only felt connection on this earth, a being unrelated by blood and one who has entered his life by a bizarre accident (her mother's death, his own mother stepping in), and whose consoling presence flickers always, at the side of his vision.

Apart from Daisy there is no one. To his brothers he writes once a year, at Christmas. Simon in Edmonton scarcely ever replies; Andrew writes back regularly, usually with a request for funds. As for Barker Flett's father, Magnus, he has fallen through a hole in the earth's crust. If by chance the old he-goat is still alive he would be in his seventies now, but it's been years since he left Canada to go back to the Orkneys, and no one has heard so much as a word from him. No one has a scrap of news or even an address. No one, if the truth were said straight out, cares about Magnus Flett's whereabouts or state of mind or whether or not the old grumbler is alive or dead.

It was always said of Magnus Flett that he led an unlucky life. Bad luck followed him in his marriage and in his dealings with his sons, and bad luck tracked him all the way to the *Louisa*, the ship that carried him from Montreal to Liverpool in the summer of 1927.

Everyone knows that early summer is a peaceful time on the Atlantic – it can be depended on – but the eight-day period of Magnus Flett's crossing was plagued with freak storms. The old man was unable to eat or sleep, and he spent every possible moment on the open deck, vomiting into an enamel basin. The days and nights fused together in a width of misery. If anyone had asked him what his wish was at that time, he would have declared that he wished for death. The image came to him one morning, as he stood retching over the railing, of the quarry in Tyndall, the sunlight striking and warming the mottled rock surface, and a good day's work waiting; he knew then what a perfect fool he was to have left. He vomited out the memory, erased it. He vomited out the sum of his pain and disappointment, his three sons, his disloyal wife; he vomited out the whole of his humiliation, so that when the *Louisa* arrived finally at Liverpool, he stepped out on to firm land light as a boy. Hurrying past the stink of the fish docks, he had himself a good feed of boiled beef and mash, a long night's sleep in clean bedding, and woke feeling more vigorous than he had in years and more eager for life.

He sent his baggage on to Thurso by train, keeping only a change of clothing, a few odds and ends, and his copy of *Jane Eyre*. At a Liverpool outfitters he bought himself a pair of stout boots and a spirit stove, having determined to walk his way up across the north of England and through the wilds of Scotland. This act seemed to him at first a defiance, then a compulsion. And then something as simple and natural as air. Nevertheless every muscle in his body tightened at the thought of what he was about to do.

The weather was with him, long soft days and evenings, and the ground dry and giving underfoot. He took his position from the sun, that only. Home; the word hummed in his ears as he walked along country roads northward, sweeter than any scattering shout of birdsong, filling him up like a meal of bread and good butter. In a ditch he came upon a rod of smoothed wood that fit his hand perfectly, and with this he beat rhythmically against the dusty surface of the road. His whiskers grew out fine and white and soft.

The hills of England, so rounded and mannerly, grew steeper once he left Carlisle behind, but whenever he felt his legs giving way, he stretched out under a tree for an hour, opened his book and read himself out of his aches and blisters. Can this really be but an island, he said to himself, looking skyward, looking out beyond hedged pastures of sheep and cattle. This wide, green, stony land, this richness of darkness and light. He thought, with happiness, of all the undated winters that had

passed over these fields, the snows, and then the slow
warming up of spring. Later, reaching the treeless moors
past Inverness, it seemed to him he was tramping on
God's broad seamy forehead. After that there was a
leveling off, an airy sensation of descent, his mind
gloriously emptied and calm.

The country hotels along the way offered a bluff,
democratic welcome, and, though not a drinking man, he
came to savor his pint of ale at the end of a long day's
walking. He bent his head low over his glass, sniffing,
then drinking. Easeful conversation flourished in the
public houses – "So what's it like out there in Canada?"
from farmers with red, rude faces – and once, in the town
of Jedburgh, the landlady of a lodging house joined him
for a few hours between the sheets. Her skin was
roughened and full of folds, but smelt freshly of soap.
Sometimes children followed him for a bit out of the
towns, curious and noisy. A young woman with a ragged
cough accompanied him for a day or two, talking about
Jesus, talking incoherently, and he was moved to give her
a few shillings before they parted.

Reaching Thurso at last, a wild wetted place with the
sky pressing down hard on the horizon, he found the
baggage he had sent ahead stored in the corner of a
railway shed. On impulse he decided against claiming it
– what was there anyway but rubbish he could get along
perfectly well without. Hadn't he proven as much? He
caught the *St. Ola* for Stromness, a short journey over a
mercifully calm sea. He was home. He took a great gulp
of air into his lungs, and at that moment a thought
formed in his head, the notion that life might after all be
made sweet. He would find himself a simple house up

near the open fields of East Bigging where he'd spent his boyhood, and make it cozy with the help of a coal-burning boiler, a warm bed, electric lights if he could manage it. And a hidey hole to sock away his store of money. He would live like a king in this snug nest. And he would go on living forever.

During all these years Barker Flett has written to young Daisy Goodwill every second month.

Well now, that comes to six letters a year for twenty-two years, making 132 letters or thereabouts. He tells himself, and sometimes others, that he feels a responsibility for the child. He does not use the word duty, as he might have had he been born a generation earlier; but, still, he is a dutiful man. He is also calm, reflective and self-critical. He knows very well what underlies the compulsive side of his nature; it is the wish to escape that which he can't comprehend, seeking safety in an unbendable estrangement. He understands perfectly – and prides himself on this knowledge – how those ancient eremites were able to live out their lives in caves, and monks in their stripped cells. Even when he is in Montreal on one of his visits, lying in the arms of women into whose bodies he has discharged his passion, he longs for the simplicity of a narrow bed and a lacerating loneliness. This is what he has to fight against – wildness, chaos. When he is not fighting, he is giddy with pessimism for a cheapened world. Not always, but sometimes, after an Ottawa dinner party, he lies lifelessly in his bed, his mouth dry, thinking: how absurd I am on these occasions, holding forth like an aged actor in tones of

fraudulent gladness. And how, afterwards, I beat back
the world with a glass of warm whisky, trying to escape it.

He is too serious, he knows that, too willing to believe
– and deaf to the comedy of mismatched couples and
unseemly flesh. To comfort himself, he imagines the
separate layers of his brain; there are spaces there,
cavities that exist between the forces of sex and work.
What is he to do with these fixed voids? Other people
know. He's never known.

His father, that austere, unfeeling and untutored man,
had insisted his sons polish their boots every evening.
Flett has learned to be grateful for this early discipline. It
kept him breathing as a boy, provided a pulse, gave order
to vast incomprehension. Later he found other ways.

He can't recall when he learned the names of the
plants in his mother's garden, but he remembers how the
exactitude of nomenclature lulled him into comfort.
Early on, he knew himself to be one of those who are
morally unhoused and in need of specific notation,
plants, animals, the starry constellations. Soon, besides
his mother's domesticated flowers, he mastered the
plantlife of the fields and woods. He had all of it quickly
by heart, common names as well as Latin. Each time he
was able to match a specimen with the illustration in
Spotton's Botanical Note Book he experienced a spasm of
strength. The green world with its varying forms brought
out an exotic tolerance in him and kept him calm. The
discovery at the age of twelve or thirteen that the whole
of the natural world had been classified, that someone
other than himself had guessed at the need for this
ordering, struck him like a bolt of happiness. He loved
particularly the pockets within pockets, the great

botanical divisions revealed and broken down into their tiniest branches, the smallest, most peninsular forms of life persisting valiantly in the bent corners of evolution. This miniature world, slime molds, algae, became his elected tongue – the genetics of plants, its odd, stringent beauty. Of his collection of lady's-slippers – one of the world's most complete, he likes to think – he loves best that one which is rarest, and of that particular bloom he values its smallest petals above the others, observing them respectfully under his microscope, memorizing the shape of the most minuscule cell, paying tribute to its position and function, and assigning it the dignity of its Latin name.

Like a chart on a wall, the complete organization of the botanic world is suspended in his consciousness. He can only suppose that the heads of other men are filled with comparable systems, with philosophies, histories, logarithm tables, texts, with points of persuasion or mapped cravings that bear them forward, as does his range of living classes, orders, families, species, and sub-species. And into this system, which is not nearly as neat and logical as he had once believed, has crept the fact of Daisy. She sits far out at the end of one of the branches, laughing, calling to him. He sometimes shuts his eyes and wishes her gone, but she remains steadfastly there, a part of nature, confused with the subtle tendrils of sexual memory; he could no more ignore her presence than erase a sub-species of orchid or sedge. He nurtures his connection from a distance, writing to her regularly and awaiting her replies. The rhythm is fixed in his life now – a support and distraction, the way in which he confirms his most human feelings.

This letter-writing of his has its ritual aspects. He takes up his pen, a dark red Waterman, on Sunday afternoons, the first Sunday of every even-numbered month – February, April, June, and so on. An observer might note that the line of his bent back and shoulders possesses a fetal curl. His tall-windowed study is quiet. At his elbow is a cup of weak coffee, rapidly cooling. His mind is aerated by acts of private embarrassment and distressing nightmare, but for the moment he brushes all this aside. He is a man writing a letter, performing an act of obligation. The date goes neatly into the right hand corner of the page, and as a sort of uncle-type joke, his lips tightening, he always puts "AD," in parentheses, after it.

Then he takes a breath and writes: My dear Daisy. The "my" troubles him, but it would draw attention to itself should he alter it now. He then proceeds with his dull and detailed paragraphs, this dullness and detail successfully blocking the yearning he feels. He completes one page and begins another, plodding away, and feeling always reassured by his plodding, which he takes to be a sign of restraint. The loneliness latent in such objects as his Waterman pen or his china saucer must be kept from view. But his face bending over the paper is ripe for heresy. He longs to cover the page with kisses and to sign the letter: your loving Barker. Yours forever. Yours only.

What he actually puts down is a plain: yours sincerely, Barker Flett. At least he has never been so blockish as to sign: Uncle Barker. Though this, in fact, is how Daisy addresses him in her letters of reply.

These replies come quickly, by return mail. It seems she shares his sense of responsibility, his dutifulness.

His heart beats rough and sore in his chest as he cuts open the square blue envelopes. Her letter paper is blue as well, and bordered with bland stylized flowers that no botanical text would deign to recognize. Dear Uncle Barker. She rattles on and on, page after page, girlishly, frivolously. At least half her sentences are apocalyptically incomplete, engineered with portentous dashes and dots, leaving him shaken, excited, exasperated. Her syntax is breathy, her diction uneven. Even after the tragedy of her honeymoon she writes (bravely?) that she is feeling "pretty down in the dumps" but hopes to be "hunky-dorey" before long. Always he is cast down after reading one of her letters; the childish banality. Disappointment lingers for days, but the weeks pass, a month, two months, and by the time he once again picks up his pen, his devotion has been restored. It is inevitable that each of us will be misunderstood; this, it seems, is part of twentieth-century wisdom.

Let it be said that Daisy Goodwill has saved every one of Barker Flett's letters; she has them still, though she would be hard put to tell you just where they are. In a drawer somewhere. Or a cardboard carton.

Her letters to him have not survived.

Nor are there any photographs of her dating from this period.

Still, you can guess how she must have looked as she neared the end of her train journey to Ottawa – although, as a captive of her own drama, she is likely to touch up this image more than a little; for instance, she sees herself as having already removed her hat – knowing full well that a woman never travels hatless – and next thing you know she's shaking out her reddish-brown hair with its eruptions of gold. The last of the sun's rays enter the train window and gather on the folds of her linen dress. (Cut on the bias. Smart by the standards of Bloomington, Indiana.) She is clasping her hands firmly together on her lap much as Barbara Stanwyck did in *The Woman in Red*, indicating sprightly female determination. And she hopes the line of her jaw, like Garbo's, conveys a similar attitude.

What will she say to him? What will be her first words?

A scene offers itself up: she is taking his hand, shaking it gravely, holding herself a little aloof so as not to alarm him. She speaks quietly, sincerely of her journey. No, she is not overly tired. It was really very pleasant. Scenery just heavenly. The miles flew by. She is anxious to demonstrate good will, while patiently waiting for candor to establish itself.

What if they have nothing to talk about? Nothing in common? Well, she must find something. She will put her mind to it.

Again she presses her hands together. Gloveless. Ringless. A stranger might guess her to be engaged in an act of silent prayer, and in a sense she is, for her concentration has a devout intensity. She is traveling to Barker Flett as to a refuge. It comes down to that. She cannot go back to Vinegar Hill to be the daughter of Cuyler Goodwill and the step-daughter of Maria, not in that house, not in Bloomington, not at her age, it is out of the question. This last year she has been in danger of becoming an eccentric or else one of those persons who does not bother to put a saucer under her cup. Her father's tiresome freestone metaphor comes back to her with all the dead weight of its evangelical offering: as with a chunk of Indiana limestone, he says, a person can split off his life in one direction or the other; the choice is open.

But no such choices are available to her at this time in her life, a woman on the verge of middle age – or so she thinks. A person arbitrarily named. A person accidentally misplaced. How did this happen? She's caught in a version of her life, pinned there.

A thought comes into her head: that lately she doesn't ask herself what is possible, but rather what possibilities remain. At this moment she is clearly on a one-way journey, though her return train ticket lies safely in a pocket of her leather handbag. Curiously, she is not afraid, knowing as she does that love is mostly the avoidance of hurt, and, furthermore, she is accustomed to obstacles, and how they can be overcome by readjusting her glance or crowding her concerns into a shadowy corner.

She closes her eyes for a moment – not Garbo eyes, no, nothing like so brave and chilly – and thinks of these last few days of travel. Everything she has seen or done has jagged edges around it. Her various conversations with strangers go round and around in her head, exhilarating but also exhausting – that man at the Falls, wasn't he the limit! All of them.

From surfeit to loss is a short line. She cannot go back. She will have to make new plans. These plans grow in her head, wild as they are, sending out tentacles, scenes, whole conversations.

How good it is to see you again, Uncle Barker.

Her lips move silently against the train window. One slender arm reaches out, shaking hands with the air. Such a pleasure. After all these years.

Maybe now is the time to tell you that Daisy Goodwill has a little trouble with getting things straight; with the truth, that is.

She had a golden childhood, as she'll be happy to tell you. Her loving adopted "Aunt" Clarentine, her adoring "Uncle" Barker. Warmth, security. Picnics along the river. A garden full of flowers. And then at age eleven finding her real father, a remarkable (everyone said so) self-made man who showered her with material plenty, as well as the love of his heart.

Well, a childhood is what anyone wants to remember of it. It leaves behind no fossils, except perhaps in fiction. Which is why you want to take Daisy's representation of events with a grain of salt, a bushel of salt.

She is not always reliable when it comes to the details of her life; much of what she has to say is speculative, exaggerated, wildly unlikely. (You will already have realized that no person in this world could possibly be as insensitive, as cruel, as her mother-in-law, Mrs. Arthur Hoad, is made out to be.) Daisy Goodwill's perspective is off. Furthermore, she imposes the voice of the future on the events of the past, causing all manner of wavy distortion. She takes great jumps in time, leaving out important matters (her expensive, private education, for instance – Tudor Hall, Long College). The acts of her life form a sequence of definitions, that's what she tells herself. Writing letters to her Uncle Barker, she elects the language of childhood, deliberately naive, wistful, girlishly irresponsible, safe. Sometimes she looks at things close up and sometimes from a distance, and she does insist on showing herself in a sunny light, hardly ever giving us a glimpse of those dark premonitions we all experience. And, oh dear, dear, she is cursed with the lonely woman's romantic imagination and thus can support only happy endings.

Still, hers is the only account there is, written on air, written with imagination's invisible ink.

Having read his Bertrand Russell, Barker Flett has long since cast off a belief in conventional morality, but, as a senior civil servant in His Majesty's government (Executive Director of Agricultural Research), he is compelled to observe a certain level of propriety. A young woman under his roof? How would this look?

A niece, he might explain, but Daisy is not really his niece. His ward? No, his guardianship has never been formalized. What is he to do? How will he explain her presence.

It occurs to him that his housekeeper, Mrs. Donaldson, who comes in daily to clean and to prepare him a cold supper, might be prevailed upon to stay overnight during the period of Daisy's visit. He asks her, delicately setting out the problem. She bluntly refuses. She has her own family, after all, to go home to; what he asks is impossible.

He sighs, immensely relieved. And then he begins to worry once again. His life with Daisy has not even begun, and already there are all these vexing problems to be dealt with.

*

"In one hour I will be there," Daisy writes in her travel journal, underlining "there" three times.

It is unbearably hot on the train, but she has managed, with the conductor's assistance, to open a window. As a result her hair is blowing about wildly, and the fading sunlight shines through it, so that she appears to be wearing a kind of halo or else a hat made of burnt fur.

To still the loud beating of her heart she stows her journal away safely, or so she thinks, and replaces her gloves. She holds herself upright, rigid. A stillness that purifies. Barbara Stanwyck with a head of foxy hair.

She is overwhelmed at times – and this is one of those times – with the wish to ask forgiveness.

Now darkness is coming on gradually, and the Ontario sky fills up with diamond dust. These particles, she senses, have nothing to do with her. The villages that rush by are foreign and unyielding. They seem to turn their backs on her. At the end of the railway car, on the other side of the aisle, four men are playing a noisy game of cards – rummy, most likely – and so engaged are they in this cheerful amusement and in the rough pleasure of each other's company, that she might be snatched suddenly from their midst and they would never so much as glance in her direction. She knows that when the train arrives in Ottawa, all of these men will hurry off into the contained nexus of their real lives, while she is about to hurl herself into whatever accident of fortune awaits her. She will accept "it" without protest, without question, for what choice has she?

She is powerless, anchorless, soft-tissued – a woman. Perhaps that is the whole of it, that she is a woman. Yes, of course.

It occurs to her that she should record this flash of insight in her journal – otherwise she is sure to forget, for she is someone who is always learning and forgetting and obliged to learn again – but the act of recording requires that she remove her gloves, rummage through her bag for her pen and for the notebook itself. This is more than she is capable of doing. And so she forces herself to sit quietly, her pulse racing, as the train rolls into the gentle, shadowy outskirts of Ottawa, capital of the Dominion (Do-min-i-on) of Canada.

He is at the station a full ten minutes before her arrival. He has allowed for this, knowing he'll need a cushion of calm in which to arrange his thoughts, his body too. "Well, well," he plans to say to her, draining the drama off the moment with his heartiness, "so you've made it all in one piece, have you?"

Or something about the heat. Or perhaps? – he doesn't know what. Everything seems suddenly at risk. Even his long legs have gone unsteady.

He wouldn't dream, though, of sitting down on one of those long, varnished benches. No, he pulls himself straight, his shoulders, his back, his hands clasped behind him, and paces the marble floor of the concourse. He pauses, staring up into the dome. A handsome building, yes indeed. He examines it carefully, its decorated frieze and fluted granite pillars with their classical pediments. He memorizes these stone surfaces, staring hard as though he may never again have an opportunity to see this clearly.

His life is on the cusp of change. Love, that sudden dissolving of art and nature, of language itself, is about to overcome his senses. He breathes deeply, and glances up at the station clock. Yes, the train is on time. On the minute. Precisely. This fact he finds deeply satisfying. Also worrying.

And there she is. Coming toward him.

Some men are described as having an eye for an ankle. Not Barker Flett. He has no eye at all. Nor any notion of what is owed him or what he may desire. This moment, this meeting, was arranged years earlier.

Here she comes, her gloved hand already extended as she moves forward, and for a moment he believes he may actually take that hand in his and shake it, a social gesture, murmuring: how nice to see you, and was the train crowded? Did you find a place next to the window? Are you exhausted?

Instead he takes her in an embrace. Not a real embrace, for there is no question of their bodies coming together. No. His hands reach out and lightly graze her shoulders, then travel down to her upper arms (these arms bare below the elbows and slightly damp), then moving upward again to her face, touching it with his fingertips, cradling it. He has forgotten all his resolve; his blood is on fire.

Her knees are shaky after so many hours on the train. The sudden light of the station unbalances her, and she can think of nothing to say.

"Daisy?" he murmurs across the combed crown of her hair, making a question of it. Almost a sob. He forgets what he said next.

*

At his age he could not face the fret and fuss and jitters of a full-scale wedding, and so they were married quickly, quietly, in a judge's chambers. August 17th, 1936. The telegram dispatched to Cuyler and Maria Goodwill in Bloomington minutes before the ceremony was framed in the past tense: "We have just been married. Letter to follow."

Both Daisy and Barker Flett felt cowardly about this announcement, and awaited a reply with some embarrassment.

The erotic realm is our nearest approach to the wild half of our nature. So thinks Barker Flett. There is a part of the human self that is unclassifiable. This is what he must learn to accept. And to be open to visitations of ardor without the thought of shame stealing in through every window. Why must everything be flattened by the iron of goodness and badness? Why?

He confesses to Daisy that he has in the past paid money for the attentions of women. She, in turn, resting her fingers lightly on his hair, confesses her true state: that she is untouched (her word), that something went wrong in her brief marriage to Harold A. Hoad; she's not sure what it was, but she may possibly have been at fault in the matter. He does not want to hear this; at this time in his life he needs all Daisy's strong feelings for himself.

These kinds of confessions, these points of honor, are almost always comic when viewed up close – and equally comic when viewed from a distance. All that unnecessary humiliation and preening honesty. And afterward, regret. Was any of it really necessary? Of course not.

One thing puzzles Barker Flett: he cannot understand how Daisy's nine years of widowhood were spent (in much the same way Daisy is unable to imagine how her father's youth in Stonewall was passed – year after year after year). He can picture Daisy darting about Bloomington, well dressed, nicely shod, prettily gloved, a healthy, hearty American girl who swims, walks, dances, and plays golf. But what did she *do*?

"I suppose you must have pursued studies of some kind. Attending lectures."

She shakes her head.

"Reading?"

Another shake.

"Of course there was your father's household to look after."

"Well" – she pauses – "we had Cora-Mae Milltown, you see. All those years. And then Maria."

"You must have done something with your time," he prods. "Charities? The Red Cross?"

She looks blank, then brightens. "The garden," she says. "I looked after the garden."

"The garden?"

"Yes."

"Ah," he says, "ah." A week later he makes an offer of purchase for a large house on The Driveway near Dow's Lake.

The house, solidly built of stone and brick, is situated on a triple lot and possesses a garden that has seen better days.

*

The Things People Had to Say About the Flett–Goodwill Liaison

The Prime Minister of the Dominion, himself a bachelor, said, on hearing of the marriage between Barker Flett and Daisy Goodwill: "Marriage is the highest calling, and after that is parenthood and after that the management of the nation."

The Minister of Agriculture exclaimed to his wife upon reading the marriage announcement in the newspaper: "Good God, Flett's got himself married. And I always thought the bloke was queer as a bent kipper."

Mrs. Donaldson, Barker Flett's housekeeper, said, bafflingly: "Out of the frying pan, into the fire."

Simon Flett in Edmonton sent a crumpled five dollar bill to his brother and the single word: "Bravo." Andrew Flett from Climax, Saskatchewan, wrote: "May the light of Jesus shine on you both."

Mrs. Dick Greene of Bloomington, Indiana, said, in a warm, congratulatory note to Daisy: "Here, in a phrase, is my recipe for a happy marriage: 'Bear and forbear'."

Fraidy Hoyt said (to herself): "She's lost her head, not her heart. I thought she had more sense. A young wife, an old husband – a prescription for disaster, if you believe in the wisdom of folktales."

Mrs. Arthur Hoad said: "Disgusting. Incestuous. Obscene. Without a doubt he has money."

The telegram from the Cuyler Goodwills said: "Congratulations and good wishes as you set out on the happy highway of life."

To himself, Cuyler Goodwill said, "He's almost as old as I am. He'll be away from home a good deal. He'll dampen passion with a look or a word. My poor Daisy."

"Bambini, bambini," Maria shouted, making a rocking cradle of her arms, and for once everyone understood what she was saying.

Daisy Goodwill's own thoughts on her marriage are not recorded, for she has given up the practice of keeping a private journal. The recent loss of her travel diary – it has never been found – caused her a certain amount of secret grief; she shudders to think whose hands it may have fallen into, all that self-indulgent scribbling that belongs, properly, to the province of girlhood – a place where she no longer lives.

Motherhood, 1947

Suppertime

PEOPLE THE WIDE world over like to think of Canada as a land of ice and snow. That's the image they prefer to hang on to, even when they know better.

But the fact is, Ottawa in the month of July can be hot as Hades – which is why the Fletts' supper table is set tonight on the screened porch. There will be jellied veal loaf, sliced tomatoes, and a potato salad and, for dessert, sugared raspberries in little glass bowls.

You should know that the raspberries are from the Fletts' own garden, picked only an hour ago by the children of the family. One of these three children, Warren, seven years old, got raspberry stains all over the front of his cotton shirt, and he has just been sent upstairs by his mother to change into something clean. "Lickety-split," she tells him, "your father'll be home in half a wink."

The two girls, Alice, nine, and Joan, five, have been encouraged to pick a small bouquet for the table, using an old cracked cream jug as a vase. Their arrangement turns out to be rather unbalanced looking, with long and short stemmed varieties mixed together, and already some of the flowers look a little unfresh. "Very pretty," Mrs. Flett pronounces, but then she's distracted because the jellied veal is stuck to the bottom of the loaf pan, refusing to reverse itself neatly on to the glass platter she's prepared. "Damn it," she says under her breath so the children won't hear, but of course they do hear. "Damn it, damn it." This recipe is torn from the pages of last month's *Ladies Home Journal*, a feature article called "Cooling Meals for Hot Days." She's followed the complicated directions meticulously, right down to the pimento strips and sliced stuffed olives that form the garnishing. "Why didn't I just buy some cold ham?" she wonders out loud.

"I love ham," Warren says dreamily, and it's true. What he especially loves is to take a slice of boiled ham and fold it over and over in his fingers and then stuff it in his mouth so that the soft sweet meat feels part of his own tongue and inner cheeks.

The tablecloth is checked cotton, blue and white. The mother's place is set at one end and the father's at the other; this is a family that tends to adhere to conventional routines and practices. At each place, just above the berry spoon, is a goblet for iced tea – even the children will be allowed iced tea tonight as a reward for having been good all day.

Being good – what exactly does being good mean in the context of the Flett family? Alice and Warren have been good because they made their own beds this morning without reminding, and, in addition, Alice has helped her mother by dusting the front and back stairs, the little wood side parts not covered by carpet. Before the war the family employed a woman to clean twice a week (a Mrs. Donaldson, famous for her indolence and sarcasm, who has since been reduced to comic dimensions), but nowadays such help – except for Mr. Mannerly who comes to help with the garden – is not to be had for love nor money, or so Warren has heard his mother say.

Little Joan has been good because she ate her eggs goldenrod for lunch (all but a little bit) and went down for her nap afterwards without whining, and because she remembered, mostly, her pleases and thank yous. And there's been a minimum of quarreling today. Mrs. Flett, the children's mother, has only spoken sharply to Alice once; there are days when Alice feels her mother likes her and days when she's sure she doesn't. Alice is always wanting to please her elders, but she's noticed that when she tries her hardest she feels sneaky and sweaty.

At last. The top half of the jellied veal drops, with a sucking slithering sound, on to the platter; the rest is hurriedly prised out with a spatula – "damn it, damn it" – and the gap hidden under pimento strips and a ruffle of garden lettuce. The platter is then covered lightly with a sheet of waxed paper and popped back into the Frigidaire so the loaf will stay firm for supper. Mrs. Flett glances up at the kitchen clock, shaped like a teapot with a little smiling mouth, and sees that the time is five-fifteen. She sucks in her breath. "Time to put your bikes in the shed," she says to her three children. "Your father'll be here in three shakes."

It's about this time that she disappears to "fix up" for dinner. Warren is always surprised how this disappearing happens without his noticing it, like a little bite taken out of the day, so quick it seems stolen. One minute his mother is standing there in her housedress with her face all damp, and the next minute she's wearing her red and white summer dirndl and a fresh white blouse with a drawstring around the neck. Her hair will be combed and she'll have lipstick on, dark coral, glossy like the licked surface of a jujube. She looks straight from the Oxydol ads, or so Warren thinks – perky, her eyes full of twinkles, her red lips pulling up, and her voice going slidey and loose. Sometimes she puts on a pair of silver-colored earrings that hang on by pinching her ear lobes hard. Warren can't help feeling proud of her when he sees her looking like this, coming down the carpeted stairs, all fixed up.

"Fixing up" is one of her girlhood expressions, one of her Hoosierisms, his father calls it. She says a number of other funny things too, like "waiting on" someone instead of "waiting for," or "having a little lie-down" instead of "taking a nap." Her voice has a cracked slant to it, slower but also brighter than other mothers' voices.

"Just a picnic supper tonight," she says to her husband, as though to confine his expectations. "Just odds and ends."

Sometimes he takes her girlishness literally, sometimes not. He kisses her cheek, feeling its cleanliness, and then he bends and kisses the tops of the children's heads, each of them in turn. Are these bright little bodies really connected to his, his old blood running in their young veins, the marrow of his bone matching theirs? Their brushed hair smells of sunshine and dust. Their smiles have a wonderful polish to them but are nevertheless tentative. He is unfailingly moved by the way their expressions have gone shy since breakfast. He touches the knot of his linen tie, considers removing it for dinner, then decides against it.

Decades of parched solitude have made him a voyeur in his own life, and even now he watches himself critically: paterfamilias, a man greeting his family at the end of the working day, gazing into the faces of his children and beyond them to the screened porch where the supper table is set. A corner pane of the folded back porch door catches a ray of sun, and he observes this with a look that is almost seigneurial, *his* porch door, *his* rectangle of golden light. "Have you washed your hands?" he hears himself asking his youngest child, and she immediately sticks them straight out for inspection, palms up. His little Joanie, five years old – who is breathless with the sense of the moment, wriggling her wrists, ready to explode. "Perfect," he tells her approvingly, making an announcement of it, but also a secret, and she hops up and down on one foot and then launches her body into a whirling off-center motion, so that he's reminded of one of those pre-war wind-up toys from Japan.

"Steady there, sweetheart," he says.

Is that his voice flowing out to her? "You'll bump your head on the doorway."

"No, I won't."

Of course she won't.

Conversation at the Flett supper table is not demanding. The children are not made to give an account of their day or to discuss "current events" or, as in one Torrington Crescent family, to speak only in French. Talk just meanders along in an unstructured way, how high the temperature went at noon, what to do about the aphids on the rose bushes, whose turn it is to clear the table. A little sigh escapes the lips of Mrs. Flett (Daisy), who is suddenly exhausted and who can't help noticing that no one has asked for a second helping of jellied veal loaf, though there's plenty to go around. "Tired?" her husband (Barker) asks quickly. "The heat," she says, fanning herself with the flat of her hand – as if that would do one bit of good – and he reminds her that the weather's due to ease off tomorrow, that's what the evening papers say, cool winds arriving from the west. "I might just as well wait till tomorrow evening to mow the lawn," he says.

She gives him a look which is impossible to read. Tenderness? Exasperation?

He is suddenly much older than he ever thought he'd be. In a matter of months he'll turn sixty-five and be forced to retire from the Directorship of the Agricultural Research Institute. A farewell banquet is being planned, with speeches and gifts and all kinds of hoopla – as his wife will most probably call it. And then what? The thought frightens him. His own father reaching sixty-five had gone strange in the head, packing up his belongings without a word to anyone and returning to the Orkneys where he'd been born, cutting off all contact with his family – not that there'd ever been much. The old devil would be eighty-five years old if he were still alive, though that was doubtful. The north winds would have got him by now, or the poisons of his own mind, though they say anger can keep a body going. What would he look like? Barker Flett can't help wondering. Only twenty-one years separate them, a mere twenty-one years. What had once seemed a great gulf has shrunk to insignificance. Their genetic structure, his and his father's, must be close to identical, long limbs, dark coarse hair, a sorrowful mouth. Nothing divides them now but geography; if it weren't for the width of the Atlantic Ocean, the two of them could stand side by side in old age, more like brothers than father and son, their blood thinned down to water and their limbs diminished by idleness.

Idleness: the notion frightens him, and so do his old temptations – solitude, silence.

What happens to men when their work is taken from them? Barker Flett thinks of his father-in-law, Cuyler Goodwill, who, though in perfect health, is reduced to the inanities of travel and the false enthusiasms of backyard projects. No, he will not allow himself to slip into that kind of dotage. A number of kind friends have suggested he write his autobiography, but, no, the surfaces of his life have been smoothed and polished by the years so as to be almost ungraspable; where would he begin? He'll work on his lady's-slipper collection instead, it's been years since he's added a new specimen. Also, there are a couple of articles he's been wanting to write, and – something altogether less academic – the editor of the Ottawa *Recorder* has asked him to contribute a piece or two, perhaps even a weekly column, on horticulture in the Ottawa-Carleton region. And he'll go back to his old habit of taking the children for weekend walks, quizzing them as they ramble along the quiet streets on the common names of trees and shrubs. He can't understand why these offspring of his are unable to retain such simple information about the natural world.

He wonders, in fact, what they do fill their heads up with. He wonders, too, if they're ashamed to be seen with a parent as old as he. A man old enough to be their grandfather, a man who's lived through two world wars and served in neither. Who almost never engages in a game of backyard catch. Who scarcely ever swings them up in the air or fills their ears with nonsense at bedtime. A man too tired to mow his lawn at the end of the day.

This day will end at eleven o'clock for the Flett family. The children will be in their beds much earlier, of course, with only a light sheet covering them, though a blanket will be fan-folded at the foot of the bed, ready to be pulled up for the cool early morning hours. The moon will have risen, a pale round peach at their windows. The branches of elms brush against the screens, and the whispery sound is absorbed straight into their dreams. Such sweetness of air. What heaven, this northerly city in the middle of its summer season. How blessed the members of the Flett family are, never mind their disparate ages, their hidden thoughts, and the fact that they have little in common.

Mr. and Mrs. Barker Flett settle in their big double bed with the Hollywood headboard, he with the latest issue of *The Botanical Journal* and she flipping through the pages of *Better Homes and Gardens*. Quietude, propriety. A single moth flits back and forth between his bedside lamp and hers. Half an hour later, as though summoned by a bell, the two of them turn, embrace cordially, and reach for the light switch. Despite the heat they drift easily into sleep, each of them feeling full of trust for the other, but then they would, wouldn't they?

Their sleep, Barker Flett likes to think, is made up of softer denser stuff than other people's sleep. There's something clean about it like scrubbed fleece. Is this what love is, he wonders, this substance that lies so pressingly between them, so neutral in color yet so palpable it need never be mentioned? Or is love something less, something slippery and odorless, a transparent gas riding through the world on the back of a breeze, or else – and this is what he more and more believes - just a word trying to remember another word.

He dreams of weeds tangled at the edge of a lake, of the breasts of a young girl, their hard tips, of an immense shaggy-flanked animal chasing him through the streets of an unknown town.

Alice

Alice's mother has explained to her the secrets of procreation. This is terrible news, shocking in all its parts, a man's peter poking inside a woman's peepee place. The explanation, meted out during a long, tense kitchen-table session, is more sickening in its way than the story Alice got from Billy Raabe who lives on the next block, for according to Billy the man goes pee inside the lady.

"No," Alice's mother says firmly, this – she pauses – this business has nothing to do with urine. The fluid in question contains seeds which are necessary if the mother is going to grow a baby inside her.

The mechanics of the exchange seem impossible to Alice.

"The mother and father lie on a bed," her mother tells her, sighing it out, "with their arms around each other."

"When?" Alice asks. Her own voice feels harsh to her ears.

Mrs. Flett's expression turns cross at this question, those three little lines between her eyes shooting up like a fan, but she clears her throat and says, "Well, usually at night."

"At night? Right here? In our house?"

"Really, Alice." Now her mother is staring down at her cuticles. The little teapot clock over the stove says half-past three. A coconut chiffon cake, freshly iced, sits on a pink glass plate.

"Well?" Alice is waiting for an answer. She will not let the issue drop.

"I don't know what to say, Alice. And I don't like the way you're speaking, your attitude, that scowl on your face."

This is becoming worse and worse. But Alice can't stop herself. "It's so icky. Why does anyone have to do such an icky thing?"

"Really, Alice."

"It's so awful."

"No, it's not awful. It's a beautiful thing between a man and woman."

"It makes me sick at my stomach."

"Well, you'll just have to believe me, it's a beautiful, beautiful thing."

Alice can feel her insides whimpering but she manages to keep the sound confined. The cloudless summer day is spoiled. Nothing will ever be the same. The house is defiled, especially her parents' upstairs bedroom with its stale powdery mysterious smell and the big hard-mattressed bed with its tufted headboard. Men and women are unclean, it was all grotesque, her mother who dresses herself each morning in her closet, the door left open a crack to let in the light, pulling on her underpants and girdle with her back turned, and hooking up her nylon stockings. Her mother actually opens her body at night to that dark hairy part of her father – Alice has glimpsed this darkness from time to time – and she allows this unspeakable thing to happen. It's like a dirty joke, the dirtiest joke she's ever heard.

Beautiful, her mother calls it, but then she'd gone on and on about the naked statues in the art gallery, saying they were beautiful too.

And other people must do it – Mrs. Raabe, Mrs. Hassel, her teacher Mrs. Strong. What about Esther Williams or Deborah Kerr or the king and queen of England? Maybe even Grandma Goodwill in Indiana. She and Grandpa.

"Do ladies," she asks her mother carefully, "still do it even when they don't want to have any more babies?"

"Well" – there was a swelling pause – "well, some do and some don't."

Alice feels a shift in the balance of the room. She and her mother have sat down at the table with willingness between them; they were going to get to the bottom of what Billy Raabe was spreading around the neighborhood. But now the discussion seems to be drawing to a close. Her mother is picking at her thumbnail, pulling a sliver of loose skin away, then glancing up at the window where the curtains are blowing inward. Alice senses that only one more question will be permitted.

"And do you – and Daddy – still do it?"

"Well –"

Alice holds her breath and waits.

"Well, yes," she hears, and then her mother adds a brave, tight addendum that seems pulled together like the drawstring of a bag, "Sometimes."

Alice is going to throw up the cream of asparagus soup she had for lunch, she knows it. She wonders if she should go stand by the kitchen sink so as not to make a mess.

"But, Alice, you must promise not to say anything to Warren and Joanie about what we've been discussing. Not until they're old enough to understand."

Warren and Joan are playing kings and queens in the backyard. Alice can hear Warren through the screen door yelling at Joan to bring him his crown and she hears Joan shouting, "Yes, your royal highness, here it is, your royal highness."

It is Alice's day to be queen, but she doesn't feel like going outside this afternoon. Let them play what they want to play.

Oh, she loves them, her brother and sister, she's never understood before how much she loves them. They are healthy, beautiful, perfect, and unbruised by this terrible knowledge. They will be able to go on looking into the faces of their mother and father, look right into their faces and smile and talk and carry on as if nothing has happened.

Warren

"How old are you?" Warren asks his mother.

She is folding sheets and pillowcases and kitchen towels on the dining room table. "That's for me to know and you to find out."

"Well, what year were you born in?"

She considers, then says, "1905."

"And now it's 1947."

"Yes."

He thinks about this for a while. "What year was I born in?" He's asked this question before, often, but is always forgetting the answer.

"You were born in 1940. In the early days of the war."

Now he remembers why he keeps pestering his mother with the same question. So he can hear that shivery phrase – in the early days of the war. The image of a rising sun swims before his eyes, blood-red in color like the Japanese flag Billy Raabe's got tacked up on his bedroom wall. He, imagines, too, a tense startled night silence broken by the high pitched rat-a-tat-tat of bullets, and all this fragmented noise is backed by a deeper, thunderous growling of guns. The War. The Second World War.

"Was that when Pearl Harbor was?" He loves the words Pearl Harbor. He loves himself for remembering them, for getting them right.

"This was before Pearl Harbor, a whole year before."

"Why was I born then?" he asks.

"Because you were."

"Alice was born before the war."

"Yes."

"And Joan, what about Joan?"

His mother's head is shrunk tight today by rows of pincurls. The bobby pins catch winks of light from the bay window. She is counting pillowcases. He can see her tongue ticking off the numbers at the same time her thumb travels down the neat stack – one, two, three, four, five. "Joan?" she says absentmindedly, "Joan was born in the middle of the war."

The war is like a wide brown tepid river the world's been swimming along in, only now, ever since Victory, there's nothing. Peace doesn't feel all that different to Warren. His body is the same body he's always had, his scraped shins and knees and bony feet, and his face in the hall mirror has the same round look of surprise. But sometimes at night he wakes up with a stomach ache and calls out to his mother, who gives him a glass of something fizzy to drink and tells him he's suffering from indigestion, that he'd be fine if only he didn't wolf down his food so fast. But he knows it's the war that gives him a stomach ache, the fact that the war is over and there's nothing to hold him up and keep him buoyant.

He and Alice and Joan are joined together like the little dolls Alice cuts out of newspaper, that's how he thinks of himself and his sisters. He's located there in the middle, always in the middle, the one who was born in the early days of the war, which is the thought he must try to hang on to. There's something thrilling in this knowledge. And there's tribute too, a place reserved for him, for Warren Magnus Flett, born in the blood-red dawn of the war.

He almost never thinks of the future, though he understands in an unformulated way that he will eventually grow up, will comb his hair back with water, and join the big boys in the back lane playing Piggy Move Up. And it occurs to him suddenly that there might be another baby born to his family, an after-the-war baby. He can't imagine why he's never thought of this possibility before, and he feels sick the way he does at the beginning of one of his stomach aches. He considers asking his mother about a new baby, but the question seems foolish. He can't think how he would broach the subject, what words he could employ. She might laugh at him or else she might put down the towel she was folding and say, well yes, of course there will be a new baby, what did he expect!

A new baby would spoil things. Where would it sleep? What name could be given to it? It would be born weak, without muscles, too weak and sick and lost to survive.

His mother seems to be reading his mind. She's done it before and today on this drowsy summer afternoon she's doing it again. "Your father and I are too old to have any more babies," she says.

Hearing this, he feels himself seized by happiness, not because of her assurance that there will be no after-the-war baby, but because his mother has offered up this information in a quiet and serious manner he's not heard from her before. Gone is her teasing voice, her usual scolding and cajoling, her singing and murmuring and chirruping tones. This new voice bursts through the others, an aberration, and yet he understands at once that he is hearing, perhaps for the first time, her real self speaking. "What?" he says.

"You mean 'pardon?'"

"Pardon."

She looks at him carefully, recognizes him, and says it again. "Your father and I are too old to have any more babies."

Joan

Joan is so full of secrets that sometimes she thinks she's going to burst. Her mother, putting her to bed at night, leans down and kisses her on each cheek and says, "My sweetie pie," and never dreams of all the secrets that lie packed in her little girl's head.

Already, at the age of five, Joan understands that she is destined to live two lives, one existence that is visible to those around her and another that blooms secretly inside her head.

There are all kinds of facts she knows, facts that no one else can imagine.

The radio for one thing. She managed one day to squeeze into that narrow dusty place behind the Northern Electric console in the living room, a radio her father describes as pre-war, and glimpsed through the mesh backing the red humming lights of a hillside village. Naturally she has told nobody about this, except perhaps a whisper or two dropped to her mother.

She has discovered how she can fill up an empty moment should one occur. When there is nothing else to do she can always walk down to the corner where Torrington Crescent meets The Driveway and there in front of Mrs. Bregman's big brown house she can roll down the grassy banked hill that runs across the front lawn. No one has said not to do this, no one seems to have thought of it. As it happens, she hardly ever goes down to the corner to roll down the hill, but she likes to keep the possibility in reserve. Or she can skip along the sidewalk in front of her own house. Learning to skip has brought control into her life. Whenever she feels at all sad she switches into this wholly happy gait, sliding, hopping, and sliding again; when doing this, it seems as though her head separates from her body, making her feel dizzy and emptied out of bad thoughts. Does anyone else in the world know this trick, she wonders. Probably not, though her mother sometimes waves at her from the window, waves and smiles.

There's a Decal transfer – a black swan swimming through green reeds – stuck to the top of the clothes hamper in the bathroom. She remembers watching her mother apply this decoration, first soaking the Decal in a sinkful of water, then peeling the transparent backing neatly away, centering the swan in the very middle of the hinged lid, and wiping it smooth with a wet cloth. Joan had thought the moment beautiful. Nevertheless, whenever she finds herself alone in the bathroom she scrapes away at the swan with her thumbnail. So far she's managed to loosen the edges all the way around, and she expects any minute to be accused, though at the same time she knows herself to be full of power, able to slip out from under any danger.

Mrs. Flett's Niece

Mrs. Flett's three children always seem to be quarreling – that's the impression she has anyway. It breaks her heart, she says, she who grew up without any brothers and sisters to play with.

But, in fact, Alice, Warren, and Joanie go through long harmonious periods, especially in the summertime when the other children in the neighborhood are away on vacation. The three of them engage in elaborate games and building projects – only last week they curtained the grape arbor with blankets and furnished the tented space with cardboard cartons and orange crates and lengths of old material from their mother's sewing cupboard. Here, in the dim filtered light with the three of them kneeling around an orange-crate table, they consume graham crackers and cups of ice water and lapse into an amicable nostalgia.

This nostalgia of theirs is extraordinary, each of them feels the richness of it. On and on they'll talk; a whole afternoon will disappear while they take turns comparing and repeating their separate and shared memories and shivering with pleasure every time a fresh fragment from the past is unearthed. Living among these old adventures is beautiful, they think. Remember swimming in Buffalo Lake, how sandy the bottom was and how the water was warm as bathtub water and how afterwards we went to a soda fountain for a root beer float. Remember going on the ferris wheel at the Exhibition, how Joanie turned green. ("Did I really?" she marvels, blissful at the thought.) Remember the time we went to visit Mr. Wrightman who was in the iron lung, the drool coming out of his mouth and he didn't even notice. Remember Billy Raabe falling off his bike in the back lane and knocking out his front tooth and his mother driving him to the hospital, how he got blood all over the back seat of the car and they never got the stains out. Remember when we had a burr war with the Jacksons, and Jeannie Jackson's mother had to cut the burrs out of her hair, her beautiful long golden hair, like a princess.

At the edge of every experience is the refracted light of recollection, snagged there like an image in a beveled mirror.

Alice, bossy, excited, takes the lead in these acts of retrieval, and Warren and Joan fill in, confirming, reinforcing, inventing too. They shudder with the heat of their own dramas, awestruck by the doubleness of memory, the hold it has on them, as mysterious as telephone wires or the halo around the head of the baby Jesus. Memory could be poked with a stick, savored in the mouth like a popsicle, you could never get enough of it.

And remember when Cousin Beverly came to visit? In the end they always come around to Cousin Beverly's visit, a visit that occurred in the distant past, a year ago, perhaps even two years ago.

No one knew she was coming. She just arrived one autumn afternoon wearing her WREN uniform, just rang the doorbell, the front door, and said, "Well, hello there, I'm your Cousin Beverly from Saskatchewan."

Of course they'd heard of Beverly, one of six girl cousins – Juanita, Rosalie, Arleen, Lillian, and Daphne were the others. They lived in a place called Climax, Saskatchewan. Their mother was Aunt Fan who was married to Uncle Andrew who was their father's brother, a pastor in the Baptist Church. Every year Mrs. Flett, the children's mother, makes up a big Christmas parcel for the Saskatchewan cousins – a new board game, flannelette nightgowns, wool gloves, a large round fruitcake – and always, when she's attaching the little name cards she shakes her head and says, "That family, they never seem to get ahead."

And now here was Beverley, all grown up – the Flett children hadn't expected that. She perched in the middle of the chesterfield and drank a cup of tea. "This is delicious," she said to her aunt in a cheerful forthcoming voice, as though they knew each other well and often sat together drinking tea like this. Alice and Warren perched on either side of her. (Where was their father that afternoon? In Toronto probably, or Montreal – he was always, it seemed, stepping aboard a train and disappearing for a few days.)

Cousin Beverly's WREN hat sat neatly on her hair, but they could see that she had short curls all over her head, probably a permanent wave or else naturally curly like Shirley Temple. She'd just come back from England where she'd been "right in the thick of things." She laughed loudly when she said that, about being in the thick of things. "Oh boy," she said, still laughing, "did we ever get our eyes opened up."

She let Alice try on her hat. It had to be put on with bobby pins, but she didn't mind a bit, going to the bother. "Hey, you look pretty cute," she told her, "a real living doll."

"Did you save any lives?" Warren asked her. He whispered it the first time and then had to say it again, louder.

Right away she laughed. "Well, I guess I saved my own skin a couple of times." Was this a wisecrack? Alice wasn't sure.

But Cousin Beverly's face suddenly lost its wisecracking look. She went sad for a few minutes, telling them about the soldiers on D-Day, flying missions in the darkness, dropping bombs on the enemy. Then she told them about an airman shot down over the English Channel. "The poor fellow," she said, "he couldn't find his parachute cord for some reason, and when they found his body they saw he'd bored a hole right through his leather jacket, he was looking so hard for it."

A human hand boring a hole through a leather jacket! In that desperate minute or two while he was falling through the sky! How do you explain a thing like that? Well, it was kind of a miracle, Cousin Beverly said, though not happy like most miracles are. Another man got both his legs blown off, but at least he was alive, at least he hadn't got his head mashed to porridge like another chap she knew –

They could have listened to Cousin Beverly talk about the war all day, but their mother interrupted. "Tell me how your parents are doing," she said. "And your sisters back home." And then she said, "Now when exactly does your train leave? We want to make sure you get down to the station in plenty of time."

Afterwards Alice couldn't stop thinking about Cousin Beverly. Cousin Beverly's visit kept running through her mind like a movie. Her beauty. Her curls. Her red mouth. Her tan hose and polished shoes. Her short-skirted WREN uniform, her quick yelp of laughter, the way she shrugged her neat little shoulders when she talked about the airman falling through the sky and boring a hole through his leather jacket. Cousin Beverly was someone in possession of terrible stories, but still she managed to walk around in the world and be cheerful and smart. She'd arrived unannounced, just marched down their street and rang their doorbell and said: here I am. But in no time at all – an hour or two – she was gone.

("So long, kids. See ya in the movies.") How far away was Saskatchewan? Alice, lying in her bed at night, seems to hear the continuous drone of great distances, a vibrating emptiness. She imagines that she can smell a rolling wave of Saskatchewan air, a smell of spice and cold.

"Is Cousin Beverly ever going to come back?" Alice asked her mother once. For some reason it took her a long time to work up to this topic.

"I wouldn't put my money on it," Mrs. Flett said slowly.

"Isn't she wonderful," Alice breathed.

"Well," Mrs. Flett said finally, "She's got plenty of oomph anyway." Saying this, she cast her eyes upward like someone trying to remember the end of an old story, and then she let out a long sigh.

When Alice looks into that sigh, or around it, she understands that there's something chastening about the sound, and also something withheld, some vital piece of information that is being kept back until "she's old enough." Nightmare, shame, revelation, judgment, the strain of failure – all this lies ahead for her. She can't bear to think about the future. It's like concentrating on your own breath: once you start thinking about the air rushing in and out of your body, your breath has a way of getting stuck in your throat so that you understand how easy it would be to fall down and die.

A Letter Folded in Mrs. Flett's Dresser Drawer

Dear Daisy,

This is to let you know that our girl Beverly arrived home yesterday afternoon after her long train journey, the train

Cuyler and Mercy, 1902

Ladies Rhythm and Movement Club

*Hannah Goodwill
(mother of
Cuyler Goodwill)*

*Aunt
Clarentine, 1916*

Clarentine

*Bessie McGordon,
Matron,
Stonewall
Orphans' Home*

Barker

Mrs Arthur Hoad

Harold A. Hoad

'Beans' Anthony

Maria

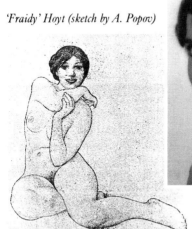

'Fraidy' Hoyt (sketch by A. Popov)

'Fraidy' Hoyt

Warren

Victoria

583 The Driveway

*Left to right:
Mrs Mannerly, Beverly, Mr Mannerly,
Angus Mannerly, Warren, Alice*

Alice

Alice Downing

Judith Flett Downing

Beth Taylor

Rain Taylor

Lissa Taylor

Jilly Taylor

Sophie Flett-Roy

Hugh Flett-Roy

was crowded with servicemen all going home and then the heating went on the blink just outside Winnipeg so that she caught herself the most awful cold, a runny nose and a real bad sore throat. I have to tell you her feelings were hurt just terribly by the way she was treated at your home, not asked to stay for supper or offered a bed for the night, just given the bum's rush, that's how she felt anyways. Maybe if her uncle had been there things would have gone different, who knows. If only she'd taken the morning train she might not have ended up sick like she is. She just can't understand it, thinking you'd be happy as can be to meet your niece from the West that you'd never laid eyes on before and who has served her Country. Her dad and I can't understand it either, maybe manners are different in the East than out here where we welcome one and all.

Sincerely, your sister-in-law,

Fan Flett

Mrs. Flett's Aged Father

Cuyler Goodwill is seventy years old, that talismanic age, and his wife Maria (his second wife, that is) has just celebrated her . . . well, no one knows how old Maria is. Mr. Goodwill, a stone carver by trade and, later, a famous entrepreneur in the state of Indiana, is now retired. He and his wife have recently sold their handsome old Bloomington house and bought a little place on Lake Lemon, some twenty-five miles outside the city limits. Why did they sell their comfortable house for this lakeside cottage? Because Maria wanted to be out in the country where she could grow vegetables in the front yard without the neighbors squawking their heads off. And Cuyler Goodwill wanted plenty of space in the back yard in which to build a pyramid.

He's been planning his pyramid for a year now, ever since he and Maria got home from their cruise on the Nile. Almost every day when they were in Egypt he sent postcards to his grandchildren in Ottawa, Canada. "Dear Alice (or Warren or Joanie), you should see the pyramids they've got out here. The biggest one has two million limestone blocks and each stone weighs two and a half tons."

He wrote a letter to his daughter, Daisy, telling her that the classic pyramid shape is based on the spreading-out rays of the sun as they fall to earth.

"Nonsense," Daisy's husband said, "the sun's rays fall straight downward, not on an angle."

"Well, never mind," Daisy said vaguely, "it's something for him to do."

The pyramid is to be two yards square, a miniature replica of the real thing. He's worked out the proportions, using the Great Pyramid as his model. So reduced in size are his stone blocks (smaller than the tip of his finger, three-eighths of an inch square) that he can hold six or seven of them in the palm of his hand. The exterior cladding will be pure white Indiana limestone, but he intends to use sandstone, marble, granite, slate, whatever, for the interior. Mortar? He's decided yes, a very thin mixture, more like glue actually. The Egyptians could build without mortar, but his stones are too small and hence too light. His aim is to use stone from around the world. He brought back lava stone from the

Hawaiian Islands where he and Maria spent Easter, and he's received stone samples from Manitoba, Ontario, Tennessee, Michigan, Vermont, France (Burgundy), Italy, Finland, and the British Isles. He's heard of limestone beds in South Africa, and he and Maria are there right now on a vacation, seeing the sights and keeping their eyes open for new quarries and new variations of stone. Shining through his thoughts, and through his dreams as well, are the warm sunlit surfaces of rock shelves as yet untouched. Here, at these newly discovered sites, he longs to tap his hammer and dislodge a sample which he will pack in wadded newspaper and carry home. (His favorite joke concerns a railway porter who asked him if he had rocks in his suitcase, it was so heavy.)

"He's obsessed," his daughter Daisy says, but she says it happily. On the whole she believes old people are better off obsessed than emptied out.

What is the pyramid for? Quite a lot of people ask Daisy this question, and she doesn't know what to say. Does he intend it as his own tombstone? No, he and Maria have already bought cemetery plots in Bloomington. Is it a sort of memorial to something? Well, maybe; no one's come out and put the question to him.

He has the self-confidence of a man who expects others to applaud his most outlandish projects. He's taking his time, too; this is a major construction, slightly more than two million tiny stone pieces to set in place. In the exact center, buried under the foundation, is a time capsule. He wrote to his three grandchildren in Ottawa for contributions. Something small, he said, and representative of the times. Little Joan, encouraged by her father, sent a two-penny postage stamp with the king on it. Warren sent a pressed maple leaf. And Alice, after much thought, sent a headline cut from the local newspaper: PRINCESS ELIZABETH TO MARRY PRINCE PHILIP IN NOVEMBER.

These items – stamp, leaf, and paper banner – Cuyler Goodwill has placed in a sealed metal box. Maria, his second wife, has contributed an envelope of fennel seeds. Goodwill himself, that eccentric old fool, has added, at the last minute, the wedding ring that belonged to his first wife.

The ring is of yellow gold with a fine milled edge. The wedding date, June 15, 1903, is engraved inside, as well as the initials of the bride and groom. Goodwill recalls exactly what he paid for the ring, which was four dollars and twenty-five cents. Eighteen karat gold too, ordered through the Eaton's catalogue. He remembers that when his young wife died in childbirth two years later, he agonized about whether or not to remove the ring before burial; what was the common practice? What did people do? He had no idea.

It was the doctor's wife, a Mrs. Spears, who urged him to preserve the ring as a keepsake; she also helped him in the removing of it, first rubbing a little lard on his dead wife's finger, then easing it off. Mrs. Spears' voice as she performed this act had been most tender. "Keep it, Mr. Goodwill," she said, her face empty of calculation, "so you can give it to your daughter when she grows up."

And this is what he has always intended to do, to present it to his dear child, making a ceremony of it, a moment of illumination in which he would for once join the separate threads of his life and declare the richness of his blessings.

But he feels, recently, that he has lost his way in life. Old age has made him clumsy in both body and spirit, and he is unable finally to bring the scene to actuality or even, of late, to imagine it. What words would he find to invest the moment with significance? And what words would his daughter offer in return? Thank you would not do. Gratitude itself would not do. Speech and gesture would not suffice, not in the thin ether of the world he now inhabits. Far less troubling to bury this treasure beneath a weight of stone – his pyramid, dense, heavy, complex, full of secrets, a sort of machine. His statement of finality. Either that, or a shrug of surrender.

Mrs. Flett's Old School Friend

Fraidy Hoyt and Daisy Goodwill Flett went to school together back in Indiana. They sat on the Goodwills' front porch in Bloomington and shared bags of Jay's Potato Chips. They went to college together too, and pledged the same sorority, Alpha Zeta, and ever since that time they've stayed in touch. That is, they've corresponded three or four times a year, and sent each other jokey presents on their birthdays and at Christmas. They haven't actually seen each other for years, but, finally, in August of 1947, Fraidy got herself on a train and went up to Ottawa for a week's visit.

While she was there she thought: here is Daisy Goodwill with a distinguished husband and a large well-managed house and three beautiful children. Daisy's got all that any of us ever wanted. Whereas I've missed out on everything, no husband, no kids, no home really, only a dinky little apartment, not even a garden. Oh, Daisy's garden! That garden's something else. She can get up in the morning and spend all day if she likes trimming and weeding and transplanting and bringing beauty into the world. While I'm sitting at work. Tied to a desk and to the clock. Missing out on this business of being a woman. Missing it all.

Or else Fraidy Hoyt thought: oh, poor Daisy. My God, she's gone fat. And respectable. Although who could be respectable going around in one of those godawful dirndl skirts – should I say something? Drop a little hint? Her cuticles too. I don't think she's read a book in ten years. And, Jesus, just look at this guest room. Hideous pink scallops everywhere. I'm suffocating. Four more days. And this crocheted bedspread, she's so gee-dee proud of, no one has crocheted bedspreads any more, it's enough to give you nightmares just touching it. I'd like to unravel the whole damn thing, and I could too, one little pull. These kids are driving me crazy, whining and sneaking around all day, then dressing up like little puppets for the return of the great man at the end of the day. Putting on a little play every single hypocritical day of their lives.

And: what can I say to her? What's left to say? I see you're still breathing, Daisy. I see you're still dusting that nose of yours with Woodbury Face Powder. I observe your husband is always going off to "meetings" in Toronto or Montreal, and I wonder if you have any notion of what happens to him in those places. I notice you continue to wake up in the morning and go to bed at night. Now isn't that interesting. I believe your life is still going along, it's still happening to you, isn't it? Well, well.

Mrs. Flett's Intimate Relations with her Husband

Deeply, fervently, sincerely desiring to be a good wife and mother, Mrs. Flett reads every issue of *Good Housekeeping.*

Also *McCalls* and *The Canadian Home Companion.* And every once in a while, between the cosmetic advertisements and the recipe columns, she comes across articles about ways a woman can please her husband in bed. Often, too, there are letters from women who are seeking special advice for particular sexual problems. One of them wrote recently, "My husband always wants to have our cuddly moments on Monday night after his bowling league. Unfortunately I do the wash on Mondays and am too exhausted by evening to be an enthusiastic partner." The advice given was short and to the point: "Wash on Tuesdays." Which made Mrs. Flett smile. She laughed out loud, in fact, and wished her friend Fraidy was here to hear her laugh. Another woman wrote: "My husband has a very strong physical drive, and expects intimate relations every single night. Is this normal?" Answer: "There is no such thing as normal or abnormal sexual patterns. What goes on in the bedroom of married people is sacred." This advice struck Mrs. Flett as less than satisfactory; as a matter of act, she isn't entirely sure what was meant.

She does believe, though, that "every night" would be a lot to put up with.

Nevertheless she always prepares herself, just in case – her diaphragm in position, though she is repelled by its yellow look of decay and the cold, sick-smelling jelly she smears around its edge. It's a bother, and nine times out of ten it isn't needed, but it seems this is something that has to be put up with. "Try to make your husband believe that you are always ready for his entreaties, even though his actual lovemaking may be sporadic and unpredictable."

Unpredictable, yes, although there are two particular times when Mrs. Flett can be absolutely certain of an episode of ardor: before her husband goes out of town (as a sort of vaccination, she sometimes thinks) and on his return. And tonight, a Wednesday in mid-September, he will be returning on the late train after a few days spent in Winnipeg. The house is orderly, the children asleep, and she herself is bathed, powdered, diaphragmed, and softly nightgowned. "The wearing of pajamas has driven many a man to seek affection elsewhere."

She wonders what his mood will be.

Lately he has been depressed. Not that he's said anything, but she can feel it. His sixty-fifth birthday is approaching; she knows retirement worries him, the empty width of time ahead and how he will cope with it. Worse than idleness, though, is the sense of being cut off in the world. Lately he has been speaking more frequently of his two brothers in western Canada, and always their names are mentioned with a ping of sorrow. Simon in Edmonton, a drunk, has been out of touch for years, and between Barker and his brother Andrew in Saskatchewan a coolness has fallen. In the old days Andrew wrote frequently, usually, to be sure, asking for hand-outs, but the last two years have brought only an occasional brisk note or a holiday greeting.

Mrs. Flett knows, too, that her husband thinks often about his father in the Orkneys. He wonders if he should write and make inquiries, but the months go by and he puts off writing, almost as though he can't bear to know what has happened. She, too, thinks often about her father-in-law, Magnus Flett, whom she has never met but who stands in her mind as a tragic figure, abandoned by his wife, dismissed by his three sons, despised, attached to nothing. In a way she loves him more tenderly than she loves her husband, Barker. What exactly had Magnus Flett done to deserve such punishment? The question nudges at her sense of charity, never quite disappearing from view.

Yet now – too late – his son, Barker, pines for reunion.

Recently, another of Barker Flett's family ties has been rekindled, the most important of life's ties – that which exists between son and mother. These last few days Barker has been in Winnipeg not for his usual round of agricultural meetings, but to attend the dedication ceremonies of the Clarentine Flett Horticultural Conservatory, a great glass-domed structure set in the middle of Assiniboine Park. The benefactor is one Valdi Goodmansen, the well-known millionaire meatpacker and financier. (Clarentine Flett, who was Barker Flett's mother, had been run down and killed by a speeding bicycle back in the year 1916, and the rider of the bicycle was Valdi Goodmansen himself, then a lad of seventeen.)

"The terrible guilt I felt at that time has never lifted," Mr. Goodmansen told Mr. Flett over dinner at the Manitoba Club. "One moment of carelessness, and a human life was erased. If only I had dismounted while turning the corner. Or if I had been traveling at a more reasonable speed. The image will be with me all my life, tied to me in my dreams and in my waking hours, your mother's poor helpless body thrown against the foundations of the Royal Bank Building, her head striking the edge of the corner stone. If only that stone had been rounded, but, alas, it was sharp as a knife. My life has been altered as a result. I've prayed to my Lord, I've tried in my way to serve others, and I've thought long and hard about a suitable monument." (Here he pulled out a handkerchief that was truly snowy, and blew into its starched folds a loud, prideful honk.) "Always, always I came back to the fact that your mother had loved flowers. You might say that she was responsible for bringing flowers to our great city, for making us aware of the blessings of natural beauty in an inhospitable climate. Of course I can never make full amends, but I do hope this little ceremony will give testimony to my terrible and continuing remorse in the matter of your mother's demise. I am only sorry that your wife, I believe her name is Daisy, could not be with us today. Of course, I fully understand how difficult it is for her to leave a family of young children to travel across the continent, and I understand, too, yes I do, how emotional an experience this would be for her. We are bound forever to those who care for us in our early years. Their loss cannot be compensated. Our ties to them are unbreakable."

But Mrs. Flett in Ottawa, lying in her bed and awaiting her husband's return, is thinking not so much of Clarentine Flett, her dear adopted Aunt Clarentine, as of her own mother who died minutes after her birth. How slender and insubstantial that connection now seems, how almost arbitrary, for what does Mrs. Flett possess of her mother beyond a blurred wedding photograph and a small foreign coin, too worn to decipher, which according to her father had been placed on her own forehead at birth – by whom she cannot imagine, nor for what purpose. She has never experienced that everyday taken-for-granted pleasure of touching something her mother had touched. There is no diary, no wedding veil, no beautiful hand-stitched christening gown, no little keepsake of any kind. Once, years ago, her father had mentioned a wedding ring that would one day be hers, but he has not spoken of it since. Perhaps he has given it to his wife, Maria. Or perhaps it has merely slipped his mind. Tonight, lying under a light blanket and awaiting the return of her husband, a man named Barker Flett, she feels the loss of that ring, the loss, in fact, of any connection in the world. Her own children are forgotten for the moment, her elderly father is forgotten, even his name reduced to a blur of syllables. She is shivering all over as if struck by a sudden infection.

She's had these gusts of grief before. The illness she suffers is orphanhood – she recognizes it in the same way you recognize a migraine coming on: here it comes again – and again – and here she lies, stranded, genderless, ageless, alone.

Tears have crept into her eyes and she dabs at them with the blanket binding. The darkness of the room presses close.

These are frightening times for Mrs. Flett, when she feels herself anointed by loneliness, the full weight of it. Wonderingly, she thinks back to the moment when as a young woman she stood gazing at Niagara Falls; her sleeve had brushed the coat sleeve of a man, a stranger standing next to her; he said something that made her laugh, but what? What?

Her loss of memory brings a new wave of panic.

And yet, within her anxiety, secured there like a gemstone, she carries the cool and curious power of occasionally being able to see the world vividly. Clarity bursts upon her, a spray of little stars. She understands this, and thinks of it as one of the tricks of consciousness; there is something almost luxurious about it. The narrative maze opens and permits her to pass through. She may be crowded out of her own life – she knows this for a fact and has always known it – but she possesses, as a compensatory gift, the startling ability to draft alternate versions. She feels, for instance, the force of her children's unruly secrecies, of her father's clumsy bargains with the world around him, of the mingled contempt and envy of Fraidy Hoyt (who has not yet written so much as a simple bread-and-butter note following her summer visit). Tonight Mrs. Flett is even touched by a filament of sensation linking her to her dead mother, Mercy Stone Goodwill; this moment to be sure is brief and lightly drawn, no more than an impression of breath or gesture or tint of light which has no assigned place in memory, and which, curiously, suddenly, reverses itself to reveal a flash of distortion – the notion that Mrs. Flett has given birth to her mother, and not the other way around.

And as for Mrs. Flett's husband – well, what of her husband? Her husband will be home in an hour or so, having in his usual way taken a taxi from the train station. He will remove his trousers in the dark bedroom, hanging them neatly over the back of the chair. These trousers carry an odor of sanctity, as well as a pattern of symmetrical whisker-like creases across the front. Then his tie, next his shirt and underwear. Then, unaware of her tears wetting the blanket binding and the depth of her loneliness this September night, he will lie down on top of her, being careful not to put too much weight on her frame ("A gentleman always supports himself on his elbows"). His eyes will be shut, and his warm penis will be produced and directed inside her, and then there will be a few minutes of rhythmic rocking.

On and on it will go while Mrs. Flett tries, as through a helix of mixed print and distraction, to remember exactly what was advised in the latest issue of *McCalls*, something about a wife's responsibility for demonstrating a rise in ardor; that was it – ardor and surrender expressed simultaneously through a single subtle gesturing of the body; but how was that possible?

The brain, heart, and pelvis of Mrs. Flett attempt to deal with this contradiction.

The debris of her married life rains down around her, the anniversaries, pregnancies, vacations, meals, illnesses, and recoveries, crowding out the dramatic – some would say incestuous – origin of her relationship with her partner in marriage, the male god of her childhood. It seems to her that these years have calcified into a firm resolution: that she will never again be surprised. It has become, almost, an ambition. Isn't this what love's amending script has promised her? Isn't this what created and now sustains her love for Barker, the protection from rude surprise? The ramp of her husband's elongated thighs, her own buttocks – like soft fruit spreading out beneath her on the firm mattress – don't they lend a certain credence? House plants, after all, thrive in a vacuum of geography and climate – why shouldn't she?

It's quite likely, with Barker Flett still rocking back and forth above her, that her thoughts will drift to a movie she went to see when Fraidy Hoyt was visiting last summer, *The Best Years of Our Lives*, a post-war epic in which a soldier returns from battle with crude hooks where his hands had once been.

What would it be like to be touched by cold bent metal instead of human fingertips? What would it be like to feel the full weight of a man on her body, pinning her hard to the world? She will ponder this, relishing the thin spiral of possibility, but then her thoughts will be cut short by an explosion of fluid, and after that a secondary explosion – of gratitude this time. Mixed with the gratitude will be her husband's shudder of embarrassment for his elderly tallow-colored body and for the few blurted words of affection he is able to offer. That men and women should be bound to each other in this way! How badly reality is organized.

"Sleep tight, my dear," he will say, meaning: "Forgive me, forgive us."

Mrs. Flett's House and Garden

The large square house at 583 The Driveway is over-spread with a sort of muzziness. The furniture, the curtains, the carpets, the kitchen floor – all have grown shabby during the war years. And now, in the post-war upheaval, there is a worldwide shortage of linoleum, though it is predicted the problem will ease fairly soon. (Mrs. Flett is already dreaming about a certain Armstrong pattern of overlapping red, black, and white rectangles.) The glass curtains in her dining room have been washed once too often, but she (Mrs. Flett) is talking about ordering pull drapes (or draperies, as she's learned to say) in a floral fabric, something to "pick up" the room, give it some vitality. What's more, she's sick and tired of the morning glory wallpaper in the living room with its numbing columns of blue, yellow, and pink; she's planning on a solid color next time around, Williamsburg green, maybe, with white enameled woodwork for contrast. And that shabby old carpet gets her down, the way it's worn along the seams so that the backing shows through, awful, like a person's scalp seen up close. To tell the truth the whole room looks undernourished and underloved, though she can't help feeling just a little proud of the coffee table which she has recently altered by topping the walnut veneer with a sheet of glass, beneath which she's positioned photographs of her three children and a copy, slightly yellowed, of her marriage announcement:

Mr. and Mrs. Barker Flett
Wish To Announce Their Recent Marriage
in Ottawa, August 17, 1936

She got this coffee table idea from *Canadian Homes and Gardens*, an article called "Putting the Essential You into Your Decor."

Every room in the house, even the upstairs bathroom, has a gathering of ferns at the window, maidenhair, bird's nest, holly fern, rabbit's foot. (These indoor ferns, in the year 1947, have an old-fashioned look of fussiness, though they are destined to achieve a high degree of chic, and ubiquity, in the mid-sixties.) The fact is, green plants and coffee table aside, Mrs. Flett is not much interested in her house. Some insufficiency in herself is reflected, she feels, in its structural austerity. Its eight high-ceilinged rooms four up, four down, have a country plainness to them, being severely square in shape with overly large blank windows. The light that falls through these windows is surprisingly harsh, and in winter the walls are cold and the corners of the downstairs rooms drafty.

She lives for summer, for the heat of the sun – for her garden, if the truth were known. And what a garden!

The Fletts' large, rather ill-favored brick house is nested in a saucer of green: front, back, and sides, a triple lot, rare in this part of the city, and in spring the rounded snouts of crocuses poke through everywhere. Healthy Boston ivy, *P. tricuspidata*, grows now over three-quarters of the brickwork (it has not prospered on the north face of the house, but what matter?); then there are the windowboxes, vibrant with color, and, in addition, Mrs. Flett has cunningly obscured the house's ugly limestone foundation with plantings of Japanese yew, juniper, mugho pine, dwarf spruce, and the new Korean box. And her lilacs! Some people, you know, will go out and buy any old lilac and just poke it in the ground, but Mrs. Flett has given thought to overall plant size and blossom color, mixing the white "Madame Lemoine" lilac with soft pink Persian lilac and slatey blue "President Lincoln." These different varieties are "grouped," not "plopped." At the side of the house a border of blue sweet william has been given a sprinkling of bright yellow coreopsis, and this combination, without exaggeration, is a true artist's touch. Clumps of bleeding heart are placed – placed, this has not just happened – near the pale blueness of campanula; perfection! The apple trees in the back garden are sprayed each season against railroad worm so that all summer long their leaves throw kaleidoscopic patterns on the fine pale lawn. Here the late sun fidgets among the poppies. And the dahlias! – Mrs. Flett's husband jokes about the size of her dahlias, claiming that the blooms have to be carried in through the back door sideways. A stone path edged with ageratum leads to the grape arbor and then winds its way to the rock garden planted with dwarf perennials and special alpine plants ordered from Europe. This garden of Mrs. Flett's is lush, grand, and intimate – English in its charm, French in its orderliness, Japanese in its economy – but there is something, too, in the sinuous path, the curved beds, the grinning garden dwarf carved from Indiana limestone and the sudden sculptured wall of *Syringa vulgaris* that is full of grave intelligence and even, you might say, a kind of wit. And the raspberries; mention must be made of the raspberries. Does Mrs. Barker Flett understand the miracle she has brought into being in the city of Ottawa on the continent of North America in this difficult northern city in the mean, toxic, withholding middle years of our century? Yes; for once she understands fully.

What a marvel, her good friends say – but it seems no mention has been made of Mrs. Flett's many good friends, as though she is somehow too vague and unpromising to deserve friendship. (Biography, even autobiography, is full of systemic error, of holes that connect like a tangle of underground streams.) The fact is, there are many in this city who feel a genuine fondness for Mrs. Flett, who warm to her modesty and admire her skills, her green thumb in particular. Her garden, these good friends claim, is so fragrant, verdant, and peaceful, so enchanting in its look of settledness and its caressing movements of shade and light, that entering it is to leave the troubles of the world behind. Visitors standing in this garden sometimes feel their hearts lock into place for an instant, and experience blurred primal visions of creation – Eden itself, paradise indeed.

It is, you might almost say, her child, her dearest child, the most beautiful of her offspring, obedient but possessing the fullness of its spaces, its stubborn vegetable will. She may yearn to know the true state of the garden, but she wants even more to be part of its mysteries. She understands, perhaps, a quarter of its green secrets, no more. In turn it perceives nothing of her, not her history, her name, her longings, nothing – which is why she is able to love it as purely as she does, why she has opened her arms to it, taking it as it comes, every leaf, every stem, every root and sign.

CHAPTER SIX

Work, 1955–1964

W. W. KLEINHARDT, SOLICITOR
Ottawa, April 25, 1955
My dear Mrs. Flett,

I am happy to say your late husband's will is now filed, and all dispersals made. Matters have been settled fairly rapidly since the document was, as I explained to you on the telephone, remarkably clear in its intention and without any troublesome conditions attached. I believe you will find everything in order.

Please feel free to contact me should you have any questions. Enclosed here along with our final report is a sealed envelope which your late husband instructed me, in writing, to pass on to you.

Yours truly,
Wally (Kleinhardt)

Ottawa, April 6, 1955
My dear,

Time is short. Dr. Shortcliffe says it will be a matter of days, doesn't he? This is not, of course, what he tells me, but what I overheard him saying to you last night, whispering in the corridor, after I was moved to the General. My hearing has remained oddly acute.

My mind, while less acute, is at ease about financial resources for you and for the children. The house, of course, is secured – for I feel sure you would be reluctant to leave familiar surroundings, particularly your garden – and there are sufficient funds as you know for the children's education.

But you will want money for travel – why is it we have not traveled, you and I? – and for small luxuries, and it has occurred to me that you might wish to offer for sale my lady's-slipper collection. I am certain it will bring a good price. I suggest you contact Dr. Leonard Lemay of Boston University whose address is in my pocket diary. I expect you will sigh as you read this suggestion, since I know well that *Cypripedium* is not a genus you admire, particularly the species *reginae* and *acaule*. You will remember how we quarreled – our only quarrel, as far as I can recall – over the repugnance you felt for the lady's-slipper morphology, its long, gloomy (as you claimed) stem and pouch-shaped lip which you declared to be grotesque. I pointed out, not that I needed to, the lip's functional cunning, that an insect might enter therein easily but escape only with difficulty. Well, so our discussions have run over these many years, my pedagogical voice pressing heavily on all that was light and fanciful. I sigh, myself, setting these words down, mourning the waste of words that passed between us, and the thought of what we might have addressed had we been more forthright – did you ever feel this, my love, our marginal discourse and what it must have displaced?

The memory of our "lady's-slippers" discussion has, of course, led me into wondering whether you perhaps viewed our marriage in a similar way, as a trap from which there was no easy exit. Between us we have almost never mentioned the word love. I have sometimes wondered whether it was the disparity of our ages that made the word seem foolish, or else something stiff and shy in our natures that forbade its utterance. This I regret. I would like to think that our children will use the word extravagantly, and moreover that they will be open to its forces. (Alice does worry me though, the ferocity of her feelings.)

Do you remember that day last October when I experienced my first terrible headache? I found you in the kitchen wearing one of those new and dreadful plastic aprons. You put your arms around me at once and reached up to smooth my temples. I loved you terribly at that moment. The crackling of your apron against my body seemed like an operatic response to the longings which even then I felt. It was like something whispering at us to hurry, to stop wasting time, and I would like to have danced with you through the back door, out into the garden, down the street, over the line of the horizon. Oh, my dear. I thought we would have more time.

Your loving
Barker

Ottawa, May 20, 1955
Dear Mrs. Flett,

I beg you to accept my sincere condolences regarding your sad loss. In the course of these last few years I have had the *honor* of becoming acquainted with your late husband, and very quickly I came to value his weekly contribution to the *Recorder*. You may be sure that the many readers of his column – and they are legion – will sorely miss their esteemed "Mr. Green Thumb." His dignified tone contributed a *rare* sense of scholarship to these pages, and yet was *never* condescending.

In acknowledgment of your husband's contribution, the staff here at the *Recorder* has assembled two specially bound copies of his articles, one to deposit with the National Archives, with your permission of course, and one which we would like to present to you and your family during the course of an informal memorial ceremony we are planning to hold at our offices here on Metcalfe Street. Can you let me know if June 1, 4:30 p.m., is agreeable to you?

Yours in sympathy,
Jay W. Dudley, Editor

P.S. Mr. Flett's demise seems particularly poignant at this time of the year when the city is ablaze with tulips. His articles on the annual Tulip Festival were among his most lyrical.

Climax, Saskatchewan, May 24, 1955
Dear Auntie,

We sure were upset to get your letter about Uncle Barker passing away. Mom and Dad and the girls send their deep felt sympathy and say to tell you they will remember all of you and him too in their prayers. But as Mom says, it can't be too great a shock for you, what with him being so much older in years. I've been thinking lately that it won't be easy for you with three kids only half grown and that big house to look after, a regular mansion if I remember right, but then I was only there the once. It seems like a dream, in fact, looking back. So in the next little while if you happen to find you need a hand in the house, maybe you could drop me a

line. I'm looking at moving East now that my husband and I
have called it quits. Drink was the main problem there. And
general laziness. Someone with my kind of pep gets driven
straight up the wall by another person just laying around. I'd
be willing to work for my room and board and forty dollars a
month. I'm a pretty fair housekeeper, if I do say so myself,
and just crazy about baking cakes, pies, buns, what have you.
Also laundry, ironing, etc. Also, I can type, as you can see,
thirty-five words a minute, it was through a correspondence course, otherwise I might of got up to sixty.

With love from your niece,

Beverly

P.S. Mom doesn't know I'm writing in regards to this matter,
so if you write back, send to Box 422, that way it doesn't go
to their place.

Bloomington, Indiana, May 29, 1955

Dearest Daze,

I wish to hell I could pour some good liquid cheer into
this envelope. I know how down-and-out rotten you must be
feeling these days. Well, no, I don't exactly know – how
could I? – but I can imagine what a misery it is to find
yourself alone after all the time you and Barker have been
together. What has it been? – I make it twenty years. Lordy,
it does go by, time that is, the filthy robber. And Alice off to
college next fall! And all this so soon after your dad dying.

Anyway I'm not going to go on and on about "remembering you in my prayers" (ha!) and "time's healing balm"
and all that razzmatazz – you'll get plenty of that from dear
old Beans – who grows more pious and platitudinous

each day. When Ma died she sprayed me with enough perfumed clichés to clog up my sinuses for a month. This note is just to remind you, old pal, that you've got lots of years left. Personally, I'm finding that being fifty isn't half as bad as it's cracked up to be – the old visage may be a bit pouchy and cross-hatched, but "everything that matters" is still in good working order, and no damn getting the curse either. So don't climb into your widow's weeds and wither away just yet, kiddo! What do you say we treat ourselves to a week in Chicago this winter. We could see a few shows, stay at the Palmer House, and eat like pigs. January would suit me – the gallery here is planning to close the last week of the month, and we're "encouraged" to clear off. Lordy, remember the terrific time we had in New York three years ago, or was it four? – that hilarious waiter and his bouncing baby lobster! – I wonder, did you ever report all that to Barker, item for item? Yes or no? Never mind replying – I can guess.

So let's hit Chi-town and put a little life into our life, what say? Surely there's someone who could keep an eye on Warren and Joanie for a few days. Give it some thought.

Love,

Fraidy

Ottawa, May 29, 1955

Dear Mrs. Flett,

We are *delighted* you will be able to attend our little tribute to your late husband. I should add that we would be very pleased to have your children in attendance as well.

And I thank you very much for your suggestion about the coverage of the Tulip Festival. We would indeed be

honored to have a few words from you; about five
hundred words would be ideal. I wish I had had the wit to
suggest it myself since rumor has it *you* are a famous
gardener in your own right.

> With sincere good wishes,
> Jay W. Dudley, Editor

Bloomington, Indiana, June 1, 1955
My dear old friend,

Our hearts ache continually for you these days. Your
burden has been unutterably heavy, losing your father in
April, bless his soul, and now your dearly beloved mate. I
feel sure that the many happy memories of your life together
will sustain you in the dark days ahead, as will the presence
of your loved ones and the prayers of your dear friends.
Time does heal, that is what you must keep in mind, though
of course we never really forget those who have played such
a large part in our lives. Dick joins me in these few rushed
words of sympathy. (After much pressure, he has accepted
the transfer to the head office in Cleveland, and now we
must face the sadness of putting our dear old house up for
sale – unfortunately the market is not booming. It seems
limestone has become a lemon.)

> Lovingly,
> "Beans"

Ottawa, June 5, 1955
Dear Mrs. Flett,

Just a note to express my thanks for the gracious remarks
you contributed to our little ceremony yesterday. I believe

I can say that we were all touched by your comments, particularly those concerning your late husband's regard for the *Recorder* and all that it stands for in our community.

And speaking personally, it was a *very* great pleasure to meet you and your three charming children, and please don't think for a minute I was offended by what your daughter, Alice, said about my necktie. I know how teenagers sometimes blurt out their thoughts and later regret it. I look forward *eagerly* to your article on the Tulip Festival. Five hundred words would do nicely, as I believe I mentioned, but please feel free to expand or contract, should you feel the need. We have a great many eager gardeners out there who will welcome your thoughts.

Sincerely,
J.W.D., Editor

Ottawa, June 9, 1955

Dear Mrs. Flett,

Just a note to let you know your *maiden flight*, as you term it, will be *landing* next Saturday in the Sports and Home section. We found the piece you mailed in to be solid in the best journalistic sense, yet full of *felicities*, my favorite being your description of thinly planted tulips looking like "ninnies marching off to a picnic." Quite so.

If you are in agreement, we thought we might use "Mrs. Green Thumb" as a byline. I am a little uneasy about this suggestion, wondering if it might seem insensitive, certainly not my intention, so do please let me know if you have any reservations.

Sincerely,
Jay Dudley

Ottawa, June 15, 1955

Dear Mrs. Green Thumb,

I congratulate you on your coverage of our fair city's annual Tulip Festival which I found fair, comprehensive, and flattering. Why flattering? Because you singled out, as being especially praiseworthy, one particular front yard on Fenton Avenue where you claim to have spotted a stand of "gorgeous Rembrandts backed by a gray-stained fence" (fourth paragraph). Since reading this, my good wife and I have persuaded ourselves that this must be a reference to our very own Rembrandts, and to our very own recently stained fence which has caught your attention and achieved the immortality of print.

Would you by any chance have an opinion on the use of fungicides to sterilize soil after an eruption of fire-blight?

> With thanks,
>
> Alvin A. MacIntosh

Ottawa, June 18, 1955

Dear Mrs. Green Thumb,

Happy to see the Tulip Festival through female eyes for a change. Liked what you said about bybloems. More people should speak out on said topic. Hope you'll continue with the *Recorder* column. Frankly, I often found the ex-gardens writer, Mr. Green Thumb, uncommitted on the subject of broken varieties. A bit namby-pamby on fertilizers too.

> Yours,
>
> Doris Griswold

P.S. I'm with you one hundred percent on the question of pastels mixed with pures.

Climax, Saskatchewan, June 25, 1955
Dear Auntie,

I've been keeping my fingers crossed for a letter from you,
but the days go by and no luck so far. I guess, truth to tell,
I'm getting sort of nervous, and the reason is, I might as well
tell you straight out, I'm in the family way, only nobody
around here knows about it, especially my folks who would
go up in smoke if they got wind of it. It's a long story, how it
happened, I mean, but now I'm starting to show and I've got
to do something real soon before everyone starts putting two
and two together. What I want to do is get way far away from
here and make a fresh start. Then when the time comes I'll
put the baby up for adoption and get a job using my typing
skills. I just know everything will work out in the end, but the
problem is I don't know how to get things started, if you
know what I mean. It's like there's this great big wheel I've
got to start rolling only I don't seem to have the muscles to
get it going. That's why I was hoping you could maybe help
me out for a few months. I mentioned room and board and
forty dollars a month when I wrote, but really room and
board is all I need. In fact I'd be grateful for that.

> With love,
>
> Your niece Beverly

Ottawa, June 29, 1955
Dear Mrs. Flett,

As you can see from the enclosed letters, your Tulip
Festival article was a great success. Everyone, including
myself, seemed to respond to your plea for bolder
arrangements and to your closing-off remark: "Beauty takes
courage. Courage itself takes courage." Well said!

We do hope – I speak for the whole staff – that you'll do a repeat performance. In fact, could you possibly see your way to doing a monthly, or even a weekly, column for us? I realize this request comes very soon after your late husband's demise, and that you may not feel up to making a firm commitment at this time. But, speaking from experience (my wife died only three years ago), I believe occupation to be *the* most effective means of dealing with bereavement.

I am returning the cheque, which you charmingly returned to me. But, of course, we *insist* on payment for *all* our writers. I only wish it were more bountiful.

Yours sincerely,

Jay

Climax, Saskatchewan, July 7, 1955

Dear Auntie,

This is written in haste. I can't wait to see you and the kiddies, and I can't thank you enough for sending the train ticket.

Loads of love. I've got this funny feeling in the pit of my stomach of my life starting all over again. So long till next Wednesday.

Beverly

Boston University, July 12, 1955

My dear Mrs. Flett,

I do appreciate your writing about the availability of your husband's fine *Cypripedium* collection which I have seen and admired, but I am afraid the collection is not complete enough for us to consider for purchase, nor is it at a standard of preservation we can accept for our museum, particularly the older specimens, *montanum*, for instance, also *calceolus*.

With best wishes and sincere condolences,
Leonard Lemay, Chairman of Botany

Ottawa, August 17, 1955
Dear Mrs. Green Thumb,

I've done like you said in last week's paper, cultivating around my hybrid teas and hybrid perpetuals, and also I've followed your advice with the bonemeal. So far so good. Now I'm wondering how you feel about staking perennial asters this early in the year.

Yours truly,
S. J. Provost

Ottawa, August 18, 1955
Dear Mrs. F.,

Many thanks for sending in another wonderful column – and professionally typed too! You do have a way with a phrase: "The succulence and snap of an apple leaf." Very nice indeed.

Hope you're surviving our heat wave.

Best,
Jay

Perth, Ontario, September 12, 1955
Dear Mrs. Green Thumb,

Here's a useful tip for your readers. If you cut back your golden glow you'll get a second bloom. Actually I try to get around to this in August. Thanks for the instructions about Madonna lilies. I've committed mine to the earth, blessed them solemnly with a sprinkle of fertilizer, and am hoping for the best.

Cheers,
Mrs. Donald Fourtier

Smith College, Northampton, Mass., September 15, 1955
Dear All,

Whew, well, I got through registration at last, and now I feel I can get through anything. Got admitted to the Russian Lit program after all. The prof – everyone calls him Zeus – said he couldn't believe I'd managed to get to this level with just two years of high-school Russian.

Yes, it's true, everyone here wears Bermuda shorts all the time, classes and everywhere. I could use a couple more pairs if Beverly's looking around for something to sew. (Hi, Beverly, hope you're feeling okay.) I was thinking a nice brown tweed (sort of tobacco shade) would go great with that lambswool sweater of mine, and maybe something in a subdued blue and white check, not too large checks though.

I suppose "Mrs. Green Thumb" is getting more famous every day. Which is really neat. Really, I mean it. I honestly didn't mean what I said about replacing Dad and forgetting his memory and all that. I was just in a lousy mood all summer hanging around the house and the heat and worrying about going away and stuff. I really honestly think this column thing could be sort of fulfilling, if you know what I mean, since you've never really done anything before, not counting the usual Betty Crocker stuff. Maybe you've truly got some latent ability, in the writing line I mean.

Gotta run before the library closes. I really truly feel I'm reaching the real Chekhov now. In his own language, I mean, cuz all of a sudden he's got TEXTURE and DEPTH that doesn't begin to show up in those stupid little translations people put up with.

Love,

Alice

Ottawa, October 5, 1955

Dear Mrs. Green Thumb,

Boy, did I get a kick out of last week's column on garden pests, including "small neighborhood boys that attack the apple trees." Thanks, too, for all the helpful hints of what to do with crabapples. I liked your last suggestion best – just throw 'em away. Great idea.

Betty Singer (A Real Fan)

Bloomington, Indiana, October 6, 1955

Dear Mrs. Flett,

We hope it won't be too much longer before your late father's affairs are satisfactorily settled, but, as you know, his investment portfolio was more complicated than most. I have tried for several days to reach his widow by telephone, but have received no answer. Her instructions have been followed regarding the division of the property, with full protection afforded your father's pyramid as a "permanent

memorial" to his life. We are anxious to procure her
signature on a number of documents relating to the will. Do
you happen to know if she is traveling at the moment, and, if
so, when she will return to the Bloomington area?

Yours truly,

Calvin K. Kopps

(Bregnam & Kopps)

Bloomington, Indiana, November 1, 1955
Dear Daze,

A quick note. No luck tracking down Maria. Georgio (my
latest) and I drove out to Lake Lemon on Sunday and found
the place locked up tight as a drum. The neighbors say they
haven't seen her around for a good month or so. Where do
we go from here? Let me know.

I'm all set for Chicago, and I've reserved our room, very
posh too, why the hell not? – have you got your train tickets
yet?

Love,

Fraidy

Ottawa, November 4, 1955
Dear Mrs. F.,

Your proposed piece on the Chicago Horticultural
Conservatory sounds *perfect* for January, also the Morton
Arboretum. I haven't visited that renowned city myself, but I
understand it is extremely beautiful, despite its reputation for
gangsters and graft. I would like you to know that if you
should ever find you can't manage a column (due to illness
or other interruption) we can always get Pinky Fulham on

the staff here to fill in for you. Although he usually covers civic events, he is a keen gardener and, incidentally, a *great* admirer of your columns.

Yours,

J.

Northampton, Mass., November 8, 1955
Dear Mother,

Let me say right off that you've completely lost your marbles about this baby business. I thought the whole idea was that Beverly was going to have it adopted and then start a new life. Here's Warren nearly 16 and Joan 14, the last thing you need is a screaming infant around the house. In no time at all they'll be in college and you'll be free to go tripping around with your old "gal" friends, which is what you've always wanted. Frankly, I think Beverly is taking advantage of your good nature. I know she helps out, especially with you going off to Chicago, and she does do your typing and all, but just think what she's getting in return. Free room and board and a pretty easy ride. And I don't see why the baby has to be in my room. What happens when I come home at Christmas? Where exactly am I supposed to sleep, if that's not too impertinent a question? As for the name Victoria, since you asked my opinion, I think it's pretentious. There's a Victoria in my dorm and she's a real snot.

Can you please send my red cardigan *soon*.

Love,

Alice

Ottawa, December 14

Dear Mrs. Green Thumb,

That was just a wonderful piece on Christmas plants, and I laughed till I cried about your struggle with your leggy poinsettia. Here's some advice you might want to pass on to your readers: keep the darn things away from gas, drafts, and radiators and they'll thrive all winter. In fact you'll get sick of having them around. Ha. Also, give the soil a stir with a kitchen fork now and again.

Happy holidays, and thanks for your weekly words of wisdom,

Hollis Sanderson

Bloomington, Indiana, December 29, 1955

Daze–

A quick note to say you'll be getting a letter from Beans who's decided she wants to come with us to Chicago. You have to believe me when I say I couldn't think of any way to say no. She had me on the spot, but you'll be hearing the whole story – I think I'd better leave it for her to tell.

Also want to assure you we got the key to the Lake Lemon house from the lawyer and checked it over thoroughly. There's absolutely no indication of what might have happened to Maria, no notes, etc., though it looks like some of her clothes could be missing. (Empty hangers in the closet and so forth.) You already know about the money she withdrew – a cool twenty thousand, though she could have taken a helluva lot more, according to the lawyer. By the way, your dad's old backyard pyramid looked kind of sweet under a layer of fresh snow. Georgio thought there might be squirrels nesting inside. How d'ya like that? – little squirrelly pharaohs.

The Christmas present was a hoot. I must be the only person in the state of Indiana, maybe in the whole Western Hemisphere, to have a reading lamp made out of a giraffe's foot – where in God's holy name did you find him (her?)? I think you're back to being the Daze of old – though I hope you know what you're doing, taking on a baby. Yikes.

See ya soon,
Fraidy

Bloomington, Indiana, January 10, 1956

Fraidy's no doubt told you what happened, Dick's little "lady friend" in Cleveland, anyway I won't go into detail on a postcard. Just gotta get away for a couple of weeks – from all these gee-dee memories. I've taken the house off the market – that's one decision anyway. See you next Tues at Palmer House.

Love,
Beans

Ottawa, February 2, 1956
Dear Mrs. Green Thumb,

Just wanted to let you know your column on Chicago gardens pushed my husband's magic button. His nibs hates traveling like all get out, but after reading about the Morton Arboretum, he's decided we've just got to go see for ourselves, so we're driving down in April. Glad you're back. Pinky What's-his-name doesn't know "nuttin" about Harrison's Yellow versus Persian Yellow.

Yours sincerely,
A Faithful Reader

Northampton, Mass., April 6, 1956
Dear All,

Sorry I haven't written lately but I've been going through a lousy time with Russian lit, also with the professor (a drip) and my roommate, Shirley, who's depressed about her boyfriend, another drip. Also it's been raining a lot. I'm thinking about changing my major, maybe Spanish. Or sociology. Or education. Everything I think of seems irrelevant.

> Love,
>> Alice

Northampton, Mass., April 20, 1956
Dear Mother,

Just to let you know I'm feeling a whole lot better and I really did appreciate you coming, especially when I know you've never flown in an airplane before and are scared to death of crashing. I think you're right, that I was feeling down because of Dad, the thing about it being just one year after he died, one year exactly. I had a long talk about it with my Russian prof who said he really truly understood how I feel and that these one-year anniversary things can hit you hard emotionally and it was okay if my term paper was late.

I've decided to stay with my Russian major. We're into Gogol. What a soul that man has, Russia's great soul incarnate.

Give my love to Warren and Joan and Bev and especially Victoria and tell them I'll be writing soon.

>> Alice

P.S. Forgot to comment on your new hairstyle which is just

the mostest. Makes your neck look thinner too. Have you
ever thought of tinting over the gray?

Ottawa, September 3, 1956

Dear Mrs. F.,

We wondered if you would care to join the *Recorder*
staffers for our annual dinner at the Press Club, September
20th at seven o'clock. Pinky Fulham always plans a superb
menu and a wonderful evening of songs and skits. Perhaps, if
you would like to join us, I could call for you and drive you
there. Do please let me know.

J.

Ottawa, November 14, 1956

Dear Mrs. Green Thumb,

At last, someone's solved my black leg problem. Any
advice on thrips?

A Faithful Reader

Northampton, Mass., November 20, 1956

Hi all. Up to my eyebrows in mid-terms. Just wanted to
say happy first birthday to Victoria. Can't wait to see her
again.

Alice

Bloomington, Indiana, December 20, 1956

Hope this reaches you by Christmas. Happy holiday cheer
to all. Beans and I are thinking of New Orleans for

February. How 'bout it? It's all over with Georgio. I got tired of holding in my stomach all the time and pretending I was his girly-girl.

Peace, joy, etc.
Fraidy

Ottawa, January 15, 1957
Dear D.,

The *Recorder* staff loved your piece on how to graft cacti – the perfect topic for winter gardeners. Pinky Fulham's done a few drawings (which I've enclosed for your approval) since he thought it might help readers follow the more difficult steps. He's a cactus man from way back, he tells me. Also very good on trees.

Affectionately,
J.

Ottawa, February 7, 1957
Dear Mrs. Flett,

Thanks for your kind words about the cactus illustrations. I think, not to pat myself on the back too much, that our readers really went for them, it kind of jazzes up the page. And as for covering the column while you're in New Orleans, it would be a pleasure. I'm always glad to pitch in. A person can get pretty sick of writing about local elections and school board hassles.

Sincerely,
Pinky Fulham

Ottawa, June 30, 1957
Dear Mrs. Green Thumb,

Loved "Getting Tough With Phlox." I've clipped it out for my files, and bought an extra copy for my sister-in-law in Calgary who'll get a real kick out of it.

> Sincerely,
>> Rose Henning, a timid-but-determined-gardener-in-training

Hanover, College, September 19, 1957

It's so noisy in the dorm I can't think, but wanted to let you know I'm settled in and surviving. Great weather down here. Great news about Beverly doing the commerce course, she'll do great.

> Love to all, especially Vicky.
> Warren

P.S. You said postcards were okay.

Ottawawawa, December 2, 1958

> *O dear mrs green, my dear mrs thumb*
> *how i love you love you for*
> *your goodness your greenness your thumb-readiness*
> *your watering can your fertilizer pellets and o how i love*
> *rustling these limp pages and finding you there*
> *always there between stamps and bridge*
> *between recipes and religion there forever there*
> *with your greenness your kindness and o last week*
> *with your dampened cloth*
> *wiping clean the green green leaves*

shining and polishing o so gently and opening
the green pores to the air it was like washing
the hands of a little child you said
dear mrs greenthumb o if i could only be
your child
scrubbed clean and pure to light and goodness
i too would be happy i too would need nothing and o
how i love you need you sweet keen clean mrs green
  thumb

Anon

Bloomington, Indiana, January 15, 1958

Daze – you're going to kill me, but I can't make Florida in Feb. Guess why – I'm getting married. Yep, married! Hope you're still standing up and breathing. Beans says I've misplaced my brains, but I think you'll like Mel. He's a lab instructor, divorced, nice hair, sings baritone in a barber shop quartet, that says it all. So instead of soaking up the sun in Florida, why don't you get yourself down here to Indiana for the wedding. It's gonna be a five-minute quickie in court, no fancy dress, but the biggest party you ever saw afterwards. Buckets of champagne. Oceans.

Love,

Fraidy

Bloomington, Indiana, January 17, 1958

Just a scribble. You've just gotta come for THE WEDDING, and then we two old maids (toi et moi) can head down south for a week in Florida. (Fraidy says you've got over your fear of airplanes.) I need some gee-dee sunshine.

Hope Mel works out for Fraidy, he's sweet but has already had TWO divorces!!!

Beans

Ottawa, March 4, 1958

Dear D.,

Wonderful piece on palms, "The Mystery Tree," and we've had a *great* response to Pinky's drawings too.

Wondered if you would care to see a performance of *Tea and Sympathy*. I've been given two tickets for March 15th.

J.

Ottawa, June 2, 1958

Dear Mrs. Green Thumb,

Your tribute to geraniums touched the middle of my heart. These sturdy, stout-hearted darlings have kept me company for the fifty years of my married life, sitting on the window sill and cheering me on while I peeled the supper spuds. My hubby was one of those who could not conceive of supper without potatoes on the plate. Well, now I'm in what they call a retirement home, Sunset Manor if you can believe it, so no more paring knife duty, but I still have my window sill full of bright little beauties. Like you, I like to rub the dead flowers between my fingers and smell the fragrance, only I never told anyone I did such a thing, it sounded so crazy.

Sincerely,
Mrs. Alice W. Keefer

Ottawa, April 27, 1959

Dear Dee,

Thank you so much for inviting me to Easter dinner. What a handsome family you're blessed with: Alice with that cloud of red hair, shy Warren, sweet Joan, and your niece Beverly and little Victoria. I had almost forgotten the pleasure of sitting down with a real family for a holiday meal – and a *splendid* meal it was! And please don't think I was embarrassed about Alice demanding to "look me over."

Yours,

J.

P.S. Hope next Tuesday is still all right.

Bloomington, Indiana, November 14, 1959

Daze–

Your lawyer phoned the other day about the Lake Lemon property. He's got a buyer interested at last, but only if they bulldoze the pyramid and re-fill the area. Can you let me know how you feel about this. Should we go ahead? Apparently they don't need Maria's signature for the sale. If she ever surfaces, they can work out some sort of compensation.

Love,

Fraidy (Mel says hello)

Bloomington, Indiana, December 13, 1959

Daze,

Merry Christmas from Mel and me. I passed on your comments to the real estate people, and, no, I don't think you're crazy. Why rush into a sale if you don't need the money, though I probably should warn you that the pyramid seems to have attracted vandals, either that or frost damage. All best wishes in the next decade. Who ever thought I'd become "the little married woman" and you'd be the "career gal." Anyway, it suits you. Beans and I are in agreement on that, if nothing else – you've found your metier!

Love ya,

Fraidy

Ottawa, April 3, 1960
Dear Mrs. Green Thumb,

Wow, you really told it like it is in "Plant Food – Yes or No." My wife and I've been bickering over this particular issue for years. So, in gratitude I'm sending you my recipe (attached) for getting the algae off your lily pond (if you have one), and keeping it off! Tell your readers they can buy copper sulphate at any nursery or hardware store.

So long and thanks,

Roman Matrewski

Ottawa, August 12, 1960
Dear Mrs. Green Thumb,

Really enjoyed your dramatic struggle with the ant colony. Also your words of enlightenment on the European leaf beetle. You've got a real gift for making a story out of things.

Gratefully yours,

Fed-Up-With-Weeds-And-
Bugs-in-South-Ottawa

Bloomington, Indiana, November 4, 1960

Hi, Just got Alice's wedding invitation. I'll be there with bells on. I'm taking you at your word about bringing "a guest." We're going to fly instead of taking the train. He's loaded.

Beans

Ottawa, December 15, 1960

Dear Dee,

Just talked to Pinky who said he'd be glad to take over the column until your daughter's wedding is over. I understand these affairs can take a lot of organizing. Pinky's got some interesting material on ferns which seem to be making a comeback. Let me know if there's any way I can help out.

Yours,

J.

Ottawa, January 22, 1961

My dear Dee,

Forgive me, but I must put this in writing. Thank you, thank you, thank you.

J.

Hampstead, England, April 20, 1961

Dear Mother,

We're so happy in this little house. I never dreamed I could be this happy. Even the address sounds like a poem: 1, Brewery Lane. How about that! I think I've been a little crazy all my life and now suddenly I'm not any more. I'm going to stay here forever and have babies and write about Chekhov and keep snug and sane. Thanks for wonderful snaps of Victoria. It makes my heart swell, just thinking of her. Glad to hear you and Beans and Fraidy have decided on Bermuda this year. Ben sends his love along with mine.

Alice

Bloomington, Indiana, May 25, 1962

Daze,

So glad we could make it for the christening. Alice looked gorgeous – my, she's mellowed – and Ben Junior is beautiful. (I suppose they're already back in Hampstead.) And it was nice meeting Jay at last. Yes, you were right, he does have a nice rich, worldly laugh. Also there's something endearing about a man who knows all the words to "Ivan Skavinsky Skavar." I couldn't help being pleased he and Mel had so much in common. Isn't it bizarre, all of us having beaux at our age, though I guess Mel doesn't quite qualify as a beau now that he's a husband. By the way, Beans and Brick are talking wedding bells. Wish I could warm to him, but can't somehow. What do you think? It isn't just his name and those godawful neckties is it? Maybe it's the way he sneers at the Kennedys. Maybe it's that Sigma Chi ring. Maybe it's everything.

Love,

Fraidy

Ottawa, June 6, 1963
Dear Mrs. Green Thumb

I agree absolutely that peonies are beautiful but stupid.
The dumbest thing about them is the way they resent being
moved – which is why my husband and I welcomed your
suggestions last week. Many thanks. You're the greatest.

Audrey LaRoche (Mrs.)

Ottawa, August 15, 1963
Dear Mrs. Green Thumb,

Your piece on hollyhocks was terrif. I liked the part about
their "frilled dirndl skirts," and their "shy fuzzy stems." I
haven't had hollyhocks in the yard for years, but after
reading your column I ran straight out and bought a bunch
of seeds, even though it's too late for this year.

Thanks a bunch,
Lydia Nygaard

Ottawa, November 25, 1963
Dearest Dee,

Couldn't reach you by phone, hence this quick note. Most
of the Sports and Home section will be cancelled next week
because of the Kennedy coverage – so we'll be using your
rock garden piece the following week. What a world this is,
everything falling to pieces.

Yours,
J.

Ottawa, January 25, 1964

Dear Dee,

I'm so sorry about this misunderstanding. I realize now, of course, that telling you on the phone was a mistake. I knew you'd be disappointed, but I had *no* idea you would take it this hard. You've been talking about wanting more time to yourself, more time to travel, maybe a trip to England to see your daughter. Hope we can get together as usual on Tuesday and talk this over like two *sensible* people.

Yours,

J.

Ottawa, February 6, 1964

Dear Mrs. Flett,

I've read your letter carefully and I can assure you I understand your feelings. But I believe Jay explained the paper's policy to you, that full-time staffers have first choice of columns. As you well know, I've been filling in with the gardening column from time to time, all those times you've been away, and, to tell you the honest truth, I've had quite a lot of appreciative letters from readers who especially like the fact that my columns are illustrated and take the male point of view. Personally, I like the feel that a regional newspaper is a living, breathing organism that resists falling into rigid patterns. Think of it this way: our readers are always changing, and so must we. After nine years of being Mrs. Green Thumb, I feel sure you too will welcome a change.

With best wishes,

James (Pinky) Fulham

February 20, 1964
Dear Dee,

I am so *terribly* sorry about all this, and I do agree the policy of the paper is ridiculous, but it's a policy that has been in force since the time of my predecessor. None of this has anything to do with your competence as a contributor, you know better than that. The issue is that Pinky, as a full-timer, has a prior claim to any regular column as long as he can demonstrate capability in the area. I can't tell you how *much* I regret all this, but I'm afraid my hands are tied.

Please let's get together soon and talk of other things. You are, if I may say, taking this *far* too personally.

Your

J.

February 28, 1964
Dear Mrs. Flett,

Thank you for your letter. I am afraid, though, I am not at this time willing to change my mind. Frankly, I've been covering city politics for some ten years and am in need of a change. Even my personal physician has advised a change. I should think you would be eager for a change too after so many years. Change is what keeps us young.

Yours sincerely,

Pinky Fulham

P.S. As I said to you earlier, I hope this disagreement won't interfere with our friendship.

Bloomington, Indiana, March 28, 1964
Daze,

Beans and I are just wondering if you've broken your
wrist. Neither of us has heard from you in ages – how about
a line or two?

Fraidy

Hampstead, England, April 10, 1964

It's weeks since you've written. Hope all is well. Spring
has come to England, glorious, and Judy's already up to
twelve pounds. Is everything okay? I'm a little worried. There
hasn't been a letter from you for weeks. Is anything wrong?

Love,

Alice, Ben, and Benje and
wee Jude

CHAPTER SEVEN

Sorrow, 1965

1965 WAS THE YEAR Mrs. Flett fell into a profound depression.

It happened overnight, more or less. Her family and friends stood by helplessly and watched while her usual self-composed nature collapsed into bewilderment, then withdrawal, and then a splattery anger that seemed to feed on injury. She was unattractive during this period. Despair did not suit her looks. Goodness cannot cope with badness – it's too good, you see, too stupidly good. A person unable to sleep for more than an hour or two at a time and whose eating patterns are disordered – this type of person soon dwindles into bodily dejection – you've seen such people, and so has Mrs. Flett, shambling along the edges of public parks or seated under hairdryers. Their facial skin drags downward. Their clothes hang on them unevenly and look always in need of a good sprucing up. You want to rush up to these lost souls and offer comfort, but there's an off-putting aura of failure about them, almost a smell.

The spring and summer of 1965 – those were terrible months for Mrs. Flett, as she slid day by day along a trajectory that began in resignation, then hardened into silence, then leapt to a bitter and blaming estrangement from those around her, her children and grandchildren, her many good friends and acquaintances.

What was it that changed Mrs. Flett so utterly?

The phenomenon of menopause will probably leap to mind, but no. Daisy Flett is fifty-nine years old in 1965, almost sixty, and her hormonal structure, never particularly volatile – according to some – has been steady as a clock – according to others – since her forty-ninth birthday. Nor does she appear to be suffering from "delayed mourning," as some of her family would have it. She remembers her dear sweet Barker fondly, of course she does, she honors his memory, whatever that means; and she thinks of him, smilingly, every single time she rubs a dab of Jergens Lotion into the palms of her hands, floating herself back to the moment – a very private moment, she will not discuss it with anyone, though she records it here – in which he had extolled her smooth-jointed fingers, comparing them to wonderful flexible silken fish.

Fish? A startling idea; it took her by surprise; at the time she hadn't completely warmed to the likeness, yet she apprehended, at least, her husband's courageous lurching toward poetry. But does she actually pine for this dead partner of hers? For the calmness offered up by the simple weariness of their love? How much of her available time bends backward into the knot of their joined lives, those twenty connubial years?

To be honest, very little. There, I've said it.

Her present sinking of spirit, the manic misrule of her heart and head, the foundering of her reason, the decline of her physical health – all these stem from some mysterious suffering core which those around her can only register and weigh and speculate about.

Alice's Theory

Something happened to me. At age nineteen I was on the verge of becoming a certain kind of person, and then I changed, and went in another direction.

The self is not a thing carved on entablature. Not long ago I read – probably in the Sunday papers – about an American woman who got up one morning and started practicing a new kind of handwriting, sloping all her letters backwards instead of forwards, concentrating on smaller and denser loops. It was almost like drawing. She wrote her name a dozen times in this variant way. She wrote out the preamble to the Constitution and then the Gettysburg Address, and by noon she had become someone else.

The change that happened to me went deeper than penmanship and far, far beyond such superficialities as a new hairstyle or dietary regime – although I did at age nineteen decide to let my hair grow long, which was not a popular style in the mid-fifties, and I did give up meat and white sugar and the smoking of cigarettes.

It was summertime. I had just returned after my first year away at college. It was the first morning back, in fact, and I woke up early in our family's large, quiet, shabby Ottawa house and looked straight up at the ceiling where there was a long circular crack shaped like the hunch in an old crone's back, high and rounded at the top, then tapering down. That selfsame crack had been there ever since I could remember, since earliest childhood. It was the first thing I saw in the morning and the last thing at night, this menacing inscription in plaster that roofed me over with dread. Not that I feared the witchlike configuration, good Christ no – I knew perfectly well that such anthropomorphizing is fanciful and solipsistic; I also knew that other people, happier people, might see a river instead of a diseased spine, or a map of a buried subcontinent or, with a little imagination, a mountain topped by a Chinese pagoda, in turn topped by a knob of whipped cream. We see what we want to see. Our perceptions fly straight out of our deepest needs, this much you learn in Introductory Psych, a required course at my college. No, what I dreaded about the ceiling crack was its persistence. That it was always there. Determined to accompany me. To be a part of me.

I dragged the stepladder up from the basement, hoping it would reach. (The ceilings in that old house of ours were ridiculously high.) On a shelf in the garden shed I found a box of plasterer's putty and mixed myself up a large sticky batch which I spread the length of the ceiling crack, using a spatula from the kitchen drawer, and moving the ladder forward foot by foot. I'd never done this kind of work before, but I read the directions on the box carefully and made a neat job of it. I've always been exceptionally neat. "Very neat presentation" was what my professors wrote on the bottoms of my term papers, also "well focused" and "full of verve."

In half an hour the plaster was dry, and I sanded it smooth, letting the fine grains drift down on top of my head and into my face, breathing in the chalky dust, tasting it on my tongue. I did not find the sensation disagreeable, quite the contrary. By four o'clock that afternoon I had painted the entire ceiling, using a roller attached to an extension handle, and just before going to bed that night I gave the whole thing a second coat.

Then I lay down in the dark, possibly a little drunk from the heavy latex fumes that swirled downward and converged in mid-air with a mad proleptic wafting up of happiness. Sleep came quickly; I welcomed it; I was eager for morning; I wanted to wake up to the early light and observe, freshly, the transformation I had brought about.

This really happened. This event, this revelation! Not one of the various members of my family raised the least objection to my determination to repair and paint my bedroom ceiling. No one even challenged me as to why I needed the ladder, why I was scrounging around in the shed for a paint roller, whether this act of mine was a momentary whim or a charged metaphoric gesture. This surprised me, the general air of permission. My mother, of course, was preoccupied with the weekly gardening column she was writing for the local newspaper (Mrs. Green Thumb was the byline she used). My younger brother and sister looked on with interest, perhaps even a tincture of envy – why hadn't they thought of improving their ceilings! – and Cousin Beverly, who had moved in with us a year earlier, gave me a hand spreading newspapers on the carpet and some useful advice about how to reach into the difficult corner angles. As for my father, had he still been alive, he might have discouraged me from assigning myself a dull and messy task, particularly on my first day home, though I can't help thinking he would have understood the impulse driving me forward.

In one day I had altered my life: my life, therefore, was alterable. This simple axiom did not cry out for exegesis; no, it entered my bloodstream directly, as powerful as heroin; I could feel its pump and surge, the way it brightened my veins to a kind of glass. I had wakened that morning to narrowness and predestination, and now I was falling asleep in the storm of my own will. My eyes would open in the morning to a smooth white field of possibility. The ceiling that had taunted me was shrunk now to a memory of a memory. It wasn't just that I had covered it over. I had erased it. It was as though it had never existed.

I next made up my mind to grow kind. I was not a kind person, but I believed I could learn.

First I burned my old diaries in the fireplace and also the letters I had written home during my year away at college, letters full of gush and artifice. My mother caught me at this, and expressed concern. You may regret it, she said, you may want to look back and see what you were like at ten or twelve or sixteen years of age.

But I knew I wouldn't need the diaries or letters to prod my remembrance. I had grown up a mean, bossy little kid. I was selfish. I liked to hurt people's feelings. I addressed my sister, Joan, as Miss Sneakypants and my brother, Warren, as Pimplenose. I ordered Cousin Beverly around as though she were an indentured servant and complained about the way her little girl cried in her early months; it was only colic, but I managed to suggest she was being mishandled or maybe there was brain damage or something. I was forever clipping out dieting articles for my mother and reading them aloud to her in a cool disingenuous voice, and invariably I referred to the newspaper she wrote for as "that parochial rag." I remember the way I was. People like to think of memory as a low-lying estuary, but my memories of myself are more like a ruffed-up lake, battering against the person I became. A nice person. A thoughtful person.

I paid attention; I listened hard to the motor clicking on and off in my head; it was like doing beads, it was very intricate work. I entered the summer of 1955 a girl and came out a woman. Women, I learned, needed to be bloody, but they didn't need to be mean.

The reverberations in my family were surprisingly minor, like the offhand ringing of distant chimes – as though all these years I'd been given the benefit of the doubt: Alice's gained in maturity, they said. Alice's a real young lady now. Alice's come into her own. Alice's calmed down. Alice's got rid of that chip on her shoulder, come down off her high horse, lost her rough edges. But then Alice always was a lump of butter underneath, wasn't she? Why, she's turned out to be a regular darling. Oh, you can count on Alice, you always could.

Well!

Here is a diagram of our family structure before and after my father's death.

Before he departed (brain tumor, malignant) we were such a sweet little family: two loving parents and three healthy children. Our father was Director of the Agricultural Institute where his work on hybrid grains was universally recognized (honorary degrees from Guelph *and* the University of Iowa), and after his retirement, never one to be idle, he wrote a weekly horticultural column for the Ottawa *Recorder*. My mother was a full twenty-three years younger than my father; that age-gap became her hobby and profession, being a young wife to an older husband – it kept her girlish, made her a kind of tenant in the tower of girlhood. There she remained, safe, looked after. She stayed home and looked after her children and sewed and cleaned the house – even though she could have afforded help – and did the garden. That garden of hers, it functioned like a kind of trope in her daily life, and in ours too. She made suppers – roasted meat, boiled vegetables, pies and puddings or molded Jello things for dessert. These meals were planned, they didn't just happen. Our family sat down at a table that was set. My mother was always concocting new center-pieces, she was part of that mid-century squadron of women who believed in centerpieces. We children had agreeable table manners. We kept our voices low. Always, after the dishes, Joanie and Warren and I got down to our homework without reminding. We took piano lessons on Wednesday evening from a woman named Myrna Rassmussen, the Royal Raspberry we called her behind her back – and the mildness of this epithet says a lot about who we were and what we were capable of. On Saturdays we went for family walks – no one else we knew went for family walks – and were taught by our parents, but unobtrusively, how to identify the various shrubs, trees, plants, and flowers that grew in our neighborhood or in the woods of the Experimental Farm.

After my father died – and even during the months following his diagnosis – things changed fast. Supper was late, or else early. Sometimes it was served in the kitchen instead of the dining room, and we had things like corned beef hash out of a can or toasted cheese sandwiches. My mother never seemed to take her apron off, we had to remind her or she would have dashed out of the house like that. She got way behind on the vacuuming. Everything. Even her beloved African violets dried up, even her ferns. Part of this household neglect can be explained by grief or disorientation, that would be only natural, but something else occurred to create all this change. A mere two months after my father's funeral, our mother took over the horticultural column at the *Recorder*, becoming Mrs. Green Thumb. She was, suddenly, a different person, a person who worked. Who worked "outside the home," as people said in those quaint days, though, in fact, she did her writing under our own roof, and mailed her column into the paper, walking down to the corner of Torrington Crescent on Wednesday afternoon to pop it into the mail box in time for the Saturday paper. Whether the editor of the *Recorder* invited her to take on the column of whether she volunteered I have never known, but all of a sudden there she was, sitting at a desk in a corner of the living room, our father's old desk, laboring over her articles, scratching away with her ballpoint pen, looking up occasionally and rubbing her forehead like someone scouring her senses for an answer that would please her readers' sensibility but remain faithful to botanical truth. Sometimes she would rise, drift over to the window for a moment, then return to the desk, settling her widening hips comfortably in her chair, ready to begin again. It appeared she had a knack for this kind of writing. It surprised everyone. It was as though she had veered, accidentally, into her own life.

Then Cousin Beverly from Saskatchewan arrived on the train, six months pregnant, big as a barn, and moved into the storeroom on the third floor. The plan was that

Beverly was going to put the baby up for adoption, but this never happened. The subject was not raised. Victoria was born, a beautiful full-term baby, and she just stayed on with the family. She slept in a basket in my room at first, but then Beverly turned the downstairs sunroom into a nursery, papering over the old ivy pattern with lambs and milkmaids.

All this happened fast. In 1954 we were a nice ordinary family, Mr. and Mrs. Barker Flett and their three tractable children. Then – it seemed like a lightning flash had hit our house – there was just one parent (distracted, preoccupied) and an unwed mother and a baby with colic and three teenagers: devious Joan, sullen Warren, and mean-hearted Alice.

You'd have thought my mother would be wildly unsettled by all this, but you would be wrong. She let the chaos that hit our household in 1955 roll right over her like a big friendly engulfing wave. She came bobbing to the surface, her round face turned upward to the sunlight, happy.

Not that we didn't grieve for my father.

He was a tall, hunched, good-looking man who, right into his seventies, kept his thick head of hair. This hair he combed straight back from his forehead in an oddly continental manner. His brow was smoothly polished, white, stony, and clean. He had a breadth of neck that took well to a collar and tie, but his long arms and legs and his rather lumbering rectitude reminded you that he had once been a country boy, raised in rural Manitoba, born in another century. Despite his gentleness, his patience, I had found him an embarrassing father, too polite, too given to clearing his throat, too uncomfortable in his body, too old, much too old, but when he died I missed him.

My mother missed him too. In the days immediately following his funeral she went slack and heavy as though she were gasping for air through an impermeable membrane, her history, her marriage, everything gone down the chute. But then, presto, she became Mrs. Green Thumb. Her old self slipped off her like an oversized jacket.

For years now she has sat down at her desk every morning, still wearing her robe and slippers, writing out her column in longhand, a first draft, then a second, then a third, and then checking over Cousin Beverly's typed copy. Her rusty-gray frizz fluffs out over her forehead and ears – sometimes she brushes her hair before settling down to work and sometimes she doesn't. She gets lost in what she's doing and doesn't even hear the phone ringing; none of us ever guessed she had this power of absorption. She'll do, say, the propagation of lobelia one week and how to air-layer your rubber plant the next. When she isn't actually writing, she's answering mail from her readers – she averages at least twenty letters a week – or else she's thinking up ideas or filing away gardening information in my father's old filing cabinet. She's done this for nine whole years, but now, suddenly, it's over.

She's lost her job. A man named Pinky Fulham has taken over the column, and my mother, fifty-nine years old, has been given the heave-ho. She got her walking papers. She's been fired – and thrown into a despair deeper and sharper and wider than she ever suffered over her husband's death or her children's misbehavior.

A year ago she was sitting at that desk with her hair buzzing around her head like something alive and her pen scrambling across the paper. She was Mrs. Green Thumb, that well-known local personage, and now she's back to being Mrs. Flett again. She knew, for a brief while, what it was like to do a job of work. The shaping satisfaction. The feel of a typescript folded into an envelope. And then the paycheck arriving in the mail. Now she's like some great department store of sadness with its displays of rejection and inattention and wide silent reflecting windows, out of business, the padlock on the door.

I live thousands of miles away in England – Hampstead to be precise – but I've left my darling husband Ben for three whole weeks, also our two little sprogs, Benje and Judy, and I've come all the way home to see how matters stand. I find my mother seated in the garden, gripping the arms of a wicker chair, her chin oddly dented and old, her mouth round, helpless, saying, "I can't get used to this. I can't get over this."

Fraidy Hoyt's Theory

You don't expect Alice Flett Downing to believe in her mother's real existence, do you?

It's true she loves her mother, and true she's a good daughter – didn't she come all this way across the drink to try to jolly her out of her current state of the blues? The trouble is, Alice doesn't know where to begin. In a curious, ironic way, she hasn't known her mother long enough, hasn't known her the way I've known her, since childhood in Bloomington, Indiana, when we were two eleven-year-old brats in pigtails – well, in point of fact, I was the one in pigtails and Daze had the naturally curly hair. Which she hated – Lord! – an ambulatory fuzzball, she called herself. Later, when the poodle-cut came into fashion, she was grateful, but by that time, the late forties, she was living up in Canada, married to a man named Barker Flett and the mother of three children, the oldest being Alice.

Alice can't help herself, she's got this fixation on work. She's not like young girls were in our era, wavering between convention and fits of rebellion; she has serious interests of her own about which she is sometimes a little sententious. She's twenty-eight years old, you'd think she'd be out there with the flower children, wouldn't you, mooning about peace and love, and lolling around in public places, strumming a guitar and smoking grass and letting her life go sweetly to hell. But no, she's got herself properly married to a teeny-weenie professor of economics, she lives in a little fairytale English house, she's produced two perfect babes, and she's published a moderately successful book called *Chekhov's Imagination* and is working on another that explores Chekhov's feminine side – this new project she's outlined for me in a letter tucked into her Christmas card. That's another thing about Alice: she sends Christmas cards; she has a compulsion to hold her far-flung family and friends in a tight embrace, and her charity extends to her mother's old girlhood pals, chiefly myself and Labina Greene Dukes, who has recently moved down to Florida and who once described Alice to me as Her Holy Miss Righteousness.

Alice addresses me in her little notes and cards as "Aunt" Fraidy, and in that aunt-ish salutation I read proprietorial claims. Also benevolent respect. Also love. The last time I saw her was at little Judy's christening in Ottawa – that's one more odd bump on Alice's psyche: she's an agnostic who nevertheless christens her children; she actually brings them across the Atlantic Ocean to be anointed by pure and holy Canadian water in the presence of pure and impure family and friends. Ceremony, she says, is society's cement; ceremony paints large our sketchiest impulses; ceremony forms the seal between the cerebrum and cerebellum. Alice has a theory about every bush and button and human gesture, sometimes several theories.

After Judy's ecclesiastical sprinkling in that wonderful Ottawa garden, Alice and I stood with our glasses of bubbly and had a good jabber about *The Feminine Mystique*. I could tell she was surprised I'd read it. Like many young people she believes we elderly types have long since shut down our valves and given way to flat acquiescence about the future. Her eyes widened when I began taking issue with Betty Friedan's exaltation of work as salvation. "We are our work!" Alice cried. "Work and self cannot be separated."

Oh, dear. I opened my mouth to protest.

"Look at my mother," Alice interrupted, lowering her voice, but not quite low enough, and gesturing toward the blooming lilac where Daze was standing in a circle of friends, her body widened out now to a powerful size eighteen, little Judy nestled in the crook of her arm.

"Before my mother became a newspaper columnist she had no sense of self-worth whatsoever. Whatsoever! Really, when you think about it, she functioned like a kind of slave in our society. She was unpaid. Undervalued. She was nobody. Now look at her. She's become" – here Alice groped for words, waving her hand toward the nodding lilacs – "she's become, you know, like a real person."

Work is work, I wanted to tell Alice, and don't I know it. Work's not just sitting in the corners of shadowy libraries and producing beautiful little monographs every couple of years. It's the alarm clock going off on winter mornings when it's dark and cold and you've forgotten to iron the green blouse that goes with the gray suit and the car's not working right and you can't afford to get it fixed this month because it's been four years since the Official Board of the Monroe County Art Gallery thought of increasing your salary or even dropping you a word of praise, and on top of that there are whole mornings when no one comes into the gallery at all or if they do they stand around griping about the exhibitions and giggle and smirk at the abstracts, letting you know their kindergarten darlings could do just as well with a pot of fingerpaint, and furthermore (hem, hem) it's taxpayers who support this kind of thing when what people really like, only they're too damned intimidated to say so, is a nice landscape, fields and sky and a horizon line that looks like a horizon line for God's sake. And what else? Well, there are meetings with the board and the books to balance and the publicity that somehow always misfires and the fund drives that peter out and the misplaced grant applications and the catalogues coming back late from the printers, and the crazies who phone at all hours and beg you to take just one little peek at their portfolio, you owe it, you owe them, who the hell are you anyway but a glorified clerk.

And then – lately anyway, since Mel left – it's home to a glass of bourbon and a scrambled egg, or maybe stopping by at the library to see what new they've got in, and going to bed early because you've got a splitting headache and sometimes just before closing your eyes you think about your old pal Daze up there in Canada with her kids and her days to herself, how she bustles along at her own speed, spreading the gospel of *Good Housekeeping* far and wide and getting her rewards through the accomplishments of others who will certainly crown her with laurels and tell her how grateful they are, in retrospect, that she was a real mother, that she wasn't out working her tail off for the holy dollar like her old pal, Fraidy Hoyt of Bloomington, Indiana.

Well, once in a while a family has to surrender itself to an outsider's account. A family can get buried in its own fairy dust, and this leads straight, in my opinion, to the unpacking of lies and fictions from its piddly shared scraps of inbred history. With the Fletts, for instance, the work ethic has always been writ large. Barker and his hybrid grains. Alice and her Russians. Warren and his music. Joanie and her – whatever the hell it is she does down there in New Mexico – and so it's only natural that they should attribute Daze's breakdown to the loss of her newspaper column. I thought as much myself for the first month or so, but gradually I've come to believe that the forfeiting of her "job" was only a trigger that released a terrible yearning she's been suppressing all her life.

Sex is what I'm referring to, what else?

Not that Daze and I ever discuss sex. Well, not for a long time anyway, not since we were young girls trying to puzzle out the mysteries of the copulative act: how long did it last? How much did it hurt? Were you supposed to talk at the same time you were doing it, whisper little endearments and so on? What did a "climax" feel like and how could you be sure you had it or not, and why did it matter anyway, and was it cheating to pretend you did even if you didn't? That kind of thing.

Then suddenly it became *lèse-majesté* to discuss our sexual lives.

I think we both wanted to; each of us, when we got together, made a few clumsy gestures in that direction, but we never managed to find any common footing. There's too much space between us, too much dispro-portion, you might say. Our awful imbalance. Daze with her plodding Barker, that epicene presence – and per-haps, or perhaps not, a brief flutter with an editor at her paper, Jay Dudley his name was, who ended up a regular shit, handing her job over to someone else like a king anointing a new lord – well, that sums up Daze's erotic experience, about one and a half bean sprouts by my count. And on the other side of the fence, here I sit with my fifty-three lovers, possibly fifty-four. I've been on the side of noise, nerve, movement, and thanking my lucky stars too, and raising a toast to my army of fifty-four – that's how I see them, a small, smartly marching army with the sun shining on their beautiful heads and shoulders.

I've kept track. This is possibly a perverse admission, that I possess a little pocket diary in which I've made note of dates, initials, geographical reference points and coded particulars, going back to 1927, such as duration, position, repetition, degree of response, and the like.

My "phantom" fifty-fourth lover was encountered just weeks ago on a train to Ottawa, no names exchanged, only a pair of ragged weepy histories. We had both drunk too much bourbon in the club car, the hour was late, and we may or may not have made love before we passed out, the two of us drearily naked on the coarse blanket of my lower berth. I have an impression of a rosy, pleated male belly pushing against me. I have a recollection, like a black-and-white movie, that we were noisy, that we made a spectacle of ourselves. He was gone – thank God – when I opened my eyes in the morning. And my body, my sixty-year-old body (Christ!), was unwilling to report what had happened, other than a soreness "down there" that could have been anything, a dryness that puzzled. A question mark went into the diary instead of the usual data. In that question mark I read the possible end of my erotic life. Something to do with shame, though I won't yet admit it.

What do women want, Freud asked. The old fool, the charlatan. He knew what women wanted. They wanted nothing. Nothing was good enough. Everyone knew that. Everyone but me.

The reason I was on my way to Ottawa was to offer consolation to an old friend in distress. She had written to me telling me not to come, that she had her niece Beverly to look after her, that she was not fit company at the moment, but of course I went anyway. I thought, wrongly, that I could carry her back to sunnier times, dredging up old stories, foolish or sentimental or touching on some spring of affection between us. And I believed we might, after a few days, open up this forbidden topic of sex, letting our thoughts out loose and fresh.

There comes a time, I've seen it happen, when women offer to decode themselves. All of Alice's shrewd sympathy would be nothing compared to a moment's shared revelation between old pals. The self is curved like space, I tried to say to my girlhood friend, and human beings can come around again and again to the sharpness of early excitations. The sexual spasm, despite its hideous embarrassments and inconvenience, is the way we enter the realm of the ecstatic. The only way. It's a far darker and more powerful force than we dreamed back when we were girls chattering on about "climaxes" and saline douches. I wanted to tell her about Professor Popkov who was my first seducer, about Georgio with his endless *sportif* variations (The Royal Gonad, I called him), about poor Mel who lasted only four years before drifting off in his wispy way. I intended to hold nothing back, not even my pitiable little encounter on the train. I persuaded myself that an open confrontation would dislodge whatever it is that has shut off Daze's happiness and made her into a crazy woman.

But the week was a disaster. She would not be coaxed out of her dark bedroom; she lay flat on her back, her neck and shoulder muscles in painful contraction and her queenly pounds dropping away one after the other. "Don't make me pretend to be lively," she said to me once when I brought her a lunch tray. "It takes too much effort."

I went home to Bloomington and wrote her a note of

monstrous good cheer. About the future. The sun breaking through. The joy of future generations. On and on.

A week later an envelope came addressed in her writing. No note, only my little pocket diary with its cryptic entries. I must have dropped it on the carpet when I was closing my suitcase.

Cousin Beverly's Theory

Ten years ago back in Saskatchewan I got myself into hot water. It wasn't enough that I was a divorced woman, and, boy oh boy, that was a real crime back then, let me tell you, but worse was to come. Two short years after I kicked my husband Jerry out (a drinker from Day One), I got boinked by Leonard Mazurkiewich who worked in the pickling plant (married, natch) whose idea of lovemaking was – well, I get the willies just thinking about it – but anyway it wasn't worth it, three minutes of grunt and bad breath, and, bingo, there I was in the family way.

I would have gone to Calgary but I was too scared. Imagine, me scared, me who served with the WRENS during the war, way over there in Britain. Bombs and everything. I lived through that. I was full of courage when I was young. And then I came home to Saskatchewan at the end of the war and the puff just went out of me. There was Jerry, hounding me to get married. And my parents. And my sisters. Everyone. Somehow they tore me apart, it happened fast. The funny thing about being married to Jerry was not being able to get pregnant no matter what kind of stunts we got up to. Ha!

– and after one midnight roll with Leonard Mazurkiewich, just one, I was up a stump. Some girls will turn to
suicide when they get themselves in a fix like that, but I
never thought of it for one minute, the reason being
I could still shut my eyes when I wanted and remember
what I was like over there in Britain, how brave and full
of pep I could be – this picture would light up for me like
something on a calendar or in a movie, the way I was, and
I thought maybe I could get it back, only I couldn't, not if
I committed suicide, that's for sure.

Aunt Daisy in Ottawa took me in. I was one of the
family. She let me paint the storeroom in the attic pink
and white and put up curtains – my own private bedroom, no one to muck things up, and later, after Victoria
was born, she said, "Why don't you fix up the downstairs
sunroom for the baby?" and I did.

Victoria Louise weighed eight and a half pounds at
birth which is amazing when you think I only weigh
ninety-eight myself, being skinny like the Flett side of
the family and also short like my mom's side. She was a
real good baby after she got through the colicky period.
She was born with this gorgeous soft yellow hair. Now
she's nine years old and what a doll! Thank God, I didn't
put her out for adoption the way I planned. I look after
her, make her clothes myself, go to the school meetings
and talk to her teacher, all that stuff, and make her pipe
down at home so she won't get on Aunt Daisy's nerves. I
also take care of the housework here, do most of the
family cooking, and earn a little extra on the side typing
insurance policies. And lately I've been nursing Aunt
Daisy who's suffering from nervous prostration.

Myself, I don't think it's her change of life that's done

it, or her allergies either. I think it's the kids who've got her down. Being a widow she feels extra responsible, I can understand that, and then again some people are just natural worriers. She used to worry about her daughter Alice who has this way of coming on strong – whew, does she ever! Then she worried for a time about Warren, who was a nice kid but sort of a drip. He had this real bad acne growing up and that made him kind of shy and drippy, but the thing is, after a certain age, no one's really a drip any more, they're just kind of sweet or else "individualistic." That's something I've noticed. Nowadays Warren's a regular young man – his skin's a whole lot improved too – and he's down there in Rochester, New York, getting his master's degree in music theory, first in his class, the Gold Medal. Aunt Daisy was planning to go down for the graduation, she even bought herself a darling little pillbox hat, kelly green, but now that's out. She can hardly lug herself out of bed, she just lays there in the dark and cries a whole lot and scrunches up the sheet in her hands, just wrings those sheets like she's wringing someone's neck. I think it's Joan she's worried about now, little Joanie, the family princess, spoiled rotten, but smart as a whip, only now she's smoking dope and doing I don't know what, whatever hippies get up to. She says she's selling jewelry down there in New Mexico, but I bet my bottom dollar she's selling more than that. Well, it's breaking her mother's heart. It kills me to see it. Aunt Daisy saved my life, that's no exaggeration, giving Victoria and me a home, and now I want to save hers, only she's the only one who can do that. A person can make herself sick and that same person has to will herself to get well again, that's my personal theory.

Warren's Theory

My mother's an educated woman but you'd never know it. She has a degree in Liberal Arts from Long College for Women, class of 1926, but ask her where her diploma is and she'll just give a shrug. Once I came across a cardboard box up in the storeroom – this was when we were cleaning up so Cousin Beverly could move in – and in the box was a thick pile of essays my mother wrote back when she was a student. One of the essays was titled: "Camillo Cavour: Statesman and Visionary." I couldn't believe that my mother had ever heard of Camillo Cavour (I certainly hadn't) or that she could write earnestly, even passionately, about an obscure period of nineteenth-century Italian history. The ink after all these years was still clear and bright – those were her loops and dashes, her paragraphs and soaring con-clusion. *Italians everywhere owe a huge debt to this mono-lithic hero who battled for the rights of his countrymen and . . .*

Where did it go, my mother's intellectual ease and energy? She has never once, that any of us can remember, mentioned the subject of Italian independ-ence to her family. Or the nineteenth century. Or her theory about Mediterranean city-states that's so clearly set out on the pages of her 1926 essay. It never occurred to me that she would care about the plight of the Italian peasant. As a matter of fact, I don't think I've ever seen her reading a book except maybe a love novel from the library or some pamphlet about how to breed better dahlias. When I think about my mother's essay on Camillo Cavour, I can't help feeling cheated, as if there's some wily subversion going on, a glittering joke locked in a box and buried underground. And then I think: if I feel cheated, how much more cheated she must feel. She must be in mourning for the squandering of herself. Something, someone, cut off her head, yanked out her tongue. My mother is a middle-aged woman, a middle-class woman, a woman of moderate intelligence and medium-sized ego and average good luck, so that you would expect her to land somewhere near the middle of the world. Instead she's over there at the edge. The least vibration could knock her off.

Joan's Theory

My mother's been sick this year, a nervous breakdown everyone's calling it, and my sister Alice sent me money so I could go home and visit. She wrote me a long, long letter saying she had thought it over and come to the conclusion I was the best person to cheer our mother up, that my presence would be like a "glassful of medicine." Which is just like Alice; she's someone who always goes around appointing people.

I expected to find my mother in a state of torpor and instead found her in a rage. It seems a man called Pinky Fulham has snatched away her newspaper column. All those hours she once put into writing about flower borders and seedlings, she now funnels into her hatred for Pinky Fulham. She can't talk or think of anything else. She's narrowed herself down to just this one little squint of injustice, and she beats her fists together and rehearses and rehearses her final scene with him, the unforgivable things he did and said, especially his concluding remark which was, apparently: "I hope this won't affect our friendship." He said it blithely, unfeelingly, the way people say such things, never even noticing how pierced to the heart my mother was, how crushed she was by such casual presumption and disregard.

Now she can't let it go. She lies in her bed and goes over and over that final exchange, how she'd gone to his office at the *Recorder* and pleaded with him, and how he turned to her and pronounced that impossible thing: "I hope this won't affect our friendship." My mother recounts the scene for me, again and again, speaking harshly, weeping, shaking her head back and forth in a frenzy, and begging me to join in her drama of suffering.

I'd only been home a few days when I realized she was relishing all this, the pure and beautiful force of her hatred for Pinky Fulham, the ecstasy of being wronged. There's a certain majesty in it. Nothing in her life has delivered her to such a pitch of intensity – why wouldn't she love it, this exquisite wounding, the salt of perfect pain?

I held her hand and let her rage on.

Jay Dudley's Theory

Of *course* I feel guilty about what's happened, how could I not, though I never actually led her on, as the saying goes. (One marriage was, I confess, *enough* for me.) I was very, very fond of her though. We had our moments, one in particular on that funny old-fashioned bed of hers with the padded headboard, like something out of a thirties movie. Well, that was fine, *more* than fine, but I could see she had a more permanent arrangement in mind, not that she ever said anything, not in a direct way. Anyway, it seemed best to put a little distance between us. I had no idea she'd take it so hard, that our "friend-ship" – and that's all it was – meant something else to her.

Labina Anthony Greene Dukes' Theory

When I married Dick Greene back in 1927 I thought I was getting a strong husband. He was straight-backed, his shirts tucked neatly into his slacks, his shoes glossy. The man played tennis. He swam for Indiana Varsity. His face was tanned and finely shaped, and I used to adore watching the way his mouth sometimes sagged open when he was listening to someone speak. That slackness of jaw held me for years in a rich, alert, concentrating innocence. He had a fastidious almost humble way of shifting his broad shoulders, as though he had them on loan, as though they were breakable.

I was the breakable one. Women always are. It's not so much a question of one big disappointment, though. It's more like a thousand little disappointments raining down on top of each other. After a while it gets to seem like a flood, and the first thing you know you're drowning.

Cora-Mae Milltown's Theory

The poor motherless thing. Oh my, I remember to this day the first time I laid eyes on her. Eleven years old, her and her father driving up to the Vinegar Hill place in a taxi cab, and myself still up to my elbows in soap and water, not half ready for the two of them, I hadn't even started on the kitchen. Where's your missus? – that's what I was about to say, but thank the Lord I buttoned my lip, because there wasn't any missus, she'd gone and passed away years before, the life went out of her giving birth to this washrag of a girl. It was Mr. Goodwill himself who told me the story. A tragedy. That was after I got to know him better.

Coming from Canada like he did, he wasn't used to coloreds, and he talked to me straight out about this and that and everything else too. "Cora-Mae," he said, "my girl needs a woman in the house, she needs to learn things, she'll be wanting a bit of company when I'm not here. First her mamma died, you see, and then an old auntie who took care of her up in Canada, and now she's got no one in the world, only me."

That's how I came to be working for Mr. Goodwill by the week instead of just Wednesdays the way the company said. That's the Indiana Limestone Company, I'm talking about, they'd hired on Mr. Goodwill and brought him all the way down to Bloomington. A widow-man and his little girl. Now this would be round about 1916, when Orren was overseas, his leg all shot to pieces, only I didn't know it then. That very fall our own Lucile was six years old and starting school, and so I said yes, to Mr. Goodwill, I'd come by early and get breakfast cooking and see that the child was dressed nice and clean for school, and look to the house and the wash and all. Two dollars a day he paid me, three dollars after they moved into the big house, and that was good pay for colored help then.

They treated me nice. Mr. Goodwill had a jokey way about him. Sometimes he'd go and leave a sack of fresh doughnuts on the kitchen table. "What's this?" I'd say, and he'd say, "Why, someone must've left those there for you, Cora-Mae, a little treat to go along with your coffee."

I'd start in on the dusting and the beds and I'd wax the furniture if it needed doing and after that I'd sit myself down with a cup of coffee and a doughnut, taking my ease. If the girl was home from school for some reason she'd sit next to me and have herself a doughnut too and a big glass of milk. Once she turned and said to me, "How come you eat your doughnut with a fork, Cora-Mae?" "I don't know," I said back, and I didn't. "I never saw anyone eat a doughnut like that," she said, all puzzled-like, and I couldn't guess her meaning, if she thought I was ignorant, if she was being fresh or just curious the way my Lucile always was. I held my tongue and tried not to scold or fret too much over the things she'd do. I'd say to myself, remember this poor child is motherless, and there's not one thing worse in this world than being motherless.

I still think that way in my mind. My Lucile lives way out there in California now and has her own family and a beautiful home of her own, ranch style, and I haven't seen her for, oh, six or seven years. She hardly ever sits herself down and writes a letter home, what with all she has to do looking after her family, and I don't hold her to blame one bit about that. Her mama's no more than a little bitty story in her life now, something from way, way back when, and that's the way my mama is for me. You can tell that story in five minutes flat. You can blink and miss it. But you can't make it go away. Your mama's inside you. You can feel her moving and breathing and sometimes you can hear her talking to you, saying the same things over and over, like watch out now, be careful, be good, now don't get yourself hurt.

Well, that's why I took to Mr. Goodwill's little girl the way I did. I'd be ironing one of her dresses or brushing her hair and I'd think: I'm all she's got. I'm not even half a mama, but I'm all the mama she's ever going to get. How's she going to find her way? How's she going to be happy in her life? I'd stare and stare into the future and all I could see was this dark place in front of her that was black as the blackest night.

Skoot Skutari's Theory

My grandfather was born in a northern Albanian village, the son of poor country Jews. When he was eighteen he left home, telling his parents he was going to walk to Jerusalem. Instead he traveled westward to the city of Skutari (and tacked that name on to his own), and caught a boat bound for Malta. From there he traveled to Lisbon, then boarded ship for Montreal. By the year 1897 he was living in rural Manitoba, traveling from township to township and earning his living as a peddler of household sundries. Abram Gozhdë Skutari was his full name, a self-made man, a millionaire, founder and owner of a nationwide chain of retail outlets.

In the early days, though, he was heartbreakingly poor, and the life of a backwoods peddler was painful to him. He was reviled by the very farmers and townspeople who depended on him to bring them necessities. The old Jew he was called. No one had the decency to ask him his name or where he lived or whether he was married and had a family. The men in the region refused to shake his hand, as though he carried lice on his body. That hurt him terribly, he never got over the insult of that.

And then along came Eaton's Mail Order, and suddenly people didn't have to deal with traveling peddlers any longer. It was cheaper and easier to send in an order to the Winnipeg store for their shoe polish and hair ribbons. But how was Abram Skutari to support his wife Elena (my grandmother Lena) and their little boy (my Uncle Jacob)?

It occurred to him to apply for a bank loan and start up his own business, selling work clothes, safety equipment, fire-fighting outfits, drilling supplies, everything, in fact, that Eaton's left out of their catalogue back in 1905. And bicycles. My grandfather had the idea that bicycles were the future. The automobile was coming in, yes, but he was looking around and seeing that every young person in Winnipeg would soon be lusting for one of the new, mass-produced bicycles that had come on the market.

He was fearful, though, about applying for a loan, having never set foot in a bank, especially not the Royal Bank, an imposing stone and marble temple situated in the middle of Winnipeg at the corner of Portage and Main. He was a man who didn't own a necktie. He spoke brokenly. It's possible he really did have lice – many people did during that era – but something happened that gave my grandfather courage. It was something he witnessed, an incident that changed his life.

This event took place in the summer of 1905 when he was in the midst of his peddling rounds, he and his horse and his wagon piled with merchandise. It was mid-afternoon. He pulled into a little town in Manitoba, a place as bleak as any eastern European shtetl, at that time a company town, stone quarrying, a particularly fine grade of limestone. On this day my grandfather happened to be driving past one of the worker's houses when he heard the sound of someone moaning, as though in great pain. He didn't stop to think or knock, but entered directly through the back door.

There he found a woman lying, unattended, in the kitchen with her legs apart, about to give birth to a baby. He could see the baby's head starting to come. He had no idea what to do. Birth was women's business – that was the way people thought in those days, especially a Jewish male raised in the old country, as my grandfather was.

Next door a neighbor was hanging out her clothes, and he hurriedly sought her help. Then he ran to the other end of the village where the doctor lived. It was a hot day. He remembered the heat and dust for the rest of his life. By the time they got back to the house the woman was dying. And it was my grandfather, Abram Skutari, the old Jew, who received her final glance – a roomful of people had gathered, but he was the one she fixed her eye upon. He swore afterwards that he watched her face fill up with his own fright; she drank it in, and then she died.

The child was still alive and breathing. It took my grandfather a minute to understand this. There was much noise and confusion in the room, and it was hot, and everyone was hovering around the dead woman. But there on the kitchen table was a baby wrapped in a sheet. Its lips were moving, trembling, which was how he knew it was alive. No one was paying any attention to it. It was as though it wasn't there. As though it was a lump of dough left by mistake.

He reached out and touched its cheek, and felt a deep, sudden longing to give it something, a blessing of some kind. He could never understand where that longing came from, but he once confessed to my father, who was fond of retelling the story, that he felt perfectly the infant's loneliness; it was loneliness of an extreme and incurable variety, the sort of loneliness he himself had suffered since leaving home at eighteen.

In his pocket was an ancient coin from the old country. He placed that coin on the baby's forehead and held it there, watching as the breath rose and fell under the sheeting. "Be happy," he said in Albanian or Turkish or Yiddish, or possibly English. Then he said it again, be happy, but he felt as though he were blessing a stone, that nothing good could come out of his mouth. He felt weak, he felt like a man made of paper and straw, he felt as though he wasn't a man at all, that he might as well be dead.

He didn't realize he was weeping until he felt the weight of an arm on his shoulder. It was the doctor, who was also weeping. They stood together like that. Their tears mingled.

Mingled – that's the word my grandfather used when he told this story, our tears mingled. The other man's arm on his shoulder felt like a brother's arm and the touch of it made him wail even louder.

After that they all signed the death certificate and then the birth certificate, even my grandfather. Everyone was astonished he could write his name. He set it down: Abram Gozhdë Skutari, and as he wrote he felt a surge of strength come into his body. He felt the strumming of his own heart. He felt he would be able to do anything, even walk into the Royal Bank at the corner of Portage and Main and ask for a loan.

But that child's sadness never left him. He swore he'd never seen a creature so alone in the world. He lived a long life and made a million dollars and loved his wife and was a decent father to his sons. But he grieved about that baby all his days, the curse that hung over it, its terrible anguish.

Mrs. Flett's Theory

Surely no one would expect Mrs. Flett to come up with a theory about her own suffering – the poor thing's so emptied out and lost in her mind she can't summon sufficient energy to brush her hair, let alone organize a theory. Theorizing is done inside a neat calm head, and Mrs. Flett's head is crammed with rage and disappointment. She's given way. She's a mess, a nut case. In the

morning light her hurt seems temporary and manage-
able, but at night she hears voices, which may just be the
sound of her own soul thrashing. It sings along the seams
of other hurts, especially the old unmediated terror of
abandonment. Somewhere along the line she made the
decision to live outside of events; or else that decision
was made for her. Write a gardening book, her daughter
Alice advises. Go on a round-the-world trip, says Fraidy
Hoyt. Take some courses at the university. Teach yourself macrame. Look into allergy shots or vitamin B
complex. Listen to soothing music, keep a diary like
Virginia Woolf, go for long walks, indulge in hot baths.
Question your assumptions, be kind to yourself, live for
the moment, loosen up, pray, scream, curse the world,
count your blessings, just let go, just be.

All this advice comes flying in Mrs. Flett's direction,
but she's too distracted to hear.

You'd think she'd be scared to death by the state she's
in, but she's not. Her hair's matted, her fingernails
broken, her houseplants withered, her day-to-day life
smashed, but sleeping inside her like a small burrowing
creature is the certainty that she'll recover. For one
thing, she distrusts the sincerity of her own salt tears,
and, another thing, she remembers how, years ago, she
and Fraidy loved to quote poor old William Blake:
"Weep, weep, in notes of woe" and how the word woe
made them fall over laughing, such a blind little bug of a
word.

Now, at the age of fifty-nine, sadness flows through
every cell of her body, yet leaves her curiously
untouched. She knows how memory gets smoothed
down with time, everything flattened by the iron of

acceptance and rejection – it comes to the same thing, she thinks. This sorrowing of hers has limits, just as there's a limit to how tangled she'll let her hair get or how much dust she'll allow to pile up on her dressing table. That's Daisy for you. Daisy's resignation belongs to the phylum of exhaustion, the problem of how to get through a thousand ordinary days. Or, to be more accurate, ten thousand such days. In a sense I see her as one of life's fortunates, a woman born with a voice that lacks a tragic register. Someone who's learned to dig a hole in her own life story.

But she's tired of being sad, and tired of not even minding being sad, of not even in a sense knowing. And in the thin bony box of her head she understands, and accepts, the fact that her immense unhappiness is doomed to irrelevance anyway. Already, right this minute, I feel a part of her wanting to go back to the things she used to like, the feel of a new toothbrush against her gums, for instance. Such a little thing. She'd like to tie a crisp clean apron around her waist once again, peel a pound of potatoes in three minutes flat and put them soaking in cold water. Polish a jelly jar and set it on the top shelf with its mates. Lick an envelope, stick a stamp in its corner, drop it in the mail box. She'd like to clean her body out with a hoot of laughter and give way to the pull of gravity. It's going to happen. All this suffering will be washed away. Any day now.

CHAPTER EIGHT

Ease, 1977

VICTORIA LOUISE FLETT is only twenty-two years old, a student at the University of Toronto, a tall stringbean of a woman with large hands and feet and straight blond unyielding hair that she bends carelessly behind her ears. So much for her coiffeur. She favors jeans and sweaters and an old denim jacket – as a matter of fact, she owns no other clothing. These clothes are dark in color and dense in weave, as though she's trying to keep the bad dreams of modern life out. To correct her nearsightedness she wears glasses with round metal frames, and her eyes behind the rather spotty lenses appear cold and serious. It is 1977; she is no longer the tenderly sheltered child of a large household; her voice, an embarrassed voice, shunts between adult censoriousness and teenage perplexity. Her emotional rhythms are sometimes uneven, as you might expect, and yet she is capable of generous insight.

She's confided to her Aunt Daisy, for instance, that she can understand the genealogical phenomenon that has burst forth all around her. She finds it moving, she says, to see men and women – though, oddly, they are mostly women – tramping through cemeteries or else huddled over library tables in the university's records room, turning over the pages of county histories, copying names and dates into small spiral notebooks and imagining, hoping, that their unselfish labors will open up into a fabric of substance and comity. Victoria doesn't believe these earnest amateurs are looking for links to royalty or to creative genius; all they want is for their ancestors to be revealed as simple, honest, law-abiding folks, quiet in their accomplishments, faithful in their vows, cheerful, solvent, and well intentioned, and that their robustly rounded (but severely occluded) lives will push up against, and perhaps pardon, the contemporary plagues of displacement and disaffection. Common sense, that prized substance, seems to have disappeared from the world; even Victoria realizes this.

Victoria's great-aunt Daisy, now retired and living in Florida, has become preoccupied in her mature years with the lives of her two dead fathers: Cuyler Goodwill, her blood parent, and Magnus Flett, her father-in-law. But Victoria's aunt pursues her two departed fathers in an altogether different spirit than the usual weekend genealogist. She's more focused for one thing, and, at the same time, more dreamy and ineffectual, wanting, it seems to Victoria, to pull herself inside a bag of buried language, to be that language, to be able to utter that unutterable word: father. It's true Aunt Daisy has read a few works of social history, memoirs, biography – quite a few more in recent years than her niece would ever imagine – but she does not go on detective outings to local libraries and graveyards, and she has not traveled to her birthplace, Tyndall, Manitoba, to visit the famed Goodwill Tower built in memory of her own mother; she imagines, anyway, that the structure has been sadly vandalized, stone after stone carried away by souvenir hunters, so that nothing remains except a slight doughnut-shaped depression in the ground. She has not contacted the Mormon Archive in Salt Lake City and has no plans to do so. She's sent off no letters of inquiry. She sits comfortably, very comfortably indeed, on the flowered settee in her Florida room (three walls of louvered glass), and thinks about her two departed fathers. That's as far as she goes: she just thinks about them, concentrates on them, dwells on them. For her grandniece, Victoria, the two fathers are described, but never quite animated; their powers are asserted, but not demonstrated. Aunt Daisy mulls over their lives. She wonders what those lives were made of and how they ended: noisily as in the movies or in a frosty stand-off? Of course, she doesn't do this all the time – only at odd moments, late in the afternoon, for instance, when the day feels flattened and featureless, when she's restless, when she feels her own terrifying inauthenticity gnawing at her heart's membrane, and when there's nothing of interest on television, just the local news from Tampa or the weather report.

Her life at seventy-two is one of ease. Three times a year she gets a good perm, as opposed to an ordinary perm, and ends up with hair springy as Easter basket grass; she's submitted (once) to a painful facial, tried (two or three times) a new shade of lipstick, thinks (every day) about having her varicose veins done. And she's bounded back from the depression that struck her down some years ago. Her physical health is good-to-excellent. She has money in the bank, plenty of it, though she lives modestly. Ten years ago she sold her large Ottawa house and moved to Florida's west coast, purchasing a three-bedroom condo in a Sarasota development nearby to where her old friend Fraidy Hoyt has settled, and not far from Birds' Key where another friend, Labina Greene Dukes Kavanaugh, lives with her third husband, Bud.

Since moving to Florida Aunt Daisy has learned to play shuffleboard and to decorate plastic headbands and bracelets with glued-on seashells – these she sends as birthday gifts to her half-dozen granddaughters scattered across England and the United States; to her grandsons, Benje and Teller, she sends leather wallet that she stitches together herself down at the Bayside Ladies Craft Club. She doubts very much whether they like or appreciate these hand-made articles, but she has always, especially since her breakdown in 1965, believed in keeping her hands occupied, filling more and more of the world with less and less of herself. Visitors notice how the balcony of her condo is crowded with the lush greenness of tended cacti and tropical plants. Her famous botanical thumb is still very much in evidence; she is a sensualist when it comes to the world of horticulture, though she complains, good-naturedly, about the sogginess of the Florida landscape and swears she'll never be able to accept the scraggly-barked, poodle-headed palm tree as anything other than a joke on nature.

Young Victoria, her grandniece, defends palm trees. She doesn't like them much either, but she feels a compulsion to rouse her aunt to debate. It seems to her this is the least the young can do for the old. She's read somewhere that the elderly learn to step back in order to see more, that their eyes squint, and crowd in new possibilities.

In the wintertime, when Victoria is up north in Toronto attending lectures and preparing papers and writing exams and worrying about her non-existent love affairs, she thinks of her elderly great-aunt so peachily settled down in Sarasota, tweezing dead blooms off her balcony plants and playing bridge and doing her volunteer afternoons at the Ringling Museum, and "bumming" with Fraidy and Labina in the boutiques around St. Armand's Key. She thinks, a little enviously, how settled Great-aunt Daisy's life is, also how nearly over it is, and she can't for the life of her understand why an old lady would want to speculate about two old men moldering in their graves: the eccentric Cuyler Goodwill, the vanished Magnus Flett. She entertains the suspicion that her aunt is really in search of her mother, that the preoccupation with her two fathers is only a kind of ruse or sly equation.

If anyone should be on a father quest, it should be Victoria herself, that's what she sometimes thinks; in fact, she doesn't give one golden fuck who her father is; her Aunt Daisy once overheard her say as much. Victoria Louise knows a little about her paternal parentage, but not much, only what her mother let slip from time to time. Her father was some jerkhead out in Saskatchewan, married, fat-bellied, probably dead now, probably a boozer, so dumb he never even knew her mother was pregnant for God's sake – and Beverly Flett didn't trouble herself telling him, just hopped on a train and came east and moved in with Aunt Daisy's family in Ottawa, and when people said to her round about the eighth or ninth month, "Aren't you going to put that little baby up for adoption?" she shook her head and said, "Nope."

This was in 1955; hardly anyone kept their babies back then.

Now Beverly's been gone for four years, cancer of the pancreas, and Victoria spends her vacations down in Florida with her Great-aunt Daisy – who mails her a plane ticket, who meets her at Tampa airport in an air-conditioned cab, who makes up the guestroom with crisp cotton sheets, who has a little African violet blooming on the bedside table, who has plans for the two of them to get all dolled up and have their Easter lunch at the Ringling Hotel – where they've got a new smoked salmon quiche on the menu with green salad on the side – and if the waitress turns out to be the friendly type, if she says, "So you two gals are out on the town, huh?" then Aunt Daisy will say, shaping her words into soft ovals of confederacy, "This is my grandniece all the way from Toronto, she's just finishing her Master's Degree in paleobotany, and, she's thinking seriously of starting her doctorate next September," and Victoria, already ill at ease in her jeans and torn T-shirt – it is heart-catching the way she adjusts and readjusts the neck of that stretched garment – will wiggle uncomfortably in her seat and think how her aunt didn't used to burble on like this, she's turned into a regular Florida blue-head with her beads and cork-soled sandals and white plastic purse, but she, Victoria that is, will also bask in her aunt's warm pride and probably, once the waitress has sashayed back into the kitchen, reach across the table and pat that dear dry old powdery hand. A hand she knows almost as well as she knows her own.

*

Cuyler Goodwill died back in the spring of 1955, the same year Victoria Flett was born. He was out working in the backyard of his house on Lake Lemon, a man of seventy-eight years, when he felt himself go suddenly light-headed. Probably he shouldn't have been out there at all in the bright sun without a hat on his head; that's what his wife Maria was always saying.

This strange dry dizziness – it was friendly enough at first, accompanied by a persistent buzzing noise and a corner-of-the-eye glimpse of bees' wings, like blurred spheres of sound, invisible. He stretched himself out on the soft grass, flat on his back, his laced shoes pointing skyward. A cool breeze came along, rippling across his forehead, stirring a strand of his thin hair, and almost immediately he felt stronger. Still he did not get up.

There's no hurry, he said to himself, I can lie here all morning if I like.

Maria had taken her big straw shopping bag and walked around the Point to the Bridgeport Grocery Store; she was out of butter. She'd announced this at breakfast – she was always running out of something or other, never having accustomed herself to the bulk-buying habits of North Americans. Her husband knew she would be gone for at least an hour; she liked to dilly dally on the Lake Road, especially now that the redbud was coming into bloom, and their young neighbors, the MacGregors, Lydia and Bill, would be out working on their new cedar deck. She'd be sure to stop by their place and pass the time of day – and never notice for a minute that she was interrupting or that the two young people were passing looks back and forth, rolling their eyes and making minute shrugs of exasperation. On and on she'd jabber, gesturing at the trees, the waves on the lake, the cloudless sky, making suggestions about the support brackets for their deck, about the loose shingles on the back of their house, about their rhubarb plants, whether or not they received enough sun, and neither Bill nor Lydia would understand one word she said.

Talk, talk, talk. Meanwhile, here he lay, an old man sprawled on his back.

The novelty of his position amused him at first, and very gradually he became aware of the warmth that rose out of the earth, penetrating first the crushed grass beneath him and then passing through the smooth broadcloth of his checked shirt. This was surprising to him, that he should be able to feel the immense stored heat of the planet spreading across the width of his seventy-eight-year-old back. When had he last lain like this on bare ground, fitting the irregularities of his physiognomy, muscles, bone, cartilage, against a bed of recently clipped grass, giving himself over to it? Only young people surrendered themselves to the earth in this unguarded way, allowing it to support them, the whole weight of their bodies trustingly held.

Minutes passed. He had nothing much to think of, so he thought about the angle of the sun, which was almost directly overhead, and about his body, his seventy-eight-year-old body, hatched up north in Canada in another century by parents now firmly erased, growing to strength there in his early years, and now, removed as if on a magic carpet to this other place, lying flat on a patch of Indiana grass like a window screen about to be rinsed off by the garden hose.

He lay in the backyard of a lakeside cottage, but one that he and Maria now made their permanent home. They'd been here for some years, since his retirement from business. The wide pie-shaped lot was landscaped with lilacs, forsythia, and mock orange, with the result that his prone body was obscured from the view of passing motorists, not that there were many of those in the middle of the day. Only locals used the Lake Road, and of course it was too early for the summer people.

He loved this time of year, April. Life shone through the latticed trees, shone everywhere – life.

Round about him robins sang in the grass. He stared at them with a thickened gaze. How important these robins suddenly seemed with their busy, purposeful movements, their golf ball heads bobbing. The sky overhead was a brilliant blue. Maria would be home any minute now, unloading her groceries on the kitchen table, clicking her tongue about the price of staples in the country stores and saying how much cheaper such things were in the Bloomington supermarkets, not that she'd go back to living in town for a million dollars. She would say all this in a dithyrambic mixture of Italian and English that he alone in the world seemed able to understand.

He attempted to rise to his feet, but powerful cramps seized his thighs and urged him to stay put a little longer. Rest a bit, he said to himself, lie still. To dull his brain he tried to conjure the sunlit streets of Stonewall, Manitoba, his boyhood town, but was, as always, discouraged by the muzziness of blocked memory. The visible walls of his father's house remained disengaged from its secret inner rooms, its beds and crockery, the jam pot on the cupboard shelf where the family cash was kept, the soft, decaying dollar bills. (Air – he needed a breath of air, this would not do.) He forced his way out through his mother's garden – a few weak rows of cabbages, some spindly wax beans – and along the sun-struck confusion of Jackson Avenue as it was sixty years ago, past farmers' wagons and the high aroma of tethered horses, the hardware store on the corner, the primary school, the Court House, the struggling civic flower beds, and at the center of town, in a trapezoid of light, the Presbyterian Church with its hard limestone adornments, now, suddenly, melted to ash.

He may have dozed off, then woke suddenly to a fear that seemed to tunnel out of childhood. What was this? His back, meanwhile, had grown stiff.

That back of his, he speculated, must be speckled with age by now; the skin would be mottled and creased and thinned out like tissue paper, but who ever sees their own backs? A person would have to wiggle and squirm in front of a double mirror, and even then there were parts of your body you'd never get a glimpse of. There are bits of your body you carry around all your life but never really own.

This thought, this puzzle, made him smile inside his head, though it brought with it a twinge of nostalgia. He remembered how as a young stonecutter in Manitoba he'd worked bare-chested in the summer months – all the quarry men did – and how, out of delicacy for his young wife, he'd let the sweat from his back dry off before slipping on his shirt while walking home to his supper, home to his beloved.

Not Maria, no, not then. Home from a day at the quarry to that other wife, the wife of his young manhood.

Even in old age he thinks of this wife at least once every day; something will rear up and remind him of that brief marriage which in time has come to seem more like an enclosure he'd stumbled upon than a legal arrangement formally entered. She is always, in his recollections, standing at the doorway, waiting for him, a presence, a grief, an ache. In fact, she had never once waited for him at the doorway, being occupied at this hour with supper preparations. He must, however clumsily, get that part right, that he had not been awaited.

But what was her name? What was her name? His first wife's name? A suppressed rapture. There is something careless about this kind of forgetting, something unpardonable. His dear one, his sweetheart. Her face had the quality of a blurred photograph, yet he knew her body, every inch, and remembers how he woke one night to the loudness of the rain with his arm across her breast. All that was good, that soft breast.

Feeling foolish, he started through the alphabet: Amelia, Bessie, Charlotte, an old fashioned name, Dorothea . . .

Emma, Fanny.

He stared down the length of his body, his neatly buttoned sport shirt, the rumple of his khaki pants, to where his feet made a kind of v-shaped frame through which could be seen the stone pyramid he had been working on when his dizzy spell struck.

How he'd grown to hate it.

For close to ten years he'd been at work on this structure, a scale model of the Great Pyramid, begun just after the end of the war, and only about a quarter of it now completed. Other men built boats in their retirement, or swimming pools or garden ornaments, Snow White and the seven dwarfs cut out of boxwood with a jigsaw and set up among the petunias. Other men saw their projects completed and then began something new, but he for some reason had allowed himself to become mired in this mocking piece of foolishness. ("One thing at a time"; how often had he uttered those words, persuading himself of their wisdom.) But this pyramid had become an eyesore, to his eye at least. A folly. The scolding voice he so often hears in the dark says: "You will never be able to equal your first monument, you've lost your touch." Furthermore, measurements taken only one week earlier, told him the structure had gone out of plumb, and that it would grow worse as he progressed. If he continued, that is.

Fanny, Gladys . . .

Most people need an envelope in which to concentrate their thoughts, and Cuyler Goodwill achieved his unique concentration regarding his pyramid through an imposed perspective, his compacted elderly spine stretched out along his own recently mown lawn, his angle of vision significantly diminished, and therefore radically altered. Something fortunate happened, a trick of perception.

He was suddenly clear, at any rate, in his decision. He would not continue with this ugly piece of backyard sculpture, pale shadow of that long-ago tower he'd raised in memory of his first wife. (What was her name?) No, he would call a halt to it this minute. Right now. Tomorrow he would telephone a contractor in Bloomington and have them send out a bulldozer. Then he'd get a truck to carry away the stone chips. It would take no more than a day or two. Astonishing. Of course there would be a terrible scar left in the middle of the back lawn, but come fall he could plant one of those fast-growing ornamental cherries in its place. A thing of beauty. Yes. In fact, why wait for fall? – he'd put it in right away; he never could understand why trees had to be planted in the fall. It didn't make an ounce of sense, it went against sense.

I'll knock her down, he said inside his throat, jubilant, anesthetized against tomorrow's faint heart and second thoughts, uncertain whether he was moving close to the center of his life or selling off some valuable part of himself. But immediately, with a shudder of joy, he knew that what might be done, could be done. Happiness coursed through him in that instant, decision's homely music.

A choice made when one is flat on one's back is no less a choice. Its force sends out random jolts of energy, and this energy struck now in the center of Cuyler Goodwill's chest, bringing with it on this fine April day the chill of midwinter. His feet and hands, he realized, were suddenly icy, separated from the sensations of his body, attached to it only by a tough filament of pain. Where was he now? What had he been thinking? – Fanny, Gladys, Harriet, Isabel . . .

He allowed the pain to occupy him – it seemed the only thing to do. It filled him up – perfectly – leaving only one small part of him empty, a portion of his mind where a question knocked. No, not a question, but something asking to be remembered. Something about the bull-dozer scraping across the grass and knocking down his pyramid, his shame, something he had forgotten in his joyous moment of decision – what was it now?

What? Snagged in a convulsion of thought, he rounded the muscle of his mouth, squeezed his eyes shut and saw a kind of cloudy steam roll over his mind, teasing him with his own dullness. What he needed to remember was a simple and concrete detail. An object, in fact, a precise object fixed in time. If he could manage to raise his hand he would be able to touch that object and identify it, but his hand, it seemed, that icy weight, had gone to sleep.

And then, lifted by a spasm of concentration, he remembered: there was a box buried under the pyramid's foundation – a time capsule no less. He had placed it there himself. A little steel box about twelve inches square, perhaps four inches deep. Of course. He remembered buying the box at a local hardware store; it was the sort of container intended for fishing tackle, but stronger in its construction than such boxes usually are. It possessed, in addition, a well-fitted lid, and even a little lock and key. Fifteen dollars, he'd paid for it. Ungrumblingly.

Isabel, Jeanette, Katie, Lillian . . .

He remembered that he had put considerable thought into what should go into the box. This was a long time ago. Since that time much had slipped out of his mind. These last ten years had been a period of disintegration; he saw that now. He had imagined himself to be a man intent on making something, while all the while he was participating in a destructive and sorrowful narrowing of his energy. Still it would be a surprise to open the box and see what he had secreted there. But he would have to make sure it was not damaged. He would have to explain carefully to the driver of the bulldozer about there being a little box just beneath the foundation; this explanation would tax his energy terribly, but it was necessary if the treasure were to be saved.

But what treasure was this?

Something tugged at the hem of his thoughts. Something of value lay secreted in the box, something that had belonged to his young wife. (What was her name?) It was so long ago he'd buried the box in the earth, since he was a young man walking home from the quarry with his shirt slung over his shoulder and the sweat on his back drying; so much had happened, so many spoken words and collapsed hours, the rooms of his life filling and emptying and never guessing at the shape of their outer walls, their supporting beams and rough textured siding.

Now he knew from the position of the sun that it must be late afternoon. Evening, in fact. The stars were streaming across the sky, a visiting radiance, bringing with them the perfectly formed image of a wedding ring. Her wedding ring. And the flickering moment when he had eased it off her dead finger. (Not that this scene takes sensory form, not that it even materializes as thought; it is, in fact, undisclosable in its anguish; there are chambers, he knows, in the most ordinary lives that are never entered, let alone advertised, and yet they lie pressed against the consciousness like leaf specimens in an old book.) His wife's wedding ring, his wife Mercy. Ah, Mercy. Mercy, hold me in your soft arms, cover me with your body, keep me warm.

The thought of his only daughter either did or did not occur to him in his final moments, a daughter who is now seventy-two years old and living in a luxury condominium in the sun-blessed state of Florida.

Victoria's great-aunt has become a wearer of turquoise pant suits. They're comfortable, practical too, and they conceal the fissured broken flesh of her once presentable calves. Her lipsticked mouth – a crimped posy – snaps open, gapes, trembles, and draws tight. Her eyes have sunk into slits of marbled satin. She looks in the bathroom mirror and thinks how that pink-white frizz around her face cannot possibly be her hair (though it's true she sometimes pats at it with deep satisfaction), or the appalling jowls or the slack upper arms that jiggle as she walks along the beach in the early evening, tossing chunks of stale bread to the seagulls. No one told her so much of life was spent being old. Or that, paradoxically, these long Florida years would scarcely press on her at all.

Everything she encounters feels lacking in weight. The hollow interior doors of her condo. The molded insubstantiality of the light switches. The dismaying lightness of her balcony furniture. The rattling loose-jointed cabs she sometimes takes when visiting Labina and her husband out at Birds' Key. Even her white plastic shoulder bag with its neat roll of cough drops, its mini-pack of tissues, and slim little case of credit cards that have replaced the need for cash.

In the foyer of Bayside Towers stands an artificial jade plant, and she is unable to walk by this abomination without reaching out and fingering its leaves, sometimes rather roughly, leaving the marks of her fingernails on the vinyl surfaces, finding sly pleasure in her contempt.

In the late evenings she's taken to watching Johnny Carson on television. She remains baffled by the mean hard outline of his mouth, a mouth that looks as though it were drawn on his face with pen and ink, but she likes his opening monologue, that quick run of jokes strung together with the wide familiar golf-swing and with Johnny's repeated transitional phrase: "moving right along."

"Moving right along" is what she murmurs to herself these days – on her way to Hairworks for her weekly shampoo and set, on her way to the post office or her doctor's appointment or downstairs to the club room for her daily round of bridge. Moving right along, and along, and along. The way she's done all her life. Numbly. Without thinking.

I have said that Mrs. Flett recovered from the nervous torment she suffered some years ago, and yet a kind of rancor underlies her existence still: the recognition that she belongs to no one. Even her dreams release potent fumes of absence. She has her three grown children, it's true, but she wonders if these three will look back on her with anything other than tender forbearance. And her eight grandchildren are so far away, so diminished by age and distance, so consecrated to the blur of the future. Perhaps that's why she is forever "ruminating" about her past life, those two lost fathers of hers, and hurling herself at the emptiness she was handed at birth. In the void she finds connection, and in the connection another void – a pattern of infinite regress which is heartbreaking to think of – and yet it pushes her forward, it keeps her alive. She feeds the seagulls, doesn't she? She telephones her grown children every Sunday without fail,

Alice in London, Joan out there in the wilds of Oregon, and Warren in Pittsburgh (soon to be transferred to New York), and despite the sometimes insane lunges and loops of these electronic conversations she manages to simulate a steady chin-up cheerfulness and repress the least suggestion of despair. She cooks herself a proper dinner, doesn't she? – a chop or a chicken breast, green vegetables. She doesn't take pills; she doesn't hear noises.

She does lie on her bed, though, in the early morning, her eyes turned toward the window, staring at the hard Florida light that creeps in between the slats of her blinds, and feeling its unforgiving brilliance. Sometimes she bunches her fists; sometimes tears crowd her eyes as she lies there thinking: another day, another day, and attempting to position herself in the shifting scenes of her life. Her life thus far, I should say – for she sees years and years ahead for herself. That life "thus far" has meant accepting the doses of disabling information that have come her way, every drop, and stirring them with the spoon of her longing – she's done this for so many years it's become second nature. The real and the illusory whirl about her bedroom in smooth-dipping waltz-time – one, two, three; one, two, three. On and on she goes.

The synapses collapse; well, let them. She enlarges on the available material, extends, shrinks, reshapes what's offered; this mixed potion is her life. She swirls it one way or the other, depending on – who knows what it depends on? – the fulcrum of desire, or of necessity. She might drop in a ripe plum from a library book she's reading or something out of a soap opera or a dream. Not often, but occasionally, she will make a bold subtraction, as when Fraidy Hoyt reported she had almost certainly glimpsed Maria Goodwill, widow of Cuyler Goodwill, in Indianapolis, walking down Ohio Street on the arm of an elderly gentleman – but this is impossible, laughable, since Maria has long since gone home to her Italian village and transformed herself into a black draped figure of mourning with a bowl of knitting in her lap.

If you were to ask Victoria's Great-aunt Daisy the story of her life she would purse her lips for a moment – that ruby-red efflorescence – and stutter out an edited hybrid version, handing it to you somewhat shyly, but without apology, without equivocation that is: this is what happened, she would say from the unreachable recesses of her seventy-two years, and this is what happened next.

It's hard to say whether she's comfortable with her blend of distortion and omission, its willfulness, in fact; but she is accustomed to it. And it's occurred to her that there are millions, billions, of other men and women in the world who wake up early in their separate beds, greedy for the substance of their own lives, but obliged every day to reinvent themselves.

In June of 1977, just two months after their Easter lunch at the Ringling Hotel, her grandniece, Victoria Flett, phoned from Toronto and said, "Hey, guess what? – I'm going to the Orkney Islands on a research project. Next week. Why don't you come with me. It would be a terrific holiday, and we can" – for some reason Victoria's voice carried a ribbon of laughter – "we can go put some flowers on Magnus Flett's grave."

"The Orkney Islands!" her daughter Joan said during their customary Sunday telephone call. "But I thought you said you were going to come up to Portland this year, you said you'd stay with the girls so Ross and I could get away for a couple of days, they were looking forward to seeing Grandma. It's always Grandma this and Grandma that, and now you're talking about the Orkneys."

"Have you looked this place up on a map?" her son Warren said. "Do you even know where the Orkney Islands are?"

"Why the hell not?" Alice said in her acquired English accent. "About time you crossed the pond. As long as you stay with me and the kids for a few days coming and going."

"Of course you'll go," Fraidy said. "I'll do your volunteer afternoon for you, and we'll cancel bridge for once."

"Leave your passport to me," Labina's husband, Bud, said. "Just get your photos done, fill out the form, and I'll drop it off at the federal building in Tampa where I just happen to have a few connections – a fellow there who owes me a favor. The whole thing'll be over and out in ten minutes flat, take my word for it."

"What you need," Labina (Beans) said, "is a proper wool suit. These Florida blends won't do in that unholy climate, not at all. I almost froze my behind off that time I was in Scotland, and that was only Edinburgh, not way up north where you're heading. A wool suit, a Perma-press blouse and a couple of very, very fine sweaters to switch off with, you won't need another thing."

"Walking shoes," Victoria said on the telephone. "Never mind what they look like."

"And an umbrella." Fraidy said. "The folding kind."

"Cancel the umbrella," Victoria said. "See if you can get one of those plastic ponchos with a hood."

"Sorry we can't get you the package deal," the travel agent in Bradenton said, "but the fact is, we need at least three weeks' notice for that, and besides, we don't have all that much information on the Orkney Islands."

"Frankly," said Marian McHenry, who lives in the condo across the hall, "I'd rather see my own country first instead of traipsing around over there. Have you seen Washington D.C.? I mean, really seen it?"

"No one needs inoculations any more for Europe," Dr. Neerly told her, "But I'm going to write you a prescription for travelers' trots. Also one for constipation. And you'll want to take along your own anti-allergy pillow, they probably still use chicken feathers over there, or straw."

"I hope to heaven you've made firm hotel reservations."

"Personally, we wouldn't dream of booking ahead, it takes all the fun out of it, we like to play it be ear, you know what I mean? Will o' the wisp, that's us."

"You honestly haven't been to Europe since 1927? Honest? .Oh boy, are you in for a surprise."

"I didn't know you'd been to Europe before." (Joan, phoning from Portland on a Tuesday night.) "I mean, you never once mentioned it."

"For God's sake, don't stay in hotels over there. Because, listen, they've got these darling little bed and breakfast thingies all over the place, they're much more homey, and you get a real feel for the day-to-day life as it's really lived kind-of-thing."

"Take my advice and avoid two things. First, bed and breakfast establishments. Some of them actually stick you between those godawful nylon sheets, yech, and serve you mushy hot tomatoes for breakfast, I kid you not. Two, don't drink the water out of the faucet. Haven't you ever wondered why they drink all that tea over there? Because tea requires boiled water – boiled, get it?"

"Travelers' checks."

"Money belt."

"Two small suitcases are better than one big one, that's the smartest thing I've ever been told."

"When we were in Canterbury –"

"The time I went up to the Lake District –"

"– fish and chips, wrapped in newspaper."

"– a little plastic case with your own soap because –"

"My great-great grandmother came from the Isle of Wight. Is that anywhere near where –?"

"If you could just pick me up one of those cute little Wedgwood ashtrays, the green color though, not the blue."

"– keep your valuables on your person at all times –"

"– these itty-bitty earplug thingamajigs, you can buy them at Winn Dixie."

"The Orkney Islands? Never heard of them."

Young Victoria, meeting her great-aunt at Mirabelle Airport in Montreal, was in a knot of nerves. "I'd like you to meet Lewis. Lewis Roy. Lew, this is my Aunt Daisy." Tonguing each word.

"How do you do, Mrs. Flett."

"Lew's going to the Orkneys too," Victoria said, her voice rising. Her face as she said this was awful. So was her hair, lank, unevenly cut.

"Oh."

"He's kind of, you know, in charge of the project. He's" – she performed a grotesque rolling shrug of nonchalance, "he's my prof, sort of."

"Really just a post-doc, Mrs. Flett. Victoria and I came up with this proposal together. It was mostly her idea." His face appeared strong, his mouth eager, ready to be amused.

On the plane the three of them were seated side by side, Lewis Roy on the aisle, Victoria in the middle, her aunt by the window. They drank some champagne and ate a dinner of chicken and sliced carrots, and in the daze and rumble of airline ritual became easy with each other. Then Lewis plunged into a long, complex account of a previous flight to Europe, and as the story progressed he fell, egregiously, into the present tense. "So the pilot makes an announcement. Hey, one of the motors is kaput. Right. We turn back. We're like all shook up. But we sit there spooning up our grub like it's just a real fun time we're having, and the next thing you know we're sitting on an airstrip somewhere in Labrador, an army base or something, and we're like stuck there for twelve whole hours, the toilet malfunctioning, and then –"

"Aunt Daisy's tired, I think," Victoria hummed.

He fell instantly silent. Gnawed on his knuckle bones, yawned hugely, glanced about.

Victoria burned with shame. She knew how her aunt must feel about this young man, his hair flowing around his shoulders like a cape of fur, his boyish narrative masking his brilliance, his extraordinary tenderness transformed to male insouciance. The stewardess, at last, brought around blankets and pillows and dimmed the lights, and they all three pretended to sleep. Victoria could hear her aunt's jagged breathing, almost a sob, and understood that this elderly person beside her longed with all her soul to be home in her Florida condo, to be anywhere but where she was, riding the night Atlantic with the little nightlight gleaming on the window frame and across her eyelids.

Victoria, the whole of her terrible radar on duty, could sense, too, the waves of sadness, of failure, emanating from Lewis Roy's stiff body. Under the secrecy of her woolen blanket she reached sideways for his hand, found it trembling, and held it tight. She had never touched him before; he really was her instructor and she his student; they were not, then, on a footing of intimacy.

After a while she reached out her other hand and placed it on her elderly aunt's tense wrist, saying with the pressure of her fingertips: everything's going to be all right, trust me.

In this way, joined together by the dolorous stretched arms of Victoria Flett, the three of them exchanged one continent for another. They may have slept a few winks during the night. Each of them believed they lived on a fragile planet. Not one of them knew what the world was coming to.

The Orkney Islands are low-lying, green, cultivated, covered with winding roads and with sheep who picturesquely graze on sloping meadows, forming a tableau that could have been painted by a watercolorist two hundred years ago, three hundred years ago. Behind and beneath this pastoral scenery lie prehistoric ruins – villages, forts, cairns, burial chambers, and standing stones which might, or might not, be astronomical observatories. There are Iron Age remains, too, another layer. And the Norse monuments, ninth century. Also the medieval, the feudal, the monastic. And other more contemporary additions – for superimposed upon the ancient and the bucolic are today's small humming Orcadian factories modestly producing such specialties as Orkney cakes (delicious) or Orkney cheeses; then there are the craft enterprises, knitting for the most part (but this is sadly in decline), the tourist thrust (booming), and the always present background buzz of daily commerce and professional necessity – grocers, stationers, lawyers, clergymen, what have you.

None of this is what Victoria's Great-aunt Daisy had expected. Moorland, bog, heather was more what she'd had in mind. The Orkney houses lay strewn about in a dozen straggling villages or in the two main towns, Kirkwall and Stromness. Even Victoria was surprised to see the hundreds of townish houses, so solidly built, so plain. She looked at the unrevealing facades of these houses and imagined women inside, standing in front of mirrors, considering themselves, or men pulling sweaters over their heads, flattening down their hair. Hardly anyone seemed to be out and about. Of course it was early in the day. Of course there was a fierce wind blowing off the sea. Rain pelted down. Despite this, Victoria and her aunt and Lewis Roy were standing in the churchyard at Stromness reading tombstones. It was Victoria, shouting, who discovered:

> *A holy lyf a hapie end*
> *The Soul to Christ doth send*
> *Where its best*
> *To be at rest*
> *Magnus Flett, born 1584, died 1616*

For some reason this inscription made all three of them double over with laughter; it seemed Flett was a common Orkney name; Fletts came popping up everywhere, not only Magnus but Thomas Flett, Cecil Flett, Jamesina Flett, Donaldina Flett; the Flett family were the undisputed kings and queens of the cemetery.

The rain showed no sign of abating, and after a minute Lew took the two women by the arm and led them across the street to a tea shop where they sat out the storm, keenly aware of each other.

"What kind of man was your father-in-law, Mrs. Flett?" Lewis posed this question in a social voice, while spreading butter on a floury scone.

"Well, I'm not quite sure."

"But you must have some kind of impression."

"An unhappy man. Aggrieved. His wife left him, you see."

"Aha!" Teasing. "One of those old-fashioned happy families."

"His three sons took their mother's part. They refused to see their father. They would have nothing to do with him."

"And this made him bitter?"

"It drove him back here." She swept a hand toward the window, taking in the drenched dark street, the black rain clouds. "When he was sixty-five years old. I can only think he must have been bitter."

"But you don't know for sure."

"Actually –"

"Yes?"

"Actually, I never met my father-in-law."

"I see." Clearly he was taken aback.

"We never met, no. And I've always felt sorry about that. That we never met in his lifetime. I've always thought, well –"

"What?"

"That we might have things" – she paused – "to say to each other."

"Not many women feel that way about their fathers-in-law."

"No, I suppose not."

"Magnus Flett was my great-grandfather," Victoria put in, wanting perhaps to share responsibility for the brokenness of families.

They drank their tea in silence. Then Lewis, determinedly bright, raised a celebratory tea cup and said, "Here's to the bones of the real Magnus Flett! We'll find him yet."

"You made a rhyme," said Victoria, who liked to see eagerness in others.

"Oh, well," Victoria's aunt said, her mouth smiling now, her chest full of heartbeats.

The next day the wind died down. The sun came on surprisingly strong, and tourists in shorts and T-shirts and summer dresses poured off the ferry and thronged the narrow streets of Stromness, eating ice-cream, buying postcards.

It was evening and the light still bright. Lewis and Victoria lingered over their shepherd's pie at the Grey Stones Hotel dining room and explained to Victoria's Aunt Daisy their reason for coming to Orkney. Lew pulled out a pencil and made a little sketch on his paper napkin, hastily executed, yet beautiful – or so it seemed to Victoria, who later folded the napkin carefully in two and pressed it in the back lining of her suitcase. The islands, Lew said, abounded with the fossil remains of small sea animals. But evidence of early plant life has been destroyed. The temperature of the earth was wrong, the plant structures too fragile. But back in Toronto, working with a set of computer-enhanced maps, the latest thing, he and Victoria had been investigating fossil patterns found in the north of Scotland, tracing a broad arc through the west of that country and up into Scandinavia – this arc, with just a little bending, passed through the outlying tip of Orkney's Mainland, persuading them that certain rock formations at Yesanby, a few miles north of Stromness, held promise. The rock was different here, harder, so much so that islanders had traditionally gone to this remote point of land in search of millstones, the rest of the Orkney rock being too soft to serve. Lewis mentioned the Rhynie chert, he mentioned Middle Old Red sandstone. He explained how he had applied to the Science Council of Canada for a travel grant, and how he had assembled his equipment and his research team, a team that consisted of himself and Victoria Flett. The two of them had twenty-one days to poke around and write up their notes before the funds ran out. Both of them brimmed with optimism; biology, Lewis argued, will always frustrate the attempt of specialists to systematize and regulate; the variables are too many; the earth is sometimes withholding, yes, but more frequently generous.

Victoria looked across the table and regarded her aunt, who appeared rested, serene, and flushed with the heat of a long day. Because of the fine weather she'd left her suit jacket upstairs in the room the two of them were sharing, and she was musing now about whether she should perhaps have a look in the local shops the following day, see if she could find a lightweight dress in her size. She'd slept soundly last night, solidly, which was just as well.

Victoria, gazing at her aunt, felt a lurch of love, and claimed for herself a share of her aunt's present contentment, her ease. She almost wished there were hardships she might save her from, gifts she might give her. Right now, right this minute, the little tongues of amity between Lewis and her aunt seemed beautiful to her, the beginning of something.

Lewis was telling her about the bicycles and backpacks he had rented so that he and Victoria could ride out to Yesanby the following morning and start their investigation. "We'll start digging for our little wonders," Lewis told her, "and leave you to find Magnus Flett."

"Did I hear you say Magnus Flett?" the proprietor of their hotel said, pausing by their table and pouring out their coffee.

The proprietor's name was Mr. Sinclair. He was a large, nobly built man, a lifelong bachelor with a clever face and a headful of fine gray hair which he was forever palming back from his forehead. How on earth had this person got into the hotel business, Victoria wondered – he should have been a movie actor with his graceful, his almost silvery way of setting down plates on a table and his sweet droll country voice. His hotel, which had only six bedrooms, was advertised as having "All Mod Cons," meaning some of the rooms were equipped with electric heaters. Mr. Sinclair in his neat gray overall, gliding up and down the carpeted stairs, was desk clerk, chambermaid, cook, server.

"Did I hear you say you were looking for Magnus Flett?" he said politely, leaning in his silvery way over the table. "Now, you will excuse me for interrupting, but I couldn't help overhearing you saying something or other about old Magnus Flett. Magnus Flett, why he's just next door, you know."

"Next door?"

"The Sycamore Manor. You must have walked right by it. It's where the old folk are, the ones as have no family that can keep them. When I was a lad there were sycamore trees in the back garden but they're gone now, of course. It was a private house before the Council took it over. That's where old Flett is. The famous Mr. Flett, I should say."

Victoria shook her head; she looked more comely tonight than she would have guessed. "Our Magnus Flett's dead," she said with a measure of solemnity. "He was born in 1862. We don't know when he died, but we're sure of when he was born because the date is on some legal documents my aunt has."

"That would be his nibs all right," Mr. Sinclair nodded, smiling. "That is if you believe he's the age he says he is, and I happen to be of one of them who takes the man's word on it. His picture's in the *Orcadian* every year on his birthday. This year they had the London papers up as well. The poor old lad was a hundred and fifteen years old, just think of that. Oh, not more than a month or so ago it was, a birthday party like you never saw. They had a cake big as this table here. Candles alight, a regular bonfire, course he slept right through it all. Why, Mr. Flett, he's the oldest man in the British Isles."

It was not his age alone that made old Magnus Flett famous. It was his prodigious memory.

In the summer of 1977, the year Victoria and her colleague, Lewis Roy, and her elderly Great-aunt Daisy visited the legendary Orkney Islands on their separate expeditions of discovery, Magnus Flett's reputation did indeed rest on those 115 years of his. This is a very great age. There is a woman in the Ukraine who is said to be 121, and a pair of brothers in Armenia whose ages are given, respectively, as 118 and 116 (with documents to support their claim). An Inuit woman living in the Anglican Church hostel at Rankin Inlet has sworn on a Bible that she is 112 years of age (she took up a cigarette habit at eighty-five, whisky at ninety). And then there is the undisputed champion of human antiques: Mr. Gee of Singapore, still ambulatory at 123, though only his wife (aged ninety-six) has actually clapped eyes on him in recent years. Proven or unproven, great old age is heartening to observe, and Magnus Flett with his remarkable span of years is a celebrity. He has been profiled in the British weeklies ("A Life in the Day of Magnus Flett," *The Sunday Times*, 16 March 1962, p. 54). And once, ten years ago, he appeared before the BBC television cameras, staring straight out at the audience and doing "his thing."

"His thing," much more so than his age, is what has made the man famous: his ability, that is, to recite the whole of *Jane Eyre* by heart, chapter by chapter, every sentence, every word. Mr. Sinclair describes this achievement to his visitors, his soft voice softened even further by awe.

An impossible feat, some people might say, people who are unfamiliar with the retentive qualities of the human brain. Probably these same people have never heard how certain devout individuals in long ago days memorized the complete New Testament. That even at the beginning of our own century it was not unusual to find quite ordinary mortals who had the Gospels by heart, though, later, Sunday School prizes were given out for such trifling accomplishments as the Beatitudes or the One Hundredth Psalm. Scholars have for years insisted that the Anglo-Saxon poem *Beowulf* was recited at banquets by a single performer who had no text to refer to. Daisy Goodwill Flett was told of his extraordinary achievement while a student at Long College for Women back in the twenties; during that same period of her life she herself committed the whole of *Tintern Abbey* to memory – not because her professor required her to, but because she felt a longing to take the oracular, rhythmic lines of William Wordsworth into her body.

Naturally, at the age of 115, Magnus Flett's memory has begun to fade, Mr. Sinclair acknowledges that. At the time of the television interview ten years ago he was able to recite only the first chapter of *Jane Eyre*, but this he did without once stumbling or hesitating. A year ago he could manage only the first page. And now, as Mr. Sinclair warns his North American visitors, the poor old fellow can handle only the opening lines of the opening paragraph.

The larger loneliness of our lives evolves from our unwillingness to spend ourselves, stir ourselves. We are always damping down our inner weather, permitting ourselves the comforts of postponement, of rehearsals. Why does young Victoria work so hard to keep old Magnus Flett out of her thoughts? And why does her Great-aunt Daisy, day after day, put off her visit to Sycamore Manor? Every evening she offers her niece excuses, saying she has been seeing the local sights, or occupied with shopping for a summer dress. The warm temperatures continue, a new Orkney record for the last week of June, and she claims she wants to make the most of this unprecedented weather. In her new cotton skirt and blouse (a solid burgundy shade) and her newly acquired walking shoes, she's braved the fields above Stromness, finding along the way heather, crowberry, various sedges and the beautiful, tiny Scottish primrose (*Primula scotica*) in all its pink profusion. "Love! tenderness! courage!" she murmurs to the tilted landscape, for no reason that she can think of. Mr. Sinclair, a connoisseur of the pastoral, accompanies her on some of her outings. After the hotel's midday meal has been served, after the washing-up is done, these two set out together in his smart little Ford Fiesta, visiting the churches and graveyards of neighboring villages, and one day they come across a tombstone whose family name has worn away, but whose date – 1675 – and brief inscription remain clearly visible: "Behold the end of life!" A single ringing declaration. (You would think this shout from the land of the dead would have unsettled Mrs. Flett, but instead she falls under its spell, as though she has seen a vision or heard a voice speaking through that exclamation point, announcing a fountain of radiance glimpsed at life's periphery.)

"Did you visit Magnus Flett?" Victoria asks each evening, returning sunburned and dusty from the rock beds of Yesanby.

"Tomorrow," her aunt promises. "Tomorrow I'll make arrangements."

The both know – even Lewis Roy knows, watching her, mute and patient with her tea cup raised – that she is preparing herself against disappointment.

Mrs. Flett is discovering that the Orkney greenness is deceptive. What looks like yards of fertile black earth is only a thin covering over beds of layered rock. Rock is what these islands are made of, light shelfy limestone, readily split into flakes and flags, and easily worked; it's everywhere. Each farm, it seems, has its own mini-quarry, and the tools of quarrying – hammer, point, and klurer – are part of every farmer's equipment. There being but little wood available, stone flags are used for roofs, for fences, for picnic tables and benches, for milestones and markers, bringing a smile to Mrs. Flett's face as she thinks of her grandchildren's favorite television show, *The Flintstones*. She imagines that the farmhouses she and Mr. Sinclair drive past are furnished with stone chairs and stone tables and even beds and dressers of stone. She recalls that her father-in-law, Magnus Flett, came to Canada at the age of eighteen or nineteen, already a master of his trade: stonecutting.

He worked in the Tyndall quarry until he was sixtyfive. A man of muscle and mechanical skills, a working man. By all accounts he had no softness to him. He spoke but little, according to his sons. Unyieldingness is the reputation he left behind. Narrowness. Stone.

He was literate; he could read the Bible or the mail order catalogue if needs be, but he was not a man who would ever have sat himself down to read a book. Mrs. Flett knows this without being told. No, it would not enter his head to read a book. Particularly not a novel. Not a novel by an Englishwoman named Charlotte Brontë. And never that jewel of English literature, *Jane Eyre*.

Impossible.

"Do you want me to go with you when you visit Magnus Flett?" her niece offers, with something like reluctance.

"If you like," Mr. Sinclair says to her, "I could accompany you when you call on Magnus Flett."

"Tomorrow," Mrs. Flett says. "Tomorrow."

But the next day she and Mr. Sinclair drove out to the Yesanby site where Lewis and Victoria were at work.

The end of the road had fallen into disrepair, and they were obliged to park the car at the East Bigging cross-road and walk half a mile over the moors to the rugged promontory. Victoria, seeing them approach, waved both her arms and called out an exuberant welcome, her cries blending with the squawks of seabirds and the roar of the waves coming in below.

The sun on the rocks was brilliant. And rising up at the edge of the shining, slippery stone terraces was the famous God's Gate which Victoria had described to her aunt, an immense natural archway through which every seventh or eighth wave came loudly crashing. (Fifty years earlier, two amateur photographers were said to have climbed into the aperture, and, before the eyes of their wives and children, been swept out to sea.)

It seemed to Mrs. Flett, blinking in the late afternoon sunlight, that she was all at once dwarfed by the huge-ness around her: the overwhelming height of the rock formation, the expanse and violence of the sea below, and the high wide-spreading desolate moorland; at the edge of her vision, outside the boom and wash of the sea winds, was Mr. Sinclair's parked car, no more than a speck on the horizon. Mr. Sinclair himself stood a few feet away, his large arms folded peacefully as wings across his broad chest, at home in his magisterial body. This lightness she felt! – her body suspended between the noise and the immensity of the world – what was it? She was unable for a minute to put a name to the gusty air blowing through her, softening her face into a smile, and then it came to her: happiness. She was happy.

Mrs. Flett's favorite niece, Victoria, and Lewis Roy, a man whose existence she had known nothing about two weeks ago, scrambled like insects on the plates of out-cropping rock, and scraped with their tiny tools at the surface of the hidden world, hoping for what? To find a microscopic tracing of buried life. Life turned to stone. To bitter minerals. Such a discovery, they had told her, would be enormous in its implications – it excited them just thinking about such enormity – but at the same time the proof of discovery could be held lightly in the palm of a hand, a small rock chip imprinted with the outline of a leaf. Or a primitive flower. A trace, even, of bacteria, fine as knitting, the coded dots of life.

So far, however, and with fewer than half a dozen days remaining, they had turned up nothing.

During the long dark nights in the Grey Stones Hotel, Victoria lies in Lewis Roy's arms.

She waits until her aunt is sleeping soundly, then rises, feels about in the dark for her slippers, and makes her way noiselessly down the narrow passage to Room 5, where Lewis lies, ready. There is an element of French farce in her nightly excursions, and Victoria values this theatrical frisson and adds it to the mound of her present happiness. The dim corridor, with its gleams and shadows, its antique chest, mirror, and grandfather clock, is softly carpeted, and its dimensions are not entirely lost to darkness since Mr. Sinclair has thoughtfully provided a rosy little nightlight for his guests' convenience. There is just enough light, in fact, for Victoria to make out the words on a pretty Victorian plate which is mounted on the wall next to the bathroom.

*Happiness
grows at our own
fireside and is
not to be picked
in strangers'
gardens*

Firesides! Gardens! Tip-toeing down the hall at two a.m. and pausing to read these words, she wants to snort with laughter.

Both she and Lewis believe the verse to be an admonition against the kind of rapture they have uncovered these last few days. Night after night, in the crisp white sheets of Mr. Sinclair's genteel establishment, they go deeper and deeper into that mystery, sleeping and waking, and bringing to life those parts of themselves they had thought stunted, disentitled. A year ago, even a month ago, each would have scorned the accidental convergence of island air, soft sunlight, long days – and the possibility of scientific miscalculation, even failure – convincing themselves that the rewards of erotic love were no more than a temporary recompense, a consolation for the poor in spirit.

She has said nothing to Aunt Daisy about her discovery, or about her plans for the future, knowing as she does her great-aunt's concern over her son Warren, his two divorces, and now Alice's bitter separation from her husband, Ben. Victoria suspects that Aunt Daisy – though how can she know this for sure? – might endorse the sentiments of the Victorian wall plate, believing that, all things considered, the gardens of strangers are more likely to bring harm than happiness.

*

"I should warn you," Mrs. Betty Holloway said, "he is completely bedridden. Incontinent naturally."

"Well, yes, I understand."

"Another thing, Mrs. Flett, he scarcely sees at all. Cataracts. Inoperable at his age."

"To be expected, I suppose."

"Surprisingly, he does have some hearing in one ear."

"Oh."

"But is completely deaf in the other. Has been for a long time."

"I see."

"He tires very easily."

"I won't stay long."

"You're a relative, you say?"

"Well, I'm not sure. I might be. On my husband's side."

"He has no family. Not around here at any rate. Sad, isn't it."

"Very."

"And, of course, when you get to his age, not that many do, well, you don't have a great many friends come visiting."

"Do you happen to know if Mr. Flett ever lived in Canada?"

"Canada? Well, I don't know now. It used to be lots of our young men would go out to Canada for a few years. Make their fortunes. There wasn't much opportunity here in those days."

"But about Mr. Flett. There must be records. Something written down."

"All we know is he was living up at Sandwick before he came here. Looking after himself. Living on his own. Growing a few vegetables, cutting his own turfs. Folk who knew him then said he was a bit of a hermit. Kept to himself. Very fond of reading."

"*Jane Eyre.*"

"Yes, to be sure, that's the one."

"But when he came here to live, he must have had some papers, some old letters perhaps."

"Not that I know of, no letters, no personal papers, if that's what you mean, birth certificates – no, nothing like that."

"A wedding ring, perhaps."

"I don't believe so, no. Of course men didn't used to wear wedding rings, now, did they? Well, things are different now."

"That's true."

"He did have one old photograph, all folded up under his clothes. We put it away for him."

"Do you think I could see it?"

"Well, seeing as you're family –"

"Oh, I'm not absolutely sure of that –"

"Now I've got that photograph here somewhere in his folder. It's a bunch of women, a sort of portrait, if I remember – ah yes, here it is."

"What a pity it was folded, the faces all cracked. Oh. They're lovely though, what I can make out. Oh."

"Yes, well, it was folded when he came in here. He must have folded it himself. We do our best to look after the personal effects of our patients."

"I didn't mean –"

"There's something written on the back."

"Oh, yes. It says . . . it says, 'The Ladies Rhythm and Movement Club.' But there's no date."

"Early in the century, I should think. From the looks of those dresses."

"A long time ago."

"Yes indeed. Well, shall I show you in to Mr. Flett's room?"

"Please."

The first thing she noticed was a milky film over his irises. And the white sheets, also the white coverlet that made him look as though he were wrapped in bandages.

Magnus, the wanderer, the suffering modern man – that was how she'd thought of him all these years. Romantically. And believing herself to be a wanderer too, with an orphan's heart and a wistful longing for refuge, for a door marked with her own name. And now, here was this barely breathing cadaver, all his old age depletions registered and paid for. A tissue of skin. A scaffold of bone; well, more like china than bone.

"It's Daisy," she said into his ear, unable to think of anything else. "Barker's wife."

A rustle from the cocoon of sheets.

"Your son Barker."

Nothing.

"You had a wife, Mr. Flett. Her name was Clarentine. Clarentine Barker Flett. Just nod your head if it's true."

No response.

"Please." She waited, feeling foolish, and worrying that she might cause his heart to stop. "Just blink your eyes, Mr. Flett. Blink your eyes if Clarentine Barker was your wife."

A few seconds passed – she let them pass – and then he opened his mouth, which was not a mouth at all but a puckered hole without lips or teeth. She had to lean forward to hear what he said: "There was no possibility" – he paused here – "of taking a walk that day." Another pause. "We had been wandering, indeed, in the leafless shrubbery –" He stopped.

"Why, that's just wonderful, Mr. Flett," she said, as though praising a young child, "But can you remember – can you tell me – if you lived in Canada at one time? If you had a wife named Clarentine?" She said again, louder. "Clarentine."

His eyelids came down. "There was no possibility of taking a walk."

"Your wife, Mr. Flett. Clarentine."

"Clarentine," he said. This word, this name, came out in the form of an exhalation, whistling, sour.

"Yes," she said, encouraged. "And your son, Barker."

The terrible hole of a mouth moved again: "Bark." The word whispered its way, leaking around the edge of sound.

"And I'm Daisy," she said.

He seemed to have stopped breathing. The silence was terrible.

"Daisy Goodwill," she said loudly into his good ear.

"Day-zee." He sighed it out, the tops of the consonants, at least the wind of vowels. He pronounced it, she could tell, obediently, mechanically. An echo – how could it be anything else? – but something in it satisfied her. She felt moved to grope under the sheet and reach for his hand, but feared what she might find, some unimaginable decay. Instead she pressed lightly on the coverlet, perceiving the substantiality of tethered bones and withered flesh. A faint shuddering. The rising scent of decomposition.

"I've come to visit you," she said, despising the merry, social tone she took. "And I've finally found you."

She would like to have said the word "father," testing it, but a stiff wave of selfconsciousness intervened.

She believes, though, what she sees in front of her. She believes the evidence of her eyes, her ears, her intuition, that mythical female organ. Naturally it will take some time for her to absorb all she's discovered. A conscious revisioning will be required of her: accommodation, adjustment. Certain stray elements which are anomalous in nature, even irrational, will have to be tapped in with a jeweler's hammer. Reworked. Propped up with guesswork. Balanced. Defended. But she's willing, and isn't that what counts? Willingness has been a long time gathering for Daisy Goodwill Flett.

The old man drifts into sleep, and she slips out of the room, feeling weakened, emptied out, light as a spirit, and seems for a few minutes to hold in her arms that weightlessness, that fragrance that means her life. Oh, she is young and strong again. Look at the way she walks freely out the door and down the narrow stone street of Stromness, tossing her hair in the fine light.

CHAPTER NINE

Illness and Decline, 1985

EIGHTY-YEAR-OLD Grandma Flett of Sarasota, Florida, is sick; every last cell of her body, it seems, has been driven into illness.

When she collapsed a month ago, a heart attack while watering the row of miniature geraniums on the south side of her balcony, she went down hard on the concrete paving and broke both her knees. Luckily Marian McHenry, whose balcony is separated from Mrs. Flett's by a flimsy bit of lattice-work, heard her cry out, and summoned an ambulance.

A double bypass was performed two days later at Sarasota Memorial Hospital (the possibility of such an operation had been discussed by Mrs. Flett's cardiologist more than a year earlier, but for various reasons postponed). A week after the surgery, just as she was beginning to come around nicely, Grandma Flett suffered what appeared to be partial kidney failure, and one of her kidneys, the left, was removed and found to be cancerous. "But at least we got the goldarn thing out sweet and clean," her urologist said, in the muddied southern tones that Mrs. Flett's family find so alarming.

Suddenly her body is all that matters. How it's let her down. And how fundamentally lonely it is to live inside a body year after year and carry it always in a forward direction, and how there is never any relief from the weight of it, even when sleeping, even when joined, briefly, to the body of another. An x-ray of her left knee reminds her just how insubstantial she is, has always been – an envelope of flesh, glassine. She lives now in the wide-open arena of pain, surrounded by row on row of spectators. The nights are endless, the morning sun a severity. Those hospital mornings! A thermometer planted between her lips, her blood pressure roughly taken, and a cardiac monitor rolled into her room, heavy, masculine, with dials like a human face, ready to condemn her vascular weakness. Her ancient feet poking out at the side of the sheet have an oyster-like translucence and are always cold, though, oddly, no one notices this, no one says, "Why is it your feet are so cold, Mrs. Flett?" Urine passes from her body through a catheter stuck between her legs and disappears along with other cloudy fluids into the unknown. Into the universe. She spits into a basin, makes obscene gurgling sounds when brushing her strong old teeth, trying to remember a time when her body had been sealed and private.

After a few days the drainage tube is removed from her nose and the intravenous needle from her arm, and she is told – with a congratulatory salute – that she has earned the right once again to partake of food and liquids. "Some lemonade'll do you good, sweetie-pie," the juice girl yells into her ear. "A person can never, never get enough fluids." This girl with her rolling cart of apple juice, milk, iced tea, and lukewarm cocoa is eighteen years old, black-faced, purple-lipped, with a high, tight, one-note laugh: oppressive.

In the early morning hours Mrs. Flett experiences nightmares that are uniquely invasive, reaching all the way to her heart's core, and their subject, which she can never recollect afterward, is violent. "It's just the drugs," her doctors tell her, "a common complaint."

In her much milder daytime dreams she drifts through scenes shabby like old backyards, dusty, with strewn trash in the flowerbeds and under piles of dead shrubbery, past streets where white-faced men and women are watering lawns choked with plantain, dandelions, and creeping charlie, lawns that because of ignorance and insufficient money are doomed never to flourish.

In the pleat of consciousness that falls between sleeping and waking she is capable of marching straight into the machinery of invention. Sketching vivid scenery. Laying out conversations, arguments. Certain phrases, remembered and invented, rattle in her afflicted head, taunting her with their rhythms and abraded meaning.

"The chaplain's here to see you, sweetie-pie."

"What?" Out of a spiral of thin-colored sleep.

"The chaplain, Mrs. Flett. Y'all feel like talking to the chaplain?"

"Who?"

Louder this time. "The chaplain. Reverend Rick. You remember Reverend Rick."

"No."

"Hey, you do so. You had yourself a real nice prayer together just yesterday. And some Bible verses."

"No."

"Hey, Mrs. Flett, don't give me that stuff – you remember the chaplain, sure you do."

"No."

"No what?"

"No, I don't want to see him. Not today."

She has a private room at the end of the hall with a wide uncurtained window. In the days following her surgery she lies, wretchedly, in bed and during her brief waking moments stares out at the pale concrete Florida architecture, pink, green, lavender, like frosted petits fours shaped by a doughy hand and set out to stiffen and dry. The sun shines down on dented station wagons, glints on the heads of young mothers cooing at their children and banging car doors, and boils into whiteness the cracked cement fence that surrounds the parking lot. Doctors park their Mercedes and Lincolns in a reserved section close to the hospital doors, and the tops of these cars gleam with the hard brilliance of cheap candy, a rainbow of hues.

"No, I won't see the chaplain today," she says with dignity, with what she believes is dignity.

"If that's what you want, so okay." Shrugging.

"That's what I want."

"It's up to you."

"I know."

"It does a world of good, though, the words of Jesus, the sweetest words there are in this crazy mixed-up world of ours."

"I'm too tired today."

"It'd perk you up. Hey, I see it happen every day, that's the honest truth. 'The Lord is my shepherd, I shall not want.' The best medicine there is and it's free for the taking."

"No, really, I don't think –"

"Whad'ya know, here's Reverend Rick now. How ya doin', Reverend? Why don'ya come on in for a minute or two. Cheer up our patient here, who's all down in the dumps."

"Please, I'm –"

"So – feeling up to a little chat, Mrs. Flett?"

"Well, I –"

"I could always come back tomorrow."

"Well –"

"I'll just stay a minute. Sure wouldn't want to tire you out."

"Oh, no."

"Pardon? What's that you say, Mrs. Flett?"

"Please sit down. Make yourself –"

"Afraid I didn't quite hear –"

"Make yourself, make yourself" – here Grandma Flett comes to a halt, pushes her tongue across the ridge of her lower teeth, panics briefly, and then, thank goodness, finds the right word – "comfortable."

"I'll just pull up a chair, Mrs. Flett, if that's okay with you."

"So good of you to come."

God, the Son and the Holy Ghost; suddenly they're here in Grandma Flett's hospital room, ranged along the wall, a trio of paintings on velvet, dark, gilt-edged, their tender mouths unsmiling, but ready to speak of abiding love. Not a sparrow shall fall but they – what is it they do, these three? What do they actually do? I used to know, but now at the age of eighty I've forgotten. It seems too late, somehow, to ask, and it doesn't seem likely that young Reverend Rick will put forth an explanation. The cleansing of sins, redemption. And somewhere, a long way back, the blood of a lamb. Something barbarous. A wooded hillside. Spoiled.

"Afraid I didn't quite catch what you said, Mrs. Flett."

"I said, it's so good of you to come."

Is Mrs. Flett shouting?

No, it only seems that way; she's really whispering, poor thing. From her trough of sheets. From her pain and bewilderment. Her tubes and wires. Her constricted eighty-year-old throat. The drugs. The dreams. Her feet, so chilly and damp, so exposed, ignored, and doomed. The pastel scenery outside her expensive window, the car doors slamming in the parking lot, Jesus and God and the Holy Ghost peering down on her in their clubby, mannish way, knowing everything, seeing all, but not caring one way or the other, when you come right down to it, about the hurts and alarms of her body – at this time in her life. Now. This minute. Go away, please just go away.

"It's so good of you to come."

Did you hear that, the exquisite manners this elderly person possesses? You don't encounter that kind of old-fashioned courtesy often these days. And when you think it's only two weeks since her bypass, six days since a kidney was seized from her body. And her knees, her poor smashed knees. Amazing, considering all this, that she can remember the appropriate phrase, amazing and also chilling, the persevering strictures of social discourse.

Never mind, it means nothing; it's only Mrs. Flett going through the motions of being Mrs. Flett.

Grandma Flett's room is filled with cards and flowers. The juice girl – it seems her name is Jubilee – makes a raucous joke of this abundance, shrieking disbelief, pretending horror – "Not a-noth-ah bouquet! I swear, Mrs. Flett! Now, you tell me, how'm I supposed to find room to set down another bouquet in this here jungle you got?"

Mrs. Flett's son, Warren, and his new wife, Peggy, have sent an inflatable giraffe, five feet tall, with curling vinyl eyelashes and a mouthful of soft teeth – it stands by the window, and wobbles slightly whenever a breeze passes through. A conversation piece, Mrs. Flett thinks, a little puzzled, wondering if giraffes hold special significance for the elderly, the infirm – or does it gesture toward some forgotten family joke? Her Oregon grand-daughters – Rain, Beth, Lissa, and Jilly – have pooled their babysitting money and sent Grandma Flett a com-plicated battery-operated game called Self-Bridge. The thought of their generosity, their sacrifice, brings tears into her throat, though, in fact, she never once takes the mechanism from its box, never collects quite enough energy to read the tightly printed directions.

And at five o'clock every afternoon Grandma Flett receives an overseas phone call from her daughter, Alice, in Hampstead, England (ten p.m., Greenwich time). Alice used to joke that her mother, when the time came, would lift a hand gaily on her way out, rather like Queen Elizabeth in a motorcade, hatted, gloved, bidding fare-well to everything, to life – this mystery, this little enterprise. But now she understands her picture will have to be reordered. Her mother is sick, helpless, and Alice, speaking on the transatlantic line, adopts a clear, quiet, unrushed voice, as though she were phoning from across the street, as though she were someone in a television drama.

"I've spoken to the doctor, Mother. He says you're doing wonderfully well. He says you have the most remarkable strength, and if you only had, you know, just a little more patience. At the rate you're going you'll be able to go home in a couple of weeks, but why push it when you're getting such wonderful care and attention, and luckily Blue Cross covers almost everything."

Alice also phones her sister Joan in Portland, Oregon, and says, plunging right in: "She can't possibly go home, the doctor says it's impossible. How would she manage? She's helpless."

To her brother Warren in New York she says, the telephone wires taut: "I've talked to the orthopedic surgeon and he says she'll never be able to walk again, not without a walker, and maybe not even that. I mean, Christ, we have to face it, this is the beginning of the end."

All three of Mrs. Flett's children feel guilty that they are not at their mother's bedside. Alice is planning to fly over at the end of her teaching term, another month. Warren's new wife has recently given birth to a Down's syndrome child – christened Emma – and he feels, rightly, that he can't possibly abandon his family at a time like this, not even for a few days. Joan has actually made one quick trip – Portland, Chicago, Tampa, and back – but she has, after all, four teenaged daughters to look after and a husband who is prone to extra-marital involvements. Mrs. Flett's niece, Victoria, writes a witty little

note every second day, but for the moment her professional responsibilities, as well as her husband, Lewis,
and the twins, keep her in Toronto. When Grandma
Flett thinks of her scattered family, her children, her
grandchildren, her grandniece, she is unable to form
images in her mind of their separate and particular faces.
The young girl, Jubilee, is more real to her now. And Dr.
Aaronfeld and Dr. Scott on their daily rounds, their
jokes, their loud, hearty, hospital laughter. And, in his
way, Reverend Rick. And faithful Marian McHenry who
has not missed a single evening's visit, never mind that all
she can talk about are her relations back in Cleveland.
And the Flowers! Where would she be without the
Flowers, who come by cab every two or three days, and
what a time they all have then!

Even when Mrs. Flett still had the drainage tube in her
nose, when she could scarcely lift her head from the
pillow, the Flowers arrived for a round of bridge by her
bedside. Just a couple of hands that first day, then
gradually increasing. You'd hardly think it possible that
Grandma Flett could concentrate on hearts and spades,
points and tricks, trumps and cross-trumps at a time like
this, but she can, she does; they all do. Lily, Myrtle, and
Glad are their names; Glad, of course, is really Gladys,
not Gladiola, but she considers herself a full-fledged
Flower nevertheless. The four of them live on various
floors of Bayside Towers, where Mrs. Flett has had her
condo all these years, and it was here, in the basement
card room, that the foursome first got together. (This
would be in the late seventies, after Mrs. Flett lost her
two dearest friends, Beans dying so suddenly, Fraidy
Hoyt going senile; a terrible time.) The Flowers get on

like a house afire, like Gangbusters. Other people at the Bayside envy their relaxed good nature, their shrugging conviviality, and each of the Flowers is acutely aware of this envy, and, in their old age, surprised and gratified by it. At last: a kind of schoolgirl popularity. Unearned, but then, isn't that the way with popularity? The four Flowers are fortunate in their mutual attachment and they recognize their luck. Lily's from Georgia, Glad from New Hampshire, the breezy-talking Myrtle from Michigan – different worlds, you might say, and yet their lives chime a similar tune. Just look at them: four old white women. Like Mrs. Daisy Flett, they are widows; they are, all of them, comfortably well off; they have aspired to no profession other than motherhood, wife-hood; they love a good laugh; there is something filigreed and droll about the way they're always on the cusp of laughter. On Sundays they go to church services at First Presbyterian and, from there, to an all-you-can-eat brunch at The Shellseekers (a sign over the cash register says "Help Stomp Out Home Cooking"); and every single afternoon, Monday to Saturday between the hours of two and four-thirty, they play bridge in the card room at Bayside Towers, invariably occupying the round corner table which is positioned well away from the noisy blast and chill of the air conditioner. This is the Flowers' table and no one else's. "How're the Flowers blooming today?" other Bayside residents call out by way of greetings.

"My husband used to say that girls with flower names fade fast." It was Myrtle who said this one day, out of the blue, and for some reason it made them all go weak with

laughter. Now, when asked how the Flowers are blooming, one of them will be sure to call back, cheerfully:
"Fading fast," and one of the others will add, with a
calypso bounce, "but holding firm." It's part of their
ritual, one of many. They have a joke, for instance, about
a beige cardigan Glad's been knitting for the last ten
years. And another joke about Mr. Jellicoe on the sixth
floor who cradles his crotch when he thinks no one's
looking. And about Mrs. Bolt who looks after the library
corner and hoards the new large-print books for herself.
And Marian McHenry and her everlasting nieces and
nephews up in Cleveland. And about the inevitability
and sinfulness of the pecan pie at The Shellseekers.
They celebrate each other's birthdays – with a bakery
cake and a glass of California wine – and on these
occasions one or other of the Flowers will be sure to say:
"Well, here's to another year and let's hope it's above
ground."

This, to tell the truth, is the joke they relish above all
others, a joke that shocks their visiting families, but that
rolls off their own tongues with invigorating freshness,
with a fine trill of mockery – a joke, when you come right
down to it, about their own deaths. Their laughter at
these moments wizens into a cackle. It's already been
decided that when one of them "hangs up her hat" or
"kicks the bucket" or "goes over the wall" or "trades in
her ashes" or "hops the twig" or "joins the choir
invisible" – that then, given a decent week or two for
mourning, the surviving three will invite the unspeakable
Iris Jackman (third floor, west wing) to fill in at the round
table, even though Iris has the worst case of B.O. in

captivity and is so dumb she can't tell a one-club hand from a grand slam.

A secret rises up in Grandma Flett's body, gathering neatly at her wrist bone where the light strikes the white plastic of the hospital bracelet, which reads: Daisy Goodwill.

That's all – just Daisy Goodwill. Someone in Admissions bungled, abbreviating her name, cutting off the Flett and leaving the old name – her maiden name – hanging in space, naked as a tulip. Fortunately this error does not appear on her hospital chart and has so far gone undiscovered by the staff and by Mrs. Flett's many visitors. A secret known only to her.

She cherishes it. More and more she thinks of it as the outward sign of her soul.

Not that she's ever paid much attention to her soul; in her long life she's been far too preoccupied for metaphysics – her husband, her children, the many things a woman has to do – and shyly embarrassed about the carpenter from Nazareth, unwilling to look him in the eye or call him by his first name, knowing she would be powerless to draw him into an interesting conversation, worrying how in two minutes flat he would be on to the cramping poverty of her mind. Mrs. Flett, who attended Sunday School as a child and later church, has never been able to shake the notion that these activities are a kind of children's slide show, wholesome and uplifting, but not to be taken seriously – though you did have to put on a hat and fix your face in a serious gaze for the required hour or so as you drifted off into little reveries about whether or not you had enough leftover roast beef to make a nice hash for supper, which you could serve with that chili sauce you'd made last fall, there were still two or three jars left on the pantry shelf, at least there were last time you looked. Committees and bazaars, weddings and baptisms, yes, yes, but never for Mrs. Flett the queasy hills and valleys of guilt and salvation. The literal-minded Mrs. Flett has never thought deeply about such matters, and why should she? The Czecho-slovakian crèche she sets up at Christmas does not for her represent the Holy Family, it *is* the Holy Family – miniature wooden figures, nicely carved in a stiff folk-loric way and brightly painted, though the baby in the manger is little more than a polished clothes peg. Jesu, Joy of Man's Desiring. It was all rather baffling, but not in the least troubling.

Do people speak of such things? She isn't sure.

But then Reverend Rick commenced his visits in the early days after her surgery and began to mention, cautiously at first, then with amplified feeling, the exist-ence of her soul, the state of her soul, the radiance of her soul, et cetera, et cetera, and now, in her eighty-first year, the rebirth of her soul through the grace of Jesus Christ, our Lord and Savior. Needless to say, Mrs. Flett doesn't mention to Reverend Rick the fact that her soul's com-pacted essence is embraced by those two words on her hospital bracelet: Daisy Goodwill.

And behind that name, but closely attached to it, lies something else, something nameless. Something whose form she sees only when she turns her head quickly to the side or perceives in the rhythm of her outgoing breath. These glimpses arrive usually in the early morning hours, taking her by surprise. She has almost forgotten the small primal piece of herself that came unshaped into the world, innocent of the least thought, on whose surface, in fact, no thought had ever shone. Nevertheless (it can't be helped) whatever comes later, even the richest of our experiences, we put before the judgment of that little squeaking bit of original matter. Or maybe it's not matter at all, but something else. Something holy. Torn from God's great forehead.

"I'm still in here," she thinks, rocking herself to consciousness in the lonely, air-conditioned, rubber-smelling discomfort of the hospital, "still here."

"She's a real honey," Jubilee says to anyone who happens to be around. "Not like some on this floor I could mention."

"A fighter," Mrs. Dorre, the head nurse says. "A fighter, but not a complainer, thank God."

"A sweetheart, a pet," says Dr. Scott.

"A real lady," says the physiotherapist, Russell Latterby, "of the old-fashioned school."

Which is why Mrs. Flett forgets about the existence of Daisy Goodwill from moment to moment, even from day to day, and about that even earlier tuber-like state that preceded Daisy Goodwill; she's kept so busy during her hospital stay being an old sweetie-pie, a fighter, a real lady, a non-complainer, brave about the urinary infections that beset her, stoic on the telephone with her children, taking an interest in young Jubilee's love affairs, going coquettish with Mr. Latterby, and being

endlessly, valiantly protective of Reverend Rick's sensibilities, which, to tell the truth, are disturbingly ambi-
valent. "She's a wonder," says her daughter, Alice,
arriving from England in time to help her mother move
out of Sarasota Memorial and into the Canary Palms
Convalescent Home, "she's a real inspiration."

Inspiration, Alice says, but she doesn't mean it. She
means more like the opposite of inspiration.

Alice is a strong, handsome woman in her mid-forties
who has thought very little about life's diminution – not
until a moment ago, in fact, when she happened to look
into the drawer of her mother's bedside table at Canary
Palms and saw, jumbled there, a toothbrush, toothpaste,
a comb, a notebook, a ring of keys, some hand cream, a
box of Kleenex, a small velvet jewelry box – all Mrs.
Barker Flett's possessions accommodated now by the
modest dimensions of a little steel drawer. That three-
story house in Ottawa has been emptied out, and so has
the commodious Florida condo. How is it possible, so
much shrinkage? Alice feels her heart squeeze at the
thought and gives an involuntary cry.

"What is it, Alice?"

"Nothing, Mother, nothing."

"I thought I heard –"

"Shhhhh. Try to get a little rest."

"All I've been doing is resting."

"That's what convalescence is – rest. Isn't that what
the doctor said?"

"Him!"

"He's very highly thought of. Dr. Scott says he's the
best there is."

"Did you tell the nurse about the apple juice?"

"I told her you thought it had gone off, but she said it was fine. It's just a different brand than the hospital uses."

"It tastes like concentrate."

"It probably is concentrate."

"It's not even cold. It's been left out."

"I'll talk to her again."

"And the gravy."

"What about the gravy."

"There isn't any, that's what's the matter. The meat comes dry on the plate."

"People don't make gravy any more, Mother. Gravy was over in 1974."

"What did you say?"

"Nothing. Just a joke."

"'Yolk, yolk,' you used to say. You and Joanie, clucking like chickens."

"Did we?"

"There's nothing to see from this window."

"Those trees? That lovely garden?"

"I liked the hospital better."

"I know."

"I miss Jubilee."

"Oh, God, yes."

"And the Flowers. Glad, Lily –"

"It's so far for them to come."

"I'm not myself here."

"You will be. You'll adjust in a few days."

"I'm not myself."

"You and me both."

"What's that? I can't hear with all that racket in the hall, that woman screaming."

"I said, I'm not myself either."

Alice has officially adopted her mother's maiden name; it appears now on her passport: Alice Goodwill. Her ex-husband's name, Downing, was buried some years ago in a solicitor's office in London, although their three grown children, Benjamin, Judy, and Rachel, retain it. And for Alice the name Flett was symbolically buried two years ago with the publication of her fifth book which received unfavorable reviews everywhere: "Alice Flett's first novel should be a warning to all academics who aspire toward literary creativity." "Posturing." "Donnish." "Didactic." "Cold porridge on a paper plate."

What was she to do? What *could* she do? She went to court and changed her name. Even as a girl Alice had complained about the name Flett, which suffered, she felt, from severe brevity; Flett was a dust mote, a speck on the wall, standing for nothing, while Goodwill rang rhythmically on the ear and sent out agreeable metaphoric waves, though her mother swears she has never thought of the name as being allusive. Alice is discouraged at the moment (that damned novel), but hopeful about the future. Or she was until she arrived in Florida and saw how changed her mother was. Thin, pale. Crumpled.

On the plane coming over she had invented rich, thrilling dialogues for the two of them.

"Have you been happy in your life?" she'd planned to ask her mother. She pictured herself seated by the bedside, the sheet folded back in a neat fan, her mother's hand in hers, the light from the window dim, churchy.

"Have you found fulfillment?" – whatever the hell fulfillment is. "Have you had moments of genuine ecstasy? Has it been worth it? Have you ever looked at, say, a picture or a great building or read a paragraph in a book and felt the world suddenly expand and, at the same instant, contract and harden into a kernel of perfect purity? Do you know what I mean? Everything suddenly fits, everything's in its place. Like in our Ottawa garden, that kind of thing. Has it been enough, your life, I mean? Are you ready for –? Are you frightened? Are you in there? What can I do?"

Instead they speak of apple juice, gravy, screams in the corridor, the doctor, who is Jamaican – this Jamaican business they don't actually mention.

When Alice reaches for her mother's hand she is appalled by its translucence. She can't help staring. Knuckles of pearl. Already dead. Mineralized. She reminds herself that what falls into most people's lives becomes a duty they imagine: to be good, to be faithful to the idea of being good. A good daughter. A good mother. Endlessly, heroically patient. These enlargements of the self can be terrifying.

"Just tell me how I'm supposed to live my life."

"What did you say, Alice?"

"Nothing. Go to sleep."

"It's only nine o'clock."

"The light's fading."

"It's the curtains, you've closed the curtains."

"No, look. The curtains are open. Look."

Grandma Flett has good days, of course. Days when she puts on her glasses and reads the newspaper straight through. Days when she is praised by the staff for her extraordinary alertness. A nurse describes her, in her hearing, as being "feisty," a word Mrs. Flett doesn't recognize. "It means tough," Alice tells her. "At least, I think so."

"I've never thought of myself as being tough."

"It's meant as praise."

"I'm not really tough."

"You're an old softie."

"No."

"No?"

"Don't call me that. It reminds me of those soft-centered chocolates your father used to bring home from his trips. I could never bear them, biting into them."

"I'm sorry." Alice has heard about the soft-centered chocolates before. Many times before.

"Nougat. Butter creams. And those other ones."

"Turkish delight."

"They make me feel sick. Just thinking of them."

"Don't think of them." Alice shuts her eyes, feeling sick herself: love's faked ever-afterness.

"He traveled a lot. I don't know if you remember, you were so young. Always going off. Montreal, Toronto."

"I know. I do remember."

"I could never understand what those trips were for."

"Meetings."

"Never understood just why they were necessary. I asked, of course, I took an interest, or at least I tried to. Women back then were encouraged to take an interest in their husbands' careers – but it was never clear to me. Not clear. Just what those meetings were about, what they were for."

"Administrative blather probably."

"It worried me. Bothered me, I should say."

"Don't think about it now."

"He'd bring a two-pound box sometimes. Oh, dear. Not that I ever let on I didn't like them. I used to give them to Mr. Mannerly. You remember Mr. Mannerly, Alice. He helped out in the garden. With the heavy work."

"Of course I remember Mr. Mannerly." Alice knows that now her mother is about to remind her how Mr. Mannerly's wife died of diabetes, how their son, Angus, went into politics.

"His poor wife died young. It was sugar diabetes, they couldn't do much about it in those days." Whispering. "I don't suppose she ever ate any of the chocolates, at least I hope she didn't. Their son Angus, he couldn't have been more than fifteen or sixteen when his mother went. Sixteen, I think. And he's done so well. Serving his third term, if I'm not mistaken. I used to see him mentioned in the papers. Angus Mannerly, a wonderful name for a politician, I always thought."

"It's a lovely name." Living so long in England has given Alice the right to use the word "lovely," and she uses it a lot.

"I'm glad you're here, Alice. I appreciate you being here. I don't mean to sound so out of sorts."

"You're not. You're –"

"It's all right, you don't have to say anything."

"I just meant –"

"Really, dear, I mean it, you don't have to say anything."

"All right."

"What was that word again? What the nurse said?"

"Feisty."

"It sounds like slang. Is it in the dictionary?"

"I don't think so. It could be."

"It sounds so terribly – I can't think of the word, it's on the tip of my tongue, it sounds –"

"Nasty?"

"No. More like superior."

"Condescending?"

"Yes. That's it. Condescending."

"You're right, you know. It is condescending. It's reductive. Insolent, as a matter of fact."

"Yes."

"We pretend to admire feistiness in others," Alice muses, "but we'd hate like hell to be feisty ourselves. To have someone call us that."

"It's got a bad smell."

"A bad what?"

"Overripe. Like strawberries past their prime."

"Exactly."

"He had a very long back, your father. I think that's why he never learned to dance."

"Dancing's not for everyone."

"I'm glad you're here, Alice."

"I'm glad to be here."

"What did you say?"

"I said, I'm glad to be here."

"Forgive me, darling Alice, if I don't believe you."

(Does Grandma Flett actually say this last aloud? She's not sure. She's lost track of what's real and what isn't, and so, at this age, have I.)

*

When we say a thing or an event is real, never mind how suspect it sounds, we honor it. But when a thing is made up – regardless of how true and just it seems – we turn up our noses. That's the age we live in. The documentary age. As if we can never, never get enough facts. We put on the television set and what we hear is the life cycles of birds. The replaying of wars. Interviews with mass murderers. And the newspapers know nothing else.

A Canadian journalist named Pinky Fulham was killed when a soft drinks vending machine overturned, crushing him. Apparently he had been rocking it back and forth, trying to dislodge a stuck quarter. Years ago Pinky Fulham did Mrs. Daisy Flett a grave injury, and so when she hears about his death she can't very well pretend to any great sorrow.

"Good God," her daughter, Alice, said, "how did you hear about this?"

"Someone told me," Grandma Flett said mysteriously. "Or maybe it was in the paper."

"Really? That's incredible."

"Actually eleven North Americans per year are killed by overturned vending machines. It was in the newspaper. I remember reading about it not long ago. Yesterday, I think. Or maybe it was this morning."

"And Pinky Fulham was one of them."

"So it seems."

"Incredible."

"I suppose it is."

Since her heart attack everything takes her by surprise, but nothing more so than her willingness to let it, as though a new sense of her own hollowness has made her a volunteer for replacement. Her body's dead planet with its atoms and molecules and lumps of matter is blooming all of a sudden with headlines, nightmares, greeting cards, medicinal bitterness, crashes in the night, footsteps in the corridor, the odors of her own breath and blood, someone near her door humming a tune she comes close to recognizing.

A parcel arrives for Grandma Flett. A bedjacket from her granddaughter, Judy, in England.

Oh dear, dear! – you know you're sick when someone sends you a bedjacket instead of bath powder or a nice travel book. A bedjacket is almost as antiquated as a bustle or a dress shield. A bedjacket speaks of desperation, and what it says is: toodle-oo. Nevertheless, old Mrs. Flett understands that her granddaughter has gone to a good deal of trouble to find this bedjacket. A bedjacket, these days, is a hard-to-find item. Major department stores might stock a mere half-dozen or so, if at all, and the sales clerks, women in their forties or fifties, look up baffled when you lean over the counter and say, "I'm afraid I can't seem to find where the bedjackets are located."

Where are bedjackets manufactured? New York? San Francisco? Maybe some little town in the middle of Iowa has cornered the market: the bedjacket capital of the nation. Of the world. But who designs this curious apparel? The lace borders, the little quilted sleeves, the grosgrain ribbons that tie under your chin? Maybe no one designs them. Maybe they simply multiply like dandelion cotton on the back shelves of lingerie factories. Another thing – why and when should a person wear a bedjacket? Is a bedjacket a private or public garment? Do you sleep in it, or take it off before retiring? Does it come with an instructions manual?

"You seem a thousand miles away, Mother."

"I was just thinking how sweet of Judy to remember me."

"She adores you, you know."

"I've never owned a bedjacket before."

"You look lovely in it. Wait till Dr. Riccia sees you. He'll be flowing with compliments."

"That man."

"He's not so bad. Come on, now. Those eyelashes, don't tell me you haven't noticed his eyelashes? He's really a perfectly lovely man. Admit it, now."

"Well."

"Well water! Personally, I find him ravishing. And, secretly, I think you do too."

"Hmmmm."

Alice does not find Reverend Rick ravishing; she knows the type. She greets him coldly, almost rudely when he turns up one day at Canary Palms, and then she makes a point of disappearing, leaving him alone to chat with her mother.

Mrs. Flett understands, without being told, that Alice wants only to protect her from evangelical coercion, from this room-to-room peddler of guilt-wrapped wares. Alice, from her middle-age perspective, believes her mother to have a soul already spotless – spotless enough anyway – and is outraged to see the spectre of sin visited upon one so old and ill and vulnerable.

However, the conversation between Mrs. Flett and Reverend Rick today takes a sharp turn away from elderly souls and the dream of redemption.

"I'm gay, you see," Reverend Rick tells Mrs. Flett. "Homosexual. I didn't know it when I studied for the ministry but then, well, I discovered my true orientation. For a long time I stayed, you know, in the closet. Then one or two people knew, then, gradually, half a dozen, now almost everyone knows – except for my mother. That's my problem. Do I tell her or not? And I was wondering, you're about the same age as my mom. Well, actually my mom is only about sixty, but for some reason you remind me of her. I don't know what to do. She keeps asking me when I'm going to find a nice girl and settle down. It's got so I hate to go home, I just know she's going to ask me."

There's a part of Mrs. Flett that longs to close her eyes at this moment and drift into sleep. And she knows perfectly well she could get away with it; her age gives her the privilege.

This is too bothersome. Too painful.

She feels a tearing sound behind her eyes, and understands that she is flattered by this confidence and also resentful. For one thing, it wounds her to be put, thoughtlessly, into the same box with Reverend Rick's mother, who is a woman she senses she might not like. As a matter of fact, she does not really like Reverend Rick, has never liked him; there's something greedy about his zeal, and then there are his slumped shoulders and his shirt collars which look oddly chewed. On the other hand, this young man has driven all the way across town, all the way out to Canary Palms – and on a murderously hot day – in order to consult with her, to seek her wisdom. This has not happened often in Mrs. Flett's life. Never, in fact. It almost certainly will not happen again.

"Have you tried," she says at last, "not being gay."

"What?" He shakes a dangling lock of hair out of his eyes.

"You know. Finding yourself a girlfriend and seeing if – well, you might surprise yourself, you may find that you really like having a girlfriend – what I mean is, it's possible you might change your attitude."

"Being gay, Mrs. Flett, is not a question of attitude."

She has offended him. Without turning her head and looking directly at him, she can tell that his whole body has stiffened. This she cannot bear. To be the cause of injury. Her greatest weakness – she's always known this – is her fear of giving injury, any more, that is, than she's already given. And so, despite her irritation, despite what she's read in the papers about Aids, she stretches out her hand to him, and feels it taken.

"Don't tell your mother," she says after a minute.

"But I can't go on living a lie."

"Why not?" Then she pauses. "Most people do."

"Not if we take our Christian faith seriously –"

"Your mother already knows." She says this crossly.

Suddenly it seems to Mrs. Flett that Reverend Rick's mother is here in the room with them, and that she really is, after all, a rather nice woman. Full of bustle and go. Full of smiles.

"Let me put it this way. Your mother half-knows. Soon she will fully know. She'll work it out. People do. It's not something the two of you will ever have to discuss if you don't want to. Not ever." (She can't help feeling just a little proud of this speech.)

"But to live with this barrier between us!" he says in a silly, whispery voice. He is weeping now. Weeping and sniffling.

"I'm afraid I'm feeling, all of a sudden, terribly tired. These pills they give me."

"It was different in your day. People were afraid to be open. They lived their whole lives as if they were fairy-tales."

"Terribly, terribly sleepy." Her throat tingles, it really does. "If you'll forgive me."

"May God bless you, Mrs. Flett."

How does one reply to God's blessing? "Goodbye," Mrs. Flett says firmly, shutting her eyes, pressing her head hard against her pillows, and then adding a moth-erly, grandmotherly, womanly, feminine tossed-coin of a benediction, "Drive carefully now."

In the middle of writing a check she forgets the month, then the year. She's gaga, a loon, she's sprung a leak, her brain matter is falling out like the gray fluff from mailing envelopes, it's getting all over the furniture. What she needs, she tells her daughter, is open-heart surgery on her head.

"Ha," Alice says obligingly.

Everything makes her cross, the frowsiness of dead flowers in a vase, the smell of urine, her own urine. She's turned into a bitter hag, but well, not really, you see. Inside she's still a bowl of vibrating Jello, wise old Mrs. Green Thumb, remember her? Someone you can always call on, count on, phone in an emergency, etc.

*

It surprises Grandma Flett that there is so much humor hidden in the earth's crevasses; it's everywhere, like a thousand species of moss. Almost every day she sees an item or two in the paper or on *Good Morning America* that brings a smile to her lips. Or else something amusing will happen on the floor, the nurses kidding back and forth, some ongoing joke. Who would have thought that comedy could stretch all the way to infirm old age?

And vanity too. Vanity refuses to die, pushing the blandness of everyday life into little pleats, pockets, knobs of electric candy. She looks into her bedside mirror, so cunningly hidden on the reverse side of the bed tray, and says, "There she is, my life's companion. Once I sat in her heart. Now I crouch in a corner of her eye." Nevertheless she applies a little lipstick in the morning before Dr. Riccia comes around, and a dusting of powder across her nose (she's had to give up her favorite Woodbury). Just how is it she finds the energy to lift her powder puff, knowing what she knows?

And she inspects her nails. It was Alice who arranged for the manicurist to drop in last week. Naturally Mrs. Flett resisted at first – she has never in her life had a professional manicure, such an extravagance! – but Alice insisted; a little treat, she called it. And so Mrs. Flett's hands were lowered into various soapy solutions, then taken into this young woman's lap and gently dried with a towel. Her cuticles were trimmed and the nails shaped into perfect ovals. "Moons or plain?" she was asked. "What do you suggest?" said Mrs. Flett. "Well, now," the manicurist began, and it was clear that this decision would require some serious thought, some discussion. A French polish was finally decided on; "It gives a beautiful clean look, nice for summer." As though Mrs. Flett would soon be attending a series of garden parties or dropping in at one of Sarasota's finest dining establishments.

She keeps her ten buffed beauties carefully under the top sheet, but withdraws them every half hour or so for inspection, spreading them out in the sunshine. She looks at them first thing in the morning and last thing at night, but the fact is, she is almost continuously aware of them. They flutter lightly at her sides, and their lightness travels up to her wrists and flows into her arms and body. They look elegant; they do! They look brand new. When you think of the slippage her body has undergone, the spoilage, you can perhaps understand her latest foolishness. But this concentration on fingernails is close to being obsessive, a distortion of normal powder-and-lipstick vanity. It shames her to think about what it means. How thin and unrewarding her life must have been, that such a little thing should give her so much pleasure. If she's not careful she'll turn into one of those pathetic old fruitcakes who are forever counting their blessings.

"Have you ever thought of having a pedicure?" Alice asks her.

Pictures fly into her head, brighter by far than those she sees on the big TV screen in the patients' lounge. A sparkling subversion. Murmurings in her ears. She can tune in any time she likes.

She is seven years old, standing in her Aunt Clarentine's garden, stooping over the snapdragons, pinching them with her fingers so that their mouths open and close. They possess teeth and tiny tongues. Do other people know about this? She picks a spear of chive and sucks it. "Daisy," she hears. She's being called in to supper. Aunt Clarentine's promised to make pancakes tonight. All this: the thought of pancakes, the hot bite of chives, the hidden throats of flowers, the sun, the sound of her own name – she is suddenly dizzy with the press of sensation, afraid she will die of it.

Snow fell on the neighborhood houses and at once they, and their small fenced yards, became whitened with soft fur, with what used to be called in those days spring sherbet. She scooped a handful from her bedroom window sill, held it against her forehead until she could bear it no longer. A test of some kind. A test of courage. The moonlight was cold and clear.

She found something beautiful. A dazzling iridescence on the road. A rainbow pressed into the paving. No one else knew it was there, this marvelous thing she had discovered. But she made the mistake of showing it to one of the older girls in the neighborhood who said, calm as can be, "Why it's only oil, just a little oil spilled on the roadway, nothing to make a fuss over."

Summer again. She took a blade of grass, split it with her fingernail, held it between her thumbs and blew. Someone showed her how to do this, she can't remember who. It was easy – making this wailing sound, like a loon screeching. You got better and better at it. You learned, and you never forgot. You were like other people, you could do the same things other people did.

The brown leaves had been raked into a pile ready to burn, and she longed to lie down on top of them for just a minute, flat on her back in the rustling leaves, staring upward. She let herself fall backward, her arms straight out, trustingly, and at once the complications of branches, fences, sheds and houses, so dense and tangled together, burst with a cartoon pop into the spare singularity of sky, the primary abruptness of blue. That's all there was. Herself suspended in a glass sphere. You could go back and back to that true and steadfast picture, hold it in your head for the rest of your life.

What is your name?

Daisy.

Daisy what?

Daisy Goodwill.

Do you know what the word "Daisy" means? It means "Day's Eye."

That's right. I used to know that. I'd forgotten.

A daisy really is a bit like an eye when you think about it, round and fringed with lashes, staring upward.

Opening, closing.

The odd thing about the pictures that fly into Daisy Goodwill's head is that she is always alone. There are voices that reach her from a distance; there are shadows and suggestions – but still she is alone. And we require, it seems, in our moments of courage or shame, at least one witness, but Mrs. Flett has not had this privilege. This is what breaks her heart. What she can't bear. Even now, eighty years old.

Grandma Flett knows she rambles, she knows she repeats herself, and Alice, bless her, never stops her, never says, "You've already told us about that, Mother."

All she's trying to do is keep things straight in her head. To keep the weight of her memories evenly distributed. To hold the chapters of her life in order. She feels a new tenderness growing for certain moments; they're like beads on a string, and the string is wearing out. At the same time she knows that what lies ahead of her must be concluded by the efforts of her imagination and not by the straight-faced recital of a throttled and unlit history. Words are more and more required. And the question arises: what is the story of a life? A chronicle of fact or a skillfully wrought impression? The bringing together of what she fears? Or the adding up of what has been off-handedly revealed, those tiny allotted increments of knowledge? She needs a quiet place in which to think about this immensity. And she needs someone – anyone – to listen.

It's an indulgence, though, the desire to return to currency all that's been sampled and stored and dreamed into being. She oughtn't to carry on the way she does, bending Alice's ear, boring poor Dr. Riccia to death. She chastises herself; she's getting as bad as Marian McHenry, always going on and on about her own concerns. Instead of thinking of others. Putting others first.

Little Emma is dead. Or perhaps she has been put into an institution with other Down's syndrome children. Mongoloids they used to call them back in a crueller time.

No one says a single word to Grandma Flett about Emma for fear of upsetting her, but she knows anyway: here, coming into focus at her bedside, is her son, Warren, and his new wife – whose name Grandma Flett cannot at this moment recall. The room has slipped sideways. The window lies on an angle. Her own tongue is coiled upon itself. She asks for a glass of water, a simple request, a simple phrase, but she can't get it right. "Mongoloid," she says instead. Alarm touches Warren's face and spreads downward through the erect, elastic column of his neck. She would like to comfort him with a look or a tender word, but her body is weighed down with its own confusion. She doesn't mean to be unkind. She shuts her eyes, concentrating, shutting out her son and his young wife, regarding something infinitely complex printed on the thin skin of her eyelids, a secret, a dream. A kind of movie.

Alice abruptly marries Dr. Riccia. She moves with him to Jamaica where they live in a beautiful bungalow by the ocean. They have a child, a little boy with long curling eyelashes and courtly manners.

No, none of this is true. Old Mrs. Flett is dreaming again.

How do these spurious versions arise?

Think, think, she tells herself. Be reasonable.

Dr. Riccia is already married and the father of two children; Grandma Flett has been shown snapshots of the Riccia family standing in front of their colonial-style house in Kensington Park.

Alice returns to England. The summer is over. Her teaching term begins next week, and she's already planning a weekend party for a dozen or so friends: Moroccan music, something curried, cold beer, herself loud and ironic in swinging earrings. She's found a buyer for the condo in Bayside Towers and she's looked after a number of minor legal matters for her mother, having been granted power of attorney. Papers have been signed. Arrangements made for the future. Alice takes back to rainy Hampstead a gorgeous Florida tan, though everyone, even her mother, warns her that Florida tans don't last. Never mind, she'll be back at Christmas. The pattern of her life is unfolding, a long itinerary of revision and accommodation. She's making it up as she goes along. This is not how she imagined her middle years, but this is the way it will be.

Something has occurred to her – something transparently simple, something she's always known, it seems, but never articulated. Which is that the moment of death occurs while we're still alive. Life marches right up to the wall of that final darkness, one extreme state of being butting against the other. Not even a breath separates them. Not even a blink of the eye. A person can go on and on tuned in to the daily music of food and work and weather and speech right up to the last minute, so that not a single thing gets lost.

She is surprisingly heartened by this thought, and can't help telling her mother how she feels.

Her mother, Daisy Goodwill, is still alive inside her failing body. Up and down, good days, bad days. She's doing as well as can be expected, that's what everyone keeps saying. She could go on like this for years.

CHAPTER TEN

Death

DAISY (GOODWILL) FLETT   Peacefully, on –, in the month of – in the year 199– at Canary Palms Rest Home, Sarasota, Florida, after a long illness patiently borne.

"Grandma" Flett was predeceased by her husband, Barker Flett, a respected Canadian authority on hybrid grains. She leaves to mourn her daughter Alice Good-will-Spanner of Hampstead, England, daughter Joan and spouse Ross Taylor of Portland, Oregon, son Warren and wife Peggy of New York City, and grandniece Victoria and spouse Lewis Roy of Toronto. She was the adored grandmother of Benjamin, Judith, Rachel, Rain, Teller, Beth, Lissa, Jilly, and Emma (?), as well as the loving great-grandmother of Madeleine, Andrew, and Mordicai, and the great-aunt of twins Sophie and Hugh.

A memorial service will be held at Canary Palms Chapel, 10:00. Flowers gratefully declined. Interment will follow at Long Key Cemetery.

Flowers gratefully accepted
in remembrance of
DAISY GOODWILL FLETT
who embraced as well as she was able
most growing things
gardens children balloons

of memory
though she feared greatly the encircling shadow
of solitude and silence
which she came to equate
with her own life

Daisy Daisy
Give me your answer true

Day's eye, day's eye
The face in the mirror is you

"It was in her bedside drawer. This little velvet box."

"What is it? It looks like —"

"That's what it is. Fingernail clippings. Hers, I assume."

"Christ."

Flett, Daisy (née Goodwill), who, due to historical accident, due to carelessness, due to ignorance, due to lack of opportunity and courage, never once in her many years of life experienced the excitement and challenge of oil painting, skiing, sailing, nude bathing, emerald jewelry, cigarettes, oral sex, pierced ears, Swedish clogs, water beds, science fiction, pornographic movies, religious ecstasy, truffles, Kirsch, jalepēno peppers, Peking duck, Vienna, Moscow, Madrid, group therapy, body massage, hunger, distinguished honors, outraged condemnation, who never drove a car, never bought a lottery ticket, never, never (on the other hand) was struck on the face or body by another being, never once perched her reading glasses (with a sigh) in the crown of her hair, never (for fear of ridicule) investigated the possibilities of plastic surgery or yoga, never gave herself over to the kind of magazine article that tells you to be good to yourself, to believe in yourself and do things for yourself. Nor, though she knew she had been loved in her life, did she ever hear the words "I love you, Daisy" uttered aloud (such a simple phrase), and only during the long, thin, uneventful sleep that preceded her death did she have the wit (and leisure) to ponder the injustice of this.

"A blessing," exclaims the noted Chekhov scholar Alice Goodwill-Spanner when informed of her mother's death.

"My mother's quality of life had been hovering at sub-zero for some time," remarks Warren Flett, musicologist for the Lower Manhattan Public Schools.

"She was worn out," announces Joan Taylor, the unemployed soon-to-turn-fifty youngest daughter of the Flett family. "Her life wore her out and then her death wore her out."

"She told me she was ready to go any time," murmurs the award-winning paleobotanist Victoria Louise Flett-Roy. "But is anyone ever really ready?"

"She had this crazy kind of adjustable intelligence. She could hoist it into view when she wanted to."

"Egregious. I heard her say that word once, egregious! It just rolled off her tongue."

"And holy smokes. She used to say holy smokes."

"Really?"

"And like sometimes she wasn't quite there. Knock, knock, anyone home?"

"Those clothes! She had this way of dressing so no one knew if she spent too little money or too much. Or if she was four years behind her fashion moment or twenty-four years."

"Ha."

"She was evasive."

"Yes, but evasion can be a form of aggression."

"Come again?"

"You heard me."

Bluebirds, Pioneer Girls in Service, GSA, Tudorettes, History Circle, Christian Endeavor, Alpha Zeta, Quarry Club, United Church Women, Mothers' Union, The Arrowroots, Mutchmor Home and School Association, Ottawa Horticultural Society, Beautiful Glebe Committee, Carleton County Heart Fund, Rideau Luncheon Series, Ontario Seed Collective, Bay Ladies Craft Group, The Flowers.

"No definitely, I do not want to have any of her body parts donated."

"It was just a thought."

"Everything about her was worn out anyway."

"I just thought –"

In Loving Memory of
Daisy Goodwill Flett
1905–199–

In Loving Memory of
Daisy Goodwill
Who in Sound Mind
And without malice
And Over the Objection of her Family
Made the Decision
After Prolonged Reflection
After Torment
With Misgivings With Difficulty With Apologies With
Determination
To Lie Alone in Death

"She left you what?" Joan shouted over the telephone. (A bad transatlantic connection.)

"Her trug," said Alice, grimacing.

"What in God's name is a trug?"

"That old gardening basket of hers. That old mildewed thing with the huge hooped handle?"

"I think I remember. Vaguely. But why?"

"I don't know. Same reason you got the silver asparagus server, I suppose."

"Lordy."

"And you know what Warren got."

"No. What?"

"Her old notes from college. And her essays. All

hand-written. Pages and pages. A big cardboard carton of them."

"She really kind of lost it at the end, didn't she?"

"Maybe just a joke?"

"She wasn't exactly one for jokes."

"I don't know about that."

"Victoria has the lady's-slippers."

"Gawd, what'll she do with those old things?"

"She wanted them. At least she said she did."

"Well everything else is in order. Her assets, and so on."

"We can thank her accountant for that."

"And her lawyer. Although he seems to have dipped in pretty deep himself."

"What about Canary Palms!"

"Oh boy!"

"I feel guilty even talking about this. Even thinking about it."

"So do I."

"But I suppose everyone feels this way."

"Of course they do."

"So what can we do?"

"Not one little thing."

Seventy-four percent of American households spent at least a thousand dollars to improve or maintain their dwellings this year. It was on the radio, the news – or else I dreamed it. Tell me, why do I need to know such a thing? Is the mind sweetened by this useless pellet of knowledge? No. Not when you're already at the stuffed, blunted end of life.

Isn't there anything else you can tell me?

The Bridal Lingerie of Daisy Goodwill Hoad, 1927

- 2 three-piece bridal sets of crêpe-de-chine and Valenciennes lace with fine hand embroidery and drawn work, shell pink, ivory
- 12 slips
- 12 two-piece French sets, chemise and step-ins, peach, cream, blue, tea
- 6 night gowns
- 6 negligees, georgette and chantilly lace
- 2 robes, 1 wool tartan, 1 corded cotton
- 6 "Flaming Youth" brassieres
- 6 "Pansy" brassieres of silk jersey and mercerized cotton
- 3 camisoles in pink jap silk
- 2 Gossard Dancelette girdles of silk jersey with elastic side insets
- 12 pairs silk stockings
- 12 pairs cotton stockings
- 3 beach pajama suits, orange satin, copen blue, ochre
- 6 kimonos, black, blue, red granite, rose, peach, and mauve
- 2 Kellerman bathing suits (all wool), black, copen
- 1 knitted beach cape
- 1 bathing cap
- 6 aprons, assorted styles

"I never knew she could embroider."
  "This is beautiful."

"Are you sure she did it?"

"There's this tiny little daisy in the right-hand corner."

"You're right, there is."

"A signature, sort of like."

"Hey!"

"The nurses were always saying how good-natured she was, a smile for everyone."

"Except that time she broke her radio. Threw it on the floor."

"It could have been an accident."

"True."

"What I can't figure out is why she never told us about this first marriage of hers."

"She must have known we'd find out after she was gone. I mean, the papers are all there. The marriage license and the report and everything."

"Hoad! His name was Hoad."

"Harold Hoad."

"Rhymes with toad. Give me strength."

"But look at that picture, will you. He was – he looks like a movie star, silent movies I'm talking about. Gorgeous."

"But why weren't we told?"

"Think about it. How could she talk about anything so – so perfectly awful."

"The shock of it."

"I don't get it. Was she embarrassed about it or what?"

"This beautiful man fell out of a window. Her lover. Her brand new husband. Think if that happened to you. Would you want to talk about it?"

"Probably she was just so, you know, broken up by it, she couldn't bear to think about it, never mind talk about it. Imagine being on your honeymoon and –"

"And at her age."

"Repression. Sometimes repression's a good thing. How else was she going to continue with her –?"

"He looks handsomer than Dad."

"And younger."

"By a long shot."

"Surely Dad must have known about – about him."

"He must have. I mean, she may have been secretive, but –"

"It gives me –"

"What?"

"Goose bumps."

"What does? Thinking of Mr. Hoad falling on his head?"

"No. Thinking of her. Her. All those years."

"All those years – saying nothing."

"She must have been reminded every year, on the anniversary of his –"

"Remember how sometimes she'd just want to lie down on her bed in the middle of the day. Not sleeping, she'd just lie there looking at the ceiling."

"Keeping it all in her head. Remembering."

"I know."

"Oh, God."

Garden Club Luncheon, 1951

Ham Rolls / Cheese Pinwheels
Mixed Pickles
Melon Balls and Seedless Grape Salad
Jelly Tarts
Assorted Cookies
Coffee   Tea

I'm still here, inside the (powdery, splintery) bones, ankles, the sockets of my eyes, shoulder, hip, teeth, I'm still here, oh, oh.

"If she'd lived in another age she might have been Ms. Green Thumb with her own TV show."

"Prime time."

"Somehow I can't imagine it."

"This mean old sentimental century. It smothered her. Like a curtain. The kind you can't see through."

"She could have divorced Dad."

"For starters."

"What? What are you talking about?"

"Why would you think that? I mean, the two of them were reasonably happy together, all things considered."

"You honestly think so?"

"Well, as happy as most."

"Whatever happy means."

"Tell me about it."

"All I know is, the past is never past."

"Is that supposed to be profound?"

'Hmmmmm."

Aunt Daisy's Lemon Pudding

4 tbs butter	1 cup milk
$\frac{1}{2}$ cup white sugar	2 tbs flour
2 eggs separated	juice and rind of 1 lemon

Cream butter and sugar, add egg yolks beaten until thick and lemon-colored, stir in flour and milk, lemon juice and grated lemon rind. Beat egg whites until stiff but not dry. Fold egg whites into mixture. Bake twenty-five minutes in buttered baking dish set in pan of hot water. Moderate oven, 350 degrees.

"Do you think her life would have been different if she'd been a man?"
    "Are you kidding!"

"Just look at this bedjacket."
    "Looks brand new. Never worn, I'd guess."

For Tuesday –
        1 can condensed milk
        1 bunch celery
        carrots
        onions
        1 pound butter
        1 pound lard
        matches
        soap flakes

2 cans corned beef
pork chops
Phone Mr. M.
new beater for Mixmaster
Warren's teeth
post office
drugstore, cough syrup, Box K
juniper

Now there's a woman who made a terrific meatloaf, who knew how to repot a drooping rubber plant, who bid a smart no-trump hand, who wore a hat well, who looked after her personal hygiene, who wrote her thank-you notes promptly, who kept up, who went down, went down and down and down, who missed the point, the point of it all, but was, nevertheless, almost unfailingly courteous to others.

"Remember Jay Dudley?"

"Who?"

"You know, that nerd who worked on the Ottawa *Recorder*. Jay Dudley his name was."

"Oh, sure, I remember. Hand-woven neckties? Ceramic cufflinks?"

"Do you think they ever, the two of them, do you think they ever – got together?"

"Naw."

"Too bad."

Black Beauty, Anne of Green Gables, Freckles, Twice Told Tales, Beautiful Joe, Mill on the Floss, Pocahontas, Helen's Babies, Our Mutual Friend, Nellie's Memories, Elizabeth and Her German Garden, Jane Eyre, The Unification of Italy, Beowulf, The Romantic Poets, In His Steps, Wild Geese, Gone With the Wind, Claudia, The First Six Years, Grapes of Wrath, Forever Amber, The Egg and I, Cheaper by the Dozen, Lust for Life, The Web and the Rock, The Skutari Saga, A Brief History of the Orkney Isles, Chekhov's Daughter, The Edible Woman, The Good Earth (large print edition), *Murder in the Meantime* (large print edition, half finished).

"What do you mean you don't think anyone's ever ready?"

"Christ, I'm ready right this minute."

"That's because you're feeling depressed about not having a job. You're not really ready at all. And I'll bet you she wasn't either."

"I don't know."

"Did you ever get a chance to talk to her about, you know –"

"Death? You couldn't talk to her about things like that."

"She'd change the subject."

"She'd put on the baffled schoolgirl look."

"Blink her eyes."

"Her mouth in a little round circle."

"Her eyebrows."

"When it comes right down to it, I freeze, too, at the thought of dying."

"It runs in the family."

"Our genes are pure granite."

"Little pellets."

"Hailstones."

"I do remember that once she said she liked pansies at a funeral. Not those dumb pansies with faces. What she liked were the absolutely pure purple ones, those deep, deep velvety petals. That's the only thing I can remember her saying apropos to death."

"She just let her life happen to her."

"Well, why the hell not?"

"It was like –"

"Like?"

"Like she was always going after some stray little thought with a needle and thread."

"Afraid to look inside herself. In case there was nothing there."

"Isn't that what Buddhists try so hard to get to?"

"The Buddhists?"

"Wanting to arrive at a state of nothingness?"

"Really?"

"What an awful thought."

"Why?"

"I don't know. I mean, nothing isn't, you know, much."

"Nothing's nothing."

"Amen."

Must Do's – Long Term

summer curtains
furs in storage
touch up back steps, fence
re-block wntr hats
lavender – restock
spray porch furniture
Stretch?
Behind stove, under ice box
cheque for Mr. M.
gas
moth balls
magazines to thrift shop
furnace
piano
poison
lamp fixtures

Colic, chicken pox, measles, bronchial pneumonia, allergies, influenza, menstrual cramps, eczema, cystitis, childbirth, blood pressure, menopause, depression, angina, blocked arteries, broken bones, coronary bypass, kidney failure, cancer, bladder infection, stroke, bed sores, ulcerated leg, incontinence, stroke, memory loss, failing eyesight, inappropriate response, speech deficiency, depression, stroke, stroke.

Daisy Goodwill, in her final illness, the illness she is reputed to have borne with such patience, was left with only her death to contemplate – and she approached it with all the concerted weakness and failure of her body. Somewhere in the course of those final dreaming weeks, there had occurred a shifting of the tide. It arrived suddenly during one of her frequent comatose periods. She entered sleep, as through a tunnel, still groping in the past, breathing in like a species of inferior oxygen the real and imagined episodes of her life, and then a kind of exhaustion took over, or perhaps boredom – in any case a rapid fading of color and of line, and a failure of the mechanism that had previously called up the earlier scenes. What pressed on her eyelids, instead, was a series of mutable transparencies gesturing not backward in time but forward – forward toward her own death. You might say that she breathed it into existence, then fell in love with it.

Her initial vision was theatrical, the usual pastel coffin, droning scripture, and shuddering pipe organ – all the stirred confetti of grief floating loose in a vividly inhabited room, loud with trashy weeping and tribute. But this was preposterous.

The brilliant room collapses, leaving a solid block of darkness. Only her body survives, and the problem of what to do with it. It has not turned to dust. A bright, droll, clarifying knowledge comes over her at the thought of her limbs and organs transformed to biblical dust or even funereal ashes. Laughable.

Stone is how she finally sees herself, her living cells replaced by the insentience of mineral deposition. It's easy enough to let it claim her. She lies, in her last dreams, flat on her back on a thick slab, as hugely imposing as the bishops and saints she'd seen years earlier in the great pink cathedral of Kirkwall. It wasn't good enough for them, and it isn't for her either, but the image is, at the very least, contained; she loves it, in fact, and feels herself merge with, and become, finally, the still body of her dead mother.

She's miles away now from her clavicle, her fat cells, her genital flesh, from her toenails and back gums, from her nostrils and eyebrows, and the bony nameless place behind her ears. Her brain is purest mica; you can hold it up to the window and the light shines through. Empty, though, that's the catch.

With polite bemusement she lingers over each detail of her frozen state, adding and subtracting, refining, polishing. The folds of her dress, so primitive and stiff, are softened by a decorative edge, a calcium border of seashells of the kind sometimes seen on the edges of birthday cakes. A stone scroll dips gracefully across her slippered feet, the date worn away, illegible, and a stone pillow props up her head, the rigid frizz combed smooth at last. Her hands with their gentled knuckles curve inward at her sides, greatly simplified, the fingers melded together, ringless, unmarked by age, but gesturing (that minutely angled thumb) toward the large, hushed, immutable territory that stands beyond her hearing. From out of her impassive face the eyes stare icy as marbles, wide open but seeing nothing, nothing, that is, but the deep, shared common distress of men and women, and how little they are allowed, finally, to say.

Her final posture, then, is Grecian. Quiet. Timeless. Classic. She has always suspected she had this potential.

Only minimal energy is required to call up her stone self and hold it in place. Deaf to all but the loudest echoes, it flourishes on its own declining curve – the whiteness, the impermeable surface – and fills the hemisphere of her vision so completely that previous strategies and arrangements are cast aside. The blameless teeth, hair, and bones of Daisy Goodwill embrace this final form, or rather, it embraces her, allowing her access, at last, to a trance of solitude, attaching its weight to her faltering pendulum heart, her stiffened coral lungs. It grows harder and colder, and will soon take over altogether. Next week. Tomorrow. Tonight.

14 Grange Road, Tyndall, Manitoba (demolished 1922)

166 Simcoe Street, Winnipeg, Manitoba (demolished 1947)

Apt. 12, 144 East Avenue, Bloomington, Indiana

6 Hawthorne Drive, Vinegar Hill, Bloomington, Indiana (Heritage designation 1975)

Alpha Zeta House, Long College for Women, Hanover, Indiana (converted to Alumni Offices 1957)

583 The Driveway, Ottawa, Ontario (subdivided into condominiums 1981)

419 East Bayside Towers, Tamiami Trail, Sarasota, Florida (condemned: failure to meet fire code 1986)

Canary Palms Convalescent Home, Marine Drive, Colmann, Florida (bought by ICW Meditation and Cognitive Study Center 1990)

Canary Palms Care Facility, 1267 Fauna Avenue, Colmann, Florida

"I am not at peace."

Daisy Goodwill's final (unspoken) words

"Daisy Goodwill Flett, wife, mother, citizen of our century: May she rest in peace."

Closing benediction, read by Warren M. Flett,
Memorial Service, Canary Palms

"The pansies, have you ever seen such ravishing pansies?"

  "She would have loved them."

  "Somehow, I expected to see a huge bank of daisies."

  "Daisies, yes."

  "Someone should have thought of daisies."

  "Yes."

  "Ah, well."

Carol Shields

Small Ceremonies

The companion novel to *The Box Garden*.

Judith Gill is writing a biography of a minor Victorian novelist.
Judith has also written a novel of her own, but is unhappy with it.
Is the plot original – or is it plagiarised? And when she discovers
her own novel has been plundered can she fairly justify the anger
she feels? In the perplexing swirl of family life are her husband,
who keeps odd balls of wool in a bottom drawer, and her son, who
shares his secrets with a penfriend.

Lacking the certainty of youth and not yet reaping the wisdom
of older age, Judith Gill is at the centre of a beautifully realised
novel that is tender, funny and unusually insightful.

'Carol Shields sings with the charm of a true siren. In her hands,
we believe, anything can happen.' – *Guardian*

ISBN: 1-85702-029-4   £5.99

Carol Shields

The Box Garden

The companion novel to *Small Ceremonies*.

Charleen Forrest's husband has left her. Gone, not only from her own life, but apparently from the face of the earth. Charleen is left with his name and their marvellously uncomplicated son, Seth. She also has a fair talent for poetry, and a job on *The National Botanical Journal* which brings her in touch with the mysterious Brother Adam . . . a man with a contagious passion for silence and grass.

Charleen's piercing gifts of observation are wonderfully balanced with her intermittent bouts of all-too-familiar feelings of incompetence that are as poignantly depicted as her gifts for love and survival.

'Carol Shields's prose is addictive' – *Sunday Telegraph*

ISBN: 1-85702-088-X   £5.99

Carol Shields

Various Miracles

Sharp, sceptical and stylish, sympathetic and always unexpected, this collection presents Carol Shields at her inimitable best in seventeen miracles of storyteller's art.

Slyly and perceptively, Carol Shields surveys a whole range of life's surprises: a leisured middle-class housewife who transforms herself into a successful saleswoman; a strange, special intimacy that binds a group of strangers at an evening class; the unexpected death of a friend. The stories collected here offer an entrancing, intriguing look at some of the various miracles of everyday life.

'Shields's outlines of lives, witty and generous, are alive with provisional happiness, a fragile incandescence glowing against the dark.' – *Independent on Sunday*

'These fictions are highly polished and made to catch light.' – *Observer*

ISBN: 1-85702-249-1   £9.99

All Fourth Estate books are available at your local bookshop or newsagent, or can be ordered direct from the publisher.

Indicate the number of copies required and quote the author and title.

Send cheque/eurocheque/postal order (Sterling only), made payable to Book Service by Post, to:

Fourth Estate Books
Book Service By Post
PO Box 29, Douglas
I-O-M, IM99 1BQ.

Or phone: 01624 675137

Or fax: 01624 670923

Alternatively pay by Access, Visa or Mastercard

Card number:

Expiry date ....

Signature ....

Please allow 75 pence per book for post and packing in the UK. Overseas customers please allow £1.00 per book for post and packing.

Name ....

Address ....

....

....

Please allow 28 days for delivery. Please tick the box if you do not wish to receive any additional information.

Prices and availability subject to change without notice.